The Earl On the Train

KERRIGAN BYRNE

One

SEBASTIAN MONCRIEFF PALMED his blade in the darkness, anticipating a kill.

He waited, listening to the boisterous night, savoring the sensation of the ground moving beneath him.

Always moving.

In fact, the only time he felt unstable was when he stood in one place.

He'd built sea legs as the first mate on one of the most famous—er *infamous*—ships in the entire world, The Devil's Dirge. Now that the Rook had regrettably retired, Moncrieff sought other ways to keep ahead of the relentless demons giving him chase.

To keep the ground beneath him from falling away.

The fastest steamships, most expensive coaches, wildest stallions, and even a novelty such as a hot air balloon provided escape from the prison to which he'd been sentenced.

For the next three days, it was the clack and sway of a train mobilizing the floor beneath his feet. The sumptuous luxury locomotive followed the tracks of the Orient Express from London to Constantinople.

He'd booked his passage with the intent to assassinate one Arthur Weller.

As luck would have it, he'd the opportunity to do it tonight, before the train even reached Paris, with no one the wiser. For the rest of the trip to Constantinople, he'd sit back and watch the resulting chaos whilst indulging in expensive cigars and baccarat, before retiring to his private car.

Where he'd sleep with the unburdened conscience of an innocent baby.

At least where Arthur Weller was concerned.

He'd plenty of sin staining his soul, and plenty of ghosts to haunt his dreams...but they'd be silent tonight.

They always were after these kills.

Arthur Weller eschewed a rail steward, preferring to be attended by his personal valet. Thus, no one stood sentinel as Sebastian let himself into the railcar, shaking the skiff of snow from his hair.

His own accommodations were three cars away, as only an idiot would murder his neighbor and not expect suspicion.

No one, however, would imagine someone would be mad enough to let himself out onto the landing of the speeding train, and proceed to climb onto the roof in order to leap several cars forward.

Few people built their strength spidering about a ship for a decade, clinging to dubious handholds while the sea did its level best to claim anyone foolish enough to be out in a gale.

Compared to a steamship in a hurricane, the roof of a train might as well have been a stroll in Hyde Park.

It had rails and everything.

Measuring his breath, Sebastian flattened his back against the wall of the Weller's first-class car and peeked

Big Duke Energy

KERRIGAN BYRNE   CHRISTI CALDWELL

AMALIE HOWARD   JANNA MACGREGOR

STACY REID

OLIVER
HEBER
BOOKS

around the corner to assure no one moved about the narrow hall. Unlikely at this hour, but one never knew if a family member needed a midnight snack or use of the necessary.

One wouldn't want a murder interrupted by something so pedestrian as a wee.

Empty. *Excellent.*

The lone lamp provided little better than a golden well for shadows, and Sebastian melded with them as he crept along the hallway.

Three doors shielded the opulent cabin suites in which the Weller family slept. According to the information he'd paid handsomely for, Arthur Weller's cabin was the last one on the right.

The knife felt like his own appendage as he passed the first door belonging to Weller's daughter, and the middle cabin in which his wife, Adrienne, slept.

He pressed his ear to Weller's door and listened for any movement before sliding it open and easing inside. The elite nobles could hardly abide squeaks, and God love the well-oiled luxury of first-class. It made stealing about so much easier.

The drapes had been left open, revealing the meager glow of the city as it reflected off the delicate flakes of snow to mingle with various lights from the train. It illuminated just enough of the cabin to outline the shadows of furniture and glint off crystal, silver, and his blade.

Tucking the knife against his cuff, Sebastian slithered closer to his mark.

The vile fuck would finally get what was coming to him. Perhaps he should light a lamp so he could watch the life bleed from Weller's eyes.

Sebastian had never been a macabre sort of fellow.

He left that to men with darker predilections. But this...*this* was personal.

Drifting to the bed, he loomed over the outline of a slim body, his every muscle coiled like a snake.

When he struck, it was with a viper's speed and precision, and before his victim could blink from slumber to awareness, he'd a knife to his throat and arms pinned helplessly to his side.

Wait.

He released one alarmingly slim arm to test a curious softness he'd not expected.

Breasts. Shit.

"Please." The feminine plea feathered over his flesh and arrowed down his breastbone, landing in his cock. "Please, no."

Lord, but he loved it when they begged.

Begged for pleasure, to be precise, never for their lives.

This was a disconcerting development, to say the least.

Sebastian snatched his offending hand away from the lovely orb with no small amount of reluctance and regret. The shape had fit his palm like a dream, the warmth of the plentiful flesh beneath a thin cotton night rail a balm to his frozen fingers. The plump nipple beaded against the cold.

Who was this, the wife or the daughter? Thinking swiftly, he returned the knife to his cuff with the swiftest sleight of hand. If he was lucky, he could rely on what he always did to get out of trouble with a lady.

His charm and general magnificence.

"Do pardon me, madam, or is it miss? I fear I have the wrong railcar." He released her carefully and straightened, hoping to convey chagrin from the shadows. "I was...invited by a woman, you see, and this is the car number she gave me along with orders to be stealthy. I dare think we both might have been had."

"Moncrieff?"

The disbelieving whisper froze the blood in his veins and his tongue to the roof of his mouth.

That voice.

He'd recognize it anywhere. Heard it in his most salacious dreams.

And the mild ones, as well.

Her features were little better than shadows, but it didn't matter. He'd committed her every feature to memory more than a year ago. The curve of her cheekbone, sharp yet delicate. The silk of her ebony hair and the cream of her skin.

The veritable perfection of her incomparable beauty.

Veronica Weatherstoke.

A woman possessed of every virtue he'd lost along the way.

She was loyal, erudite, patient, measured, clever, strong...

Kind.

It was rare for such a beautiful woman to develop such deep wells of compassion, rarer still a countess. Hers was not a refined sort of empathy.

She'd been born into this merciless world with a tender heart, soft eyes the color of the finest jade, and a full, kind mouth...

The *kind* of mouth he often pictured stretched around his cock.

His astonishment gave her time to sit upright, clutching the covers over her pale, high-necked gown.

"Sebastian Moncrieff, what the devil are you doing here?" she hissed in a loud whisper.

7

'I told you, seducing the wrong woman, apparently." Or the right one, if fortune favored his cursed soul.

'With that knife you hid up your cuff?"

'Saw that, did you?" Fortune, he remembered, was a fickle bitch.

'One does not forget the feel of steel against one's throat."

Sebastian had never before put a blade to her lily-white throat.

Which meant someone else had.

Just as he was about to inquire as to the name of the dead man walking, she said, "Tell me the truth, Moncrieff. What are you doing here?"

'Attempting to kill Arthur Weller," he answered blithely. "What are *you* doing his cabin? Wait..." He swallowed a surge of bile as he calculated the possibilities with abject disgust. "Tell me you're not warming his bed. I'll slit my wrists right now if you and he—"

'I'd rather warm my innards with a hot poker than the likes of *Arthur Weller*." She said the name as if it tasted rotten in her mouth.

Thank Christ. He'd known she had more scruples than to take such a cretin as a lover. Did she have a lover? He wondered. Was she in need of one?

He certainly would apply for the position.

For *every* position she would allow.

'W-what will you do now?" she asked, a tremulous hint of vulnerability escaping on her voice. He could see her clearer now, the outline of her dark braid, the motions of her lips. Just shapes and shades, and no less alluring for it.

'I've hardly made up my mind," he confessed, wondering what she'd do if he kissed her.

Would she submit to his seduction, yielding that soft body to his skillful caresses?

Or would she knee him in the nads?

With a jerking, almost violent motion, she tossed the bedclothes off and scrambled to her feet, standing before him with her shoulders thrown back in challenge. "I *refuse* to become a prisoner of yours again, do you hear me, you villainous troll?"

"*Technically*, you were a prisoner of my captain, the Rook," he corrected indulgently, placing a hand over his heart to advertise where she'd wounded him.

If he were possessed of a heart.

"And...*troll*?" he tutted. "I *hardly* believe that's an apropos comparison. Trolls are unsightly and unwashed, famously living beneath bridges and such nonsense. Whereas I am fastidiously clean and have been told I'm at least tolerably attractive." Words like masculine perfection, Adonis, Eros, and even the title *handsomest man alive* had been bandied about, but manners dictated he remain humble. "Let us find another villainous creature to assign to me."

"Ogre, then," was her next suggestion.

"My Lady, I don't mean to hound a point, but surely you're aware ogres and trolls are in good company together. Might I suggest—"

She splayed her hands against his chest and pushed with all her adorable strength. He even let her budge him a little, to soothe her ire.

"Whatever fiendish demon you find acceptable, I care not! Either kill me or... Get. *Out*."

Sebastian hissed in a breath through his teeth. "I'm in a bit of a conundrum, you see, as I can't seem to do either! We *both* know I won't kill you..."

"Oh, do we?"

When he realized she might not be able to read his sardonic look in the dimness, he made an audible sound conveying his impatience. "Secondary, I cannot allow you to alert Weller to my plans...so what to do with you,

9

is the question." He tapped a thoughtful finger on his chin.

"You do nothing *with* or *to* me, you piratical bastard. Touch me again and I'm going to scream until my breath runs out."

Bastard? She had no idea.

"Go ahead." He shrugged. "The first person who comes through that door catches my blade. So, I very much hope it's no one you're overly fond of."

"You pigeon-livered ratbag!"

Reaching out, he caught her hand before it connected with his cheek. "Come now, don't let's dwell on the past. Tell me where Weller is, I'll slit his throat and be out of your hair before dawn."

She snatched her fingers away cringing toward the bed. "My *God*, but you're cold."

"Trust me, woman, if you knew Arthur Weller's sins, you'd be sending him to Hell yourself."

"No, I mean, you're as frozen as a corpse."

"Apologies. It is beginning to snow out there, and I had to use my hands to steady myself so as not to fall off the roof."

A beat of silence passed. Then another. "The roof?" she echoed, as if she'd never before heard the word.

"How else would I attain entry to the car undetected?"

"I—I couldn't say." Lifting her hands, she scrubbed them over her face a few times, as if to wipe away stress, or sleep, or the sight of Sebastian, himself. "Why do you want to kill Arthur Weller?"

"For all the reasons you don't seem surprised, I expect," he replied darkly, as he realized that a provocative question had yet to be answered. "You never told me what you're doing in his bed."

She snorted with derision. "This isn't his bed, it's his daughter Penelope's."

Sebastian swallowed once. Twice. Momentarily paralyzed by lascivious images of what she and Arthur Weller's young daughter got up to in bed. "I never took you for a Jack the Lass... Lucky Penelope."

She instantly crossed her arms. "No, you rank *pervert*, I'm both her chaperone on this journey to meet her betrothed in Bucharest, *and* I'm designing the wedding trousseau."

"Hmmm..." he drew out the speculative sound. "Do you suppose there will still be a wedding once her father is dead? What is the requisite mourning period in Romania?"

She stared at him with her arms crossed over her breasts for an uncomfortably long time. The silence ate at him, as it was wont to do. The stillness swirling with the ghosts of his sins ready to catch him up.

He needed to move. To do something.

And here they were in the dark, with a bed. Him, shivering with the cold, and her, all warm and soft and effectively naked. What rotten fucking luck. The one woman who would likely never permit him to touch her.

The one woman he did his best to forget...if only his dreams would allow it.

"Moncrieff..." She hesitated, and his breath refused to draw at the sound of his name on her lips, spoken with a return of her innate gentility.

My name is Sebastian. He wanted her to say it. Over. And over. And again. He wanted her to sigh it. To moan it.

To scream it.

She ventured a step closer, beguiling him with the whisper of cotton against the bare skin beneath. "I'd say

11

after everything you put me and Lorelai through, you might agree that you owe me a boon—"

"Come now," he interrupted. "I was properly careful that not one hair on your head was harmed on that ship—"

"Could you kill him tomorrow night, instead?"

Two

IT TOOK a great deal to stun Sebastian. Most often something cataclysmic. But hearing such a request from her lips did the trick. "Let me make certain I'm comprehending you, my lady." He held up a hand. "You're not asking me to spare Arthur Weller's life. Only to wait to murder him until tomorrow night."

"You heard correctly."

He cocked his head, thoroughly bemused. "I've never been more curious in my life as to someone's motives. You are not a murderer. In fact, I remember you begging the Rook to spare my life after I organized a mutiny against him, and abducted his wife, your sister-in-law, as collateral."

"I fully remember what you did," she said crisply. "But as you mentioned, Arthur Weller is a man who deserves the worst a villain like you could do to him. In fact, I have already hatched a plan to spirit his wife and daughter away. All I ask is time to do so before you send him to Hell."

A villain like you.

Sebastian had always been more than happy to play the scoundrel. He'd never let his roguish reputation

13

bother him in the least—in fact, he'd nurtured the status with vigor, until he was considered the perfect mélange of Guy Fawkes, Sir Francis Drake, and Cassanova.

Most women found him irresistible.

But not Veronica Weatherstoke.

Sebastian remembered watching as the Rook slid a dagger into her husband's brain. Her reaction to the murder had been horrified.

And yet, she'd not shed a single tear for the man.

The Earl of Southbourne, Mortimer Weatherstoke, had shanghaied an injured boy and sold him to a captain in need of a crew. The boy who'd become the Rook, the most terrible pirate in this century. Mortimer had broken his own sister Lorelai's leg over a toy, and killed her beloved pet rabbits before feeding them to her in a stew. He'd separated the Rook and Lorelai for twenty years on a cruel whim.

What must he have been like as a husband to Veronica?

As it always did, the thought hit him like a hammer to the guts, and the urge to commit murder surged to a fever pitch. "Where is Weller now?" he growled.

She flinched, and he instantly tempered his rage. "He's with his mistress somewhere in second class."

"Excellent. Why don't I simply find him and kill him tonight, and then his wife and daughter no longer have to worry? We can all sip Tuica in Bucharest by week's end."

Veronica shook her head vehemently before he'd finished his sentence. "Penelope doesn't *want* to marry the Romanian count to whom she is promised. The ink is dry on the contract. The dowry already sent. But if we can lose her in Paris, she can be married quickly to the man she truly loves, and on a ship bound for America by the time she is missed. Penelope is with him now, going over the plans for tomorrow night one last time."

"You trust this boy?" Sebastian asked.

She nodded. "He will care for her. He's young, but from a good family with plenty of means and, furthermore, decency. I know them from...from before."

"From when you were a countess?"

"From when I was nothing more than a shipping magnate's daughter with an obscene dowry of my own."

He made a soft sound in his throat. "I forgot you were not born nobility."

"I was *never* allowed to forget." The bleak note that stole into her voice tugged at the empty hole in his chest.

"Do you know the Wellers from then also?" he queried, Weller being a shipping magnate of his own.

"I had heard of him. He and my father were friendly rivals."

Sebastian's lip curled with distaste. "Did your father *also* take refugee and immigrant children and sell them to deviant men on far continents? Did he use his ships to smuggle stolen sarcophagi, relics, and pillaged art?"

"Of course not," she answered, horrified. "My father was an honorable man, but Weller is a brute and a bully. What he does to his own family is shameful enough, but to learn that he...that he is cruel to children..." She passed a hand over her eyes and then turned to him. "Are you, a *pirate*, really passing judgment? Do you see yourself as better than scum like Weller?"

"We were not those kinds of pirates," he defended. "We *took* from men like Weller. We had no quarrel with refugees or the poor, and often we freed them from such ships, and even added several to our crew."

"Oh *please*, don't make yourselves out to be some sort of Robin Hood figures. There is no such thing as a *good* pirate, and your lot were among the worst of them.

The Rook, at least, was redeemable because he'd been forced into the life, and everything he'd done was for Lorelai's sake."

Bending closer, he inhaled the scent of orchids and amber radiating from the warmth of her skin. God, but he hungered for a taste of her. Of every part of her that opened and bloomed. "I never claimed to be good, my lady—if anything, I am one of the most wicked men you'll ever know."

She retreated one step, which was all the space the tight quarters would allow. "I know you are wicked, which is why I don't trust you."

"I didn't ask you to."

"What do you mean?"

"Trust is a dangerous fallacy. The only thing I trust is that a person will always act in their own self-interest. Because of that, my lady, you can rely on me to keep my word in this respect. What is that old adage? The enemy of my enemy is my—"

"We are *not* friends."

"Uncomfortable allies, then," he offered. "You do what you have to do, Countess, and then I will rid the world of Arthur Weller."

"I'm not a countess any longer. I'm a dowager...little better than a seamstress now."

"Modesty doesn't suit you," he quipped. "You're becoming quite a name in the world of fashion."

"How do you know that?" The rank skepticism in her voice brought out a teasing smile he wished he could turn on her.

"Well, you kidnap a person once or twice and you tend to get attached," he admitted. "Tell me you haven't experienced something of the same issue. That you have not looked for mention of me here or there?"

She groaned with more disgust than the moment

warranted, in his opinion. "I'd all but forgotten you existed."

Lies.

Sebastian had many skills, and the chief among them was being able to tell when someone fed him a falsehood.

"Will I ever be anything but the villain to you, Veronica?" The question had left his lips before he could call it back.

"How could you not be?" She gestured wildly. "You turned on your captain and took my sister-in-law and best friend hostage during a mutiny. You threatened to kill her!"

He rolled his eyes. "I wouldn't have *done* it. Everyone knows that. I only needed to make a point."

"No one knows anything of the sort! How the devil did you escape prison? I was *certain* you'd have hanged for your crimes by now."

His brows met in confusion. "Surely you've heard."

"Heard what?"

She really didn't know? Oh, this was a *lark*.

"How long have you been on the Continent?" he asked.

"Since Ash married Lorelai, and don't you *dare* change the subject."

Ash. The Rook. His captain. His brother. His best friend. He'd have died for that man. He'd killed for that man. He'd hung his future, such as it was, upon the life they'd built at sea.

Only to have it disintegrated by the Rook's forgotten past. Ash had bound himself to a lost love and a brother he'd been twenty years without.

And Sebastian, his first mate and his most loyal friend, was set adrift.

And he might have acted...hastily. Now that time had separated him from the debacle, he had regrets.

Especially when it came to Veronica.

"I agree that I owe you this boon," he granted. "I will wait to assassinate Arthur Weller until you have carried out your plans."

"Thank you."

"Let us shake on it." He offered his hand.

"I'd rather not touch you."

Another lie.

Interesting...

"I'm glad we met again, Veronica. I didn't like how we parted." He couldn't remember the last time he'd said something so genuine. It made him feel exposed. Vulnerable.

He'd certainly not make a habit of it.

"You mean you disliked being led away in irons by Chief Inspector Morley?" she clarified with a syrupy sarcasm.

"I meant I regret you saw me like that. On the day I lost everything."

"On the day you *surrendered* everything," she corrected. "You brought it all on yourself, you know."

He knew.

It was a truth he often ran from, which meant he needed to get moving.

Yet, his feet didn't seem inclined to obey. He wasn't a man to look over his shoulder at the past, and yet... here she was. One of his most intrusive, pervasive memories.

So close.

So dangerously, alluringly close.

His heart sped. His breaths intensified as a dagger of dread threatened to skewer his tightening throat. If he thought about what he wanted to do, he'd take the deserter's road. He'd been many things in life, but a coward wasn't one of them.

Then why fear this? Fear her? What power did she have over him?

None.

Power was given or taken.

She wasn't the sort to take it. And he'd die before he gave it up. So, he needed to do this. It was what they both deserved.

"I'm sorry." The words tasted foreign and foul on his tongue, but he managed to spit them out.

It wasn't that he expected a parade or procession. Hell, he hadn't really even imagined forgiveness was forthcoming, but he thought she might have said *something* in return.

He groped about to fill the resulting silence. "I'm sorry," he repeated. "The thought that I might have frightened or distressed you offends me in every way."

"Thank you." Her reply was colored with astonishment.

With a practiced bow, Sebastian turned and eased the door back open, trying to ignore the warmth of her gaze on his chilly skin.

"Moncrieff," she called after him in an elevated whisper.

He paused, unable to turn around, half afraid she'd found the words to rebuke his apology.

"Do be careful on the roof. The snow is getting worse."

Sebastian didn't bother to fight the grin spreading across his face as he once again melded with the shadows.

Veronica Weatherstoke didn't want him to fall to his death from a speeding train.

And *that* felt like progress.

Three

VERONICA THOUGHT she'd reached the upper limit of irritation at Sebastian Moncrieff.

Yet here she was, mere *hours* after their nocturnal encounter, seething at him with uncharacteristic vigor. Even in his absence he was a sliver beneath her skin.

An unrelenting prick.

She'd rolled like restless waves in the night, doing her best to escape fevered memories of the man. Recollections that became lurid dreams, once she'd finally wrestled sleep into submission.

Though morning had been her nemesis since she was a girl, Veronica was particularly fond of breakfast. Coffee and scones, biscuits and bacon, soft boiled eggs in their little cups, and toast drenched in butter. These were the things that beckoned her from the warmth of her bed each day.

And Sebastian Moncrieff, that arrogant bully, had deprived her of that pleasure this morning.

Had stolen it, like the knavish pirate he'd been.

That he apparently still *was*.

Because, though she was seated in one of Europe's most opulent first-class dining cars, sinking her teeth into the butteriest croissant she'd had in ages, she could hardly taste a single morsel.

His scent had taken her olfactory senses hostage, filling her with the extraordinarily masculine flavors and aromas that were distinct to *him*. Warm, wild, and clean. Like bergamot and citrus...both sharpened and sweetened with notes of honey.

Should she bottle the essence, she'd make a bloody fortune.

Damn him for being free to walk the world she inhabited! For confining them into a space from which there was no escape. Were she to flee, she'd run out of track.

And even were she to leap from the train, he'd find her still.

She intrinsically knew that, somehow.

In her unbidden thoughts, she had often wondered if their paths would cross again. Of course, she'd always immediately rejected the idea. He'd been arrested by none other than Carlton Morley, the Chief Inspector at Scotland Yard. She'd watched as they'd led him away in irons.

Surely he'd have been tried for kidnapping, theft, privateering, even murder. As it was more than a year after his capture, he should have had his neck stretched by a rope.

Which was one of the reasons she avoided British papers. She found she didn't want to know. Because in all reality she *should* be relieved that justice had been done.

And yet...

A sudden cold dread clenched in her stomach, and she glanced across the table to see Penelope Weller's eyes widen in her elfin face with a brief flash of unmasked trepidation.

Veronica was horrifically, *intimately* acquainted with all that was hidden behind that very expression. The instant physical tension at the approach of an oppressor. The shattering of any pretense of inner peace. The anticipation of humiliation or condemnation. Of punishment and peril.

During her marriage to Mortimer Weatherstoke, the Earl of Southbourne, Veronica learned to read the most insignificant indications of emotion. Such as the tremble of Mrs. Adrienne Weller's teacup as she returned it to its saucer. The tight, compulsive movements of Penelope's throat as she worked to swallow her fear more than once. Hoping her voice wouldn't reveal the chaos within. The returning of both women's hands beneath the table, to grip at each other. To draw strength from a fellow captive.

Veronica steeled her own spine, measuring her voice and breath the moment before Arthur Weller joined them.

"And here I rushed to breakfast, beset with worry that your food would cool whilst you waited for me." He scowled down at his wife and daughter's breakfast plates, on which the food had been more poked and nibbled at than consumed. "I see I needn't have bothered."

This was how Weller expressed his disapproval. Sneering over the spectacles perching on his hawkish nose, he expelled the politest words from his mouth.

Yet they landed like a threat.

The subtext always being: *You will suffer for my displeasure.*

Men like him had so many vast and varied ways of collecting their dues. The range was incredibly wide, spanning from slight cuts and pinpricks of hurtful words, to physical blows that would beat a grown man into dust. Men like Arthur Weller didn't just break bones, he reached inside the people he should have protected and broke their spirits as well.

To say nothing of their hearts.

"I'm sorry, Papa," Penelope whispered, her gaze never leaving the table.

Because his wife and daughter could not speak up, Veronica did it for them, taking perverse pleasure in doing so.

Arthur Weller was always pleasant in public.

"Lend us your pardon, Mr. Weller, we were uncertain if you would join us this morning, as you did not yesterday." She kept her tone conversational, as if oblivious to the fraught atmosphere between the entire Weller family. "In fact, I didn't see you in your cabin at all, so it was assumed you'd awoken early and breakfasted already, seeing as how breakfast began a quarter hour past." Picking up a muffin, she slathered it with preserves and bit off an unladylike mouthful, chewing it *at* him.

This one tasted like strawberries and spite.

Veronica didn't have to look at him to recognize the wrath burning down at her from his dark eyes. Her attention remained firmly affixed to her food, not only because she didn't want to give Weller the satisfaction, but because she disliked the sight of him. He wasn't unsightly, *per se*. A wealth of silvering hair and an impressive mustache bracketed by muttonchops were affixed to rather mild features, weathered by his early years as a seaman. He'd kept that lean, rangy figure into his fifties, and stood taller than most men. Though he'd a volatile intensity about him that she'd noticed cowed people beneath him and his peers, alike. But he hadn't a build she would describe as intimidating.

Not when she'd stood in the presence of leviathans such as The Black Heart of Ben More and the Rook.

Of the tremendous titan that was Sebastian Moncrieff.

"How extraordinary you are, Countess," he replied in an indulgent tone. "Most women so devoted to fashion take care not to eat so much or so often. Though I suppose you are lucky to be possessed of the skills to let out your own gowns as the need, no doubt, arises."

Veronica offered him a smile she hoped did not bare as many teeth as she desired. "Dowager Countess," she corrected. "I know you were not educated with nobility, so I don't mind reminding you that it is commensurate to address me as 'my lady.'"

His eyes narrowed as his smile widened into something that would be accompanied by a snarl in the wild. "Ah yes, how very sad. You are often so jolly, I forget the man who lifted you out of the mire of mediocrity was murdered."

And so shall you be.

The savage thought astonished her.

Veronica was feeling less and less conflicted about his impending demise, and she'd only spent a matter of minutes in his company.

This man sold women and children, or so Moncrieff had mentioned. Just when she didn't think he could be any more evil...

Weller snapped his fingers at the staff and demanded his breakfast, cutting off any need for a reply. The Weller women didn't touch their food again until he'd received and dug into his own, and even then, they chewed as if the delicacies tasted of ash.

"I learned something from a...loquacious companion this morning," Weller said around a bite. He obviously referred to the mistress with which he'd spent the night, intending to embarrass or hurt his wife.

24

Men like him rarely realized that their absence was, in fact, a relief.

"You don't say, darling," Adrienne replied dutifully, batting her pale eyes at her husband in a most disarming way. She'd been a scandalously young bride, thereby possessed of an eligible daughter before her fortieth year. However, marriage to a man like Weller, and eight subsequent failed pregnancies, had pinched deep grooves into her forehead and bracketed her tight frown. Shadows haunted the skin beneath her eyes which sagged from exhaustion, and even her honey-colored coiffure seemed to droop in his presence.

Veronica remembered that self-same expression in the mirror.

Lord, but she wished she could take Adrienne with them, but like so many women she insisted on staying with her husband.

"What did you hear, Papa?" Penelope asked overbrightly, a white pinch encircling her smile and the skin on her knuckles as she stirred her tea.

He puffed out his chest. "Not only are the Duchess of Lowood and her daughter aboard, but also is the Erstwhile Earl. I met him in the observation car last night. Capital fellow, not at all like one hears in the papers."

Veronica froze.

The Erstwhile Earl. She'd heard that moniker before. When the Countess of Northwalk had mentioned it in regard to Sebastian Moncrieff.

Earl of Crosthwaite, she'd called him.

As tempted as Veronica had been to investigate the matter over the months since she'd encountered the man, she'd never allowed herself to do it.

To look into his past would be to admit that Moncrieff had a powerful effect on her, enough at least to arouse curiosity.

"Why do they call him the Erstwhile Earl?" she couldn't help but ask.

"Oh, you don't know?" A victorious chuckle washed her in revulsion. Men like Weller delighted in schooling the uninitiated. "Crosthwaite's father died when he was a lad away at boarding school. The title is old, granted back when a York held the throne, but old Henry Moncrieff lost the last of the fortune and began to parcel off the land to pay debts. Most everything else was taken in taxes upon his death. So, the boy never returned to the drafty ruin that even the Crown didn't want to bother with taking from him."

"He became a pirate, instead." Moncrieff's voice was as smooth, cold, and lethal as his blade from the night before.

Veronica nearly dropped her cup and was unable to avoid a slosh into the saucer as it landed with uncontrolled clatter.

Awareness poured down her spine, and every hair on her body vibrated at an alarming frequency. The electric sensations skittering through her threatened to set her aglow.

It was what his nearness always did to her.

She didn't turn to look, choosing instead to be completely absorbed by her breakfast plate. Yet, she knew exactly where he stood behind them, as if every nerve in her body recognized the proximity.

"My lord." Weller stood, wiping his mouth and turning to greet the Erstwhile Earl. "You'll forgive my idle gossip; I was regaling the ladies about your exploits. You're rather a legend."

"No forgiveness needed," came the amiable reply. "Though my deeds are hardly proper breakfast conversation."

Veronica witnessed his approach through Penelope

Weller's reaction. Her irises, dark like her father's, gave way to dilating pupils. Her pert nose flared, and her delicate jaw went slack as she arched her neck back, and then further, in order to take in the man's sheer immensity. A hand went to her hair, fluttering like a butterfly over the honey curls before smoothing over a lush green morning dress of Veronica's own creation.

Why did the girl have to look so comely in it? So young and unfettered?

Veronica blinked herself back to sanity.

Why the devil did it matter?

"Would you join us for breakfast?" Weller offered Moncrieff, snapping at a waiter and pointing at a chair he wanted taken from another table.

Don't accept. Don't say yes, Veronica pleaded inwardly. *Please just move along.*

"I've already dined," he answered, allowing her to expel her relief on a breath she hadn't known she'd been holding. "But how could I refuse at least one cup of tea with such lovely companions?"

Drat and damn and blast! She dug into her recollection of even more foul curses when the hem of his grey morning suit jacket found her periphery as he stepped to the table.

What in God's name was he doing? A man bent on murder should *not* be seen dining with his intended victim. How could he smile into Weller's face all the while expecting to slide a knife into him at the first appropriate moment?

"My lord, allow me to present my wife, Mrs. Adrienne Weller, and our daughter, Penelope." Arthur Weller swept a hand across the table as the women in question struggled to stand.

"Please, don't get up my account," was Moncrieff's pleasant reply. "I'll sit."

Weller made a grand gesture at Veronica who sat on his other side. "And this is the Dowager Countess Southbourne, the Paris fashion prodigy we've engaged to make Penny's wedding trousseau."

He loved to parade her in front of important people.

"My lord," she murmured in greeting. She could no longer avoid looking at him without drawing notice to her odd behavior, so she steeled her spine and lifted her gaze.

Instantly, she regretted it.

The shadows had been kind last night, concealing the full force of Sebastian Moncrieff's presence.

She'd forgotten he didn't belong to the darkness. That he was this lambent creature of almost blinding splendor, possessed of the depraved sort of good looks that one would ascribe to a pagan god of opulence and sensuality.

On a ship beneath the open, endless horizon he'd been an exceptionally large man.

But on a train where space was at a premium, he took too much of it for the comfort of regularly built people. Like Goliath, he was both a giant and a philistine.

With the scruples of a tomcat.

"A dowager countess employed by a shipping magnate?" Eyes the color of Brandywine lazily touched every part of her visible above the table. Veronica felt quite molested once he'd finished. "My how the world has changed in my years at sea."

Veronica's jaw went slack.

How casually he addressed his crimes. Wore his scandal on his skin and bared it to the world—nay, displayed it in pride of place, as if mischief and malice might be awarded a trophy.

A chair appeared behind him, and he rucked up his

trousers as he sat, making room for his powerful thighs. Dismissing Veronica, he turned the full weight of his charm toward Adrienne and Penelope. "I understand felicitations are in order on your impending nuptials, Miss Weller."

"T-thank you," the girl breathed, her cheeks staining a soft shade of pink.

It took nothing more than a slight smile in the direction of the staff to incite a parade of food and drink in an elegant dance performed only for men of his rank and power.

Ultimately, he ended up choosing an Irish breakfast tea, and pouring an offensive amount of cream and sugar into a cup that looked preposterously small in his hands. "Tell me, Miss Weller, who is the lucky groom?"

"A Count Gyürky in Bucharest," her father answered for her. "He's a direct descendant of Catherine the Great. Much like many of our own noble houses."

"A count, you say?" Belying his words, Moncrieff's sip of tea was decidedly unimpressed. "Ah, well...if you can't find nobility close by, it's worth looking abroad to the Continent."

"Yes—well—Gyürky's holdings are the size of Hampshire," Weller spluttered, not immune to the implied insult.

Veronica leveled Moncrieff with a scathing look, one he summarily ignored.

How abominably he was behaving. Did he not know that the pique coloring Weller's features would be felt by his family? That he'd take it out on the women as if his mortification were their fault?

"He's wealthier than so many of our impoverished noblemen," Weller said with a sniff.

"Yes, I'm certain his goats are well cared for," Moncrieff chuckled, then shrugged. "At least he's not an American."

"Or a *pirate*," Veronica said, finally drawing his notice.

"We were more privateers, my lady," he corrected with a solicitous smile, one that turned her insides rather slippery and soft. "Regardless of reputation, we generally pillaged according to the rules of maritime law."

"Generally?" Veronica wrinkled her nose and clenched her thighs. "Last I checked, the Royal Navy is not at war, nor was the Devil's Dirge under contract with the crown."

"Semantics." Moncrieff waved them away as if they held no bearing whatsoever. "It could be argued that any attack on a British vessel could be considered an act of war."

Was that how he'd wriggled out of trouble with the law?

Or was it because he'd turned the incomparable power of his pulchritude on the queen herself, and the besotted woman granted him full pardon?

Un-bloody-believable.

A handkerchief drifted on an invisible breeze, landing like a silken snowflake at Moncrieff's feet. It heralded the arrival of a strawberry-haired beauty, thrust into view by an older woman with similar features, but which drooped at the jaw like the jowls of a hound.

"Jessica, you are too clumsy," berated the matriarch, with overwrought affectation.

"Allow me." Sebastian bent in his chair and retrieved the scrap of fabric, offering it back to the girl, who was scarcely old enough to have been presented to society.

"Thank you," she demurred with a coy bat of her

lashes. I'm ever so much obliged."

Obliged? He returned a scrap of fabric, not the stolen family jewels.

"Think nothing of it," he replied to the moon-eyed girl, whose entire face bloomed crimson at his wink.

"A true gentleman," the mother cooed from behind her daughter.

Veronica lowered her lashes to hide the complete orbit of her eyes. Surely, she couldn't be the only one to notice that all available debutantes seemed to be thanking him for his mere existence.

"Few who know me accuse me of being a gentleman, madam." His eyes glimmered with merriment as he took another measured sip of his tea.

"I see you don't recognize me," the elder woman addressed the table. "I am Heloise de Marchand, Duchess of Lowood."

This time, the assemblage stood with alacrity. One did not remain seated in the presence of a duchess until she gave her leave.

"Your Grace," Sebastian executed a perfect bow as the duchess nudged the girl forward with alarming blatancy.

"This is my daughter, Jessica."

"A pleasure, Lady Jessica." He caught the girl's forearm and slid his hand down until her gloved fingers curled over his as he bent to press a kiss over her knuckles.

Veronica's own hand curled, her nails biting into her palms.

"I am Sebastian Moncrieff, the Earl of—"

"We are well aware of you," the duchess interjected, as a woman of her age and standing was excused for lapses in manners, so long as they seemed to have done so on purpose. "One does not travel without knowing the importance of one's fellow passengers."

"Indeed." Sebastian flicked a glance at Weller. Or was it Veronica? They stood close enough in the cramped space it was impossible to tell. "Allow me, then, to make presentations to—"

"We've not the time, Moncrieff." The duchess sniffed toward the table, her only recognition of the existence of other people thus far. "Now that we've been introduced and you've proven yourself a gentleman, I'd like to invite you to our private car for breakfast."

His eyes lit with interest, and Veronica felt her own demeanor darken.

He's a bloody pirate! She wanted to scream. How could a woman—*a duchess*—be throwing her young, buxom daughter at the man? Did she not know his seat was in ruins? His family in shambles?

He'd been arrested only a year past!

"It would be rude to leave the lovely Wellers and the Dowager Countess Southbourne's company."

The duchess finally glanced over at them as if they were mud she'd scraped from the bottom of her shoe. "I'd have invited the Countess if she'd not regrettably returned to her origins in *trade*."

"Oh, I don't know," Moncrieff slid Veronica a speaking glance. "Fashion is more of a passionate hobby than anything. Much like the Duchess of Trenwyth does with her paintings."

Veronica's fingers itched to curl around his obscenely thick neck.

Opening her fan, the woman used it as a shield against the now awkward assembly. "The difference is vast, dear Moncrieff. The Duchess of Trenwyth's painting hangs in the Queen's own private quarters. She does not lease her services to *new money*."

New money. The phrase encompassed and oppressed the social standing of entrepreneurs such as manufacturers, transporters, and merchants who were quickly amassing fortunes, often far greater than those held by the landed lords.

Veronica couldn't see Weller's features, but his neck turned an alarming shade of purple.

"You are wicked," Moncrieff teased indulgently, though she noted that his smile was confined only to his lips. "Men like me are forced to dowry-hunt amongst new money, so I cannot share your sentiments."

The duchess's eyes glinted. "Follow me, Moncrieff, there's more to discuss on the topic of dowries." Her head gestured toward the door before she flared her skirts and sailed away, her diminutive daughter trailing in her wake.

Affecting a regretful expression, Moncrieff turned back to the table. "It seems noble duty calls." Rather than hurrying away, he bent and kissed the hand of each lady at the table, leaving Veronica for last. He reached across Weller to envelope her fingers, lips only hovering above her knuckles.

"It's been a rare pleasure," he said before sauntering away.

They all watched, mute, until he was forced to tilt his shoulders to the side in order to fit through the door.

"Insufferable man!" Weller threw his linen on the table and sat down in a heap. "I didn't like him from the moment I laid eyes on him," he said, as if he'd not been close to licking Moncrieff's boots only a moment before.

"I don't think he meant us disrespect," Penelope murmured, her voice painted with awe. "It's impossible to refuse a real-life duchess."

33

"Do you mean to disrespect me by defending him?" Weller snarled, his knuckles whitening as they gripped the side of the table.

Adrienne placed a hand on her daughter's shoulder, as the girl had gone several shades of green. "She meant nothing by it, Arthur. I'm certain we were all overwhelmed by our first brush with a woman of such rank and an earl of such...such..."

Weller leaned forward, his cheeks mottled with barely-leashed rage. "Such. *What*?" he asked from behind clenched teeth.

"Such infamy," she finished quickly.

His nostrils flared for a fraught moment, and then he leaned back into his chair, taking up his cutlery. "One wonders how a body would fare being thrown from a train at this speed," he speculated, apropos of nothing. "Do you think the snow would cushion a fall?"

Veronica didn't remark on the ill-concealed threat, directed at no one in particular. Her entire being was focused on the piece of rolled-up paper Moncrieff had tucked into her hand.

Four

SEBASTIAN most often found anticipation a delicious form of torture.

However, that was before he'd had to wait in the third cargo car back from second class, wondering if Veronica Weatherstoke would be the first woman in his personal history to deny an invitation to meet him.

Rather than luggage, his surroundings were dedicated to freight and shipped goods of every imaginable kind. Copper pipes lashed to the right wall gleamed in the wan light from the window. Across from them, bolted shelves propped up gluttonous bags of barley and seed. Crates of frozen butter were stacked neatly by fragile boxes of wine glasses.

There *would* be a battalion of wine glasses. Their next stop was Paris, after all.

When the far door opened, he breathed a sigh of relief and flattened his back to the wall, hoping the shelves and shadows would provide him cover.

Veronica swept in and turned instantly to lock the door against the winter wind, before glancing at the gloom of the interior. Her attentions were immediately diverted by a tightly packed pile of worn furniture.

Chairs with torn velvet upholstery were stacked upon three-legged tables and the corpses of armoires, all secured by leather straps and chains.

As she'd not yet alerted to his presence, Sebastion took the opportunity to observe her in an artless, uninhibited moment. She inspected every piece of abused antiqued furniture as she pulled her peach gloves from each individual finger.

Why he found the action unbearably erotic, he couldn't say.

It was bloody cold in these unheated cargo cars, why would she be taking off her gloves?

Oh... Oh fuck.

Questioning fingertips entranced him as they tested the textures and details of several pieces while thoughts and opinions escaped her throat in slight speculative sounds. A wordless murmur of discovery, a crestfallen sigh, a small *oh* of surprise as she discovered something unexpected.

He'd been a fool to suggest they meet in such confines, though he did note that it was safer than anywhere with a bed.

Not that he'd ever needed a bed to enjoy sex. Any surface would do, really.

Carefully, almost reverently, Veronica stroked the scratched, pocked surface of a desk, her fingers finding the grooves and following them to their fruition. Closing her eyes, she indulged in a private moment, as if she shared a memory with the desk that caused her to gain three shades of peach to her cheeks.

Sebastian had flirted with, fondled, and fucked an untold number of beautiful women. He was a hedonist at heart, and did his utmost to live up to his reputation at every turn. A man driven by desire, by the indulgence thereof, he consumed whatever pleasure a moment could provide, stretching it out to the final drop.

In the bacchanalia that had been his life, he couldn't ever remember wanting a woman with such ardency.

Truly, it bordered on violence.

Not violence *toward* her, so much as a ferocious, primitive reaction slamming into his body with the power of a war hammer. Skewering him with wicked lances of lust before mocking him with her indifference.

Not only did this leave him intensely perturbed, but also uncharacteristically perplexed. Though painfully ardent, this was no rutting need to throw his hips forward into a warm orifice with a pretty face.

His hands itched to build things for her. To break what insulted her. He wished for a bullet to throw his body in front of. Or a tyrant to topple in her name.

These almost sophomoric desires and drives hadn't been a part of his intentions toward women since he was a lad of fourteen, desperate for a dragon to slay to win his damsel.

As a man, he'd become the monster.

Still was, in her eyes.

Driven by an intensifying inquisitiveness, he crept forward, no longer hiding himself, but also not calling attention to his presence.

Something about the old desk had absorbed her notice so thoroughly, he'd moved close enough to reach for her and she'd yet to register that she was not alone.

He adopted a sprightly tone, so as not to startle her overmuch. "What a lovely old piece. I was fond of one very much like it in my quarters on the Devil's Dirge."

Veronica whirled toward him, pulling her hand away from the surface of the desk as if it'd burned her.

"How did you get in here?" she demanded breathlessly.

37

"Same door as you."

"You mean...you've been here all along?" Her winged, ebony brows met in a scowl. "You did not announce yourself upon my arrival."

"I hope you can forgive my wickedness," he murmured, thinking of all the multitudes of meaning that statement could convey. "It is only that you swept into the gloom looking like a Caribbean sunrise, and I was too breathless to greet you."

Her wary gaze had yet to meet his, and he was getting the idea she found his flirting more aggravating than amusing. His compliment did not go entirely unappreciated, he noted, as she smoothed an idle hand down her bodice and scrutinized the drapes of her lovely skirt before tugging at them.

"What do you want with me?" she inquired of the ground with no little amount of impatience. "Because of your shameful behavior today, I'm keen to stay close to Penelope and Adrienne as Arthur Weller is now in a rotten mood and likely to take it out on them."

"I've been told Weller is in the casino car with his young mistress...the Weller women are safe from his moods for the moment."

"Excellent," she clipped, reaching out to pick at a sliver from the edge of the desk. "I don't want to keep you from courting the duchess's daughter, so if you'll just state your business, I'll be on my way."

His lips twisted into a grimace at the thought of the vapid lady Jessica and her militant mother. "They're courting me, more like. I'd rather leash my life to a leathered old sow."

"Even with her excessive dowry?" she asked, lifting a skeptical brow.

"You forget, my lady, that I've a pirate's hoard of treasure, and no one's whim but my own to spend it on.

I need a debutant's dowry like the lake district needs more rain."

"Oh." She blinked rapidly. "But I've been told your estate and finances are in ruin."

"Come now, Countess, do you believe everything the gossip mill has to offer? Besides, why restore a defunct ruin when I could spend my ill-gotten gains on myself rather than a legacy I'm not likely to sire."

Though his response seemed to trouble her, she still refused to lift her eyes above his cravat. "I suppose your answer in that regard shouldn't surprise me. So, if you please, would you tell me why you've summoned me, and we can both return to the business of the day."

"That very business is why I'd like to speak with you," he said. "I awoke curious as to exactly how you plan to spirit poor Penelope and her lover to America. And also to offer my assistance, such as it is."

"Why would you do that?" she asked suspiciously.

Because Arthur Weller was a dangerous man to cross. Because the conscience he thought he'd buried whispered that her broken trust in him was a fault he needed to work to regain. *Because* something about her overrode every selfish instinct he'd carefully cultivated over the decades.

He could say none of this out loud.

"Because, dear lady, I cannot do my part until yours is done, and impatience is chief among my vast assortment of flaws."

"I see." His answer seemed to mollify her. "Well, the plan is a simple one, really. Once we pull into Gare de Lyon, I've a contact that will conduct us in his coach to Le Havre where they're booked on a steamship to America under pseudonyms."

"I'm impressed." Sebastian examined her with different eyes. She was so shrewd for someone so gentle. A ruthless mind did not often maintain such a soft heart, encased in all that exquisite loveliness.

Lord but she transfixed him.

"You said 'us' when discussing the journey to Le Havre. Does that mean you're going with them?"

"Yes."

The idea of such distance curdled like bad cream in his gut. "To America?"

"No, to the ship. I want to see them off safely, but I also want to come back for Adrienne. She doesn't know that she'll be alone in this world once her husband and only child are gone."

"What if Weller does something to subvert this elopement?" he asked. "Do you have contingencies?"

"Of course." She rolled her eyes, crossing defensive arms over her chest, doing lovely things to her decolletage. "It will be night when we pull into Paris, so in the unlikely event that Arthur Weller disengages himself from his mistress to prevent us from leaving the train, I suppose I'll just have to create a diversion."

"That, at least, will be simple, as I'm certain you're aware you're one of the most diverting creatures on the planet." He reached toward a wayward ringlet that'd come loose from her coiffure and fallen in front of her eyes.

She jerked her head back before he could touch her and retreated several steps. "Please don't."

His hand froze mid-air. Several dark suspicions swirled about in his chest, ones that condemned all those of his sex into a lake of eternal hellfire. A fire he'd often the mind to stoke himself. "Veronica, why can you not look at me?"

"I *am* looking at you."

"My throat does not count. Look at *me*."

Her brows knit together, and even in the dimness

her cheeks flared a color vibrant enough to rival her dress. 'Do not presume to tell me where to look or what to do, sir. You are not my keeper nor my master."

'On the contrary, my lady," he murmured. 'I am but your humble servant."

Her gaze latched onto the desk against which his hip now rested. 'Are we finished? Or was there something else to discuss?"

'Something has driven you to a pique," he observed. 'Was it Weller?"

'It was not."

'Was it me?"

Her silence answered for her as she scratched at a wound in the wooden desktop.

As much as he desired it, he made no move to go closer to her. 'Do I frighten you?"

She scoffed. 'Not in the least."

Lie.

'Come now, I know I've been a cad and a rogue the whole of my life, but are you really afraid that I'll hurt you?" He held his hands out, offering himself up for scrutiny. Surely a woman with your fashion sense would deduce that a man with such a light-grey suit wasn't planning on getting any blood on it. And the fit of it didn't at all allow for tight maneuvering— he'd split the seams.

'You're a criminal and confessed pirate, Moncrieff," she stated with a droll huff. 'Your crew was rather famous for hurting people."

'Never women," he asserted, holding up his finger to make the salient point. 'It was a veritable creed of ours that women and children would always be spared much possible distress from our pirating. One of Rook's sticking points, with which I heartily agreed. You and

41

Lorelai were among the first ladies to ever board the ship."

To his utter astonishment, she snorted. "You are a filthy liar."

"Uncalled for," he admonished her without letting his good nature slip. "How do you figure?"

She gaped at him as if he were the largest, dimmest bulb she'd ever had to contend with. "Our second night on that ship, the captain brought a veritable contingent of prostitutes to entertain the entire crew."

Laughing that away, he waved his hand at her. "That doesn't count—our anchor was down."

"Gah!" She threw her arms up and shifted as if she wanted to pace the length of the aisle. "You are the most ridiculous, infuriating man. How you avoided the noose is one of the great mysteries of our time."

"It really isn't." He chuckled, enjoying how lovely aggravation made her, even in the pallid, grey light of winter filtered through the grime of the window. "I was given an ultimatum, of sorts. It was either declare myself the Erstwhile Earl of Crosthwaite, take up my political seat and lordly responsibilities...or prison, and likely the noose. I will tell you it was one of the most difficult decisions I've yet made. The life of a lord is tedious in the extreme. There are days I would have preferred the gallows."

A noise, half disbelief, half frustration, burst from her chest. "This is why everyone hates the aristocracy."

"Says the countess."

"Dowager!" she cried. "And I never *asked* to be a countess, I fell for Mortimer Weatherstoke before I knew he was an earl's son."

Now it was his turn to be incensed. "If you tell me you loved that cretinous bastard, I'll pitch myself from the train right now."

"Tempting as that outcome may be, I cannot claim to have loved Mortimer Weatherstoke. I found him charming whilst we courted. He was one of the handsomest men I'd met in society, and never revealed the rot he'd festering in his soul until it was too late."

Questions crowded into Sebastian's throat until they choked him into silence. He wanted to understand her damage. To not merely patch up the holes perforating her soul and spirit...but to truly mend them.

How can someone as broken as you fix her? queried his conscience. *She is better than you will ever be.*

This whisper was precisely why he'd locked his cursed conscience away some time ago, and never planned to set it free again.

What fucking key did this woman hold to spring his better self from its carefully maintained prison?

"I did not desire a title," she continued. "I wanted to be a wife. To bring my family pride. To care for a grand home and devote myself to various philanthropic causes. I wanted to raise kind sons and strong daughters. I wanted... Why are you looking at me like that?"

"Because I'm going to kiss you," he blurted. "I thought that was bloody obvious."

"You are *not*."

Except...she didn't step back this time.

"You want me to."

Her luscious mouth dropped open. "I *never*."

Gigantic. Lie.

"And why not?" he asked, mindful of the fact that many people lied to themselves, most of all. Especially when it came to affairs of the heart.

Or any affairs, really.

Her eyes lifted above his tie, for once, but stalled on his lips. "I know where that mouth has been." She made a disgusted face.

"As they've always been attached to my face," he teased, "I can vouch for their whereabouts exclusively. I vow they've never ventured where they ought not."

"I know they've found their way between the thighs of a common strumpet," she accused. "They could be diseased."

"Have they?" He scratched his head, thoroughly enjoying himself. So, the countess was a gossip? What fun —he'd found a delightful flaw they could share. "There are simply too many strumpets to remember them all, though I'm not at all in the habit of paying for anything considered common."

"How could you forget?" She threw her hands up in the air as if giving up. "You were feasting—nay —fiending on her that day in the ship. I thought you might be in danger of losing your tongue in her—"

"You. Watched?" Every muscle in Sebastian's body clenched at the very idea. Not with anger or embarrassment, no, with something much more dangerous than that. Suddenly his desire had teeth and claws, ripping his skin and his uncultivated self-discipline to shreds.

Luckily, she was too irked to notice. "I was looking for an escape! I certainly didn't install that lens between your stateroom and my prison."

"It was hardly a prison," he defended. "That bedroom boasted the most comfortable mattress on the entire ship. The crystal alone cost—"

"The door locked from the outside!"

"Only to keep you from doing yourself a mischief. You were threatening to leap into the ocean in the middle of a storm to attempt an impossible swim back to shore."

"To avoid a fate as offensive as that poor prostitute had to suffer beneath you."

Sebastian remembered the encounter, because he'd

been so inflamed by the woman in the next room, he'd selected a strumpet with similar hair and blazing green eyes. He'd feasted upon her, and then he'd filled her every orifice with the singular enthusiasm he'd felt toward this particular prisoner.

He'd watched the wall that separated him as he'd come, not knowing that she was pressed to the very oculus they used to keep an eye on their captives.

Watching him in return.

He'd be damned if that didn't send every available drop of blood straight to his cock.

Luckily, he'd spent twenty years learning to layer indifference over any other emotion as he interacted with the world. "As a point of clarification, I wonder just what about my performance offended you so?"

"The entire bloody thing offended me," she exclaimed. "From start to—to—finish."

I've got you, he thought, unfurling the smile of a Cheshire cat.

"One must wonder, my lady, if you found what you saw as offensive as you claim, then why watch the entire display?"

It was cruel, really, to remain silent while she sputtered and groped for an answer she likely didn't understand. But the discovery was too delicious not to dine on for a few moments before taking pity on her. "There's nothing to be ashamed of, Countess, we've all a bit of a voyeur inside of us...some more than others, apparently."

"I am *not*—"

"I've a point of contention, however." He held up a finger. "At no time was that woman—or any woman of my intimate acquaintance, for that matter—in a state of suffering. Were you watching closely, you'll notice I pleasured her to fruition at least twice before allowing my own. That is a personal point of pride for me."

Wrapping her arms around her middle in a decidedly protective gesture, the Veronica still didn't cave to his excellent point. "Women like her are paid to stroke the ego of a man. They can manufacture their pleasure as well as any wife."

He did not miss her inadvertent admission there, but smoothly avoided picking at it. "I've paid a woman to stroke many parts of me, madam, but my ego has never been in need."

"Now *that* I believe," she said acerbically. "Though I suppose your overinflated sense of self would not allow you to imagine that a woman might have faked her enjoyment of your attentions."

"Never happened."

"So, say you all," she challenged. "But I know there are ways to manufacture one's enjoyment to appear like the real thing."

"Certainly," he agreed. "But there are ways to tell, so many men ignore it, either because of ignorance or simple selfishness. These are impossible to fabricate."

"If you say so."

"If a man is simply searching for writhing yips, then he could certainly be fooled," Sebastian conceded, lowering his voice and leaning toward her. "But, like so many untamed creatures, a woman's desire is so often conveyed with unspoken, incontrollable signals. Take, for example, the dilation of her eyes. The plumping of her lips with blood and the tightening of her nipples. Her breath will come more quickly, and her delicate nostrils will flare."

Sebastian very much enjoyed the fact that she did her level best to measure her rapid breaths and tuck her full lips against her teeth.

"The same could be said of a frightened woman, as an aroused one," she said, in a voice husked with sensation and tightened with strain.

"If I cannot tell from a woman's reaction if she is aroused, then it is indisputable that her sex will reveal all."

"You're...you're being absurd," she accused.

If he reached out and touched her cheek in that moment, Sebastian might have diagnosed her with a fever. She was ripe and primed, and that likely contributed to her temper.

A gentleman would allow her a moment to recover.

But he never claimed to be a gentleman, and the predator within him could scent her arousal like a shark sensed blood in the water.

Now was no time for a retreat.

Instead, he splayed his hand close to hers on the desk and leaned down until his lips hovered above the shell of her ear. Not one part of them touched the other.

But every nerve in his body was alive with the feel of her. Attuned to the very vibrations of her atmosphere. "Your intimate skin flushes with color," he continued, in a voice barely above a whisper, threatening to be swept away by the rhythmic cacophony of the train. "The hood of delicate flesh becomes swollen, engorged, revealing the clever, magical button it protects. That delicious little place where so much of your pleasure is contained. The folds will be slippery with desire, and if paid the correct attention, you'll release a flood of moisture upon your climax that would take me two swallows to contain. Your muscles would clench at my cock with powerful, chaotic little spasms. Trust me, my beauty, these are things that cannot be feigned. Surely you know that."

She said nothing. *Did* nothing.

In fact, they stood like that for so long he straightened and pulled away to examine her with a twinge of concern.

"Do you know that? Have you ever..."

She stared down at their fingertips splayed on the desk, as close as they could be without touching. Breath sawed in and out of her with marked difficulty, unsteady with the force of her trembles.

These were no small vibrations, Sebastian noted. But great, bone-wracking tremors, wrought by overpowering emotion.

He knew the answer, and the heart he claimed to have left on some deserted island somewhere broke at the injustice.

*"*Veronica. Look at me."

She flinched, but didn't retreat. Perhaps he was being unintentionally crueler than he realized. He wanted to torment her with arousal. But...what if arousal was a torment for her?

What if Mortimer Weatherstoke created wounds that were still taking time to scar?

Swallowing a surge of rage, he slid his hand closer, allowing the energy to arc between them before the pads of their fingers touched.

*"*Look at me," he pressed, gentler this time.

With infinite slowness, she tilted her neck back until their gazes met and held. Even in the dim light, her eyes gleamed the color of the most exotic eastern jade.

To Sebastian's astonishment, something within him calmed.

In the past, he'd been told that to look into the eyes of the right woman was like falling, losing oneself in their color, or perhaps drowning in their depths. The earth would move, the planets would align, and all that melodramatic, romantical nonsense.

How intriguing to learn they'd been wrong.

This was neither falling nor drowning. Quite the opposite, in fact.

The earth had ceased to move entirely.

For once in his bedeviled life, Sebastian quieted. He stilled. Cords of velvet and silk encircled his limbs and secured him to this spot, to this moment, forcing him to remain in one place long enough to catch up with himself...

And take a breath.

A slow, easy inhale, flavored with notes of orchid and amber, bloomed inside of his chest with the languid deliberation of a sunset. Refusing to bend to the will of Man, God, or the relentless influence of Time itself, the sensation struck him dumb and stripped him of the wits upon which he so heavily relied.

Miraculous.

There was no other word for it. With each breath taken deeper into his chest, the consistent tightness eased, replaced by another need that surprised him as precious little did in this world.

His desire, though all-consuming, had lost its violent edge. The possession and provocation thrumming through his veins paused in his chest to expand and melt, before flowing in languid, honeyed beats to the rest of him, carrying a foreign substance as dangerous as any toxin.

One to which he couldn't subscribe an exact identification.

Tenderness, perhaps. Vulnerability. Need, in its most generous form.

The need to worship the parts she kept hidden, even from herself. To adore what had never even been appreciated. To give to her what had only been taken.

He knew the bliss of unrepentant indulgence. He'd

tasted the sweetness of discarded inhibitions. He'd drenched himself in pleasure so heady it'd bled into pain and become all the more intense for it.

And this vision of desire had never even been allowed a taste?

In-fucking-tolerable.

"Veronica." Lord how he loved to say her name. How he hoped he could whisper it against her sex. "Let me make you come."

Five

"I AM *NOT* HAVING sex with you." It wasn't a sentence Veronica imagined she'd be forced to utter today.

Or ever.

Especially not to this man.

Furthermore, she'd never even considered that the denial would be a difficulty.

Sebastian Moncrieff had her pinned down. Not physically, but in every other conceivable way. Somehow, he'd guessed at the desire she'd discovered more than a year ago, as she'd witnessed him fornicate with another woman.

On a desk very much like this one.

His head had danced between the woman's thighs, and drawn by a macabre curiosity, Veronica had watched in fascination as the woman had cried and strained and screamed beneath his attentions.

Veronica's disbelief had been accompanied by another distressing discovery. One that'd made her thighs clench on an aching pulse accompanied by a yawning chasm of emptiness deep in her womb.

The sight of his naked body had intensified the

51

ache. The play of muscle swelling and cording in his arms and shoulders. The flat of his tongue on forbidden flesh. The strain of his taut abdominals as he hammered her into the desk.

It was the first time she'd watched a woman climax. That she'd known such a thing was possible.

Her body had responded by releasing a rush of wet desire, and the ache had been so overwhelming that even the friction of her thighs with each step was impossibly, *unbearably* sensual against the slick thrum of need.

She'd resisted him then, and hadn't had to contend with such unwanted sensations in the time since.

Until today, when he insisted upon invoking the wicked memories, along with her body's reaction to them.

He'd explained her own desire to her, which should be the most aggravating factor in the entire world.

And yet, here she was, a pulsing puddle of slick arousal, her legs ready to give out at any moment.

She refused to give him the satisfaction.

"I'm never doing *that* again," she vowed. "I know you think you are some legendary sort of lover, and I'm sure you've honed your skills with untold multitudes of women, but I will not yield. You can look to take your pleasure elsewhere—am I understood?"

Closing her eyes, she wished her voice carried the same strength as did the words, but alas, her voice trembled as pathetically as her legs did.

"I think it is I who am misunderstood by you, dear Veronica," he said. "I'm not after taking pleasure, only giving it."

She did her level best to wither him with a look. "I have not given you leave to address me so informally. It is 'my lady' or nothing at all." She wasn't the sort that insisted on such proprieties, except when her hackles were so thoroughly engaged. She needed space. Air. A moment to think! All of which was in short supply in his presence.

"Seeing as we're contriving a murder together, I reckoned we were past such distinctions."

"Well…" She groped about for a witty rejoinder and came up with exactly nothing. "We're not. It is just such distinctions that keep us civil."

"Fine—then allow me a kiss, my lady?"

She eyed him warily, unstitched by the dimples beneath his puckish smile. By the width of his jaw and the roguish sparkle in his otherwise lethal eyes. He was the embodiment of carnality. Temptation incarnate sent from the Devil himself, to entice her.

"Only a kiss?" What was she doing? Surely not considering this madness. "You'll expect no…no pleasure from me?"

"You have my word."

"Words are empty," she said on a hitch of breath as he lifted a finger to her lips, tracing whisper soft trails of fire on the outline of her mouth.

"One finger." That finger traced down her chin, the tiny buttons of her high-necked gown, down the center of her throat, awakening nerve endings she was unaware she'd possessed. "And a kiss. That's all I ask. If I touch you with anything else, you have my permission to cut the offending appendage off."

Curiosity overcame her contrariness. "One finger?"

"So long as it has free rein to roam where it likes."

Intimate muscles gave an involuntary clench. "I don't know…"

"It is a proposal of zero risk, my lady, with only pleasure to be gained. To be guaranteed."

"But what if…" She paused, a familiar insecurity gripping her.

Mortimer had always been angered at her lack of response, her grimaces of pain, and her general discomfort in the marriage bed. He'd humiliated her in front of doctors and mocked her openly about her frigidity. After so long, she'd been beyond caring what disappointed the brute, let alone what pleased him.

But this man? Something told her she would not withstand his disdain. Could not risk it.

"What if I am not able?" she whispered.

A storm gathered on his features that somehow made him all the more beautiful. "Woman, during this impossible and purely hypothetical event, the fault would entirely be mine. I would have failed us both and would immediately request another attempt."

It wouldn't be her fault.

None of this was her idea, responsibility, nor was it incumbent upon her to even perform her duty of *receiving* the pleasure...

How many nights had she lain awake, beset with the memory of that woman writhing beneath him? How many times had she wondered? Wanted? Yearned?

For a mere taste of what he did to her.

"One finger," she acquiesced.

The splendor of his victorious smile blinded her, and it took an embarrassingly long time for her to figure out just why he patted the top of the desk. "I would help you climb up, but alas even *my* finger is not so strong."

She opened her mouth to verbally protest, while her body moved to comply, sliding onto the desktop until her feet swung above the floor.

Eyes gleaming like a predator who only stalked at night, his mouth descended, claiming hers before she could change her mind.

Six

IT WAS JUST AS WELL.

His kiss melted away any objection with a suffusion of instantaneous warmth. In contrast, his lips were cool and dry as they swept and slanted across her stunned mouth, quietly unraveling every knot of her taut, anxious muscles. She'd expected passion from him—skillful, artful seduction, and dominant, masculine impatience.

What she found instead was a coaxing, tender exploration. Unhurried and uncomplicated. Even though he carefully held his tremendous body away from her own, he somehow imprinted upon every inch of her.

And yet...she was not distracted by roaming hands or the fervent press of his demanding arousal.

Her entire being was focused on the firm, shifting pressure of his mouth as he nibbled at the corners of her own before exerting the tiniest sucking tension, pulling her passion-plumped bottom lip to roll between his.

Lord but it was lovely and—*oh!*

A velvet swipe of his tongue against the seam of her mouth stole all breath from her body and all the thoughts from her head.

She lost herself in the seductive heat of this act. So familiar to a woman once married, and yet so foreign. This man was different in every way to her husband.

The shape of him, the scents and sentiments.

The safety.

That word gave her a moment's pause. This man exuded danger. Radiated wicked disregard for all things reliable and reasonable.

For heaven's sake, he was there to murder a man.

So why did she suddenly want to enfold herself against him? To crawl into his arms like a child and make a cradle of his strength...

When his seeking tongue once again tested the topography of her mouth, she opened for him with a sibilant sigh, before fully realizing what she'd done.

Alarmed, she braced herself for the invasion. The wet, smothering plunge that would create a mash of lips against teeth and a gagging sort of fullness in her throat.

She nearly expired when he met her own tongue with his before retreating, testing the curve of her lips as he did. That soft sucking motion invited her tongue into his mouth, enticing her to explore the warmth there.

He tasted divine.

Both bitter and sweet, like the finest, darkest chocolate. He made way for her exploration while caressing and teasing her with silky darts and swirls. It was not a dance to which she knew the steps, but he led her with a precision and expertise she relied upon.

Hollow, guttural noises and deep, appreciative sounds encouraged her on, vibrating across her lips, into her mouth, and down her spine to land at the very core of her desire.

So absorbed was she in the kiss—the first kiss that truly curled her toes—she'd been oblivious to his other designs until cold air kissed the tender skin above her stockings.

Ripping her mouth from his with a gasp, she clutched at the pile of skirts he'd gathered above her knees.

"Yes, do secure them there, that will be ever so helpful," he urged with a playful tone, though something both savage and devious glinted in his eyes.

"This isn't—what the devil are you—I don't think we—"

He pressed that infernal finger to her lips. "Now is not the time to think, Countess, but to *feel*."

Hot breaths exploded around the flat of his finger and arrested his gaze, while she trembled and struggled with her desires, her past, and her crippling anxieties. "I don't know what I feel," she confessed, unable to keep the wobble from her chin. "I don't know how to feel. How to do any of this in the way that—"

He smoothed the back of his knuckle over her chin, hooking the finger beneath it to lift her face to meet his.

"Do nothing," he said firmly.

She shook her head, but he didn't release her. "I don't understand."

"I've a delightful task to perform. However, *your* entire—and might I say delectable—body has but one job. To think and do as little as is possible. Do not feel on my account, only yours. Don't go looking for pleasure, let it find you."

"But—"

"Do your best to resist me, to remain unaffected. Do nothing at all, if you are so inclined."

"But then you won't be able to make me—"

His hand left her mouth and stole its way beneath her skirts. The fingertip traced the seams of her stockings against her thigh robbing her of the ability to speak. To breathe.

"Doubt me all you dare," he said darkly against her lips. "But do not rush your satisfaction, my lady. I am eager for the challenge."

He stole what was left of her sanity with another kiss, this one more ardent and impassioned than before. It drew from her a surprising form of impatience as he unleashed the full force of his seductive prowess upon her unsuspecting, insignificant defenses.

A spin of his tongue accompanied the rasp of his rough finger against the edge of her stockings. A barely-there nip of his teeth drew her attention from the line he traced up her thigh.

When he found the seam of her drawers, she couldn't tell which of them uttered the deep, needy moan. Though he was gentle and methodical, she could still sense the pace of his heart, hammering with a rhythm as furious as her own.

And then he was *there*.

One finger, true to his word, stroking through intimate hair and delving into soft, wet flesh.

She liquified beneath his touch, her legs melting further apart, her pulse abandoning its vocation and her lungs emptying of breath. She needed none of it to survive...

Not when the slippery warmth of his hand suffused her with such electric sensation.

With life.

Crooning soft, unintelligible words against her skin between worshipful little kisses, he smoothed his lips over her hairline, her eyes, her nose, her chin, and her cheekbones before dragging his mouth down the sensitized curve of her jaw, igniting erotic sparks of sensation over her entire body.

His leisurely explorations through engorged ruffles of her feminine sex was a turbulent lesson in frustration. Not only had her anxieties fled, she was instantly overtaken by a demanding urgency.

One he apparently seemed inclined to ignore.

"Dear God, but I could do this all day," he groaned against her ear. "You are so sweet, so slick, so abidingly perfect."

She couldn't summon the words to reply. Not only because of what his diabolical finger was doing to her, but because of the deliberate depth of his voice. The gratification she identified in the words and the fervency of his tone.

It was suddenly as if someone else had taken control of her body. For surely, *she* would not undulate her spine forward, rolling her hips against his finger, seeking the one touch that he couldn't seem to give her. She was not the sort of woman who squirmed and gasped in wordless, artless physical pleas.

It was only that the aggravating man had touted his skills so adroitly, and all he seemed to be able to do is build some sort of throbbing, arching, aching, almost painful pressure to a fevered pitch.

Sweat bloomed on her body and her spine cracked with her next demanding arch.

"Why?" the question ripped from her dry throat.

He lifted his mouth from her throat. "Why what, my darling?"

"Why won't you just..." She had no idea what he needed to do. To move, to find that place that throbbed and release it before she screamed.

"Oh, my poor lady, I am being exceedingly cruel. Selfish even."

"Why?" she whispered again, hating him a little. Wanting him a lot. Needing him more than she liked to admit. Craving what he was doing to her. Among other things.

'Because I didn't think that you'd come apart so easily...so quickly. I hoped to play for longer..." Upon a reluctant sigh, his clever finger did something that made her entire body jerk before pulling back.

Play? Was this recreation for him? When he was so obviously not the focus of the game, but the arbiter of it... How could he be enjoying it so much?

She rolled her hips in a display beyond the reach of shame. 'Please." The plea escaped on a desperate sound, closer to a whine than she cared to admit.

"This is why you are dangerous," he growled, as if to himself. 'No matter what I want, it seems I am powerless to deny you anything."

With that, he unleashed an erotic assault upon her sex that appropriated what was left of her dignity. Carnal strokes evoked torturous shivers that built upon themselves until they coalesced into clenching pulses. She cried out. Her arms reaching for him, clutching at his shoulders with helpless claws as wave after wave of unencumbered ecstasy threatened to drag her out into an ocean of lust and languor. Just when she thought the moment might pass, it escalated into another thrilling, soul-searing burst until the sensation became so exquisite, she could no longer distinguish the difference between pleasure and pain.

When she began to writhe, to seek escape, the pressure of his finger lifted but did not leave her. He let her down slowly, bringing her back from the brink and allowing her to float upon the smaller waves as they pushed her back toward the shore.

When she returned to herself, bedraggled and half-drowned, Veronica realized that Sebastian had kept his word. He'd not touched her with aught but his mouth and one finger.

One magical, maniacal finger.

She, however, had attached herself to the thick column of his body as if he were the only thing keeping her from being swept away and lost.

Realizing that she was clinging to him like a ridiculous ninny, she disentangled herself from him, suddenly tentative and shy.

His arms moved, as if to hold her in place, but he stopped short of touching her.

"My God." If she had to ascribe a word to his tone, it would be *marvel*. "I've been to every place claiming to be a wonder in this world. I've handled treasure you wouldn't believe existed. I've toured galleries and museums with the greats, names you would expire to hear. And never in this lifetime have I witnessed anything so beautiful as your body arched in climax."

A strangled giggle escaped her, and she placed a hand on his chest to halt the kiss he intended for her lips. "You needn't flatter me," she assured him.

He made a wry sound. "I have never flattered you, Countess. Were I a sculptor, I'd recreate it so you could agree with me. But, alas, I was born without talent in that regard."

She couldn't be so certain of that. She'd been nothing more than a boneless, shapeless heap in his hands, and with untold skill he'd...

Well, he'd transformed her.

The realization was a bitter one. She didn't want something so irrelevant to him as a passing tryst in a dusty cargo car to be a formative moment in her life.

But here she was, adrift in a storm of her own making.

Up until now, her entire existence had been about

what she could do for others. How she appeared to them. She'd been so aware of her every movement, what her features conveyed, how to modulate her voice and moderate her words in just such a way. She'd been the creation of her social-climbing parents, her finishing school, the rigorous life of a countess, and ultimately the quick temper and heavy fists of her husband.

For one surreal encounter, Sebastian Moncrieff had stolen that capability.

No, she was being unfair.

He'd *relieved* her of that *obligation*. Had converted her into a creature of need and hunger and unfettered pleasure. A pleasure he'd offered. Gifted. Without so much as a whisper of *quid pro quo*.

What kind of man did such a thing? Here she thought she had his measure. That she'd peeked into his empty heart and found it beat only at his pleasure.

Was there more to the Erstwhile Earl than even he realized?

Pulling back, she arched her neck to look up at him.

The taut mien of his skin pulled across hungry bones made him look older and even more dangerous. His gaze was feral and greedy, his jaw hard.

When his lips parted, fear lanced through her, turning her pulse to thunder.

The Devil was about to demand his due. What would he do to her if she refused?

"Let me use my mouth. I could coax another from you if you'd let me."

She blinked. Once. Again. Uncertain she heard him correctly. He wanted to give *her* another climax. With his mouth?

Unbidden, her eyes traversed the length of his body to find the barrel of his erection straining the front of his trousers.

Lord but he was large.

"Don't." The snarl rumbled from deeper in his chest than she dared to venture. "Don't look at me like that. Don't touch me or I—" He cut off, taking a long moment to compose himself. "Just let me taste you?"

"I can't." Her tight throat worked over a swallow. "I can't right now."

"Oh, trust me, Countess, you can."

"No. I mean..." She struggled with her skirts, shoving them back over her knees and sitting straight. "I have to go to Penelope. There is too much to do... Weller could be returning for them."

He pushed himself away from the desk with a tortured groan. "Say the youngsters escape without a hitch and are on their cheerful way to America. *Then* would you consider my offer? If I don't taste you, I'll probably expire of thirst."

"I'll be going with them."

Pursing his lips, he considered this. "I'll meet you in Le Havre. There's a lovely grand hotel—"

"I'm not going to have intercourse with you." She wriggled away from him, doing her best to ignore the curious pulses and aftershocks of what he'd done to her.

"You've said that already," he reminded her with a solicitous smile. "It's a stipulation I've unenthusiastically agreed to."

Veronica attempted to stand on legs now made of wet clay and shot him a look of disbelief. "Then why offer to—that is—what do you get out of it?"

He shrugged. "I've had plenty of orgasms. This was your first. You have some catching up to do. I promise you'll enjoy yourself."

She pressed her hands to fevered cheeks. "The question is why *you* would enjoy it when I'm giving you nothing in return."

"Because..." He lifted his finger and pressed it between his lips, his eyes never leaving hers as he drew it out slowly. "You have no idea how divine you taste."

"Dear God, don't do that." She seized his elbow and tugged on it.

His smile was utterly wicked. "You cannot stop me unless you relent. This cannot be the last time I appreciate flavor of your—"

Surging forward, she slapped a hand over his wicked mouth. "Christ," she huffed.

"Blasphemer." The accusation was muffled by her palm, which he licked, playfully.

Snatching her hand back, she closed her eyes and pinched the bridge of her nose, actively refusing to be charmed. "You're impossible."

"Come now, Countess, you must admit. The danger is splendid, isn't it?"

Her head snapped back up. "What are you talking about?"

"It makes everything better. More intense. The secret meeting in a place we might be discovered. The excitement of a clandestine adventure to facilitate two young lovers. I can see it in your color, in the brightness behind your eyes. You are made for this, and you are magnificent."

"And *you* are categorically mistaken."

He laughed at her then before swooping in for an intoxicating kiss.

"Until tonight, my lady," he vowed before sauntering out and leaving her in the chill of the cargo car, still trembling with the memory of his heat.

And the impossible hunger he'd awakened inside of her.

Seven

VERONICA DIDN'T ALLOW herself to breathe until she spied Penelope Weller and her lover, Adam Grandville, making their careful way toward her on the train platform.

Parisians and travelers blurred together in the colorful chaos of the Gare de Lyon, performing a polite waltz as they either disembarked or boarded the train. Any other day Veronica would have enjoyed the spectacle, but she couldn't allow herself a moment's peace until the train pulled away from the station and the young couple was out of Weller's reach.

Pasting on a smile at their approach, she felt it melt immediately from her face as she took in their identical expressions. "What is it? What's wrong?"

Rather than answer, Penelope and Adam stepped to the side, revealing a third companion.

Adrienne.

She'd a carpet bag gripped in two hands and even the veil of her emerald velvet hat couldn't hide her swollen lip and blackening eye.

Blast and damn. While Veronica was dallying with

Sebastian in the cargo car, the poor woman had been suffering her husband's violent displeasure.

"Please don't be cross with us," Adam pleaded earnestly, swiping his fine hat from his dark head to clutch in front of him. "But Penny and I couldn't leave her. I kept thinking...what if she were my own mother? I'd do anything to save her from such a monster."

Veronica had to blink back tears, so touched was she by Adam's decency. A kind heart was often hard to find. Gentlemen abounded these days, but a truly gentle man?

A rare treasure, indeed.

"Adrienne..." Veronica paused, struggling with the secrets she held. "What if I told you that you might very soon become a widow? Would you still want to go? To give up everything your husband might leave you?"

"My husband has nothing but vices and debtors, my lady," the woman answered with downcast eyes. "His wealth has become sham. I will be left with less than nothing...but if I stay, I will become nothing."

"I'm so sorry," Veronica hugged the fragile woman to her.

"Dear Adam has invited me to live with his family in Boston. They've a summer home somewhere called Montauk, right on the sea." The little spark of hope in Adrienne's voice ignited something inside of Veronica as well.

Struck with anxiety, she pulled away. "Of course, you can have my seat on the coach to Le Havre, but are only two tickets on the ship. Your cabins—"

"We'll manage." Adam said with confidence. "This is a trip I've taken often in my life. I can navigate preparations easily."

Veronica found a new appreciation for the lad. He

might look boyish and a bit innocent, even for his age, but he'd the steady gaze of a capable man.

"What about your travel papers?" she remembered with alarm. "I only have two forged copies for Penny and Adam. Should anyone look at the register...they'll know where to find you. Furthermore, you won't be able to board the ship without them."

"I don't care if I'm found, I won't return." Adrienne's eyes blinked against instant panicked tears. "But...*he* keeps my papers and all money. Somewhere in his cabin. He wouldn't tell me where."

Adam stepped forward. "I will go back and get them."

"No." Veronica put a staying hand on his lean chest. "You won't be allowed near his car, as the porters and ushers don't know you. But I've been Penelope's companion since London and will gain easy access." Taking the bag from Adrienne, she pushed it into Adam's hands and pointed to the coach in which she'd hired three seats to Le Havre. "You two help settle her into the coach and let me search for the papers."

Whirling on her bootheel, she dashed back for the train, weaving in and out among some rather incensed travelers.

Lifting her skirts to ascend the steep, unsteady steps to the train, she grasped the large hand that reached down to lift her up and came face-to-face—or face to chest, rather—with Sebastian Moncrieff.

"You came back." His pleased smile broke over her like the rays of spring sunshine dawning over a late winter's night. "Couldn't wait until Le Havre to collect on my promise?"

His what?

A tongue smoothed over his full lip, reminding her what he intended to do.

Oh... No. She couldn't think of that now. Couldn't allow the inconsequential parts of her to awaken when she had such an important task in front of her.

Which was?...

Papers! Dear God, how was it a man could be so handsome he made her forget what she was about?

Scowling up at him, she snatched her hand from the warmth of his enveloping grip. "Adrienne Weller took my place in the coach. She's leaving him."

His smile became impossibly brighter, revealing both rows of even, white teeth. "Excellent. I applaud her decision. I've been thinking, I could take my blade to Weller now, and then maybe you and I should find a bed here in Paris. It's a city for lovers, after all."

Veronica blinked up at him in disbelief for a split second before shoving her shock aside. "I hardly have time for this—please move." She made to shoulder past him, unsuccessfully.

"What's happened?" he asked, sobering only slightly.

"Adrienne needs her travel papers and I have to retrieve them before the train takes off again."

Sebastian checked a fine watch hanging from his silk vest. "We hardly have time."

"That is precisely what I just said!"

"So it is. What can I do to assist?"

"You can stay out of my way."

To her utter astonishment, he turned to the side like an opening door, making a sweeping motion for her to pass.

She shot forward, painfully aware that she needed to traverse three cars of crowded hallways...

Drat. She should have stayed on the platform and boarded on Weller's car, though a look out the window told her the platform was no less congested than the halls.

'Don't follow me," she snapped to Sebastian over her shoulder. 'It's conspicuous. Suspicious, even."

'But it isn't," he corrected. 'I'm often seen following pretty women."

For some reason, his words tasted both sweet and sour. 'You should keep your eye on Weller," she muttered. 'That is how you can help."

'I was, but he is busy doing what I'd rather be doing with you."

She turned with an aggravated growl that only seemed to amuse him further. 'Might you not be—whatever this is?" She hadn't the words for it.

Charming? No, too infuriating for that.

Romantic? No, too wicked for that.

'I beg you to be silent so that I might focus on the task at hand."

To her surprise, he said not another word, but remained her shadow. It occurred to Veronica to be incensed at his audacity, but then his presence was actually useful. The crowd parted for him like a biblical hero—or plague—making way for the width of his shoulders and the force of his presence. Sebastian Moncrieff didn't merely occupy space. He claimed it. He owned it. He was the master of whatever ground he walked upon, and she was currently under his protection.

A part of her wanted to resent that fact.

To begrudge the feminine pleasure it brought her.

But there wasn't the time for that, either.

When they reached the Weller car, she went straight to Arthur's cabin and began to rifle through the few drawers bolted to the wall by the expensively appointed bed.

In contrast, Sebastian flipped over the mattress and checked within every pillowcase before lifting Weller's entire trunk and dumping the contents on the bed.

That was one way to do it, Veronica supposed.

Finding nothing, she pulled open a cupboard and froze.

"Blast and damn it all! The papers must be in this safe." Stronger curses perched on her lips, but she didn't allow them to escape.

"Say it." The dark command rumbled so close to her ear, she could feel the warmth of his breath tease at wisps of her hair.

"Say what?"

"The word that's itching your tongue. Say it. I imagine it's something like... *Fucking hell*."

That word.

In her ear.

From behind.

Fucking.

"I don't say such things," she informed him, her voice stiffer than her melting legs. "I'm a lady."

"It'll make you feel better," he promised.

Needing him to back away before his scent overwhelmed her, she elbowed him in the chest. Not hard, but enough to feel like she might have elbowed a statue made of granite or marble. "What would make me *feel better* is getting into that safe."

"I could do it, rather easily," he boasted.

She turned around, finding his mouth entirely too close for comfort. "I-I don't believe it."

"Please, this thing is child's play." He lifted one sardonic brow, before drawing his finger down the ridge of her nose as if she were an adorable child. "You *can't* have forgotten I'm a pirate."

She slapped his hand away archly. "Then do it."

"First you have to say it."

"No."

"All right," he almost sang the words while making a dramatic show of checking his watch once more. "I think we've only ten more minutes until we pull away from here. I suppose I should leave you to your—"

She seized his elbow. "Are you really going to abandon—"

He turned back with a sinful smirk. "Come on, my lady, say it."

Fine. Fine she would say the bloody word! *"Fucking hell* but you're impossible."

His laugh was low and rich and exasperatingly victorious as he crouched in front of the safe to inspect it. Holding his hand back to her without looking up he said. "I need one of your two-pronged hairpins and that hat pin with the golden feather.

Veronica put her hand up to her braided knot held in place by three stick pins and topped by a little fascinator of dark gold skewered through with a single feather pin.

"The quicker the better, Countess," he prodded.

Plucking the pins from her hair, she took the hat from her head and smoothed her crown with anxious motions. His large fingers made astoundingly deft motions with the delicate pins in the lock and the safe was open in less than half a minute.

Veronica reached in to find the papers conveniently tucked into a well-labeled leather file.

Heedless of the mess, they both burst out the door and made for the rear of the car. Just as Veronica would have leapt from the train onto the platform, she was bodily lifted from around the waist and set behind Sebastian in one graceful sweep.

"Unhand me, you oaf, I have to—!"

Sebastian plucked the papers from her grasp. "I'll get it to them faster."

"But—"

"You go up the train four cars and wait for me there," he instructed. "I don't want you here should Weller wander back whilst I'm gone."

"But you don't know where the coaches are."

"Yes, I do, I saw you return from them."

"You don't know which one the Wellers are in." She swiped for the papers, but he held them out of her reach. "There's no time for this argument, Moncrieff. Give them back."

"Have some faith in me, Countess," he prodded. "A little trust."

"*Me*. Trust *you*? That's rich!"

He looked truly wounded for a moment, which made her angrier.

"Go check on Weller," she suggested. "What if he returns before the train pulls away?"

"I left my valet to watch him," he shrugged.

"You what?"

"Brannock. You met him on the Devil's Dirge. Now, I am not commanding you, but I'm beseeching. Go to my car. Just as a precaution."

He was asking. Not ordering. Had a man ever done that before?

He softly caressed her cheek with the back of his knuckles. They were too rough to belong to an earl, abrading her soft skin enough to lift goosepimples all over her body.

And yet, his eyes were so gentle. So sincere.

With a lithe motion of a sailor, he swung down to the platform, skipping the steps altogether. "I shan't let you down, Veronica," he vowed before surging toward the line of coaches at the end of the vast concourse.

Veronica...

She'd corrected him before. And wanted to again, as he shouldered his way through the crowd.

Because her heart did a little extra beat each time he said her name.

Eight

SEBASTIAN BROKE into a run as the train chugged into motion.

He bounded around travelers and leapt over porters and their carts of attaché cases. Never having been an apt French student, he only recognized the curse words hurled in his direction and summarily ignored them.

If anyone stood in between him and the raven-haired woman on the platform of his car, their fate was a fault all their own.

Veronica stood clinging to the rail, her eyes owlish with fear as her lips moved in encouragement.

Had she no faith? He would get to her. He would not leave her to face the aftermath of this adventure alone.

Besides, he'd a promise to collect on.

He might have leapt onto one of the cars next to him, but he wanted to reach her. To grip the hand she stretched out, and have no one in between him and the lush bed on the other side of the door.

Spurred by that thought, his legs churned faster beneath him, and his heart pounded in his chest, feeding his body the speed and stamina to leap into her arms right as the platform fell away.

She made a soft squeal of shock as he hauled her into his arms, tugged at the latch to the door, and swept her inside. Throwing the lock, he shut out the East Parisian winter, the Wellers, and the anything that might bring her to her senses before he could get his tongue between her thighs.

The locomotive accelerated beneath them, but Sebastian's own engine was already purring and thrumming, anticipating a rhythm of his own.

He could feel it in her, as well. A pulse of expectancy, the gnawing of primitive hunger awakened.

She'd been given a satisfying appetizer...a mere taste of what he could do.

And now she was ravenous for the meal.

Except he was the one with the watering mouth. *He* was the diner and *she* the feast. And now that he'd done a bit of sprinting, he'd worked up an even greater appetite and warmed up his body to perform.

Trying not to dwell on how perfectly she fit in his arms, he lowered his head to claim a kiss, and was stopped by her fingertips against his lips.

"You saw them pull away?" she asked, anxiety overshadowing the excitement dilating her lovely eyes.

"And turn the corner," he said against her fingertips before gently nibbling on them. "There's no way Weller or anyone else would know where they've gone."

She went lax with relief in his arms, her fingers dropping away from his mouth.

Thus liberated, he took her lips in a searing kiss as he carried her to the lavish coverlet of burgundy velvet embroidered with gold. He draped her across the foot of the bed, her skirts a river of golden silk over a sea of the most luxurious wine. The tableau was so appealing Sebastian stood for a moment to take it all in, seriously questioning for the first time how much self-discipline he'd be able to maintain.

Her sumptuous body, constricted by so many buttons and contraptions to conform an unnatural shape, called to his fingers to unravel the fashion she hid behind. She could craft that image for the world, and it was a lovely picture, indeed. But he wanted her unbound and undone. Exposed to his gaze alone, her beauty unfettered and undeniable.

He wanted it with such violent fervor, he forced himself to stand still. To remind himself of her fragility, of her permissions and her desires. Her past and her fears.

The gods, for some benighted reason, had seen fit to grant him this rare taste of Heaven. He didn't bloody deserve it, but by Jove he would fucking drain every drop. Extend every moment so that he might take the memory and lock it away in that shallow vault of truly joyful reminiscences.

Perhaps this hadn't been a celestial gift to him, but an ultimate, inevitable torment. He'd know perfection, only to have tasted what he didn't deserve.

What he couldn't keep.

Her delicate throat worked over a swallow as she lifted herself onto her elbows, apprehension leaking into her gaze. Her hair had loosened from where he'd taken the pin, and he decided to begin there. It was that or drown in the verdant infinity of her eyes.

"This is one of the first times I've seen you look so serious..." she ventured, as he released the rest of her braids to fall from their confines. "Are you reconsidering—"

"Have you ever enjoyed a book with such delight, that you're afraid to open it again because the turn of each delicious page brings you closer to the end?" He could hardly look at her as he said it, because he meant it too keenly to laugh the truth away. He was forever turning sentiment into a jape, because if it was real...

It was terrifying.

"I—I've often been afraid of losing something so much, that I didn't allow myself to reach for it. I denied myself altogether." She reached up for him, gripping the lapels of his jacket and tugging him down. "What fools we both are."

Her lips rose to meet his in a searing, soul-stealing kiss. This one containing the desire she'd long denied and the hunger long unfulfilled.

Soft, questing hands tucked into the shoulders of his jacket and smoothed it down his arms until it landed in a puddle on the floor.

When her fingers went to his collar to tug at the knot there, Sebastian broke the kiss and gently enfolded both her busy hands into his own. "If you touch my skin, I'll be lost," he confessed, pressing her back to the mattress before making a titillating journey down her body to where her knees draped over the edge. "So you lie back, my lady, and let me play."

"What if I'm already lost?" she asked the ceiling as her chest worked over hastening breaths.

"I hope you lose yourself more than once before I'm through..." As he lowered to his knees before the bed, he smoothed his hands up the silk of her stockings, lifting her skirts along the way. Charting a course over shapely calves, he paused to kiss the dimples by her knees and caress the soft places behind them. Eventually reaching her undergarments, he pulled them over her hips, down her legs, and had to free them as they caught on the hooks of her short boots.

Sebastian loved nothing so much as the sight of a

beautiful naked woman...but somehow the idea of her coming while wearing those boots threatened to drive him out of his mind.

He didn't force her legs apart, merely kneaded at the taut muscles there, eliciting a little whimper as she allowed them to splay open. She couldn't see much over the mountain of skirts he'd rucked up to her waist, and it was just as well.

For surely he looked like a man who'd found an oasis in the middle of the Sahara, and perhaps the intensity of his regard might have overcome her.

The sight of a glistening cunny bared by parted thighs was a thing he always enjoyed.

But this.

This.

It wasn't the usual enchantment he experienced. Not merely a delicious thrill of discovery, but something far more powerful.

Indescribable.

Veronica was pink and peach and perfect.

He indulged in the sight for so long, she began to tense and squirm with violated modesty. "Moncrieff? Is everything..."

Her question died on a moan as his fingers petted through the soft triangle there, awakening little quivers that twitched and trembled through her entire lithe body.

God she was so responsive. So prone to unrestrained movement erupting, alongside sighs and sounds so primitive and visceral they mesmerized him. Veronica was a self-possessed woman naturally, but she was also honest.

And good. So fucking good. In every imaginable way.

Sebastian generally left good girls alone. He wasn't

one to delight in deflowering the virgin or teaching the uninitiated. He tended to bed women who could contain his wickedness, and demand a few things of their own.

Why was she different?

Someday, when he wasn't about to taste her sweet sex, he'd take the time to figure it out.

Lowering his head, he dragged his lips across her inner thigh, where the skin was thin and alive with nerves. Once she'd seemed to recover from the shock of his attentions there, he drifted to the seam of her leg and her hip, nuzzling the softness there, before moving to the very core of her.

He hovered for a breathless moment, heart pounding in a rough staccato.

Every muscle knotted with craving.

Sebastian was a man always battling the rule of his fathomless desire, lest he become overwhelmed by them. Tonight...he knelt at the altar and pledged his fealty to a hunger that now demanded his surrender.

Closing his eyes, he drew his tongue up the seam of closed lips, parting them with sinful slowness.

Christ she was, in a word, delectable.

Veronica's entire body jerked, but she made no sound. Not until he reached that soft bud at the apex of those folds. He thought he might have to coax it out, to play in the little pleats and ruffles of flesh until it revealed her need.

But she came to him ready. Not just once, but twice in a day.

Perhaps her heart had been too broken to know desire, or to identify it, but her body... *oh*, her delicious body was a conduit for pleasure. She'd been crafted to tempt, to entice, to lure, and to make love.

She'd been wasted on a cruel man, and her real

tragedy was that she'd ever lived a life without someone to worship her. To make her sing this throaty melody he'd coaxed from deep within her as he nibbled and supped at the edges of her folds, tickling her with his breath. Teasing her with playful lips and gentle flicks of his tongue. Pressing vibrating moans of encouragement against her wet flesh.

So wet. So sweet. A nectar only rivaled by ambrosia...

And even then.

Between her trembling thighs, he felt like a god. And soon, he'd convert her to belief.

Not in the divine, but in *him.*

I'll worship your body, my lady, he thought. *But you'll be praying to me before I'm through.*

Apparently, she'd had enough of his teasing, because she slid impatient fingers through his hair. Pausing, she seemed unsure whether to pull him closer or push him away.

Her features contorted into a mask of misery, but the noises she emitted were raw with pleasure.

Taking pity on her, Sebastian splayed her open with his fingers, thoroughly exposing the little peak of her sex. With slow and tender precision, he pressed the flat of his tongue over the pulsating opening of her body, coating it with her slick desire before drawing it up against the quivering bud.

She made a sound that shot straight to his already aching cock. It kicked against the confines of his trousers as she tugged on his hair with just enough strength to cause a delicious sort of pain.

Fuck. He might not survive this.

Drawing upon every ounce of—admittedly under-developed—willpower, he let his tongue slide over and around the delicious little hardness amidst all that soft, pliant flesh. Touching it. Flicking away. A languid stroke. A gentle glide.

She shuddered beneath his ministrations. Said things in a language he didn't recognize. Maybe one that never existed.

His hands had to move to her thighs as he dined, using his strength to keep them plied open so he could work. She bucked and trembled, jerked and moaned, as if he were an inquisitor and the lashing was meted out by a weapon more painful than his tongue.

"Moncrieff," she finally sobbed. "I—I can't—Please. *Please*."

He lifted his head to look up over her body, glad and also bemoaning that he'd kept them both clothed.

Her lush ass fell back to the bed and her legs splayed in an exhausted collapse.

"Sebastian," he said, his breath feathering over her core, causing it to visibly throb.

She seemed unable to speak, blinking down at him in obvious, foggy-eyed confusion.

"I want you to say my name when you come," he ordered in a growl he didn't recognize as his own. It was everything he wasn't. Dark. Demanding. Possessive.

She nodded, curling her pelvis forward in a wordless plea for release.

Lifting a finger, he drew wet little circles around the entrance to her body, probing the tight flesh there until she made a plaintive little sound.

"Say it," he commanded.

"S-Sebastian." Her broken whisper filled him with an emotion he couldn't begin to identify. Something he knew he'd been seeking but didn't know what to do with now.

True to his word, he parted his lips over the little

pearl of her pleasure and insinuated his finger deep into the recesses of her core.

Fuck.

Fuck! He wished he hadn't done that.

Even as her hips surged up with a sob of bliss, he accepted that he was a fucking doomed man. He'd forever regret knowing what she felt like from the inside. What hot depths of slick velvet pulled at him with such exquisitely feminine flesh.

Everything that had ever happened before, everything that might come to pass after this, dissolved beneath the devastating perfection of the moment. He suckled and slid, licked and laved, all the while rocking his finger inside of her, letting her body drench him with the gripping, pulsating release that took her much too soon.

Thighs clamped against his shoulders and her hands fell to the bed beneath her, bunching and ripping at the coverlet. She screamed in breaths and sobbed his name —or at least raw, broken syllables of it. Over and again. Both an invocation and a benediction, a plea for mercy and a hymn of praise.

Beautiful spasms clenched his fingers, inviting him deeper as she bowed and writhed like a wild creature set free after so long in captivity.

A devil's whisper slithered through him in the dark. *Seduce her. Claim her. Release your cock and finish making her your own.*

She will not stop you.

Nine

SURGING AWAY FROM HER, Sebastian stumbled to the small water closet and stuffed himself inside, slamming the door.

Panting as if he'd only just run for the train, he braced both of his hands on the tiny sink and stared at someone he didn't recognize in the mirror.

He'd the same sand-colored hair, once kept long but now cut fashionably tame. The same pale whisky eyes and sunbaked skin, weathered over his brawny bones just enough to leave winsome grooves that deepened when he smiled.

Except now, they were carved with something he'd never spied on his own features. Something he did not battle often. If ever.

Fear.

Stark and sinister, it glared back at him, creating an ugly portrait of features so often and so frankly admired.

In his entire life, he'd given over to indulgence. To a rebellious rejection of all things considered decent. Tasting the vitality of life had become a tonic to the rigid rejections he'd experienced in his youth.

And yet, he'd always known what he was doing. What his actions might do to him. He took risks, knowing the outcome always tended to turn in the favor of people like him. Strong. Handsome. Proud. Teutonic. Charming. Male. Skilled. Noble. Educated. Wealthy.

Ruthless.

Indeed, he generally only need smile in the direction of a lady to entice her, and it took a few inviting compliments to see her legs parted.

He couldn't remember the last time he'd been denied something—someone—he wanted.

And here he was, wanting someone more than he could ever remember, and apparently her favorite word was *no*.

It should have been enough.

This taste of her. This pleasure he'd promised. He was a libertine and a hedonist and all the things of which she'd accused him.

By choice. The vices and violence, the pleasure and the pain had been measured and controlled by palatable doses. He'd seen so many other men have their sins turned against them. Losing their money to wagers. Their health to sexual disease. Their dignity to drink or the drugging euphoria of other substances.

He'd flirted with all of it and promised himself to none. He was ruled by his passions, not owned by them.

Until now. Until *her*.

Veronica Weatherstoke was a dangerous phenomenon. An obsession he could feel building in his blood, threatening to overtake him completely.

His entire life he'd spent bedding women who could have no claim to him. Not to his body, his money, his time, nor his heart. Neither did he seek to keep them once he'd had them. Not even a mistress. A handful of lovers had been amusing enough to dally with more than once. But even upon that rare occurrence he'd made certain feelings were never involved.

And the moment a woman twitched a possessive eyelash in his direction, he'd disappeared like smoke in the sea mist.

A pirate's life was lucky in that respect.

Lucky... And lonely.

Why did she make his loneliness feel less like freedom and more like a consequence?

A soft knock on the door caused him to flinch, though he should have known it was coming. He'd left her so abruptly, he couldn't even remember if she'd been finished with her orgasm.

"Moncrieff?" came the hesitant call from the other side.

"I'll be a moment longer," he croaked out, turning on the water to wash his hands and splash over his face, hoping to cool the fever there.

What was he going to tell her?

The woman already didn't trust him, for better reasons than he'd admitted to her. If he told her the truth now, she would run from him in terror.

How could he explain that he'd become so overcome by lust he'd almost lost his humanity? That the sight, and scent, and taste of her pleasure had driven his tattered dignity into the dirt... That he found a quickly fraying thread of decency and used it to shut himself in here.

He'd wanted to take her, in every possible way. To steal her. Claim her. Own her. Possess her.

Only her.

Always her.

He'd wanted to thrust himself inside of her body, so that the last man who'd had her was not the monster she'd married. A beast Sebastian carried forward from the seed of his Viking ancestors convinced him he could fuck the memory of any man out of her. Could turn her into a vessel for him, alone. To shape her to his cock...

And even *that* wasn't the worst of it.

Images of her, wrapped in the richest fabrics he could provide and adorned in gems he'd draped over her, glittered in his mind's eye. While he'd had his tongue buried in the most wicked parts of her, his imagination had summoned other fantasies.

Ones he'd never before entertained.

If he could make her come, could he make her laugh? Could he make her feel safe and protected?

Could he make her happy?

Make her *his*?

Groaning, he ran his hand over his face, doing his best to wipe away the lunacy.

He was not a man a woman would want to keep.

The knock sounded again, this time more urgent. "Is everything...are you all right?"

Categorically not.

Sebastian looked down to where his cock throbbed painfully against the placket of his trousers. Even the fine fabric felt like sandpaper against the sensitized flesh.

Perhaps if he relieved his pent-up desire, some of the madness would abate. At the very least, he'd be able to think more clearly.

"I'll only be a—" He gasped in relief as he undid his trousers and released the shaft into his hand.

"Sebastian?"

Yes. Say my name. The column flexed in his grip, a bead of moisture trickling from the head.

"A moment, Countess, *please*," he implored. I can't—"

The door slid open, and there she stood, silently taking stock of him.

His brain stalled completely at the sight of her. Flushed with passion and her pale skin painted with shadows, she was the purest vision, and he was a vulgar catastrophe.

And yet, Sebastian could do nothing but remain as he was. One hand on the sink, the other around his sex.

God, but even the calluses on his palms was torture.

His gaze lowered to her hands. So soft. Supple.

"I need you to go," he gritted through clenched teeth.

Rather than turn away, she took a step forward, eyes both hot and soft. "I *know* what you need."

Sebastian had always been a man of action, but he found himself transfixed to stillness as she reached for him, first touching his shoulder, her fingers warm and tentative through the thin shirt. Both of their eyes followed her questing hand as she stroked down the curve of his bicep, to his elbow, and traced the veins in his forearm down to his wrist.

They both caught their breaths as her cool fingers joined his. Her touch seared through his shaft like a shock of lightning, pulling his balls in tight to his body and causing an involuntary convulsion of pure, electric pleasure.

He released himself to her softer, smoother grip with a helpless, wordless sound.

She joined him in the mirror, her features at once serene and knowing. Benevolent and bold. The most beautiful woman on Earth. And he?

Checking his own reflection, he quickly looked away. Who was this creature he'd become? Wild-eyed and flushed with reckless dread. A sheen of sweat at his hairline. Every muscle tightened over his thick bones in a mask of agonizing bliss.

Just when he thought he could take no more, her head lowered, disappearing from the view of the glass.

Releasing the sink, his body turned to face her as she blocked the door with the pool of her golden skirts as she sank to her knees.

Holy God.

Usually, he'd be goading a generous lover on with sinful encouragements, lacing his fingers through her hair and massaging her scalp. Touching her mouth, sinking his fingertips into it.

But he did none of those things as her hand remained gently locked around him, her mouth tantalizingly close.

When her breath caressed the throbbing tip of his sex, his knees weakened.

When she slid soft, curious lips over the thick head, they buckled completely.

He caught himself by slamming his palms into each wall at his side, pressing out like Sampson—hoping these barriers would hold.

Nothing about her ministrations were particularly skilled or confident, and in that he found even more satisfaction. Her lips were full pillows of pleasure, her mouth smooth and hot, slick and succulent. Her tongue, tentative and curious, found thrilling little ridges and sensitive veins beneath the thin skin stretched over steel. Each stroke sent delirious sensations surging through him to dizzying effect.

He searched his empty mind for something to say until her eyes locked with his. The need to speak died as something so tender and profound passed between them, he dared not profane it with words.

After her initial exploration of his sex, her motions became bolder. Her eyes blazed up at him, eternal wells of jade desire, as she took him as deep as possible, then sucked with a gentle brutality as she drew her head back. The many inches she could not take, she stroked with her palm, moistened by her mouth and his need.

Sebastian panted like a wolf after taking down a fresh kill. Blessing her and cursing her as his emotions varied violently from heart-rending tenderness to demanding desperation. Nothing in this world could be so sweet as this goddess on her knees, tending to his cock.

When she used her tongue to swirl around his head in rhythm to her strokes, he caved in upon himself a little, seeking to pull away before the pressure gathering in his spine found its escape into her awaiting mouth.

"Stop," he rasped. "If you don't, I'll—"

She gripped him harder, increased her pace as he grew larger against her lips. The desperate pull of his muscles locking down tore away the last vestiges of his control as his climax gathered in his blood.

He threw his head back with a primal roar as his hips jerked once, twice, and then his entire body was imprisoned by pleasure. Incapacitated by pulsating ropes of velvet and silk.

He belonged to her now.

She'd drained the very substance of his life and swallowed it. Consumed him with warm little licks and soft, encouraging sounds until he was nothing but her leftover scraps.

Happily so.

She could discard him at her will. Throw him to her hounds, and he'd lie there and yearn for her as he was ripped apart. For another touch. For another kiss. Just one more taste.

When he was able, he reached down and hauled her to her feet, crushing both her body and her mouth to his.

This time, she met him with equal fervor, her

tongue sparring brazenly as they melded the flavors of the other into one irresistible sexual delicacy.

Never in his life had Sebastian savored anything so sweet.

By the time she broke the kiss they were both struggling for breath. She tucked her head against his chest as she visibly sought control of her lungs.

Calling upon one final, rational thought, he disengaged his hips to tuck his sex back into his trousers, chagrined to discover he was still half-hard. After such a powerful release, he'd expect to need at least half an hour to fully recover.

As it was now, he wasn't certain he ever would.

"You didn't have to do that," he said, concerned by the tension in her body against his.

"I needed to," she said, her forehead still pressed into his clavicles as if she couldn't extricate herself to face the enormity of what they'd done. "I-I wanted to."

Swamped with compassion, he smoothed unsteady hands over her shoulders. "Tell me what you are thinking," he murmured, pressing a kiss into the wreck he'd made of her tidy hair.

She still didn't look up, so he had to strain to hear her. "Would it be possible to—I know this isn't what— that *we* aren't—but... I..." Several unformed sentences died with a trembling sigh.

Hooking a finger under chin, he pulled away so he could lift her gaze to his. "Tell me what you need."

She pressed her lips together, gathering strength. "Would you...hold me?"

"Woman, if you asked me to, I'd hold up this train."

He turned her around and did his best not to stumble as he directed her toward the bed. It was difficult not to sweep her up and carry her, but something stopped him. Not just the lack of available space in a railcar, but also a sense that she needed her physical autonomy just now.

Taking the initiative, he sat on the bed and reached for her, allowing her to slide between his open legs and once again tug at the silk knot at his throat.

"I know I'm ridiculous," she said with a self-effacing smile. "But I can't relax knowing this is tight and confining."

"Undress me at your leisure, my lady," he teased, hiding a spill of bittersweet warmth in the cavern of his ribs.

"I *won't* be undressing you," she informed him crisply. "I just need you to be comfortable."

That warmth... It spread like sun-warmed honey through his limbs as he sat with uncharacteristic stillness, submitting to her ministrations.

Her eyebrows drew together as she plucked and grappled at the loops he'd secured rather tightly.

I need you to be comfortable.

How many women had told him they needed him? Too many to remember.

In fact, he'd forgotten every single one... Every woman who'd ever needed him. To fuck them. To adore them. To pleasure, arouse, and excite them.

Women were often very generous, especially in bed. It was one of the things Sebastian loved about them the most.

But never in his life had one offered something so genuine and uncomplicated as this. A consideration of his simple comforts.

Sebastian could not detect one hint of sex or seduction in her movements, no coy glances from beneath her lashes. No moistening of lips. Just concentration, and eventually, victory, as she finally grappled it loose and slid the offending tie from his neck.

He swallowed, unencumbered by the garment, and still something threatened to choke him with a suspicious heaviness in his throat. Something concerning.

Terrifying, even.

Women had undressed him before. Had stayed for a cuddle, a drink, or even a night.

But never in his life had he felt such intimacy. Such immense vulnerability. This was no prelude to wickedness, but a quiet aftermath.

Something a wife would do.

Unstitched by the thought, he reached for her, smoothing his hands over the shape of her slim waist confined in her corset. "Should I unlace you?"

She shook her head, parting only a few buttons of his collar and splaying it open before she nudged him to lie down.

Sebastian did as she directed, stretching long across the bed and creating a cradle for her head in the divot between his shoulder and chest. She settled in exactly the place he'd hoped, fitting against him like a missing piece of a puzzle before resting a hand on his breastbone.

How strange to be so tranquil and unnerved at the same time, he thought as his arms encircled her.

They lay there for a silent moment, their muscles melting together, breaths slowing and eventually synchronizing as Sebastian watched the play of the lantern light on the canopy above.

Never in his life had he sat in silence with a woman, not contentedly at least.

What was Veronica Weatherstoke doing to him? What sort of man would she make of him if they spent more than these precious hours in each other's company?

It was a question he couldn't allow himself to ponder. So, he posited one to her instead, one he'd been contemplating since rediscovering her on this train.

"What keeps you from allowing me to make love to you?", He kept his tone casual, as if the answer meant nothing more to him than any passing curiosity. "Are you afraid I'll get you pregnant?"

Her head shook against his arm. "It isn't that... In fact, I don't think you could."

He grunted. "I assure you, Countess, I come from a *very* fertile line of—" He felt tension steal back into the hand at his chest, bunching her shoulders closer to her neck.

Not everything is about you. He chided himself, feeling like an absolute ass. "You mean you are not able to..."

"I don't think I am," she said matter-of-factly, though the tension didn't abate as she idly plucked at a button on his shirt. "Surely you don't want to talk about sad things just now."

His hand stroked up the soft arm of her gown, and he lifted it to her hair to finish unraveling the few onyx braids that remained intact. "I find I want to know all your secret joys and sorrows."

She nuzzled in deeper, allowing him more access to her hair. "More sorrow, I'm afraid," she admitted without dramatics. "Though I'm learning to find joy. To...allow myself the opportunities for discovery and the liberties of pleasure."

"I suppose children are not conducive to liberty," he postulated.

"Though I know they can become great sources of joy." A long breath left her deflated against him as he finished with her braids. Meticulously, Sebastian combed thick fingers through the silken waves of her hair, sifting through little knots or tangles with infinite care, and then massaging the scalp. It was something he'd enjoyed when his locks had been long, and he sought to give her the same shivering delight.

"I am sorry that you were ever denied joy..." he whispered.

A kiss tickled his rib through the thin cotton of his shirt. "I conceived once," she confessed after another silent beat. "Early on in my marriage. But in my third month, Mortimer...he...he kicked me in the stomach, and I lost the child."

A red-hot rage poured through Sebastian's entire being, setting his cursed soul on fire. He took out the memory of Mortimer Weatherstoke's death and relived it with effusive, savage delight.

Thank God the bastard had never been able to procreate.

The dark, selfish thought was accompanied by shame.

Sebastian himself was proof one didn't turn out like one's father. And perhaps a child would have made her life less frightening and lonely. Or conceivably she'd have been subjugated to the hell of a mother forced to watch her husband hurt their child.

The very idea tore through him with claws and teeth, shredding the sweet languor he'd enjoyed only moments before. He shouldn't have asked the question, not only for his own benefit, but he was certain she'd rather not relive the agony.

Veronica smoothed patient hands over his shoulder. "I don't want your fury," she said, low and gentle. "It is done. He is gone from this world, from my life, thanks in part to you."

"I only regret it was not my hand that wielded the blade." He didn't realize he'd spoken the wrathful wish until she replied.

94

"The Rook had more reason. I'm glad he took his vengeance."

Sebastian didn't argue the point, Mortimer had kept Ash and Lorelai from each other for almost twenty years. He was the reason the boy had become the Rook...had survived the pits of Hell to bring his damned soul back to the woman he'd loved as a child. To inflict his wrath on the foul fiend who'd separated them for no reason but his own cruelty.

But Mortimer Weatherstoke spent a handful of years *hurting* the woman that Sebastian was—

Was what?

He couldn't even think the words... Could not turn the strange maelstrom of his emotion into a tangible thing.

He didn't know how.

What he did know was that she'd asked him to stow his anger. She needed his deference. His gentility. His understanding. He could grant her those things and indulge in his own rage later.

It was the least he could do.

"You don't have to tell me anything," he said, measuring his voice. "But it might do you some good to unburden your mind."

She took in a preparatory breath. "I never conceived after that. Some doctors said my womb was too small, others that my body temperature was too low, or things weren't...shaped correctly inside of me. I was examined in all manner of ways, and no one could give me an answer."

That did less than nothing to abate his ire. "What about your husband? Was he examined?"

The question seemed to startle her. "No one...no one suggested that the fault might lie with him."

"Unbelievable," he snapped. "There's every chance the infertility is his."

95

'Oh? Are you a doctor as well as a pirate and an earl?" she asked, with surprising levity.

'Obviously not. But surely if a woman can...malfunction internally, it stands to reason that a man would as well. There's no way to look inside of our bodies, so who is to say what...pipes and channels and bits and bobs could be defective. It only stands to reason."

'I love that you think that, but the medical community seems to agree that if a man can finish then he is able to breed."

He snorted his naked derision. 'I think they'll someday figure out that I was right, and then I'll delight in telling you that I had once informed you thusly."

She let out a soft little sound of mirth. 'I look forward to you finding me on that day."

Finding her? Where would she be?

Then it dawned on him, stealing his breath with the bloody obviousness of it all.

Of course, they would go their separate ways. Would she even want to see him again after this?

Was tonight all they had?

There was a man he needed to murder several railcars away. A room they'd ransacked that would be discovered before morning. Questions regarding a missing family that would most certainly arise once the patriarch was found dead.

Pure unmitigated chaos would ensue.

Would she disembark the train now that Penelope and her intended had escaped? And even if Veronica remained until Constantinople, they'd run out of track eventually. What then? Back to her life at Southbourne? Paris? London?

Swallowing a surge of unexpected misery, he allowed

himself to ask another question burning within him for the past year.

"Do you see them often, Lorelai and Ash?"

"All the time. She is my closest friend and I find I like Ash the more I am in his company."

"And..." He drew little circles around her knuckles with an errant finger. "They fare well?"

"They are disgustingly happy."

He was glad to hear it. Truly.

"Why are you not with them? It will be Christmas soon."

She shifted as if the question had made her uncomfortable. "They're newlyweds, and I wanted them to adjust to life together without me being a dark cloud over their happiness. Reminding them of just how it had fallen apart in the first place."

"Lorelai fought for you. She adores you. And the Rook—Ash—is used to having people to care for. He wouldn't mind you sheltering under his roof, beneath his wing. I know him well."

"I believe you, but I left for selfish reasons, as well. When two people are so entwined, being an outsider is almost cruel, and I wanted some space from Southbourne. I'd been a prisoner there for so long, I'd seen very little of the world. I wanted to travel, design and make my dresses, and fall in love with other places in the world. To see women of beauty in every shape, color, and culture. To find textiles made in foreign and exciting places. To find other passions..."

"Other men?"

She scoffed. "I have very little use for other men. The last thing I considered is confining myself to another husband. I have enough money to live on the rest of my life, if I'm frugal, and my creations are lovely supplements to my income."

"How very independent of you."

Lifting herself onto her elbow, she frowned down at him. "Don't be cruel."

"I mean it." He reached up to sift fingers through the silken waterfall he'd made of her hair. "I admire your ambition. I do not blame you for wanting to remain free. I have always lived just so and realize now more than ever what a privilege that is. It is why I joined up with the Rook in the first place. Why that part of my life was so important to me."

His answer seemed to mollify her, but then she blinked down at him with naked speculation.

"Then why did you betray him?"

Ten

VERONICA BECAME SUDDENLY afraid that the truth would drive her from his arms.

She didn't want that. Not yet.

What kept her pressed against him was the certainty she felt that he would tell her the truth. She was coming to learn that Sebastian Moncrieff was many things, but not a liar.

Even if that honesty was cruel, as truth often tended to be.

In the pregnant silence that followed her question, she took the moment to truly appreciate the sumptuous railcar splashed in the golden glow of lamplight. The sway of the train beneath them had lulled her into a gentle torpor cocooned in immense masculine heat. Somehow, it'd made her feel safe enough to speak about the past and the pain she'd left in it. And for once in her adult life, she'd allowed herself to trust the sense of security she'd found in his embrace.

It was beyond reason, really, when he'd been such a villainous figure in the lives of those she called family. Ash had been so angry at Sebastian, it'd taken an act of God to keep them from spilling each other's blood.

But Veronica had learned that villains were often the protagonists of their own narratives.

She remained silent as she watched a plethora of emotion darken his resplendence, and gave him the time he needed to truly contemplate her question.

She'd been married to a villain, and though she'd considered Sebastian a diabolical, even deviant degenerate, the word "villain" never truly stuck.

Even when she was the one to hurl it at him.

It was why she'd been able to do what she'd done for him, even after vowing that life would never again find her on her knees for another man.

He didn't ask her to. Didn't push her head down toward his lap, nor did he make her feel guilty for her pleasure when she offered him none in return.

Sebastian Moncrieff had kept his word and respected her wishes... He'd asked nothing of her and delivered what he'd promised.

Of course, he was a beautiful specimen of a man, but that fact was what had made him truly irresistible to her.

Her entire life she'd been expected to exist at the whims and for the pleasure of men. How easy it had been to offer *him* pleasure, when he'd not demanded it from her. How delightful she'd found his astonished reaction.

When she'd found the act otherwise demeaning, she found power on her knees. She'd known, somehow, that he was her creature. Her beast.

Her villain.

Finally, after the silence stretched into a tangled, uncomfortable place, the man beneath her tilted his chin away and studied the canopy while a long exhale deflated him.

"You don't have to tell me," she recanted, searching for a way back to their intimacy of before.

"It's a question I often ponder," he responded, his fingers still tangled in her hair, though he couldn't seem to meet her gaze. "And all the answers that present themselves feel inadequate and pathetic."

She knew he'd done wrong by his friend, and by hers, but the despondency in his voice tugged at a deep-seated sympathy in her soul.

"If I've learned anything in life, it's that anger is little more than fear, pain, or grief wearing a protective mask." She fidgeted with the finely stitched hem of his collar. "You were so furious at Ash," she recalled. "Was it because he'd hurt you, he'd taken something from you, or he'd made you afraid?"

"Do I have to pick only one?" he scoffed.

"Of course not." She waited patiently for him to gather a few more thoughts, discovering the soft golden hairs fleecing his breastbone with curious fingertips.

"You asked me once how I'd escaped a prison sentence," he said stonily, his dazzling eyes dulled as they remained locked on the canopy above them.

"You're changing the subject," she gently chided.

"Not really."

"What do you mean?"

He hazarded a glance at her, and what she read in it broke her heart. She'd expected defiance and excuses and his singular sense of blistering humor.

What she found was a bleak, fathomless indignity.

His gaze skittered away when he spoke again, as if he couldn't both look at her and examine himself at the same time.

"I'm not the Earl of Crosthwaite," he confessed to the shadows above. "My mother, may she rest in peace, was trapped in a loveless marriage to an impotent earl. She had a lover, several in fact. None of them noble."

"Do you know which one of them sired you?" she queried.

"I don't even think she did, or she died before she was able to reveal it to me or the earl."

"And the earl always understood you were not his progeny, for obvious reasons..."

Sebastian shifted, and when she would have raised herself to give him more room, his arms tightened around her, keeping her close. "He hated me for it, but he hated worse the cousin that would inherit. Though, to save face, he named me his heir, and publicly claimed me as his own. Privately, I lived my youth as a prisoner of his rage."

"That's awful," Veronica murmured, pressing a hand to his chest.

"It wasn't so bad. The earl trotted me out when he was supposed to. Granted me the education due my station—er—his station. All the while, he pissed away any inheritance, ruined my childhood home, and dismantled all other properties that might have provided income. I swear to Christ, he even salted the earth in the fields. And so, when he died, I was seventeen and left with nothing but tax debt and a title I'd usurped through no fault of my own. I was the Earl of Nothing."

"That must have been so lonely," she commiserated, resting her chin on the meat of his chest.

He summoned a wan smile that must have meant to be cheerful, but fell short of the mark. "I've never wanted for company," he boasted, more out of habit than pride, she thought.

"Yes, but don't you find that sometimes a crowded room is the loneliest place in the world?"

He tucked her hair behind her ear, stroking at the little diamond bob in her lobe. "Stop looking into my soul, Countess, especially when I'm trying to bare it to you. Sometimes it feels you know me better than I know myself."

Driven by a quick impulse, she pressed a soft kiss to his cheek. "So, you took to the sea to find your fortune," she prompted.

He gave her an arrested stare before continuing. "Fortune found me on the Devil's Dirge, where I climbed in rank rather quickly as I proved my usefulness to the Rook. Eventually we formed a kinship. The Rook violently obtained things, and I violently enjoyed those things.

For me, pirating had begun as a rush of life-affirming exhilaration. The freedom of calling no man king and no country home. And then, it was about something bigger than myself, as well. Revenge on the very system that still took liberty from others. The seas are such a dangerous and wild place...not only because of nature, but because of the types of men that move goods around the world. It was the Rook's own tragic story that tied me to him so utterly."

"Which brings us to the betrayal in question," he said, seeming to notice the confusion wrinkling her forehead. "What the Rook didn't know—what I'd never told him—was that he'd become a brother to me. We'd planned to follow that ancient Roman treasure, the Claudius Cache, to the end of the world, and then retire to paradise. We'd even spoken of doing exactly what I do now, finding the bastards who make a living off the broken backs of shanghaied men, and helping them from this world, starting with your late husband."

Suddenly it all made sense to Veronica...and she finished the story, herself. "But instead, he found Lorelai—and me—and in doing so, he connected with his past and the brothers he'd left there, neither of whom were fond of you or his life as a pirate."

His jaw hardened as he dipped it in verification of her assessment. "I knew the life he was thinking of building with Lorelai, Blackwell, and Cutter had no room for me or the rest of the crew of the Devil's Dirge in it. The future we'd been working toward was quickly disappearing and...and I did something drastic to—I don't know—to snap him out of it all, I suppose. But Lorelai was never truly in danger, I simply figured If I took her with me to find the Claudius Cache, he'd see her next to it and realize what treasure truly was."

"Which he did," she said gently. "Just not in the way you intended."

"I never understood the decision he made..." He lifted his hands until they both cupped her jaw with infinite tenderness, his eyes bright and fervid as he gazed up at her.

"Until now."

Eleven

THE KISS WAS one of equal fervency and mutual need.

Veronica couldn't say which of them had made the first move or the response to it. Their mouths simply met.

Melded.

And the rest of them seemed to follow. Their torsos, hips, legs...

Hearts.

The man beneath her was no longer a creature of charm and mirth or of mischief and wickedness. He was real. A man with arcane depths and the capability for profound compassion.

He'd bared that part of himself to her, which had somehow made her want to see more.

To see everything.

As they devoured each other, her fingers found the buttons of his shirt, and began to tug restlessly, freeing them one by one.

His hands buried themselves in her hair as a guttural groan urged her on.

Finally, she laid the shirt open, displaying an impeccably sculpted torso dusted with hair only slightly darker than his mane. Her fingers slid over taut skin, jolted by an almost electric sensation that coursed through her entire body, landing heavy and hard in her core.

Pulling back, she broke the kiss, momentarily entranced by the glisten on his swollen lips as he watched her with rapt eyes. Motionless. Vigilant. As if she were a bunny that might bolt into the underbrush at the first sign of danger.

Emboldened, Veronica smoothed both hands over his wide shoulders and meandered down the mounds of muscle on his chest and lower, discovering the spectacular corrugations of his torso.

The tendons of his neck tensed and flexed, his jaw clenching and grinding against a powerful need.

Pausing, Veronica glanced down to the bulge straining against his trousers.

Never again. She'd once vowed. Never would she lie beneath a man and let him rut and sweat and dump his seed inside her. Never would she be made to feel like some rubbish receptacle after, lying used and discarded on the bed in a puddle of her own tears and shame.

And yet, today seemed like a day for breaking those vows. She'd also promised never to be on her knees before a man, and she'd enjoyed every moment she'd had him in her mouth. His scent, his taste, his heat and girth and shape. The circumference of him matched his own impressive dimensions, and still she was not afraid.

She was not afraid...

A myriad of emotion swirled within her. Arousal, excitement, curiosity, hope...

But not a single hint of fear.

She'd tasted the ocean on his lips when he'd kissed her after. And he'd tasted his own release as well, lingering on her tongue. Their release had created a heady mélange of flavors and erotic delicacy that undoubtedly belonged together.

Her body fit so perfectly next to his, soft and round where his planes were hard and unyielding.

So far, he'd surpassed every previous interaction she'd had with her husband, the only other man with whom she'd been intimate.

Could he pleasure her from the inside as well?

"I want you," she whispered, her body suddenly thrumming with the truth of those words.

He levered up to sit, the motion doing intriguing things to his abdominals as she melted away from his chest to kneel across from him. "What are you saying?" He eyed her warily.

"I want you, Sebastian Moncrieff," she told him, her voice stronger this time. "I want you to take me like that woman on the desk."

He reached out to caress her face. "Not like that, Veronica, not you. I will be gentle and—"

"No." She reached for the lapels of his shirt, yanking them down the cords of his impressive arms as a violent maelstrom gathered within her. "You've shown me gentle. You've given me that. But I don't feel gentle anymore. I want you to take me like you took the women whose stories made you one of the most infamous lotharios in the Empire." Climbing into his lap, she straddled him. "I can't explain this... the violence of this hunger, but it has eaten at me since the day I watched you with that woman and hated her for having what I wanted. What I was *afraid* to want."

She bracketed his face with both her hands, gazing deep into Brandywine eyes, alight with a fire she now understood. "I don't want to be afraid anymore. I want to meet you as an equal, do you understand? I want to feel the full force of your desire, whatever that is."

His nostrils flared as he sat beneath her, every muscle rigid as even the air seemed to still around them. "You have to be *sure*."

She kissed him. Hard and fast. "I'm sure."

A demonic smile toyed with the edge of his lips, as the banked coals in his gaze became a pagan inferno. "So be it."

Without warning, he reached up and rent her bodice down the middle, sending little pearl buttons scattering to the whims of fate, their clatter eaten up by the sounds of the train. In several rather deft and mystifying motions, he'd stripped away the torn fabric, corset, and chemise, and tossed them into the shadows.

Before they landed, she was suddenly on her back beneath him, looking up in limp, open-mouthed astonishment as he divested her of her skirts and undergarments, peeling them from her body with unholy expertise.

Veronica didn't know whether to be impressed or jealous as he discarded it all to the foot of the bed. And then, she forgot what she'd been thinking about when his trousers and boots disappeared.

He was on her before she could recover, a low growl reverberating through his throat as he looked at her as if he'd unwrapped the only gift he'd ever desired.

A hand closed over her breast, his palm abrading the sensitive peak budded from the winter chill and the ferocity of her arousal. He stroked and caressed her, molding her like clay in a sculptor's hand, as his lips found the protuberant nipple and teased it into an almost painful peak.

She'd already been wet for him, ready, but now she released a river of need, her loins melting and pooling in preparation for him. With a throaty sound she didn't recognize as her own, she arched into his mouth, fingers digging into his scalp.

After ravishing one breast, and then the other, he dragged his mouth down a few of her ribs, angling for her sex.

'No.' She tugged at his hair to stop him, and he looked up over her body with a wordless question. 'Just... Just... Be with me?' Her cheeks burned as she manifested what she wanted into words. Words that now seemed almost inadequate for what she asked of him.

He kissed the thin, sensitive skin beneath her breast with a mischievous smile. In one, smooth, graceful, ever so predatory motion, he moved up her body, lifting her knee to wrap around his hip.

His thick sex slid into the folds protecting the tender opening to her body. 'I am with you, Countess.'

'Then...please.'

'Please, what?' he gritted, as he paused above her to search her face. The muscles in his neck seemed tight enough to tear, and the brackets around his neck were now deep grooves of restraint.

The bastard was going to make her say it. 'Fuck me.'

With an animalistic sound, he buried his face in the curtain of hair next to her ear, and buried his cock deep in her body.

A strangled gasp of surprise wrenched from her, as little jolts of discomfort accompanied the pleasure.

He hovered for a moment above her, his arm bunching with strength as he supported his weight, the other gripping her thigh, as she wrapped it tighter against his waist.

'Sweet fuck, you're wet. Warm. Tight. Perfect.

God." Each word escaped on a breath as he remained still, allowing her to adjust to his intrusion.

How had she never known it was supposed to be like this? No sting or struggle. No pain or bearing down against the clench of her body. She was so struck by the disparity between this moment and the act she'd suffered with her husband, tears burned behind her eyes.

Happy ones.

This was what it was like to welcome a man into her body.

Veronica luxuriated in the fullness. The tensile heat of him above her, inside of her. Hard and smooth and hot everywhere. A feverish beast of flesh and steel.

A sudden, primal need to move overtook her, and she opened wider beneath him, lifting her hips in an invitation to move.

Sebastian choked on a groan, but he obeyed her silent command, rocking his hips at first, testing her reactions with motions both careful and sure. Her name tore from his throat, raw and untuned, lost to the sounds of the storm gathering around them both.

She clung to him, lifting her other leg to take him deeper, hooking her calves around the curve of his muscular ass.

Sebastian didn't kiss her. He didn't croon sweet nothings or smooth at her hair.

He watched.

Every twitch of her muscles, every flutter of her lashes. When she parted her lips, and how fast her breath sawed in and out of her as he moved. Modulating his rhythm to her silent instructions, he went deeper, harder, faster until she was a wild, inarticulate thing only made of chaos and bliss. Her nails bit into his arms and raked down his back, her teeth bared at him more than once until he finally snarled back his reply, slamming his hips against hers in a merciless war for release.

Her ascension was like the train beneath them. Rhythmic, unstoppable, storming through her with all the speed man could muster, and letting every vessel and sinew, top to toe, aware of its ephemeral presence.

Dimly, she heard a guttural roar above her. Felt him clench and tremble as his motions became less measured and more frenzied.

Then they were clenched in a freefall like eagles, the ground rushing toward them.

Let it. She didn't care. She could be dashed on the rocks and not feel a thing but the molten pleasure of her blood and bliss of his hot seed spilling against her womb.

Veronica was nothing but a limp puddle of exhaustion when his forehead finally came to rest against hers. They breathed together in the silence for a moment. Eyes open. Bodies joined.

After a tender kiss buttoned closed the wildness of their joining, he lifted himself away from her and went into the washroom. Returning with a cloth, he washed her, saying soft things she couldn't understand, let alone reply to.

He left again and returned without the cloth to extinguish the lights and slide them both beneath the sheets. Arranging the covers around her, he made a nest with the curve of his body and pulled her into it.

Nestling in, Veronica realized she'd barely slept since London. Due to anxiety over the Wellers and the success of this plot...

Fear and uncertainty hovered in the cold outside of their cocoon. There was so much still unsaid between them.

'Don't do that," he breathed against the crest of her ear, nibbling at it without teeth.

'Hmmm?" She still couldn't summon the strength to form actual syllables.

'Don't start dreading tomorrow. The light will dawn, my lady, and all will be well. We will say the things we cannot say in the dark."

That's what he didn't understand, she thought as she wriggled closer to his big body, allowing the hairs on the tops of his thighs to tickle her backside.

She could tell him anything in the dark. That she was becoming attached to him. That she'd been thinking of him. Mourning him. Missing him. Fantasizing about him. These were little secrets she could share under the cover of night.

But the light of day was for truths. And the truth was that Sebastian Moncrieff might think of her fondly as a one-time lover...

Veronica, however, would never stop yearning for the safety of his arms.

For this.

She would never stop wanting him, even as he walked away.

Twelve

VERONICA HAD awoken wrapped in Sebastian's dark scent and the luxurious memory of their lovemaking. Momentarily, she'd forgotten that the world was waiting to tear them apart, until she reached over and found his side of the bed empty.

Now she raced as fast as a body was able down the dark, cramped hallways of the train, praying she wasn't too late.

They were pulling away from Venice in the wee hours of the morning. A scant few passengers were up and about. They peered at her as if trying to figure out if she were a ghost or a madwoman as she ran, barefoot and clad in naught but her chemise and a belted velvet smoking jacket she'd found in his wardrobe.

What if it was already too late? What if she couldn't change his mind? What if—

An arm snaked around her waist from behind, and she was hauled into a cabin with two benches facing the other. Only a stunned squeak escaped before a large hand clamped over her mouth.

"What the hell are you doing?" demanded a familiar voice from behind her.

Sebastian. Thank God.

She wriggled and writhed until he loosened his hold and took his hand from her mouth. "I came to find you."

"Dammit, Veronica, I could have been in the middle of—"

She seized his lapels. "Tell me Weller is still alive."

"Why?" He eyed her skeptically. "There's no decent reason to wish him so."

"I realized something when I woke and you were not there," she panted, noting an indefinable flare in his eyes as she struggled to regain her breath. "You've been going about this all wrong."

His gaze became as flat as his tone as he replied, "Is that so?"

"Weller may be higher up in this Shanghai operation, but he's not the head. Perhaps the neck, or even the hands—it doesn't matter." She waved the metaphor away. "What is important is the information he could give you. If your design is to dismantle the entire system, you'll need names, places of contact, ports of refuge for these criminals. You are an earl with a seat in this empire and a voice that demands to be heard. Not only are you wealthier than most men can imagine, but you are a born leader." She shaped her hands to his jaw and stared hard into his eyes, willing him to mark her. "You have power, Sebastian, *use* it. Use it to do good. To be better."

He covered her hands with his, pulling them away from his face and encompassing his fingers in her own. "I told you, I'm not a good man. I'm wicked and—"

"I know!" She jerked her hands from his grasp. "But you can be wicked and still do the right thing sometimes. Yes?"

To her amazement, he laughed. Low and rich with a mercurial glimmer in his dazzling eyes.

"I fail to see what is so funny," she said testily, trying not to lose her hope.

"I can't lie to you, my lady." He reached for her hand again and brought it to his lips to press a reverent kiss on the knuckles. "The authorities are holding Weller in Venice until Scotland Yard can send someone to oversee the extradition. He will be tried for his crimes... and interrogated as to his associates."

Stunned, she stared at him as the lights of the Italian coast played havoc with his skin and bounced off the fair streaks in his untidy hair. They'd not spoken of this. Last she knew his plan was to murder the man. "Why— why did you do that?"

"Because I knew you'd want me to." Sliding his thumb into her clenched fist, he pried her fingers open and dragged his lips against her open palm.

"Ohhhhh..." She hadn't meant to moan that.

"And..." He drew the word out between playful samples of the delicate skin on the underside of her wrist. "Because it was the right thing to do."

"The—the right thing?"

He released her hand and took a step back, holding her only with a solemn gaze that sat stark and strange on a face as splendid as his. "I realized something as well, Countess, when I woke to find you beside me."

Lanced by anxiety, she hitched in a preparatory breath. "Oh?"

"I know you never want to feel beholden to another man, and that is your prerogative. But I am yours, Veronica Weatherstoke. Body, heart, and soul. I give myself to you freely and without reservation, to do with whatever you wish."

Her heart sputtered, stalled, and then kicked over in her ribs twice as fast as before. Surely she was misunderstanding. "But...you have often said you are not a man who wants to be tied down."

He shrugged. "Historically—metaphorically—that's been true, but in the strictest sense of the word, I very much like to be tied—" With one look at what must have been a distressed expression, he apparently decided not to finish the thought. "We can discuss that later. Listen. Veronica...I'm in love with you. I think I have been since that time you slapped me on the Devil's Dirge."

She shook her head in disbelief. Love? Him? Could he truly love anyone but himself?

"I thought I'd already lost any chance at being with you because of all the reasons you have so eloquently stated against me," he continued, with a wry quirk of his brow. "But I wonder if we could move past all that. If we might see where this journey could take us."

Just as she'd begun to recover her breath, it was taken again. "Where...where would you want it to go?" she fretted. "Neither of us really have a home."

"I never have, and I believe your spirit is much like mine. We don't have to settle anywhere, you and I. We can make the entire world our home if we like. Or we can plant our flag if we reach a place that calls to us."

"Sebastian...think about what you're saying. About what this would mean. Can you truly be a faithful man? Because that *is* what I want—what I need. I have a plan already, one that involves my work. I love what I do, and I only want to get better at it. I cannot allow a husband to eclipse that part of myself. The fashion world would certainly bore you."

His arms stole around her, and she stepped into the embrace, daring to hope this wasn't all a fever dream called forth by her inner most yearnings. "I am a sailor, a drifter, and all I need is a North Star, someone to guide me when it is dark." He feathered kisses over her temples, her brow, her hairline, and worked his way down to her lips. "But I am also a man of my word. I will walk in your wake and watch you take flight. I will never raise a hand or even a voice to you. I will cherish and adore you and try to make you fall in love with me every day until you do. I'll let you win arguments at least eighty percent of the time, even though I'm usually right. I will give you two orgasms *at least* to every single one of mine—"

A harried giggle escaped her, and she pressed her fingers to his lips in order to take a silent moment to listen to her heart. "What would I do with such a wicked man as my—?"

Oh God, she'd almost said *husband*. They'd not even discussed what this arrangement would look like on paper.

He held those fingers to his lips, only pulling back to speak. "I would make you a countess again, if you'd allow it. Give you a new name, even if it shouldn't belong to me."

"I would love that more than anything," she sighed, unable to help being swept away by the fervency of her reaction to his words. "With everything that's happened to us both...do you think we could truly ever trust each other?"

"I will strive to earn your trust," he vowed. "But it will take time...time I'm willing to give. As long as you need. Forever, if that is what it takes."

A brilliant smile broke over her features and reached in to set her heart aglow as she saw an identical joy lift his lips. "I think...I would look forward to forever. I'd be much more interesting with you at my side."

"Lovely!" He kissed her, lifting her against his chest. "Let's get married, then! Today, if you like."

She laughed in earnest this time, squirming to be let down. "Do you call that a proposal?"

'I call it a suggestion until I can get a ring." He rubbed his jaw, now rakishly prickled by a night's growth of beard. 'Shall we go buy one at the Turkish Bazaar? Or perhaps I should take you to Antwerp or—"

"Take me to bed first?" Sliding her arms around his neck, she stretched up to seal her lips over his in a searing kiss, while rubbing her body against him like a hungry cat. "We could stay there until the train runs out of track...then decide what happens next."

That wicked smile spread over his breathtaking features, the one that'd first arrested her attention so many months ago. "My lady, your wish is my command."

More by Kerrigan

A GOODE GIRLS ROMANCE
Seducing a Stranger
Courting Trouble
Dancing With Danger
Tempting Fate
Crying Wolfe
Making Merry

THE BUSINESS OF BLOOD SERIES
The Business of Blood
A Treacherous Trade
A Vocation of Violence

VICTORIAN REBELS
The Highwayman
The Hunter
The Highlander
The Duke
The Scot Beds His Wife
The Duke With the Dragon Tattoo
The Earl on the Train

THE MACLAUCHLAN BERSERKERS
Highland Secret
Highland Shadow
Highland Stranger

To Seduce a Highlander

THE MACKAY BANSHEES

Highland Darkness

Highland Devil

Highland Destiny

To Desire a Highlander

THE DE MORAY DRUIDS

Highland Warlord

Highland Witch

Highland Warrior

To Wed a Highlander

CONTEMPORARY SUSPENSE

A Righteous Kill

ALSO BY KERRIGAN

How to Love a Duke in Ten Days

All Scot And Bothered

About the Author

Kerrigan Byrne is the USA Today Bestselling and award winning author of several novels in both the romance and mystery genre.

She lives on the Olympic Peninsula in Washington with her two Rottweiler mix rescues and one very clingy cat. When she's not writing and researching, you'll find her on the beach, kayaking, or on land eating, drinking, shopping, and attending live comedy, ballet, or too many movies.

Kerrigan loves to hear from her readers! To contact her or learn more about her books, please visit her site or find her on most social media platforms: www.kerriganbyrne.com

Loved and Found

CHRISTI CALDWELL

Prologue

LONDON, ENGLAND , YEARS EARLIER

THE GIRL WAS HIDING.

Or, ten-year-old, Thaddeus Phippen *thought* she was hiding. She kept sticking her auburn head out of the doorway and peering back and forth down the hall.

He knew, because at that precise moment, he was hiding, too.

If *she* was, she was doing a deuced bad job of it.

If she wasn't...then Thaddeus had no idea what she was doing.

But then, girls were peculiar creatures.

And he said that, as someone with a sister of his own.

Just then, the girl ducked her head out for a fifth time and peeked about the double-glazed, robin's-egg blue, curved door panel.

Aye, if she was intent on hiding, whoever was searching was most certainly going to find her.

And Thaddeus, son of a bricklayer, and worker under his father's employer, the builder, Mr. Webb, found himself...intrigued.

Because it was his first assignment working for Mr. Webb, and it was also the first time in the whole of his ten years of existence Thaddeus had ever *seen* a lady. At least up close, and this small.

With emerald-studded hair combs in her auburn hair, and a lacy white dress, she positively sparkled and shined like Thaddeus hadn't known a person could. She was certainly too grand to talk to, and yet Thaddeus couldn't make himself look away.

He certainly should.

Mr. Webb was conducting a meeting with the Duke and Duchess of Huntington, after all, on the upcoming renovations to their townhouse, and while he did, Thaddeus was supposed to be out in the barn.

And he'd surely be sacked if his employer—or if anyone—discovered him hiding in the household belonging to a duke. It was just that Thaddeus had never before seen a nobleman's home, and he'd been intrigued enough to sneak off and slip inside when his employer had been conducting business within.

And the house was nothing short of a palace, with each room large enough to fit fifteen or more single-room homes, not unlike that which he shared with his family of five.

The windows gleamed, letting sunlight come streaming through: bright slashes of golden rays. Living with his family in their own hovel, in the toughest part of London, it was often cloaked in such thick, heavy fog, he'd not known sun was even a reality in England.

They had shiny porcelain statues of little people and sheep tucked upon various mahogany tables.

So many sheep.

Yet, with all that he'd found himself most intrigued, he was riveted by that little girl hiding.

Because he'd also not known that fine little ladies who belonged to a duke and duchess did something such as hide, like he did.

"Thaddeus?" That furious whisper came from somewhere in the corridor. "Thaddeus?" It grew more frantic, and frustrated.

His elder brother, Martin. The one who'd gotten him this job, and the one who took the work he did for Mr. Webb as seriously as if he himself were the builder.

Silently cursing, Thaddeus forgot his curiosity with the little lady and leaned back inside the parlor he'd taken refuge in.

He caught the faint tread of approaching footfalls.

"You're going to get yourself sacked," Martin whispered as he neared the place Thaddeus had shut himself away.

And for a moment, Thaddeus suspected he'd been found out, and by his elder brother, no less.

He held his breath, keeping the air trapped in his chest, until Martin's footfalls grew closer and closer, and it became harder and harder to not exhale the breath he still kept lodged inside.

And then those footfalls grew more and more faded, and then diminished altogether.

Thaddeus waited a moment more and then released that painful breath he'd been holding.

He scrunched up his mouth.

He should go.

He really needed to.

After all, it would hardly be fair to his father and brother were Thaddeus to be discovered lurking about the home of Mr. Webb's client.

With a sigh, and unable to resist another look, Thaddeus stole a further quick peek out the doorway.

"Are you hiding, too?"

Thaddeus frowned, as those crisp, polished tones, belonging to a proper lady, echoed around the hall.

And then he found her.

She was still hiding in the room across the hall.

She stared back with the widest, biggest blue eyes he'd ever seen.

Curious eyes.

Except—Thaddeus frowned—she couldn't be staring at him. He was hiding, and he was the best at it.

If there were any doubts, however, that he'd been found out, and by a little lady, no less, the answer was made clear a moment later, when the girl darted out from the room opposite his, and raced headlong for Thaddeus and his hiding space.

The moment she reached him, she pushed the door closed; the hinges didn't so much as squeak, and the quiet click as she shut the panel, was the only telltale sound.

And up close, she was more magnificent than anything or anyone he'd ever seen in his whole ten years. And Thaddeus wasn't one to note girls. But this one... this one was unlike any one...any person he'd ever seen.

Her auburn curls kissed by streaks of gold were the same shade of that streaming sun that rarely made an appearance in London. Thaddeus widened his eyes. And her skin. Why, it was the finest, softest looking *any-thing* he'd ever seen, but she had freckles upon her rounded cheeks. Her skin had a faint bronzed color, like she played in the sun, and the gods had graced her with the same sheen as those golden statues the fancy toffs stuck in their households.

The girl cocked her head. "Can you talk?"

Of course he could.

He opened his mouth to say as much.

But she'd tipped her head, and those curls bounced, and he found himself just as intrigued by those ringlets because he didn't know hair could curl that way. Like a perfect corkscrew.

So he managed nothing more than a nod in answer to her question.

"Who are *you* hiding from?" The slight emphasis she placed on that particular word indicated he'd been right in his thinking. She was hiding.

"You knew?" he blurted.

She puzzled her little brow.

"That I was there," he said, reminding himself to speak in a complete sentence, and not to keep staring at her like a dunderhead. It's just...he'd never seen a person like her this close, in his life.

"Since the moment you snuck in," she said, with a proud puff of her chest.

Thaddeus frowned.

And here he'd thought he was better than that. He was. He'd just been sloppy this day, and given where he was, and the work he did, it was perhaps the most dangerous time to be sloppy.

"You're hiding from my mother and father, too," she predicted.

"Who...are your mother and father?" he asked, dread pitting in his stomach; even as he asked, he knew. Because the girl before him could only be the daughter of a duke or prince, but with the way she shined, certainly nothing less.

"The duke and duchess," the girl muttered, with a regret to rival his own.

Thaddeus's gaze slipped over the top of her head, and he swallowed hard...and loudly.

Oh, trouble on Sunday.

Hiding with the duke's daughter, his employer's client's daughter? This was bad.

"You're hiding from them, too? Aren't you?" she asked a second time.

"In a way," he said gruffly, glancing at the doorway,

that pit in his stomach, growing to the size of a boulder. If this girl had discovered him, it was certain anyone else could, too.

This would be bad.

Very bad, indeed.

For him and for Martin and their father and entire family who was dependent upon the wages they earned from Mr. Webb.

"They *always* find me," the girl was saying, drawing his thoughts away from the panicky fear of discovery. Then a mischievous little glimmer lit her blue eyes. "Eventually," she whispered.

With an equally impish smile, the girl skipped past him, heading over to the high window that sat ajar.

She skipped.

It was an odd detail to note when his entire future and his family's security hung on the proverbial line... but it was one that held him...intrigued.

"Is this how you came in?" She directed that whispered question at the window, ducking out the crack and leaning down.

He nodded before recalling she could not see him.

"Hmm...a ladder. I suppose if I run away, a ladder outside would be just the way. But my chambers are too high."

"You talk a lot," he blurted.

The girl sank back on her heels. "I know." She ducked back inside the room and blew back a curl that had fallen over her eye. "My mother says I really must stop the improper habit."

Improper habit?

Talking.

These nobles sure were a peculiar lot.

"I like it," he said sincerely, and he may as well have

fetched her a star and presented it on his palm, for the way her eyes lit.

"You do?" she whispered. She didn't await his answer, just prattled on. "Because my governess insists I not be so talkative and agrees with Mother that ladies aren't garrulous, but I am, and Mother insists I stop being so loquacious..."

Well, he didn't know what the word garrulous *or* loquacious meant, but he knew he liked the way she spoke: all quick, like she'd seen and heard exciting things and had to share them fast out of fear she'd lose them but wanted to make sure that her secrets were passed on forever.

"Who are you hiding from?" she asked, when she'd finally let on about her mother's determination to elucidate the improper out of her—whatever that meant.

"Mr. Webb."

She cocked her head.

"My employer," he explained, and puffed his chest out. "He's the master builder."

Or it'll be "former employer," if you keep tarrying any longer with the duke's daughter.

Her eyes widened even further, in what he'd have thought was an impossible feat. "You *are*?"

And no one had ever looked at him the way she now did, as if he were someone of interest and intrigue, and not just any poor boy from the East of London.

He nodded.

The girl clasped her hands under her chin; her gaze grew dreamy and far off, the way his mom looked when she scrubbed their laundry early in the morn before he and Martin and Papa went off to work.

"Been working for him four years now," he said, because he really wanted that look in her eyes to last forever. "But this is my first time on assignment."

In the past, he'd merely been tasked with collecting bricks that were to be used for projects.

Only, whatever he'd said caused that spark to go out of her eyes, and her brow dipped. "Four years? How old are you?"

"Ten." He paused. "Almost eleven."

Her eyes grew round again. "You've been working since you were a small boy."

Boys in his side of England weren't ever small. The babes who managed to survive went on to become full-grown people in a matter of moments, or else they perished.

She opened her mouth to say something more, when frantic footfalls echoed from the corridor.

"I saw her at the foyer, Your Grace...and then she just disappeared..."

"Girls do not just disappear." Those cold, regal tones could belong to none other than Her Majesty herself, or someone close to it.

A duchess.

The duchess.

Thaddeus felt the blood leave his cheeks.

Oh, hell.

This was bad.

This was very, very, very bad.

A small hand slipped into his, and the girl gave his fingers a tug, bringing Thaddeus's gaze whipping down to hers.

"Come," she whispered, and then was pulling him back towards the window he'd climbed through, and—

He strangled on his own spit. "You can't climb out the window," he blurted.

Except, he spoke in vain. For the girl was already out and over the doorjamb and several rungs down.

"You did," she pointed out, looking down, and not up, and he remained frozen, once more, his jaw slack, because he'd never known a lady could climb a ladder, but this one did. And—

She glanced up. "And you should, too," she whispered. "They're going to find you."

They were going to find him.

And then it would be all over...and not even just his employment. Likely his life.

Because it was one thing to go sneaking about his employer's client's household. It was another to be caught doing it with the employer's client's daughter.

Springing into motion, Thaddeus heaved himself outside, taking extra care to not jar the ladder and send it rocking so that he inadvertently sent the girl tumbling to the stones below.

Not that he needed to worry.

She, moving as quick as the fleetest London pickpocket, had already reached the bottom.

Planting her hands on her hips, she stared up at him. "Hurry," she whispered.

He wanted to tell her to hush, but he'd only bring more noise and further raise the risk of discovery.

And then he was down, beside her and free. Almost free.

Catching the ladder under his arm, he took off racing...

And he felt air brush him, and then widened his eyes, as the duke's daughter went racing with him.

Nay, not with him. Past him.

Goodness, she was quick.

For a girl.

And a princess, at that.

And even more, in skirts?

And Thaddeus had never been one to be impressed by little girls. But this one...did.

He quickened his strides, returning that ladder to

where he'd found it, earning not so much as a look from the other men employed by Mr. Webb as they moved about the bustling courtyard, focused on their tasks for the latest assignment.

The little girl raced ahead to the barn, slipping inside, and he stared after her.

She'd not even said goodbye.

Of course she hadn't.

She wasn't a friend.

She was almost royalty.

Almost royalty didn't play with the help.

They—

The girl ducked her head from the stables, and then gave a frantic wave, flicking her four fingers towards her chest, motioning. For him?

Thaddeus touched a finger to his chest.

She rolled her eyes. "Of course, you," she mouthed, her voice silent, the meaning of her words clear.

He sprang into motion a second time, hastening after her, and then he joined her in the stables.

The scene of horses and hay surrounded him. And quiet.

It was so very quiet. A manner of quiet he'd never known existed in London.

"I checked," she whispered. "No one is here."

Thaddeus glanced about, some two dozen mounts all housed in generous spaces. Why, even the duke's horses had a grander home than his own.

He stopped beside one of the stalls, and catching the edges, he looked in.

The little girl drew herself up by her hands, and dangled there beside Thaddeus. "He is mine," she said proudly.

Thaddeus stared at the grey pony, its head down as he munched on hay.

"He's pretty splendid," he said quietly.

"Do you have a pony?"

Thaddeus shook his head. He barely had a house.

"You want to ride mine?"

It took a moment for her question to register.

He glanced over.

"Her name is Pixie," the girl said. "You can ride her."

Thaddeus grunted. "I can't." He'd be sacked for sure. And he also didn't know how to ride.

"Ride?" she asked, all wide-eyed, and unlike before when he'd felt proud at her awe, now he felt the sting of shame and embarrassment.

Color flooded his cheeks.

The girl slipped her palm in his once more, twining their fingers. "Come with me." Hers was a quiet command, and he found himself being pulled forward as she led him inside the stall.

"He likes to be petted here," she said, scratching the pony. "This is his shoulder."

Thaddeus cocked his head. "Doesn't look like a shoulder."

She giggled. "It's a horse's shoulder."

Which were apparently different than human shoulders.

"You can pet him," she offered.

He shook his head. "I shouldn't," he said, his voice gruff. "I should get back to work."

Her face fell. "But I don't want you to go back to work. I want you to stay with me. I like you."

Thaddeus opened his mouth to tell her she didn't even know him, but something in her eyes called back the words that he knew would wound her; they were all wide and trusting and innocent.

"We can be friends," she ventured hesitantly, and when he didn't immediately respond, she glanced down at her slippered feet. "Most people aren't my friends because my father is the duke," she said. "And my brother Crispin, is busy with *his* own friends. He has a girl who is a friend, so I can have a boy who is one, too."

He couldn't be her friend. His da was a bricklayer and Thaddeus had soot under his nails and a belly that was usually empty.

"My name is Thaddeus."

She considered that a moment. "I like that name."

He was glad one of them did.

He'd always thought it was too fancy for a boy like him.

"My name is Edith Rose."

Edith Rose.

She sighed. "I like Rose but *hate* Edith."

"Edie," he murmured. That suited her far more. It was a name of a girl who was approachable and real... just as she was.

Her face brightened, and she clasped her hands to her chest. "I quite like that." She took a step towards him. "Can we be friends?"

No.

Leave.

Run.

Go.

And yet, he couldn't make himself.

He didn't want to.

Thaddeus nodded. "Friends."

She smiled. "Forever!"

Friends, forever? That was...a bit much. As it was, they were already pressing it with this. "We can't be friends, forever, Edie," he said slowly. "You're a duke's daughter."

She scoffed. "That won't change anything. You'll see!"

And in the days and months that came, with he working for her family, and she stealing time away with him as he did, and then when that work was done, and he sneaking off to visit her through the years, it almost felt that way.

As if nothing would change.

Until he fell in love with her...

And then everything did change.

Everything.

One

SHE WAS ABOUT TO DIE.

Lady Edith Peregrine, the Marchioness of Bourchier, clung to the sides of the carriage, gripping it with all she had and for all she was worth, as it pitched and swayed and careened along the icy, snow-covered road.

A panicky laugh built in her throat: the irony not at all lost upon her.

After enduring far too many years of marriage to a miserable, emotionless cur of a husband, and answering to his whims, she'd finally found herself set free in his death: free to go where she wished without his oppressive thumb over her. Free to spend the winter away from London with her brother and his family in Oxfordshire.

Only to at least leave but find herself about to die in a carriage accident.

Her driver's frantic shouts and pleas to the horses filled her ears.

If he had moved to pleading with the team, they were, indeed, in trouble.

The team's hooves slipped and slid as they galloped; she felt it in the way the carriage slid forward.

Faster and faster.

Clenching her eyes shut, she prayed.

And she regretted that she'd not prayed in so long, and that those prayers were so rusty.

But God hadn't made it a point of answering her pleas before, and she'd gotten tired of asking and talking to him, and well, now she could really use some help.

And this moment, her death, was so very consistent with how her life had gone when she was living.

And then, suddenly, the carriage was careening sideways, sliding to the left and then right, zigzagging back and forth: crisscrossing in a way that brought her gaze colliding with the horses who were moving in an arc.

The driver cried out, and she joined in, and then screamed until her throat hurt and her lungs burned. Edith pitched sideways, and then flew forward.

She slammed hard against the opposite bench, expelling all the air from her lungs, leaving her too winded to do anything more than attempt to breathe.

But, the carriage had stopped.

She'd survived.

She lay there, draped across the opposite bench, her skirts flipped over her knees, the way she'd used to hike them when she'd run about London, sneaking away from her family's townhouse, and racing about freely with *him*—Thaddeus.

Edith froze.

Yes, mayhap she was dead, after all.

Because she'd known in death, she would again see him.

Thaddeus Phippen.

The boy who'd been her friend, and then the young man who'd been her lover, and then the lover who had left.

Her chest ached, with a pain that had nothing to do

with being tossed about the inside of her carriage. A pain so deep, as fresh as it had been when he'd stopped coming around, and just fallen out of her life.

Aye, this was no heaven, after all.

Because she still hurt. And surely there wasn't hurting in the great beyond.

If there was even a great beyond?

The door was wrenched open, and a blast of cold filled the conveyance.

"Your Ladyship!" Stanbridge cried. "Are you—"

"Fine, Stanbridge," she interrupted, hurrying to assure the loyal, crimson-clad servant, who'd expressed reservations about their setting out in the storms they'd been having, but who'd been forced to do so anyway because of her and her whims and wishes. "Just fine." Pushing herself upright, Edith let loose a gasp as her shoulder screamed in protest.

He cried out again. "Your Ladyship!"

She bit her trembling lip. "Fine," she lied, through her gritted teeth. Her shoulder throbbed and ached with the likes of a pain she'd never before known or felt.

That was a manner of vicious physical agony, different than the previous ache in her heart that hadn't hurt any less than this misery.

"Are you well?" she asked the servant.

"Aye. Not so much as a scratch." He flinched and snatched his cap from his blond head, and drew it against his chest. "Sadly, I'm not able to say the same for the carriage."

Her stomach dropped, and she scooted herself along the bench, allowing Stanbridge to help her from the conveyance.

Her booted feet were immediately swallowed by several inches of snow, and she gasped: not from the bite of cold, wet snow as it penetrated the fabric of her skirts, but from the agony that jarring motion caused her shoulder.

Tears smarted her eyes, and she caught her elbow, bracing her arm to keep it as still as possible.

Stanbridge took a step forward, but she fluttered four of the that cradled her elbow.

"What do we do?" she asked the young driver, her voice strained to her own ears.

Worry creased his brow, and as the young man stared off into the distance, the concern deepened in his eyes. "Well," he said slowly. "I...hope the other carriage realizes we are not following."

The other carriage containing her maid, and trunks.

"But...I've not caught sight of it for some time now."

Nor would they have. The other carriage had continued on at an earlier hour in hopes of arriving before Edith, so they might have the country residence readied.

Edith's teeth chattered from the cold. "Wh-what now?" she managed between chattering teeth, the warm sough of her breath leaving a little puff of white in the night air.

"The nearest inn is some ways back, and...I'm not certain of how far forward..." the driver went on.

And then...it began to snow. Again.

A single snowflake fluttered and danced slowly down, before landing on her nose.

Edith's eyes went cross as she stared at that blip of moisture.

That tiniest of flakes was soon followed by another and another.

"*I love the snow...!*" That long-ago, whispered avowal floated into her consciousness.

She and a little boy, sprawled flat on their stomachs,

in the dead of night, outside the entrance of the stables, their legs kicked up behind them.

He'd gathered up the untouched snow, gathering it into a small, perfectly formed ball.

"Ices...?" he'd whispered, offering her that snow-fresh treat, like he'd been handing her an ice from Gunter's, and it had been even more special than the confectionaries at that place in London, because it had been him, and—

"My lady?" Stanbridge's concerned query cut across those long-ago musings, and Edith gave her head a shake to dispel the past, and focus on the more alarming present.

It'd been years since she'd let herself think of him. When she'd been miserable and lonely and longing for him, she'd sit with the memory of him and the times they'd shared.

This however, was decidedly not the time for wool-gathering.

"What do you pr-propose?" she asked, reflexively rubbing her gloved hands together to bring warmth to the digits, and then a hiss of pain slipped through her teeth as agony shot down her arm. Stars danced behind her eyes, and she sucked in an uneven breath.

"Lady Bourchier!" Stanbridge's cry cut through the night sky: the winter still, and quiet of the snowfall making it even louder.

"I'm f-fine," she lied again through her chattering teeth. "J-just cold." It was another falsehood. She was in pain from the blow to her arm and from the bite of the winter chill. "Wh-what are we to do?"

"There was a residence we passed a short while ago. Not so very far from here. We can go there and ask for their hospitality. I'll return afterwards for the team."

Ask for their hospitality? At this point, she'd have begged Satan for a hand on Sunday.

Collecting her valise, Stanbridge led the way, and Edith followed close behind, and what was "not so very far from here" proved a long, slow, arduous walk.

As the snowfall increased, the flakes swirled in the air around them, and Edith squinted, searching for any hint of the household they'd be begging for sanctuary from, and finding no sign of it. She burrowed deeper into the folds of her fur-lined cloak in a bid to escape the frigid cold, silently crying at the pain that trembling wrought to her arm, each quaver as miserable as the steps that she took.

"Y-you are c-certain you saw it?" she asked, feeling tearful and hearing the fear in her own voice.

"Not much farther," Stanbridge promised for the sixth time since they'd set out.

And then, wonder of wonders, they stumbled upon it: the massive stone keep.

Edith stopped briefly in her tracks. The completely dark, massive stone keep...the manner in darkness, without so much as a single candle flickering in the window, or smoke from the chimney, belonging to a roaring hearth.

Nothing.

Stanbridge doubled back and stopped beside her. Shielding a hand over his brow, he peered off into the distance. "I...do not think anyone is home?"

"No," she said. "I-it...appears that way."

Forcing her chilled feet to keep moving, she set out once more; every step that brought her closer left a buoying lightness in her chest, her relief growing and growing and then promptly dissolving as she reached the foot of the mammoth household.

And up close she understood why no one was home.

She took in the shattered window frames where lead or glass panes should be.

So. Many. Shattered. Windowpanes.

So heavily damaged as to only indicate not a vacant household, but rather an abandoned one.

And one likely to offer little warmth from the elements.

"Come," Stanbridge urged. "I expect we can make a fire."

She expected *he* might be able to.

She, on the other hand, hadn't the first inclination of anything to get them warm.

As her driver led them in, straight through the old oak doorway, the hinges groaned.

She blinked to adjust her eyes to the dim surroundings.

Abandoned.

Yes, there was no hint of life, not so much as the squeak of an errant mouse.

Why, those tiny creatures had likely also found somewhere far warmer to go than the current abode Edith and her driver had commandeered.

Her teeth clacked together noisily. "W-we should s-split up and see what we might f-find," she said, and as he dropped a hasty bow, taking off in the opposite direction, Edith made a long, slow climb abovestairs.

The bottom of her skirts, damp from their trek through the snow, dragged slowly and heavily as she made her ascent.

As she walked, she peeked inside empty room after empty room...until she found an abandoned bedchambers.

She wandered inside and breathed a steadied sigh of relief as her gaze snagged upon a surprisingly soft-looking velvet coverlet, draped over the four-poster bed, at the center of the room.

Edith stopped beside the bed, and clutching her left arm close to her chest, she lowered her right hand, and stroked the bed.

The fabric wore the chill of the night air, and yet...it was warm, and there was a stack of blankets, and she sent a prayer of thanks skyward.

Releasing the fabric, she did another cursory sweep of the room...and her eyes landed upon a tattered trunk, one that showed its age and wear.

Drawn over to the old, forgotten article, she unlatched the clasps, and lifted the lid.

Several rows of garments still lay neatly within, and she sifted through those things, searching for something belonging to the former owner that she might use for herself.

The shirts were of fine quality: a soft lawn, the trousers a serviceable wool.

Edith continued wading through the articles, and she awkwardly lifted a long, dark, heavy wool cloak.

She let the article fall, and with frantic movements, proceeded to unclasp her own wet one; it collapsed to the floor, landing with a thwack.

Her arm still throbbing, she awkwardly lifted the dry article as best as she was able, and draped it over her shoulders.

A hiss sailed through her teeth, and a curse along with it, that echoed off the walls, from the agony that movement caused her.

And she paused, taking in several slow, uneven breaths, until the pain abated, returning to that dull, aching throb.

With a greater carefulness to her motions, Edith drew the long wool cloak about her shoulders, awkwardly fiddling with the clasp at the throat...until she had it.

She turned to go...but a bright flash of red caught her eye, and she glanced down.

Her gaze alighted on that bright crimson garment within, and with a suitable reverence and respect, she reached for, and carefully lifted, that military jacket in her right hand.

Brass gleamed upon the shoulders; medals adorned the front.

A military man had once lived here.

Who had he been?

And what's more, what had happened that he'd left behind forgotten his—

"My lady?"

She gasped, losing her grip on the jacket, and she spun about.

"My apologies," Stanbridge said from the doorway, his arms laden with wood. "I found another chambers with blankets at the end of the hall." He grinned and nodded to the logs he still held. "And this in the kitchens. I'm happy to say they'd left the household well-stocked with kindling and wood and means to start a fire."

And for the first time since she'd begun the trek from London, free of her dead husband and the constraints of that stifling place, she found herself smiling.

"We are going to be all right, after all, aren't we?"

He returned her smile. "I expect we are."

Two

SOMETHING WAS AMISS.

A problem, rather.

Former Lieutenant Thaddeus Phippen's ability to ferret out problems was a skill that had eluded him as a child, but fortunately found and honed during his years fighting in the King's Army.

The celebration of his brother, Martin's marriage to Lady Christina, was still in full swing.

The voices of the guests, who'd gathered at Lady Christina's sister's household for a scheduled winter house party, and who'd instead found themselves attending an impromptu wedding, filled the room in song.

Every member of the party present stomped and raised their voices, singing "In Sweet, Rejoicing." Over the tops of their heads, Thaddeus peered at the butler eyeing the collection of guests, his concerned focus still on Martin, his features strained. As if he needed to interrupt but regretted being the one to infringe upon the celebration.

A little hand tugged at his, and he glanced down at

Lady Christina's young daughter, Luna. "You aren't singing, Uncle Thaddeus?"

Thaddeus leaned down and whispered, "I didn't want to drown out your angelic voice."

The little girl's eyes filled with happiness, and drawing in a deep breath, the daughter of the newly married young mother, erupted into an even louder, more boisterous song.

From the corner of his eye, he caught sight of the butler starting across the room. "Keep singing," he urged, heading for the servant, and intercepting him. "What is it?"

A palpable relief at being spared from bringing his problem to the bridegroom filled the servant's eyes. "There is...smoke across the way," the butler whispered. "At...the residence across the way, that is."

Thaddeus stiffened. "Smoke?"

"It appears a chimneys was lit, and...one of the footmen spied it and thought it...odd."

Odd because he and Martin had been made guests for the formal house party being thrown.

The residence across the way being the investment property he'd stumbled upon and purchased on behalf of his brother: London's premier builder. The properties had been in shambles, and needed extensive repairs, and yet Thaddeus had seen through all of that to the potential. Broken windows could be fixed, and walls plastered and painted.

It could not, however, recover with a same ease were it to be burnt to the ground.

From across the room, Martin snagged his gaze; concern lit his brother's eyes, but Thaddeus gave a slight wave of his hand, reassuring him all was fine.

"I'll see to it," he said, already starting from the room.

The butler followed close at his heels. "I've had Mr. Phippen's mount saddled and sent along several servants to assess in the event of...fire."

A short ride later, Thaddeus found himself dismounting outside the residence he'd purchased: one that would no longer be sold, and would now become home to Martin, his new wife, Christina, and her four children.

Having lived in the worst end of London, he'd witnessed all manner of disasters: oftentimes involving careless fires set in hopes of people finding warmth, but which had ultimately taken down entire streets of buildings and hovels serving as homes. That familiarity with the perils of fire had been further witnessed during his time fighting in the King's Army.

And yet, as Thaddeus handed the reins of his brother's horse to a waiting servant, he scoured the horizon.

The pungent, acrid scent of a raging fire did not hang in the night sky.

Rather, the fire was contained to a single chimney flute.

With a frown, he climbed the uneven and cracked stone steps.

The moment he reached the foyer, one of his new sister-in-law's servants, headed down the steps. "There... is something you should see, Mr. Phippen. Trespassers."

Trespassers.

Trespassers...

The cool, clipped tones of the young Englishman's words mingled and merged with different tones: those belonging to another, spoken in foreign tongues that Thaddeus had been forced to pick up or perish if he did not.

"Intrus, tirez..." *Trespassers, shoot...*

The rapid echo of gunfire pinged in his mind, sucking him from the present and placing him in the past, and his breath grew shallow and rapid in his ears—

And as the servant spoke, his words continued to blend with the warnings of others. "Down several doors...Phippen."

Down, Phippen...get down...

Sweat beaded his brow.

"Mr. Phippen? Mr. Phippen?" That person speaking his name, his tone grew more strident, more concerned, and Thaddeus slogged his way through the hell of the past.

Mr. Phippen.

Not Lieutenant Phippen.

Think.

Why aren't they calling you "lieutenant."

Because you aren't there.

He was here.

Back in England.

Safe.

The present came whirring back, and Thaddeus blinked rapidly, the cobwebs lifting, and he stared at the servant.

The young footman looked back at him with concern-filled eyes.

A dull flush burned Thaddeus's neck, and he gave thanks for the cover of darkness provided by the dark foyer. "Which room?"

"The fourth upon the right, Lieutenant Phippen."

The fourth upon the right.

The rooms he'd taken in this place as his bed-chambers.

Avoiding the young man's eyes, Thaddeus directed his focus forward, and made the climb, concentrating his attentions on the task at hand and not the demons that were still with him: the ones that would always be with him.

As he approached his temporary bedchambers in this place, heat spilled out into the otherwise chilled corridors, growing increasingly warm, until he reached the door.

It hung slightly ajar, having been left open a crack by the servant who'd done an inspection of his own.

Stiffening, Thaddeus clasped the handle, and slowly pushed the panel open, gradually, so as to not lend the hinges any further squeak.

An impressive fire blazed from the hearth.

He stepped into the room, doing a sweep as he went.

A slight snore rented the quiet, and Thaddeus wrenched his gaze over to the figure sprawled in the center of Thaddeus's bed.

Curled on his side, the tiny figure lay, with his legs drawn up and his diminutive form swallowed by a cloak.

Nay, not just any cloak. Thaddeus's cloak.

Pity tugged at his breast, as he moved closer towards the "trespasser."

But then, how many times had he himself been a "trespasser." Stepping foot on properties he'd not any right to be, but one he'd been hopeless to stay away from, and then not even because of the material possessions or warmth to be had there—though there'd been that, too.

Thaddeus reached the side of the directoire white-painted sleigh bed and stopped.

He stared down at the pathetic little creature curled within the lumpy mattress, in desperate need of feathers or being replaced.

'Should we find a magistrate, Mr. Phippen?" the forgotten servant quietly called from across the room, and Thaddeus pulled his gaze briefly from the boy and cast a glance over his shoulder to the young man waiting.

Waiting for the one word that would see him off to find the law.

One word that would alter the child's future and fate.

He shook his head. "I've got this," he said, dismissing the young man.

The servant bowed, and then hurriedly stepped from the rooms.

Bowing to him.

How quick a fellow's circumstances changed. A poor soldier, hired to work for his brother, a brother who'd, in turn, in less than ten days of arriving at this place, had met and married the widower sister of a baron, and thereby elevating Thaddeus just by chance of their shared blood.

Giving his head a wry shake, Thaddeus turned his attentions back to the still-slumbering intruder.

The faded reddish-pink coverlets rustled, as the young boy stirred.

Nay, he'd never been one and never would be one to condemn a man outside the ranks of the peerage to a life of drudgery and hell, all because they'd sought to steal themselves such much-needed reprieve from the elements and the viciousness of the world. Not when he himself knew firsthand what it was to be at the mercy and kindness of an otherwise merciless world.

"Take these to your family, Thaddeus..." Those whispered words, spoken in a singsong voice, whispered forward from the deep corners of his mind.

Of her.

Edie.

Edie, with an armful of blankets and food for his family that she'd snuck from her family's household.

Memories of a woman he always kept pushed to the side, but they were always there, floating on the periphery.

It was hard not to think of her.

The one friend he'd had in London. The friend who'd then become a lover.

But also, the one friend who'd needed him to make more of himself, and whose parents had paid for his commission in the army at their daughter's behest, they'd said. And while he'd went, attempting to make more of himself, and for them, so he could rise up in ranks and worth—feats he'd accomplished—she'd also done the same. For, upon his return, he'd discovered in his absence, she'd made that same climb herself—all the way up to the rank of marchioness.

His gut muscles seized and clenched.

Funny, that time didn't dull or blot the blow of past betrayals and losses and hurts.

Just then, the intruder in his bed groaned, and Thaddeus closed the remaining space between himself and the bed.

He knew the mind-numbing terror of sneaking into another person's household, and the fear of discovery that made it fully impossible to relax in peace.

He'd let the boy stay on for the night, and then advise him to go next door to the kitchens for food, a place to stay, and then he'd add him on to his and Martin's staff of workers, overseeing the reconstruction of this property.

Suddenly, the boy rolled onto his back, and the hood of his cloak slipped back, and a tumble of reddish-brown curls spilled out, a lion's mane of tangled tresses that covered the face and revealed but a dainty chin and—

Thaddeus froze.

For it also revealed his intruder was, in fact, not a boy, but rather, a woman.

A woman who just then pushed that jumble of hair back from her eyes, parting the curtain it had made, revealing a heart-shaped, freckled face.

His heart stopped beating.

For hers was a very familiar heart-shaped, freckled face.

And surely it was because he'd been thinking about her.

Surely it had been the intrusion of her memory moments earlier to account for his seeing her even now.

He blinked several times, trying to blot out the image of the woman before him and replace it with whomever the person was who'd stumbled across this stone keep.

Confusion filled the largest, most enormous blue eyes he'd ever seen.

Nay, he'd seen eyes that large before.

"Thaddeus," she whispered, her voice husky from sleep, similar to the way it had grown husky when they'd made love, with the stable floor hay as the only mattress under them. But then, that was all he'd been good for.

And he narrowed his eyes.

For she, the intruder of his recent properties was none other than Lady Edith. He curled his lips into a cold smile. "Well, well, well. If you aren't a regular old Red Riding Hood."

None other, than Lady Edith—the woman who'd broken his heart.

Three

WHEN EDIE HAD BEEN YOUNG, she'd dreamed of Thaddeus Phippen, often and always.

He'd been such a part of her waking and living thoughts, she'd not been able to separate what was real from the dreams of him—nay, of them—that lived within her head.

Those dreams had lasted only until the nightmares began.

The nightmare that had been her marriage to that mean, old letch.

In the earliest days of that torturous union, she'd clung to the memory of him still. When he'd gone to fight, her parents had used her love for Thaddeus against her. In order to keep his family safe and secure from her parents' threat to destroy them, Edith agreed to marry a cold-hearted marquess.

The day she'd found out Thaddeus had left, Edie had wept as though her soul had been crushed.

And that was how it had felt. As though with his leaving, all the joy and life and light had been sucked from her body, leaving in its place, a vast, empty void of loss and loneliness.

She'd thought nothing could hurt more than his being gone.

Until her parents had come to her.

Until they'd demanded she wed that decrepit, old marquess...and the failure to do so would see Thaddeus's family destitute.

The brother whom he'd loved.

The parents who'd had so little, that to lose even more would have consigned them to death.

And so she'd married.

All the while she'd done so, she'd vowed that when he returned, she'd run away with him.

That they could go somewhere, together. Another country. Some place. Any place. Just as long as they two were together.

That dream had sustained her...and she'd waited until his return...waiting, waiting, and then seeking him out.

Only to find when she'd visited him, he'd proven a good deal less forgiving of her circumstances.

She'd done what she'd done...for him.

She had waited for his return, hoping desperate that they might leave together.

Only to be rejected by him.

Because he was an honorable man; and he'd not understood her desperation. She'd not revealed the depth of the cruelty she lived every day. But then, he'd not been willing to listen.

And she'd loved him so desperately that she could not have blamed him. Until...his visage had faded. Because it had been easier to let him go. She had put walls up around her heart, shutting away her feelings, wants, and desires for Thaddeus.

He'd not remained buried in her thoughts forever.

At the oddest times, and in the oddest places, he'd crept back in.

It had been so long since she'd not thought of him, she'd believed all her hopes and dreams of him were gone.

It was why she was surely imagining him.

Here.

Of all places.

Or she'd died.

Yes, that made more sense.

The wild carriage ride...and the accident, and then there'd come thoughts of him in those last moments.

She groaned. "I am dead."

It was better this way. He was here. Because in the worst days of her marriage, she'd imagined being united again with Thaddeus...even if it was one day when they both drew their last breaths.

A cold smile formed on his mouth. "Oh, no. You are very much alive, *Lady Edith*."

Her heart stuttered. Or mayhap she'd died and gone to hell, after all. Because that was the only way she'd recalled this frosty, steel-eyed version of the man from her youth.

He narrowed his eyes. "Or should I say, Lady Bourchier now? Isn't it?"

A vise twisted her heart. She'd tried to tell him why...but he'd not wanted to hear her out, and in truth, she'd not truly been able to get all the words out. For even as she'd done what she had for Thaddeus and his family, she'd been ashamed for asking him to run away with her.

When he ordered her gone, she'd waited for him to cool his temper, and come to her.

But he'd never come.

He, this man, who she'd thought knew her so well.

If only he had known her as she'd believed had, he would have gathered she'd was miserable and come to her rescue as he'd vowed he would always do.

The same ache of regret struck painfully in her chest. "No, Thaddeus," she said softly. "Edie will do. Just...Edie. We"—we are friends, after all— "were friends, after all." She handed those words to him as an echo from a long-ago time, the same ones she'd once uttered.

He stared at her through stricken eyes.

What else did you expect when all he saw was that you'd married another?

"Friends," he echoed with a quiet wryness that went straight to her heart.

She pushed herself up onto her elbow and then bit her cheek to keep from crying out, as her arm screamed in protest. She stabilized her arm, and awkwardly scooted herself out from under the blankets. The moment she managed to shimmy out, she lay there: her skirts and his cloak hiked up, and her lower limbs exposed.

And she felt Thaddeus's gaze slip from her face and slide lower to her bared flesh.

And something shifted in the air: the anger evaporating under the presence of something that had always been more familiar with this man—desire.

Only, things had changed.

Everything had changed.

She had.

He had.

With hurried movements, she shoved her skirts back down into place, and then swung her legs over the side of the bed so that her skirts fluttered to the floor.

"What are you doing here, Edith?"

Edith.

159

God, how she hated that name. It was the one her parents insisted on using, and then the one her husband had called her, and then also one all of Polite Society did, too. Now, Thaddeus did.

That made her want to cry most of all.

"My carriage was...stalled by the snow," she said, glancing down at her feet, and then she picked up her gaze. "Is it really you?" Her heart and mind struggled to understand seeing him again, and finding him here, of all places.

He quirked his lips in another harsh grin. "One and the same." He touched a hand to his brow as if in salute, and she recalled just why he'd gone.

And her gaze slid to that trunk she'd been rifling through. A trunk not abandoned but belonging to this man, of all men. Her eyes locked upon the crimson jacket she'd left partially draped over the edge, and now she saw those epaulets and metals in a new light.

"You managed your dream," she said, her voice wistful to her own ears. It was why she'd been unable to begrudge his leaving for the army. He'd deserved to escape.

"Aye. The dream." Something in that latter word: harsh, cold, and hollow brought her gaze sliding back over to his.

She searched his face, but unlike the boy and then man whose every emotion she could read from his features, she could make no sense of anything. He may as well have been chiseled in granite.

A glorious granite. His features were still strikingly sharp angles: a chiseled nose, a cleft in that nobly squared jaw. He'd always been tall, several inches past six feet, and possessed corded muscles from a life of labor.

And she hated that her body should tremble at the remembrance of his embrace, and the ways in which he'd brought her to pleasure: gliding in and out of her, until she'd shattered in those glorious little deaths that only he had ever done.

'See something you like, my lady?" he asked in a whisper of whiskey and sin..

A cold, mocking glimmer glinted in his eyes.

One that said he'd noted her study of him.

And she hated that her body should respond to him so, when he clearly only held her in antipathy.

It had been one thing knowing he'd sought a better future and gotten himself freedom that she'd so craved.

It was another knowing the time they'd spent together had mattered not at all.

Four

THE DREAM, she'd called it.

And for a long while that was what it had been. He'd imagined a life in the military, rising to the ranks so that he might make more of himself...so that he could be more for her.

Back when she'd assured himself that she didn't need more. That he was enough.

Until her father had come to him with the truth.

The words Edith hadn't spoken but had instead been presented by the duke; of the need for him to go so that he could be worthy. Only to wait until he'd gone and then marry another. A man of the peerage, a man with a title and gads of wealth and influence, in short everything Thaddeus had not been, nor would ever be.

And yet, even with all the hurt of past betrayals, he couldn't stop himself from drinking in the sight of her.

She was as trim as ever: her waist nipped, her breasts a perfect size for a man's palm. And those auburn tresses, loose corkscrew curls as defiant as the lady herself, had fought free of her coiffure and hung down about her shoulders. Unbidden, an image slipped in: those same curls spanning the makeshift pillow he'd made of his discarded shirt, as she'd stretched her arms up towards him, pleading for his kiss, and his body, and his body cared naught for her defection, as a wave of desire bolted through him.

As if she felt the wicked direction his thoughts had traversed, a delicate blush stole across the high slashes of her cheekbones.

She blushed as easily as if she were the innocent girl who'd earned his heart.

And then, she tipped her chin up: defiance blazing in those enormous pools of her blue eyes. "See something you like, Thaddeus?" she shot back, turning his own jeering words back upon him.

He held her gaze. "Aye," he said, his voice husky with desire. "That I do, Edie."

Her jaw slackened, and her lips parted, as surprise rounded out her eye all the more.

And he smirked at having managed to unsettle her.

Outrage glinted in her eyes, making them harder than he'd ever seen them, harder than he'd ever known this gaze to be. "You're making light of me." Fire flashed in those endless pools of blue.

He tipped the brim of his cap. "Aye, that I am."

The fury was replaced so quick with a flash of hurt, and he felt like Johnny Trowber, the bully in East London who'd gone around kicking all the cats, and it made him feel as small and awful as when he'd been a child who'd tried—and failed—to stop that abuse.

"What did you think I should be—happy to see you, Edie?" he snapped. "Do you think I should have just forgotten that you"—sent me off to war— "married when I'd been gone?"

Her mouth turned down, and she held her mouth so tightly, little white lines appeared at the corners.

"No," she whispered. "I don't think you'd...have forgotten that."

And with that, another memory slid in...of the earliest days of his return, when he'd been in the new home, bigger than the hovel he'd left behind, struggling to find his way—through the nightmares, and back to a new norm—when she'd suddenly shown up, her eyes alight with joy, and urged him to run away with her. Run away...because she'd already been married.

His lips curled in a reflexive sneer. "What? That you'd come to me, ready to take me as your lover." But never her husband. She'd given that right to another. He took a step towards her. "That I wasn't good enough for you to marry, but certainly good enough for you to bed."

She jerked like he'd struck her; her features went deathly white, and even as he knew she was deserving of his fury, he hated himself for hurting her. "It was never that way, Thaddeus," she whispered.

"It was always that way, Edith," he said, unable to keep the regret from creeping in. He'd never had a place even thinking he had a right to a woman as fine as a duke's daughter.

Edie looked away first, glancing down at the floor. "Forgive me," she said tightly. "I should not have come here." Her features pulled in a grimace. "I would not have...had I known that this was your home." With stiff, regal movements, she headed for the valise that sat next to the hearth.

And the sight of her draped in his cloak...was so jarring, because of how right it was seeing her small form swallowed by his garment, and it sent a wave of longing through him.

And he didn't deny himself the feel of her.

He stretched an arm out, drawing her loosely against him, and she went.

Thaddeus lowered his mouth close to hers, hovering it there, and then stopped.

Her golden-red lashes fluttered.

"Do you want my kiss still, sweet Edie?" he whispered, teasing her...and tormenting himself.

Her lush lips trembled, and she gave a slight, tight nod of ascent, and with a growl, he kissed her. Kissed her as he'd dreamed of doing, and she moaned, parting her lips, and letting him in, and he went...sweeping his tongue inside. Desire burgeoned within, as he tasted of her. That delicate pink flesh toyed with his in return, and he and Edie dueled, in a familiar dance they'd done in the past.

In the past.

Before her betrayal.

With a curse, Thaddeus wrenched away, and took a quick step back.

Dazed, Edie blinked her wide eyes rapidly, even as she touched a trembling hand to her mouth.

"I trust Lord Bourchier would take offense to his wife kissing another man," he said frostily, his voice surprisingly steady given the fire that still raged within.

"Lord Bourchier died six months ago, and I'm a widow." She paused. "Nor would he have cared either way." She added that last part, as more an afterthought for herself.

She was...a widow.

It shouldn't matter.

She was no longer tied to another.

Footfalls echoed in the hall, and dumbly, Thaddeus wrenched his gaze from her, and looked to the entranceway, just as a crimson-clad servant appeared. "Your Ladyship, servants have—" The young man's words trailed off as he caught sight of Thaddeus, and then the servant returned his focus to his mistress.

Edith promptly dropped her fingers from her lips.

The young man narrowed his eyes, and then in a show of loyalty for his mistress, he rushed forward, hurrying to place himself between Thaddeus and Edith.

"You needn't worry, Stanbridge. I've not come to any harm. Lieutenant Phippen...was a friend from long ago."

A friend from long ago.

Aye, they'd been that. And lovers.

"Mr. Phippen," Thaddeus clipped out that form of address.

"Mr. Phippen," she murmured. "Forgive me." She returned her focus to her servant. "If you'll collect my things, I'll be down shortly."

Stanbridge's eyes bulged. "But, my lady, the carr—"

Edie quelled the remainder of those words with a look, and the young man cleared his throat. "As you wish, my lady." Reluctantly, the driver collected Edie's valise, and with a last, long suspicious look for Thaddeus, hastened from the room.

With her right hand, Edie unfastened the clasp of his wool cloak, and let that garment slide to the floor.

And all the breath lodged in his lungs at the sight of her: her lithe frame draped in a rose-colored satin gown, adorned with gold lace accents. She was a siren: tempting and bewitching, and he ran his gaze over her, too weak to keep himself from committing this new sight of her to memory for all time.

Garbed in a shimmering fur-lined cloak, and with diamond hair combs haphazardly tucked in her shimmering tresses; those jewels were finer than anything he'd ever seen, and never, even when he'd been off fighting, had he felt any more divided from her.

Edie, on the other hand, remained wholly oblivious to his appreciation. Instead, she stooped down to retrieve his cloak.

A hiss exploded from her lips, and she immediately caught her lower lip to keep that sound of suffering in.

It was too late, however.

The initial shock of seeing her now lifted, Thaddeus took in those other details he'd previously failed to note; her wan features he'd attributed to guilt, were strained and stretched. The corners of her mouth taut and her eyes glittering with pain.

"You are hurt." With a frown, he was immediately across the room.

"I'm fine," she gritted out, even as she brought her right palm up to cradle her left elbow. "The carriage hit a patch of ice, and careened, and I happened to hit the opposite wall."

His heart seized and spasmed as an image slipped in, of her being thrown about a carriage, her body broken and battered and—

He gave his head a firm shake, attempting to dislodge those torturous imaginings. He sharpened his gaze on that telltale gesture, and all past hurts and resentment were instantly forgotten. "Let me see, Edie," he urged.

She tightened her mouth and angled her opposite shoulder towards him. "I said I'm fine."

"You always were a terrible liar," Thaddeus muttered. He held her gaze. "May I?"

Edie hesitated; within the strains of suffering in her face, he saw the indecision there, too: a battle she fought with herself.

This prideful side of the woman before him was new. And he wondered at all the other changes which had befallen her in their time apart.

Finally, Edie gave a terse nod.

More than half-afraid she'd change her mind, Thaddeus immediately searched his fingers along her arm, gently feeling her forearm and then the point of her shoulder. All the while, his fingers burned from the heat of her satiny soft skin. It was a body he'd touched countless times before, but the awareness of her had never faded, and it never would.

This, however, was different. Now, he probed the delicate protrusion of her bones, in search of—

She sucked in a small breath, and his gut clenching, he stopped. Damn it to hell.

"I told you, it is fine," she said, her breathing slightly labored.

"It is not fine. It is dislocated, Edie," he said gently.

If possible, her cheeks turned a whiter shade of pale. "Oh," she said weakly.

She cleared her throat. "Well, again, thank you for allowing me the use of your rooms...I will not infringe upon your hospitality any more than I already have." With that, she bowed her head, and headed for the door.

Thaddeus's brows dipped.

She...actually believed he'd let her go out like this? Hurt and injured?

Marching over, his longer legs easily overtaking her smaller strides, he placed himself between her and the doorway.

Edie frowned. "What are you doing?"

"I'm seeing to your arm."

She drew that wounded appendage closer. "You most certainly are *not*."

That rejection hit him square in the chest: the evidence that she'd rather suffer in silence and leave than allow him to help her.

But should you expect anything different? When you've been coldly jeering and cold to her?

That had been before, however. Before he'd known she was hurt.

And despite whatever betrayals she was guilty of, he'd have sooner lopped off his own arm and handed it to her than see her suffer in any way.

"Edie," he said gruffly. "Let me help you."

She continued to eye him with that same palpable indecision, warring with herself. "Fine," she said between tightly clenched teeth. "But the moment you are done, I'll leave."

Absolutely she would not. Old hurt and pride aside, there was no way he was sending her out with her arm injured, and in that godforsaken weather.

But his wartime experience had shown him there was a time and place for every battle, and this, her finally having capitulated and allowing him to tend her injury, was decidedly not that moment.

Thaddeus motioned to the bed she'd previously commandeered.

Edie hesitated a moment, and then tilting her chin up, glided gracefully across the room, and sailed onto the edge of the mattress.

Nay, not just any mattress.

His mattress.

And as he went and joined her, his hands trembled, and he shook inside at that reminder of the place she now occupied.

For it was a place he'd always wanted her, in his bed. But that would have never been enough. He'd wanted her in every way: in his life, as his wife, the mother of his babes.

Thaddeus forced himself to thrust those futile longings and lamentations of the past away.

He again gently probed the area of her shoulder,

praying his earlier assessment had been wrong—she moaned softly—and finding he hadn't.

"Edie," he said, using the same measured, calm tones he'd adopted with the men who'd answered to him in the army. "Your arm is dislocated. I need to put the bone back in place. It"—*oh, God*— "is going to hurt."

She offered a sad smile. "I'm not afraid of pain, Thaddeus." I've been hurt before...

So in tune with her thoughts, even all these years later, he heard the words she did not speak.

Who had hurt her? The man she'd married?

She came to you when you returned.

But after she'd shared the news of her marriage in his absence, begged him to run away with her, as his lover, he'd not heard her out beyond that. What if there'd been more she'd had to say? What if the bastard had hurt her?

His gut muscles clenched and twisted, and he forced himself to clear his mind, and focus on Edie. She needed him now.

Thaddeus made himself take in a slow, steadying breath. "Lay on the side of the bed," he urged, guiding her down onto her back, so that she rested with her injured arm at the edge of the mattress. "I'll be a moment." Concentrating on the task at hand, and not the clamor of questions roiling in his mind, Thaddeus rushed downstairs to collect a flask and a piece of kindling. He hurried back upstairs, more than half-afraid she'd left. Even more afraid he'd merely dreamed she was back in his life.

Instead, he found her precisely as he'd left her, with her gaze on the ceiling.

The moment he returned, she turned her eyes onto him.

They were more serious, and sadder than he'd ever

recalled them, and that change which had befallen her ravaged his heart, made a mockery of his earlier coldness towards her.

"Here," he said gruffly, sitting at the head of the four-poster bed, he helped her up. "You're going to want to drink this."

She protested the moment he put the flask to her mouth. "I don't drink spirits, Thaddeus."

"You need this, Edie," he insisted, pressing it closer.

"I—"

"Trust me."

Edie stiffened, and then relented. "Very well." She took the silver flask in her right hand, tipped it back—

"Slow—"

It was too late. She promptly choked on her swallow, spraying spirits at his garments and the floor.

He laughed, even harder when she glared at him.

"You're trying to kill me," she accused.

"Anything but. You need the liquid resolve."

"I don't," she shot back. "I'd rather deal with the pain than the misery of drinking this rot."

"Edie...drink...but slowly."

She eyed him through suspicion-laden eyes, and then lifted the flask to her lips, and took another drink —this time, as he advised, more slowly.

Her features pulled with distaste. "I'll have you know the second sip was as miserable as the first."

"How about the third and fourth?" he asked after she'd taken several more pulls from the flask.

"A good deal less pleasant."

He sat watching her as she drank. "How was the tenth and eleventh?"

"Very smoooth." The slight slur indicated the spirits were having their intended effect, which meant it was time to get started.

He'd helped any number of fellow soldiers who'd suffered falls from horses, running across battlefields, and dislocated limbs, into which he'd had to pop those joints back. But never before had he needed to inflict that same suffering upon...this woman.

His hands shook, and to steady them, he helped himself to the flask, collecting it from Edie's fingers.

"Heyyy," she protested, her cheeks flush from too much drink.

He took a swig, searching for the strength to do this thing. "Here," he said, handing the bottle back over. "Now, I'm going to need to reset your arm, Edie. Do you know what that means?" he asked quietly.

She shook her head; a curl tumbled endearingly over her brow, and he reached out and brushed it back, tucking the loose tress behind her ear.

Thaddeus went on to explain what he'd be doing. When he finished, Edie stared back with wide eyes. She blinked several times, sweeping those long, reddish-gold lashes down and then up.

"I trust yoooou," she said, a slight slur contained within that avowal.

And his gut clenched again.

He was going to hurt her. He needed to help her, but in so doing, he'd bring her pain, only to find all these years spent hating her, that he'd rather cut himself than make her hurt in any way.

Trying to tunnel his thoughts on what he needed to do, and not how much it would gut him inside, when in his quest to help care for her, he ultimately hurt Edie instead, Thaddeus fetched the short twig he'd collected from the corner of the room.

"You're going to want to bite on this," he said, holding the thick twig out to her.

Edie giggled, but made no move to take it; instead,

she availed herself to another long swallow of whiskey. This time, she didn't grimace. "Th-that is silly." She wiped the back of her right hand over her mouth.

"Edith," he said, with a gentle insistence.

"Oh, verrry well." She sighed, and then opened her mouth.

The moment Thaddeus placed it there, her teeth closed around it, and she giggled. "Thiffissilfy, she said around the stick.

"This is necessary." Thaddeus grunted. "It is going to hurt, Edie."

"I'mgooodathandlingpain."

At that revealing admission, freely handed out, no doubt a courtesy of the spirits she'd quickly consumed, his chest again constricted.

Don't think about it...you need your wits about you.

Because of what he was about to do, and because of how he'd been hurt by loving this woman as much as he had...

"I need you to lie on your back, Edie."

She flung herself backwards; that jarring motion sent the mattress bouncing; it jarred her arm, and Edie spit the stick out.

Oh, God. She'd hurt herself even more. Thaddeus took a quick step forward. "You've got to move slowly when you have this type of inj—"

"You called me Edie," she whispered; her voice quiet, and the most steady it had been since before she'd drank the spirits.

"I've called you Edie before now," he said gruffly.

"But not like you meant it." Her lower lip trembled, and she rolled herself up onto her left hip so she was seated partially upright. "I missed being 'Edie,'" she said, as she collected the flask. Then, with a noisy sniffle, she tipped back the silver drink decanter, and downed another—very long —swallow.

As she lay there drinking away, Thaddeus contemplated her.

She'd missed being "Edie." As a marchioness, and the daughter of a duke, since he'd gone to war and she'd gone on to marry, she'd likely never had anyone who'd shortened her name the way he had.

It had felt natural to do so.

Edie had been his special name for her.

A moniker reserved for a young girl, and then young woman, who was approachable and warm, and not the stiff, pompous peers whom he'd invariably begun working for, with his brother, Martin.

A stiff, pompous peerage amongst which Edith now belonged.

Nay, she always belonged to it.

That silent reminder steadied him, dragging him back from musings of anything they'd shared before. With the passage of time, he'd not known her more years than he had. She was a lofty stranger, certainly beyond the reach of someone like him.

"I believe that is enough," he said, his tones clipped, as he relieved her of that flask.

She pouted. "You were never onnnnne to killll fun."

"I was one to work," he said flatly, even as he knew trading volleys with a woman nearly three sheets to the wind was futile. "Now, lay, down," he urged for a second time.

This time, heeding his earlier advice, Edith slowly, albeit awkwardly, lowered herself back down onto the mattress.

She lay there: her auburn tresses a cascading water-fall about her shoulders, fanned his pillow, and he swallowed hard, as unbidden the images of her conjured different long-ago ones.

Those brownish-red strands falling like a silken curtain about her shoulders as she'd lain, draped over him, taking him deep, and riding him, while he'd gripped her hips, urging her—

Edie widened her eyes, and heat instantly rushed from his neck on up to his cheeks at being caught baldly watching her.

She shot a finger up. "The twiggggg."

He cocked his head as she reached out, fishing around the blankets, and retrieving that stick.

Edie jammed it between her teeth. "I'mreaffffy."

Thaddeus gave his head another slight, hard shake. What in hell was he doing, lusting after her like this? Especially an injured Edie Ferguson.

Except, she's not Edie Ferguson, a voice taunted, jibing him with that reminder. She now possesses a new surname, and a title which she acquired when she married another man.

Sobered by that reminder, Thaddeus firmed his jaw, and fixed on the task at hand. The sooner he saw to her injury, the sooner he could get himself away from her, and the memories of all they'd shared, and built back up those high walls about his heart with which he'd used to protect himself.

"Now, lie back down, my lady."

"Hate when you callfmemylaffee," she muttered around that stick.

He'd never called her "my lady."

Ever.

Until now.

"I'm going to take your wrist with both hands," he explained, ignoring that personal observation she'd made. The moment he folded his larger hand around her smaller one, he froze. Despite himself. Despite his focus, and every reason he knew why he had to focus, he remained unable to fix on anything other than the feel of her palm in his. Satiny soft where his was rough and callused. Smooth and unblemished where his bore scars from his time fighting.

Edie smoothed her thumb along that place between his thumb and forefinger. "Whohurrrt you," she slurred, her voice hushed. "Tellllmeand I'll make them payyyy."

You did.

The agony of her betrayal far greater than any mark left by his enemies in war.

"You need to keep your arm straight, my lady." He spoke in clipped, no-nonsense tones as he disentangled his hand from hers. "And keep it level with your body. Let your forearm and hand face downwards. Good," he praised when she had herself in the requisite position. "I'm going to begin with your arm at your side, then I'll slowly move your arm towards your head. As I do, I'll bring it around in a small circular motion." Even as he gave those directives, Thaddeus was already bringing her arm up into the requisite position.

Her teeth clicked noisily upon the stick.

From the corner of his eye, he caught the white lines that formed at the corner of her tense mouth, and the pain bleeding from her eyes.

Oh, God.

Don't look at her. Focus on what you need to do. Otherwise he wouldn't be able to see this through...

That in mind, Thaddeus made a firm pumping motion, up, several inches...down several inches. He continued that until her injured arm was at the height of his shoulder.

A little moan, stifled by the stick but not silenced,

filtered around the room, ramming him straight through his heart.

Do it...do it...do what you need to...

That much-needed mantra roiled in his head, as he found the resolve to continue moving her arm until it rested at a ninety-degree angle with her body.

He paused. "Are you doing all right?" he asked, glancing down at her. And then promptly wishing he hadn't. Tears glittered in her eyes, turning the blues of her irises into shimmering pools of misery.

Teeth tight around the twig, Edie nodded her head, in an apparent lie, and despite himself, despite his vow to hate her, he found an admiration stir deep down inside for the strength she evinced.

"I'm going to continue," he murmured.

She nodded once, and then slowly, he began rotating the limb...over and over...repeating that movement.

Thaddeus guided her arm up, closer to Edie's head. He paused, with that injured limb extended high up, and then he rotated—

Edie cried out, the tortured sound of her misery echoing sharply from the walls and ceiling and in his ears: a sound he knew he'd forever carry into his mind. One more torturous remembrance that would never be buried, added to the chest of miseries he'd brought back with him from his time in the army.

Oh, God. It was a prayer inside his head.

Through pain-filled eyes, Edie stared accusingly at him. "You're trying to hurt me."

She may as well have cut him open with the bayonet he'd marched on the fields of Europe with. "Never," he whispered.

"Yessss you are. You said you hoped I'd be missserable."

177

He'd said that long ago, lashing out at her because the agony that had come from losing her.

"Not like this," he said, his throat moving up and down painfully. "I'd never want to see you suffer."

"Thasssa lie," she said, her words all rolling together, but clear to him, all the same: each word a lash upon a heart that, against all better judgment, damned well still beat for her.

"I've finished," he promised. "You should drink more." Reaching for the flask, he helped guide her up a bit, so she might consume more of those spirits.

This time, unlike before, Edie didn't resist. The swallow she took this time was generous, and didn't end in the same grimace that had accompanied her first sips.

"They are not so bad, after all," she slurred, her eyes and voice equally dreamy.

"What's that, love?"

"Spirrrits. They are quite niiiice, you knowwww." As he carefully wound her arm, until it was settled into a neat little sling, she giggled. "Of course, you know. You toold me to trink it. That was silly of me, wasn't it, Thaddeus."

He found his lips twitching. "Very silly, Edie," he said gently.

Suddenly, her eyes went wide, and her mouth tremulous. "Love."

He stared blankly at her.

"You called me...looooove." She sighed, and then motioned him closer. He put his ear close to her mouth. "I still dream of that, you knowww. You calling me love and maaaking love. We were so good together. Weren't we?"

"The best," he said hoarsely.

Suddenly, tears filled her eyes, and the sight of those crystalline drops hit him like a ball to the chest. "But I know it's just a dream, because you hate me." She sniffed.

"I don't hate you." And in the ease with which that assurance slipped out, he realized...he meant that. It wasn't a lie. In this moment, faced with the sight of her suffering, he realized even resenting her as he had, and hating her for giving herself to another, he loved her still. He always would.

"I did it for you, you know. Marrryhim." Her eyes grew heavy and her voice faded. "It was all for you."

He stiffened. "What are you saying?"

Alas, it was a question that would remain unanswered.

A little snore escaped Edie's lips, and he sat there for a moment, studying her slumbering frame. Then, ever so carefully, Thaddeus drew the coverlet back into place.

Five

THE FOLLOWING MORNING, as Edie struggled to open her achingly heavy eyelids, she had confirmation of the truth—she had died, after all.

She'd not survived the carriage ride.

All of it, from the blow she'd taken to her shoulder, to Thaddeus's unexpected arrival at a foreign keep, caring for her injury proved nothing more than a dream she'd carried with her into the afterlife.

But it had felt real...and it had been so very glorious being reunited with him, even if it was only for a short while, and even if he'd been as angry, in her imagining of him, as he'd been the last time she'd seen him in the living.

Except...he'd not been at all angry this time.

This time, he'd cared for her.

And put her back together, and—

"You're awake."

At that quietly spoken pronouncement, Edie gasped.

Her heart thudded wildly against the walls of her chest as her eyes went to him—a man she'd not imagined in death, after all.

Thaddeus.

He was here.

Kneeling beside the hearth, he stoked the fire raging in those grates.

"What happened?" she asked, her tongue heavy, her head aching, her mouth dry, and her voice as thick as her head at the moment. She instantly groaned, at the pain caused by simply speaking aloud, and clutched her head....and promptly gasped as her left shoulder screamed in protest of that movement.

Thaddeus was instantly there. "You had an accident yesterday. You hurt your arm. I set it."

That was right.

There'd been spirits, and a stick to bite upon, and then the effects of the spirits.

Her thoughts still dulled from drink sought to assemble the disjointed words from her exchange with Thaddeus last evening.

"You called me your love..."

"I don't hate you..."

"...dream of making love with you..."

Edie recoiled. Good God, what had she said? Nay, what else had she said.

She groaned as that particular statement whispered forward; and then promptly winced as her head throbbed all the more.

Thaddeus was immediately there, at her side. "Take it slow," he urged in soothing, gentle tones, mistaking that groan as one of pain and not pained mortification, and she was too much a coward to disabuse him of the conclusion he'd reached. "In a few days, you'll likely be well enough to no longer use the sling, and within a couple of weeks, I expect it should heal completely."

Edie ran her gaze over his beloved features: those sharp, angular plains; his aquiline nose, and honey-brown eyes, which had always danced with love and laughter...until they hadn't. Until anger had replaced all that warmth. "You've acquired even more skills in our time apart, Thaddeus," she murmured softly. Not now. Now, there was a worry and warmth within their depths.

"A man picks up all manner of useful skills in the military," he said, and his gaze slid away from hers, shifting to a point over the top of her head, and she angled her eyes upward...this time catching the sea of tumult in those revealing irises...before he completely mastered and then concealed that volatile emotion resurrected by thoughts of the past.

Because of what he'd seen, a voice needled. War had changed him, and it had changed him because her parents had coordinated his going away.

It was just one more reminder of why she and he could have never again be...all they'd been to one another.

It had been foolish and selfish for her to think as much when she'd gone to him after his return from fighting.

With that raw and powerful reminder echoing in her heart, soul, and mind, Edie swung her legs over the side of the bed, and stood.

Thaddeus frowned. "Where are you going?"

"I thank you for assisting with my arm, and for allowing me to remain the night."

The lines at the corner of his hard mouth, deepened. "You're leaving."

Why, he almost sounded disappointed. As soon as that thought slid in, she pushed it back. Hers was merely wishful thinking. "I've infringed enough upon your hospitality, Thad—" She stumbled and faltered. She felt her face fall as she remembered their last exchange: a

volatile one, recalling all over again she'd no right to his
name. "Mr. Phippen." Edie made to step around him,
but he slid into her path.

"Your carriage is broken, Edie," he said gently.

Edie.

There it was again.

That shortened version of her name that only he
had ever spoken, one that had always made her feel soft
and wonderful and more than a cold duke's daughter.

"I have to leave, Mr. Phippen." *Desperately.*

He grunted. "And you can call me Thaddeus. I
didn't mean my outburst earlier. I was just taken off
guard."

How bloody contrary he was. And suddenly the torrent broke. Because how dare he...? How dare he have
accused her of being grasping, and for not forgiving her
for marrying while he'd been gone. "You are restoring
my right to use your name?" she asked, unable to keep
the bitterness at bay. "This when I thought I was no
longer permitted that familiarity or honor?"

He winced, his cheeks paling slightly. "Edie," he said
gruffly.

Her lower lip trembled. And yet, he'd use that special moniker for her. And she hated that her name, still
falling from his mouth in that way, did strange things to
her heart.

A quiet groan rumbled in Thaddeus's chest, and he
reached a hand out to caress her cheek, and her eyes slid
closed, as she turned reflexively into that still coarsened
hand. She'd always loved how very real his hands had
been. He'd always been so gentle with his touch. Unlike
her husband, who'd been mean and rough in those
times he'd come to her bed.

Tears filled her eyes, and she blinked them back.
"Edie," he groaned.

And the sound of pain packed within those two syllables ripped viciously through her, and she took in a deep, shuddering breath. "My carriage will be fixed, and if it is all the same to you, Mr. Phippen, I'll wait while it is." Because she could not survive being in these close quarters with him, and recalling everything she'd wanted, and everything that could never be.

"Where will you wait?" he asked quietly, his gaze moving over her face.

She bit the inside of her cheek. "If there is a horse—"

"I'm not lending you a horse to go out in this weather, Edith," he said, his tone slightly chiding. "Come with me."

Her heart stuttered.

Come with me...

That had been the dream that had sustained her when he'd been gone, the words she'd wished he'd spoken in that last meeting with him. And it was suddenly impossible to draw a breath or speak or breathe.

In the end, she was spared from answering.

"Uncle Thaddeus!"

Those excited shouts went up at the front of the room, and she and Thaddeus started, both looking as three children came streaming in.

Dumbly, she took a step away from him as two adorable little boys and an even more adorable little girl came pouring in, and over, surrounding him. All their little voices rolled together.

"We were looking for you!" the small girl cried exuberantly, throwing herself at his legs.

Thaddeus immediately caught her to him, and that natural way with which he caught the child wrought a different havoc on her heart.

"Grandmère said it was in bad form for you to leave

the wedding," the taller of the boys chimed in, and then flashed a naughty smile. "Which only makes me like you all the more."

And then...just what that boy had uttered made Edith go absolutely still.

Uncle Thaddeus.

The wedding.

He was...married.

And *just* married, at that.

Oh, God. This she could not bear.

She had to leave, to flee the agony of this, and yet, she was trapped, witness to the tableau of a newly married Thaddeus, and three children whom he was so very good with. Children he deserved of his own. Something she could have never given him, anyway, which was mayhap what the universe had known when he'd returned...why it had been for the best that he'd rejected her.

"Who is this?" the little girl's question cut into her thoughts, and she became aware of four sets of eyes landing on her.

Edith's mind went blank. "I—" She looked desperately to Thaddeus.

"Are you a friend of our uncle?" the wide-eyed child pressed.

Thaddeus rescued her. "She is. Luna, Logan, Lachlan, allow me to introduce Lady Edith Peregrine. The Marchioness of Bourchier."

God, how she despised that name and title.

"It is so very lovely"—lovely but painful— "to meet you," she said softly to the group still gawking at her.

"What happened to your arm?" the boy, Lachlan, asked bluntly, dispensing with formalities.

"My carriage broke, and I injured my arm." She moved her gaze back over to Thaddeus. "Your uncle was good enough to help me." Apparently, on his wedding day, no less.

A vicious agony more painful than the injury she'd sustained lanced through her.

Oh, God save her. She would not survive this. She'd been widowed only to find him now married.

"Uncle Thaddeus is ever so good at so many things," Luna praised, smiling adoringly up at Thaddeus.

"He is, indeed," Edith murmured.

Apparently, that consensus was not enough, as the little girl proceeded to prattle on about a list of his many accomplishments. "He's incredibly good at charades." She'd not known that. "And splendid at making animal noises. And he is *most* wonderful at snowball fights."

A wistful smile formed on her lips as long-ago memories danced in of she and he racing throughout the streets in London just outside her family's townhouse, tossing snowballs at one another. "Indeed, he is."

"Have you played snowballs with him?" Logan, silent until now, asked, curiosity in his voice.

"We did," she said softly. "We were...friends, long ago." Edith felt Thaddeus's gaze upon her, but this time, she was too much a coward to look at him.

"Annnnd," Luna added. "Uncle Thaddeus picked this castle out, and he's fixing it up."

This time, Edith looked at Thaddeus. "Are you?" she asked.

He nodded. "It is, was, an investment for my brother, but it is now going to be their home."

Luna clapped excitedly, her chubby cheeks flush with happy color, and in that instant, for all the pain, regret, and suffering, there came a flash of joy.

It hadn't been all for naught.

He worked with his brother, then.

His brother, who'd apparently become prosperous

enough to purchase, and fix up, an old estate, and make it his own. And employ Thaddeus.

"Are you coming back to the wedding celebration," Luna asked. "It promises to last for days, my mother told me, and there are so many guests, and if you join us, then you can join the snowball fights, and—"

"I'm afraid I cannot," Edith interrupted. It would destroy her being with Thaddeus and his new bride: destroy her in ways that she'd managed to never break apart, even during the miserable marriage she'd endured. "I should be on my way."

"But your carriage is broken," Logan pointed out.

"And there's games," Luna exclaimed, clasping her hands together, and bringing them against her chest.

"What is this of...games?" The owner of that low-rumbled voice, filled the doorway; similar in coloring, and equally tall, there were similarities between Thaddeus and the powerful figure before them. His gaze went from Edith to Thaddeus, before landing once more on Edith. "Hello."

The children immediately shifted their attention to the tall, broad bear of a man, and happy cries went up as they raced over. "Uncle Thaddeus has a friend!"

The man narrowed his gaze upon her. "Does he?"

"My lady, may I present my brother, Mr. Martin Phippen." So this was Thaddeus's brother. "Martin, Lady Edith, the Marchioness of—"

"Just Edith with suffice," she interrupted quietly, hating that title, and not wanting it uttered by Thaddeus one more time. "Mr. Phippen," she murmured. "It is...a pleasure."

It was singularly odd to have been linked so very closely to him, his career having been forged and sky-rocketed through her marriage, and yet, there was proof once more that her suffering hadn't been in vain. That others had found happiness from that sacrifice.

Mr. Phippen touched the brim of his hat in a belated gesture. "Likewise." He glanced over at Thaddeus. "You were missed at the festivities."

And just like that, another jagged hole was ripped within her heart. She cleared her throat. "Forgive me. Despite it being his wedding, Lieu—that is, Mr. Phippen was gracious enough to help me."

"Uncle Thaddeus got married?" Luna asked, her little brow puckered with confusion. "And Mama did?" A frown formed on the girl's mouth. "Why didn't you invite anyone, Uncle Thaddeus?"

"You didn't get married?" Edith whispered, before she could call that question back.

"No," he murmured, his gaze locked with hers. "That honor belongs to my brother." And in this instant, as he spoke to Edith, it was as though everyone else had melted away and only they two conversed. "Martin was married just yesterday to Luna, Lachlan, and Logan's mother, Christina." He paused. "I'm not married."

I'm not married.

Edith's heart slowed, stopped, and then picked up a rapid cadence. Even as it shouldn't matter. If he wasn't married now, one day he would be, and it wouldn't be to her, but in this moment...he wasn't. And she was selfish enough to prefer him this way, at least as long as he was back in her life. A tremulous smile formed on her lips.

"Martin, tell Lady Edith she must come to celebrate," Luna exclaimed, and the moment was shattered. "Her carriage broke, and I want her to play games with us."

Mr. Phippen looked over the top of his daughter's head.

'I could not,' Edith demurred. 'I've infringed enough upon your—'

'Of course you haven't. The snow is deep. Please, join my family and I,' Thaddeus's brother graciously offered.

'I...' Edith warred with herself. It was folly to go, and put herself in the same quarters as Thaddeus, and yet...her options were also limited. Her carriage was broken. 'Very well,' she murmured. 'I would be...grateful for your offer,' she said.

And a short while later, Edith left with Thaddeus and his family, certain she'd made one of the greatest mistakes of her life...but too desperate for more of him to care in these moments.

REPAIRS WERE slow on Edith's carriage, and even if the conveyance had been fixed, a winter storm had rolled across the North Yorkshire countryside, making the roads impassable and impossible for Edith's carriage to depart.

As such, she'd been with Thaddeus's family for four days.

And in those three days, she'd not come out of her rooms.

That was, she'd not come out of her rooms when he was near.

According to his niece and nephews and new sister-in-law, Christina, and her sister, their hostess, Claire, the lady had not only joined them, she'd been gracious and funny, and really it was just him who'd not seen her.

Which was why, on the fourth day of her arrival, Thaddeus stood halfway down the hall of her guest chambers. And waited.

Arms folded at his chest, his foot kicked up, braced against the wall...and continued to wait.

She'd said...too much for them to not again speak of it. Granted, she'd been three sheets to the wind, but he'd oft found that was when too many men were most truthful...and they needed to speak. Or he did, anyway.

She seemed quite content to not so much as step in the same room as him.

"Are we going to talk about it?" a voice drawled, startling Thaddeus.

With a curse, he dropped his right boot to the floor, and turned to glare at his brother.

A wry grin on his lips, Martin strolled over. "I don't think I recall you glowering like this since I'd stolen your building blocks when we were boys and pasted them with Mr. Duckworth's glue."

"Well?"

"Well what?" Thaddeus muttered.

"I asked if we were going to talk about 'what'?"

"Talk about 'what'?"

Martin chuckled. "Oh, I don't know. I was going to say your familiarity with the lady discovered at our new properties, and then your subsequent placement outside her door. But is there, perchance, something odder than even that which I've missed that we would be talking about?"

Heat climbed up Thaddeus's neck. "She's just someone I...know...from a long time ago."

"A lady," his brother said flatly.

He nodded.

"A duke's daughter." And now a marchioness. The agony of that loss hit him squarely in the heart all over again.

"And now you're just waiting outside that same lady's rooms?"

His face went several shades redder. "She was injured, and I wanted to ascertain that she is well."

"Ah," Martin said, his expression deadpan. "If that is

the case, then you need have just asked. The day Lady Edith arrived, Christina and Claire summoned a doctor who has looked after her. You set the injury well, and the arm is hardly paining her. She's already lost her sling, and Dr. Graves expects she can be on her way...that is as soon as her carriage is fixed and the snow abates." Martin stared innocently back. "Given that information, I trust you can feel comfortable abandoning your sentry post?"

Thaddeus should be glad. The only part of what his brother had shared that he should be focusing on was the fact Edie was on the mend, and yet...

She was going to leave.

As soon as the snow let up.

Of course she would.

So why did that reminder weigh his eyes shut and leave him bereft. "We did work for Mr. Webb," he said into the quiet. "I was sneaking about, trying to steal a look inside a duke's household, and she was hiding, and..." He drew in a shaky breath. "And we remained friends, and then...became more." Lovers. They'd been lovers who'd talked of marriage and imagined a future together.

His brother settled an arm on his shoulder and squeezed, and then it all came flooding out, a torrent set free. Thaddeus went on to speak the words aloud that he'd never shared with anyone. The secrets he'd kept about himself and Edith. The dreams he'd carried, a man who'd seen and suffered the world now knew they could have never existed as anything more than mere dreams. She may as well have been a princess to his pauper, each of them born on other sides of the universe.

"She came to me. Asking me to run away with her. Wanted me as her"—he struggled to form the word—"lover...but not her husband." He was unable to keep the acrid bitterness from creeping in. 'I wanted more than she was willing...or able to give me." Until he drew his last breath, he'd forever see her stricken eyes, and agonized features at that rejection. 'Letting her go was the hardest thing I've ever done," he said quietly. And he'd been a man who, in the name of war, had to take lives.

When he'd finished, Martin remained silent for a long while.

And then, he spoke. 'So she was...not in love with the marquess."

Thaddeus stared blankly at him.

'I've only ever loved you. I will only love you, Thaddeus...you must know that."

Her long-ago pleadings danced in his mind.

'She chose—"

'Another," Martin interrupted. 'Yeah, I heard all of that. The thing of it is," his brother went on, in more careful, measured tones, 'when I came here, not even that long ago, and I'd first heard Christina was on the market for a husband, I judged her, and I judged her mightily." He paused. 'At first. But then, she reminded me, Thaddeus, that, well, the world isn't always so fair to women. Christina had children and didn't have the money or means to care for them. She was reliant on the generosity of her family's charity...or marriage."

'Edith came from an affluent, powerful family." He grunted. 'It isn't the same."

'No," Martin agreed. 'I expect being the daughter of a damned duke is a good deal more...and worse." His brother took a step closer and lowered his voice. 'Do you really think the marchioness had more freedoms than a lady born outside the peerage?"

Something dark and insidious swirled in his belly.

Only, Martin wasn't done with him.

'If you loved the lady as you said you did, I expect

you would have questions for why she married...and if you're looking for her...you won't find her in her bedchambers. She's outside with the children."

She was outside with the children?

He'd missed her already.

With a curse, Thaddeus turned and stalked off, his brother's laughter trailing after him.

Pausing only long enough to collect his cloak and hat, Thaddeus headed to the terrace.

All the guests' children had gathered, with their parents and respective nursemaids and governesses as well, watching on as the girls and boys played.

Through the swirl of falling snowflakes, Thaddeus searched for Edith amongst the gathering of adults, and frowned.

Where in blazes was she?

He'd missed her already.

He—

Laughter filled the air, bell-like and clear, ringing with the same joyousness that he'd carried with him in his memories when he'd gone to fight, and pulled out when the torture of what he'd witnessed, done, and suffered haunted him.

Turning slowly, Thaddeus found the owner of that mirth-filled laugh, and the air froze in his lungs, and he just stared.

As his brother had said, she'd mended enough that she no longer required a sling. She danced playfully about the terrace, launching snowballs at the children, pausing only long enough to replenish her missiles before going after the boys and girls, alternately pelting her and one another.

Just then, Luna sprinted over, and slipped her hand so very naturally into Edith's, and the pair of them raced off: Edie adjusting her strides so they were smaller so the younger girl might keep up. The two of them took sanctuary behind a Doric column.

Edie ducked out and assessed their opponents, who'd lost them when they'd been attempting to replenish their pile of snowballs.

She glanced down at Luna and touched a fingertip to her lips, and Luna matched that gesture.

And God help him. With that bloom on her cheeks, and light in her eyes, Thaddeus fell in love with Edie all over again.

Nay, he'd never not loved her.

He'd loved her even when she'd come to him and shared that she'd wed another. He'd loved her even as he'd rejected her appeal to be her lover. And he loved her all the more now watching her engage in a snowball fight with children whom she'd only just recently met.

"Uncle Thaddeus!" Luna cried, and motioned for him. "You must come help me and Edith."

He felt Edie's gaze, saw the way her smile wavered, dipped, and then fell.

And he trotted over, his boots kicking up snow as he went.

The moment he joined them at the pillar, he spoke: "Never tell me it is you two against all of them."

"And me." A tiny voice piped in, and he glanced down at Lord and Lady Bolingbroke's small daughter, Portia, hiding there.

"We've been hiding her," Luna explained, and as if letting him in on their secret and on their team. Edie touched a fingertip to her lips, compelling him to silence.

A smile returned to Edie's lips, as if she were happy to see him, and lightness suffused his chest.

"We absolutely shan't give Ruby's place away," he

vowed, his breath leaving a little cloud of white upon the winter air.

Edith's smile widened, dimpling both her cheeks as they'd always done when she'd been most happy.

Bending down, Thaddeus proceeded to create for them an arsenal.

Edith dropped to her haunches beside him. "You should be having a care with your arm," he murmured, as she joined him in gathering up snowballs.

"It is much better," she promised; she paused, lifting her gaze, sparkling with merriment and mischief. "And you know I was never one to resist a good snowball fight."

And he felt a silly grin form on his lips. "Nay, I didn't forget."

She dipped her gaze, almost shyly, back to the ground and her efforts.

Making his features into a suitably solemn mask, Thaddeus straightened, and rested his back against the column.

"They're over there!" Logan cried.

Ruby's lower lip quivered. "They'll find me."

"Worry not!" Thaddeus whispered.

"Thaddeus will keep you safe. Just you see," Edie whispered and flung an arm around the girl's shoulders, and the sight of her and the small child together filled every corner of him with warmth and light. It filled his mind with images of Edie and bright-eyed, dimple-cheeked daughters of her own.

"Uncle Thaddeus," Luna whispered, tugging frantically at his leg, bringing him whirring back to the present. "They're coming."

"Here," Edie whispered, handing him several snowballs.

Refocusing his efforts on the battle at hand, Thaddeus took those missiles from Edie, and then darted out from behind the column, with a playful roar.

Edie's laughter melded with the younger girls' excited squeals as Thaddeus turned loose his snowballs on the boys.

The boys erupted into matching shouts of mirth as they threw their snowballs at Thaddeus.

He dipped and swayed, left and right, evading several of those shots from the unruly boys. Two of those projectiles slammed into his lower legs, spraying his black coat with white; he took blow after blow until their opponents were empty-handed and gleeful.

With a cry, Edie popped out, and charged forward, followed closely by Ruby and Luna. The girls proceeded to launch a volley back at the celebratory boys, silencing those triumphant shouts, and driving them back.

With Edie close at their heels, the boys raced back towards the cover of the adults at the opposite end of the terrace, watching on.

Gathering up snowballs as he went, Thaddeus set off in pursuit, hammering the boys with hastily made missiles as he went. Edie and Ruby clapped, cheering him and Edie on.

"Heyyyyy," Lachlan cried, even as he laughed, breathless from amusement.

The party staggered to a stop before the small gathering of parents.

Christina folded her arm around Lachlan's shoulder, with Martin matching that gesture with Logan. "It is time to return inside," his brother's new wife called out, and the children let out similar groans and protestations. "But I have it on authority from my sister that there is hot chocolates and ciders and pastries waiting."

The terrace immediately swelled with an eruption of

cheers, and as the collection of adults trailed after the stream of children, Edie started after them.

Until only Thaddeus and Edie were alone. The chilled air hung with a heavier silence, made all the more powerful by the absence of the children's laughter that had since faded.

And he mourned the loss of the carefree woman she'd been moments ago. He wanted to bring her back to the point where laughter had spilled from her lips, and her cheeks had bloomed red, not just from the cold winter's air, but from joy and mirth as well.

Instead, the walls had come up, and she avoided his gaze.

She lingered there a moment more, before taking a step forward.

"You still throw as impressive a snowball as you ever did," Thaddeus murmured, rubbing his hands together, and watching her as they continued at a more sedate pace. "You've had practice over the years."

"Not often," she said softly. "Just the times I visited my brother and his family."

She didn't have children of her own, then. A different pang struck. Even as he loathed with every fiber of his person the thought of her laying with another man, she'd deserved babes. She would have been so very good with them.

The only glimpse he'd had into her marriage had been that afterthought statement that he'd not have cared about, had she been discovered kissing Thaddeus. But how could that be true? What man would have not been mad with jealousy and fight to keep her for his own? "And...what of your husband?" he asked before he could call the question back.

"Did I have snowball fights with my husband?" a humorless laugh spilled from her lips and, chilled him far more than the cold of the North Yorkshire winter storm raging around them. "My husband was three decades my senior, and wouldn't have done anything as outrageous as throw a snowball."

It was the first she'd spoken of her husband...outside from the fact that she'd shared his title when she'd come to him.

Three decades her senior? That would have meant when she'd been a girl of eighteen, her husband had been nearing his fiftieth year.

In those earliest days, after she'd come to him, wanting to run away, he'd found his way outside their palatial household. Finer than any homes he'd worked on or in, and grander than he'd ever set foot within. He'd caught sight of the marquess as he'd been riding out.

He'd had silver streaks at his temples: a distinguished-looking chap. And Thaddeus had despised him at first sight.

At the time he'd been filled with a bitter resentment over the fact that Edith had traded an uncertain life with him for a comfortable one with a fine lord such as her husband.

The wind knocked Edie's hood back, and her auburn girls stood out like a flash of fire upon the stark white canvas made by the storm around them.

"Here," Thaddeus murmured, drawing that fur-lined hood up, back into place.

"Th-thank you," she murmured, stammering. From the cold? Because their bodies were so close, that the fabric of their garments nearly kissed?

"I expect there was a reason ..." His brother's murmurings from long ago danced to the surface.

"You said you did it for me..." he began.

She stiffened. "I don't know what you're talking

about." With that lie, Edie stalked off, making a beeline for the terrace doors.

With his gaze, he followed after her as she made a quick, proud march, the silver fabric of her cloak whipped furiously about her ankles.

She'd always been a terrible liar.

Thaddeus set off in quick pursuit, his longer legs and strides rapidly eating up the distance she'd built between them.

He arrived at the door before her; clasping the handle, he drew it open.

She paused. "Thank you," she said tightly, sailing inside, and continuing her swift retreat.

Like bloody hell she would.

They'd been apart longer than they'd been together. And the pain of losing her would always be the greatest blow and loss he'd ever suffered. But he'd now all these years of clear-headedness that he could hear her out. And he needed to.

"Edie," he said quietly, catching her lightly by her uninjured arm.

She ground her feet to a stop, and glared up at him.

"There's nothing to talk about."

"There's everything to talk about."

"There was everything to talk about when I came to you, Thaddeus," she cried, her voice pinging off the stone walls and ceilings of their host's ancient keep; that charge echoed and lingered, and Edie's eyes immediately went wide, and she glanced frantically about in search of any nearby guests. When she verified they were alone still, she looked back at him, and this time when she spoke, she lowered her voice. "I tried to speak with you," she said in a more measured way.

And he'd not listened. "I'm listening now," he said quietly.

Her rosebud-red mouth quivered, that plump flesh he'd dreamed of and longed for, trembled: not with joy but with pain, and the sight of that suffering cleaved his chest in two. "Please, don't, Thaddeus," she entreated, and he'd rather don his uniform and march off to those hellish battlefields of yesteryear than be the cause of her pain now. Or ever.

But he needed to know more.

"You said you did it all for me, Edie?" he repeated. "What did you mean?"

Seven

EDITH'S HEART HAMMERED; it thumped away between her ears, a slow and steady throbbing, and she pressed four fingers against her right temple to rid herself of that query he continued to put to her.

Why was he asking these questions now?

Why should he care now when he hadn't cared then?

Why, when it was too late for them?

Too late for different reasons.

The irony was not lost on her; years ago, all that had stood between her and Thaddeus had been her marriage to another man. Now that cruel, heartless bastard was gone, and she could no longer have Thaddeus for altogether different reasons.

She closed her eyes, willing back the memory of him playing with Ruby and Luna and the other children. How very good he was with them. He was a man who deserved to be a father. And she was a woman who could never, ever give him those children.

The fact that not once in her marriage had she ever given her husband a single son or daughter was proof of that.

Feeling Thaddeus's penetrating gaze like a physical touch, she looked away, training her eyes to a place beyond her shoulder, staring at the stone walls of varying shades of grey.

But he needed to know. And then, mayhap he could finally understand, and they could be free of the chains that bound them.

"My parents intended to marry me off," she began quietly, recalling those long-ago moments, the panic that had threaded through her, and the desperation to make them understand why she couldn't. "They...found out about you."

"They offered me my commission."

They'd paid to send him off to war, and she'd cried until she'd thought there weren't any tears left to be shed.

"You said you wanted to go," she explained. "You saw it as—"

"A way to make more of myself," he murmured, those familiar words he'd whispered when they'd lain there in a tangle of arms in one of the horses's stables.

"I hated the idea of you fighting."

"I remember," he said quietly. "Your father came to me." There'd even been a letter from Edith given him by the duke. "He said you told him I wished to carve a life for myself in the military. There was a note you yourself wrote."

"Because my parents knew you would have never believed those words if they'd come only from my father. Your going into the military was the *last* thing I wanted for you." She spoke those words before he'd even finished concluded his. "And I didn't want you to be anything more than who you were. You were perfect to me, in every way. I didn't give my parents the idea. To present you with a commission. They had that idea all on their own." Hatred and resentment soured her tongue like so much vinegar being splashed upon that flesh.

Her parents had hated so very much the idea of her and a commoner like Thaddeus, that they would have only sent him away in the hopes that he'd perish on the battlefield. Only, he hadn't. He'd survived, against all odds. Against all dangers he'd faced.

She hugged her arms tightly around her middle, the satin crunching noisily.

"I cried when you left," she said, her voice a pained whisper, and she closed her eyes, returning herself to those days, the agony of loss. Back when she'd imagined there could be no greater agony. "I shut myself away in my rooms and refused to attend any events. I told them I'd wait for y-you." Her lower lip trembled, making it hard to form words that were steady, a quiver that turned everything into a stammer. "I t-told them there w-was nothing they could do to compel me to marry. Not when I loved you. Not when I only wished to be with y-you." Her voice broke on a sob, and she sucked in a quavering breath. Oh, God. How was it possible for the pain to be as fresh and as raw as it had been all those years ago? *Because you love him: even now as you did then. You never stopped. You never will.*

Thaddeus was the other half of her soul.

A pained-sounding groan slipped from Thaddeus, and he was immediately there, when he hadn't been in so long. He gathered Edie up into his arms, and the tears fell freely because it had been so very long since he'd held her, and she'd never imagined knowing the feel of them around her.

In his embrace, she'd always felt safe and warm and wonderful, as though all the constraints the world had placed upon them didn't matter, and that they could do anything and be anything...as long as they were together.

But that isn't true.

She knew it now.

Even so, Edith let him hold her that way, stealing the bliss of being in his arms, this way...anyway.

They remained like that, with Thaddeus lightly stroking her back, in smooth, small, soothing circles that he traced upon her, and then reversed. Back and forth. And she found herself steadied enough to step out of his arms.

This time, when she spoke, her voice was again steadied: hollow and empty to her own ears. "I was so very certain there was nothing they could make me do to betray you because I loved only you." She steeled her jaw, her teeth coming sharply together, clenching and unclenching until her temples ached, and she welcomed that sobering pain. "But my parents, Thaddeus, they were ruthless. They are people who were never told no, and I was so very certain that with you gone, they couldn't do anything more to hurt me...or you." She slid her gaze to his, making herself look at him. "I was wrong," she whispered. "So very wrong."

Thaddeus's heart thudded with a dull, slow, thickening thump against the walls of his chest.

Her eyes reflected an agony so raw and so real, he wanted to run from it.

He who'd faced down thousands of men, in count-less battles, upon so many fields, with guns blazing and the fog of smoke hanging in the air, wanted to escape from the torture there.

"What did they do?" he asked quietly.

She continued to scrabble with her lower lip, her teeth worrying away at that tea-rose-red flesh, and with her uninjured arm, she hugged herself in a sad, little, uneven embrace.

And then, she dropped that limb back to her side. "They threatened to destroy your family," she said in haunting tones.

A chill crept into the room, descending like a blanket of ice over him, that sucked out all warmth, and threatened to leave him frozen forever.

"What?" he repeated dumbly.

And then the words came, falling fast from her lips, each one marching through his mind, pounding away with every viciously evil and ugly and agonizing part of the missing-until-now story. *It was only missing because you let it be. You turned her away. You rejected her, and refused to hear her out.*

"They were going to have your family turned out of their home, and your father and brother removed from their posts, and I knew they wouldn't survive, Thaddeus," she implored, as if begging him to understand why she'd done what she'd done...whereas, all the while, she'd *only* done what she had for him, and his family.

A groan, low and tortured, rumbled in his chest, trapped there by the pain of it.

"My parents thought they were the only ones in control." Edie's eyes hardened, and it was a hardness that had been absent in their youth but had been wrought by betrayal and hurt, and he wanted to rail and weep at that change: one brought about because of him and his family. "But I would be damned ten times to Sunday if they had all the power. I knew your brother's ability. I knew what he could do as a builder, and I vowed the only way I'd see the marriage they wished for me was if they moved your family to a new home, and if they secured work amongst their powerful friends."

He froze.

Martin's entire career, his livelihood that had resulted in his vision, a fortune, and connections...but it would have never come to be if it hadn't been for this woman. "Edie," he said, her name emerging as ragged as his soul. "I..." *I'm sorry. I never deserved you.*

She drew in a steadier, more measured breath between her teeth, and shook her head. "Now you know," she said.

Now, he knew.

And he would never, ever be the same.

She turned to go.

Only, he'd been a coward and the worst sort of dastard and bastard for turning her away. "What of your husband?" he asked, freezing her in her tracks.

"My husband?" she asked, as she wheeled slowly back around. She cocked her head. "What of him?"

"Were you...?" Happy. He needed to know there was some happiness after Thaddeus had rejected her pleas to run away together. "Happy?" he managed to get the word out.

"Happy?" She flared her eye slightly, and a little, mirthless laugh slipped out. "My husband had an affinity for bedding any woman who walked past. The only reason I was spared his attentions was after five years of cruel efforts, he failed to get a child on me."

His breathing grew shallower at the dark images that slithered forward, the punishing imagery of Edie on her back, while some monster, who'd never deserved her, rutted between her legs.

Closing his eyes, Thaddeus groaned; agony threatened to double him over, and he hunched to escape it.

"But...there did come some good from my marriage," Edie murmured, and he forced his eyes open.

"What?" he implored, taking a step towards her. "What?" he repeated, desperate to know. Desperate to know there'd been something good, anything good because she deserved only joy and had suffered so much.

Because of me.

Because she was doing it to protect you and your family...

Every stark reminder rolling in his head was another lash upon his heart

"I always wanted to be with you," she said. "I wanted us to have children together."

"Yes," he rasped. "Yes, I wanted that, too."

Her eyes grew sad. "And I would have never discovered I could not give you...give us...those children had it not been for my marriage." A sob slipped out, and she caught it behind her fist, stifling the sound of her misery.

He stared at her, stricken. "I don't care about that," he whispered, ravaged by her suffering and her assumption. "I only want you."

"But *I* care about that," she said, ignoring that latter assertion. Edie drew in another slow breath through her lips and took one more glance about.

"Edie," he implored, stretching a palm towards her.

Blinking so very slowly, she stared at his outstretched fingers, and his hand ached, empty, longing for hers.

"I...I feel better now that you know," she said, making no attempt to touch him, and he dropped his arm to his side. He deserved that rejection. "Thank you for listening."

She'd thank him for listening?

And with that, Edie lifted her skirts a fraction, gathering up her damp hems, and marched off.

Immobile, Thaddeus stared after her, wanting to go to her. But unsure how to.

Because he did not deserve her.

He never had.

He'd always known he'd been unworthy of her, only to find it hadn't been his birthright that'd been what made him undeserving but who he had been as a man: because of his failure to listen and to hear her out, and to believe in her.

Thaddeus groaned: the crushing weight of pain and loss and shame were too much, and he crumpled under it.

He collapsed to his haunches.

Now that he'd heard this...he could not unhear it. Nor did he deserve that. Nor did she.

As the implications of what she'd done—nay, of what she'd had to do—threatened to suck him into an eddy of despair.

She'd married another man—a cruel one—to save Thaddeus's family: his powerless family, without any influence, who'd have been quashed as easily as a bothersome insect.

Instead, she'd sacrificed herself, seen them moved to a better home, and his brother allowed to rise and thrive as a builder. What Martin had managed to accomplish would have never been had it not been for Edie's sacrifice.

Herself. She sacrificed herself.

His breathing grew shallow and ragged and raspy in his ears.

And she came to you; she came to you to escape. To flee a cruel husband and a miserable marriage, and you turned her away. You rejected her. Because of your damned pride and your own honor.

He hadn't wanted to sully her with being a mistress and not a wife.

Shame and grief and regret brought his eyes weighted shut, and sinking his chin against his chest, he gave in to the crushing ponderousness of grief and despair.

He sobbed until his eyes burned and his chest and side ached.

And he continued crying until there was not another drop within him.

He loved her.

He always had.

And despite the fact he'd no right to her, he wanted her: in his life and in his arms and in his bed—forever.

He wanted to spend the rest of his days attempting to make her smile and bring her joy, and atone for all the ways he'd failed.

Even as he knew deep in his soul...there was no atoning.

There was no forgiveness he was deserving of.

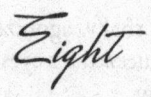

Eight

THAT NIGHT, sleep eluded him as it so often did.

Only, this time it wasn't the demons of war that kept rest at bay, or the sins he'd committed all in the name of survival.

Rather, it was a different sin, and an even greater transgression. An unforgivable one...against the one woman—and only woman—whom he'd ever loved, and would ever love again.

"This is for the best, Mr. Phippen, and we trust someday you will understand that."

At the time, he'd been so blinded by grief and hurt and betrayal that he'd not heard what her parents had truly been saying.

Until now.

Nay, not until now.

Until Edie had revealed the truth.

And he'd realized that of the two of them...she'd been the only one wronged.

He'd believed the absolute worst of her, when he should have only trusted in her, and gone to her with that note and words her parents had thrown at him. And he should have fought for her.

For them.

He sucked in a shaky, agonized breath, and rolling onto his back, he squeezed his eyes shut.

He'd been wrong.

He'd been wrong about so much, where she was concerned.

When she'd come to him upon his return, he'd been so damned proud and resentful and jealous, he'd turned her away and sent her back to a miserable marriage.

Everything within him hurt all over again: a vicious ache that robbed him of breath and hurt from the inside out.

He felt her before he heard her.

And lying in his bed, Thaddeus waited, holding his breath with the same anticipation he had as a young man, yearning for her. Wanting for her to come. Knowing she deserved more than a quick coupling, but assuring himself that he'd give her more, some day.

That some day had never come.

Not because of her.

But because of him.

Click.

But she was here now.

A slight flicker of light from the sconces in the hall filtered into the room, and then was swallowed a moment later as she shut the door behind her.

Nay, behind them.

Laying on his side, he stared at her wearing a satin, pearl-encrusted night wrapper; the fabric shimmered and gleamed as she started forward.

He lay there, watching her under hooded lashes, waiting for her to make the move. Needing her to make it. Needing her still, all these years later. Even as he didn't deserve her. He never had.

Only, it wasn't because of his birthright, but because he'd failed to believe in her.

He saw that now.

Thaddeus shoved himself up into a seated position, and he squinted in the dark, damning the shroud over the room that obscured her features. Or mayhap it was better. Because he was too much a coward to see what she was surely thinking about him.

Hello, love. My heart, my soul.

That had been the greeting they'd always offered one another. A lifetime ago. It sat on his tongue, wanting to be spoken. But he'd surely lost that right to her.

Edie picked her way across the room, and then she reached the side of his bed, standing over him. He ran his gaze over her face, attempting to make sense of what she was thinking.

His throat worked painfully. "Ah, Edie," he said hoarsely. "I am so so—"

"Shh," she whispered, touching a finger to his lips and stifling that useless apology.

And yet, even as she climbed into the bed, he slid an arm around her waist, and drew her down upon him.

"Thaddeus," she whispered, his name a breathless exhalation, and he swallowed the last remnants of it with his kiss. Covering her mouth with his.

And there was nothing chaste or quick in this kiss.

Years of hungering and longing came together, consuming him with a fire of want, and he devoured her lips. Slanting his over that flesh, again and again. And she parted her mouth, letting him in, and he swept inside, tasting of her.

She sighed, and brought her hands up, pressing her palms against the naked wall of his chest.

"I have missed you," she moaned, between kisses.

And he'd missed her, too.

"Oh, God, I've missed you, too," he rasped, leaving

himself bare and vulnerable. "So damned much." And it had been all his fault.

In one fluid motion, he caught her by the waist, and rolled her under him.

He slid her night wrapper open, and pushed the bodice of her nightshift down, baring her breasts.

His desire climbed, as he drank in the sight of her: generous breasts, rose-tipped, and with a groan, he closed his mouth over one of those pebbled peaks.

She gasped, as he suckled the sensitive flesh as she'd so loved.

"You still like that," he breathed against her chest. Even as he already knew the answer. Felt it in the way she trembled in his arms, and in the way her heart raced near his lips.

She bit her lower lip and nodded. "Only because of you, Thaddeus. Only when you kiss me."

It was a reminder that another man had known her, and he wanted to rail and mourn and lash out that someone had done so, and yet it was only his own fault. Had he remained and fought a different war, a battle for her heart and their future, then she'd only have ever belonged to him.

Instead, he'd consigned her to hell and misery and—

"Stop," she entreated. "I don't want him here. It is just us, Thaddeus. You and I."

"Just us," he whispered, catching her wrist and dragging it to his mouth, he kissed the place where her hand met her arm. "Just as it was meant to be."

Ordained by time and fate and love.

He didn't want either ghosts or that bastard here in this moment. Thrusting aside so much regret, Thaddeus returned his attention to her breasts: licking the crest, swirling his tongue around it, until Edie was moaning and panting incoherently in his arms, so that the only words he could make out were desperate pleas for more.

He needed to feel more of her.

Reaching between them, Thaddeus found that soft thatch of auburn curls, damp from her desire, and as he slipped a finger inside her sodden channel, he groaned. "You are so wet," he praised, teasing and toying with her nub.

She bit her lower lip, and lifted her hips, arching into his touch.

And he gave her what she sought. Slowly at first. And then he added a second finger, stroking her, in and out. In a slow, deliberate, rhythmic pattern that mimicked the motions he denied himself.

Because he wanted this moment to last forever. Because he wanted to take his time with her, when in the past they'd always had to hurry.

"Please, Thaddeus," she begged, not wanting that same slowness. She arched and twisted upon the silken sheets, arching her hips frantically.

And he'd always been wont to deny her anything.

Thaddeus shifted, covering her body with his, and in one smooth stroke, slid himself deep inside her.

They cried out with a reciprocal relief.

Sweat beaded his brow, and in an instant, he was reduced to the green boy he'd once been with her, wanting to move, needing to.

"Make love to me," she panted, lifting her hips up, making the decision for him, and setting him free.

Gripping her hips hard, he leveraged himself, pushing himself deep, and then retreating.

She moaned just one word: his name, over and over again.

They moved in perfect tandem. Edie lifting and him lunging forward.

There grew a franticness to their movements: their bodies growing slick with perspiration, and he sank his fingers into the soft curve of her hip. He'd yearned for this moment so long. Ached for it. It had been the stuff of dreams that he'd pull out when the nightmares had been worst, and the longing for her had been so very great. He couldn't wait much longer. "Come for me," he begged.

Edie sank her teeth into her lower lip and suddenly, her eyes went wide, and she flung her arms wide. "Yessss," she screamed, coming, her channel gripping his length. "I love you, Thaddeus."

And with that avowal ringing in his ears, he groaned and pushed deep inside the warmest, wettest place, a place he needed to be, and he spilled himself inside her.

It was so damned good.

So fucking good.

He buried his head against her shoulder, as a pleasure the likes of which he'd never known consumed him, and he continued to drive himself deep inside her, wanting this moment to go on forever, wanting to be swallowed whole in their desire for one another.

With one final thrust, he spent himself completely, and then on a sharp rasp, he collapsed, catching himself by his elbows to keep from crushing her.

Edie brought her arms up, and wrapped him in a tender embrace, and held him: held him as she'd once done, but then those embraces had been all too brief as the fear of discovery had stolen those blessed moments after they'd made love.

Their breaths grew less ragged, less rapid, and settled into a smooth, even cadence.

Withdrawing from her body, Thaddeus rolled onto his side, and drew her close.

"I love you," she whispered.

Thaddeus tightened his embrace about her. "I love you, Edie. I always have." His throat worked painfully. "I never stopped." He never would. His soul had been tied with hers long, long ago.

A happy smile danced on her lips. "Am I dreaming this?"

"If so, we're having the same dream, love," he teased, taking her lips under his once more, and this time it was a gentle, tender meeting.

This time, however, there was no fear of her parents, or some servants, discovering them. This time, unlike before, they didn't answer to anyone.

And for the first time, since he'd gone off to war, he closed his eyes, and with a smile, Thaddeus slept.

Twelve hours later.

Whistling a merry tune under his breath, freshly bathed, and more well-rested than he'd been in...well, ever, Thaddeus headed for the breakfast room...in search of Edie.

She'd managed to slip off before he'd awakened.

Of course, she couldn't have stayed. Not without having brought scandal, or gossip.

And she deserved more than that.

But he didn't want them to be sneaking about.

And soon, they wouldn't have to.

Soon—if she'd have him—they'd marry, and that would mark the end of their days hiding their love of one another.

"I love you, Thaddeus."

He came to a stop.

She'd cried out those glorious words at the height of her passion.

She loved him.

She loved him, still.

All these years later.

She always had.

He wasn't deserving of that, but he was grateful for that gift, and he didn't intend to squander it.

He caught sight of his visage in the looking glass and the silly smile he wore.

Springing into step once more, he resumed whistling, and headed for the breakfast room.

Martin stopped in the doorway, and frowned.

The empty breakfast room.

He consulted his timepiece.

Of course it was late. He'd slept several hours past when breakfast was served.

Turning on his heel, he went in search of her.

And after checking room after room, he was still searching.

Unease stirred low in his gut, that same ominous warning to proceed the darkest moments he'd faced on the battlefield...and he fought back those memories, and that sensation, because it didn't have any place in his life with Edie. Those demons were different. She was all that was light, and good, and—

"Thaddeus," that quiet greeting brought him spinning on his heel.

A quiet greeting belonging to a different woman.

"Mrs. Gray," he said, dropping a quick bow for his hostess, his brother's new sister-in-law.

She waved off that formality ."We are family now."

It was a generous extension granted him...a bricklayer's son. He'd always seen his worth intrinsically tied to his birthright. Only to find that he'd been attempting to be more, not for Edie, but because he'd accepted himself as not worthy. It was why it had been so easy to believe the lie her parents had fed him.

"You are...looking for someone."

Hers wasn't a question.

"Lady Edith," she ventured, and he felt his cheeks go hot. He'd been so very obvious. But then he'd always been hopeless at keeping his love for her secret.

Only, he didn't want to keep his love for her secret any longer. He wanted them to be free with their relationship...one that he wanted to include marriage.

"Aye," he said gruffly.

Something flashed in her eyes, an emotion that looked very much like...pity. "I...am sorry to say that Lady Edith left."

It took a moment for those words to penetrate.

He saw Claire's lips moving, and heard the words she spoke, and yet, they did not...penetrate. Because he could not let them penetrate.

He shook his head dumbly.

"Left...where?" he asked, his voice garbled.

"The house party," she said, and there was a gentleness to that admission: one that hit him like the musket ball he'd taken to the shoulder when he'd been away fighting, and it had the same agonizing feel of it, too.

He sucked in a shuddery breath.

She left.

Claire nodded, confirming that he'd spoken aloud, and this time, he saw the lady's lips move, but her words came all muffled in his ears, like he was swimming underwater, struggling to make sense of what was being said above the surface.

She'd gone.

Why had she gone?

Because why should she want you after you failed to believe in her? That voice taunted. *She was true, and you were content to believe she betrayed you, when you knew what her soul was.*

Oh, God.

He'd not survive this.

"When?" he rasped, and Claire stopped mid-sentence of whatever she'd been saying.

"Before first light. Somewhere around five o'clock."

Five o'clock.

His gaze shot to the hall clock.

Seven damned hours.

She had seven damned hours on him?

He froze.

And what was more...he'd no bloody idea where she was going. Pain rippled through his entire being, and his shoulders sagged under the crushing weight of this loss of her a second time.

A small hand touched his shoulder, and he blinked...coming to the moment. Forgetting he wasn't alone.

"She asked permission to use one of my carriages, as hers is still not repaired."

His entire body sagged, and his eyes slid shut.

The ache in his chest burned and throbbed, and he rubbed ineffectually at a pain that would never quit.

"I, of course, granted her the use of the carriage."

Of course, she had. It would have been rude not to, and the woman before him was nothing, if not gracious and kind.

Claire cleared her throat. "I also took the liberty of asking where she was going."

He froze.

"Her brother's estates are not far from here," she explained. "The Duke of Huntington's properties in Kirkbymoorside. Though, it has begun to snow heavily a—"

He was already on his heel, and racing for the stables.

He had to get to her.

He had to tell her everything he carried in his heart, and pray it would be enough to keep her.

A short while later, in the midst of the latest onslaught of snow, Thaddeus was on his way to Kirbymoorside.

EDIE HAD LEFT Thaddeus's side before he'd awakened, and before first light.

One day and a handful of hours days ago.

She'd known even before she'd entered Thaddeus's rooms to make love to him that she would not stay.

She'd known the moment she'd seen him with Christina Phippen's children that she could not stay. That she could not have a future with him.

Because he deserved those babes, who'd grow to be small children.

Because he was so very good with them.

And because she could not give him that.

She'd been gone not even two full days, and the pain of losing him a second time had not lessened.

Tears smarted her eyes.

She always loved spending time with her brother, Crispin, and his family.

Because she loved children and had always wanted a passel of babes of her own.

Because she loved that her brother had found happiness with his wife...even if there'd been times she'd envied him that happiness.

And yet, seeing them in their joy, all three of their small children racing about, so happy, cleaved her heart: reminded her all over again of what she and Thaddeus would not have, because of what she could not give him.

It was why she'd retired to a different parlor, and opted for a seat at the window, staring out at the snow-covered hills. The storm that had come on and off these past days had abated, leaving in place of the grey-white storm clouds, a crisp, cheerful blue sky.

A figure appeared in the lead windowpane, and she glanced back. "Crispin," she greeted her brother. Somber as he'd not been in so long. Not since he'd married his wife, whom he loved, and not since the pair had welcomed their two precocious children. A sinful envy sluiced away at her. "Never tell me you fell out of the hoop-rolling first?" Usually played outside, only her brother and his wife had thought to convert the ballroom to a makeshift space to play that game in the winter, too. "You who were always the best in our family."

A small smile formed on his mouth. "Alas, I've reared three little ones who are even better than I. May I join you?" he asked, motioning to the place on the window seat beside her.

"Of course." She wanted to be alone. She wanted to sit with her regrets and her misery and wallow until she was all wallowed out. Even as she knew there was no end to the pain of losing Thaddeus a second time.

Crispin settled himself onto the corner of the floral upholstered portion of the window bench.

"You are quiet," her brother remarked.

She'd been miserable company. She should have stayed in London. "I'm sorry—"

"Don't apologize for it, Edith," he gently rebuked. "You aren't happy."

His wasn't a question. Tears stung her eyes, and she blinked them back.

"You haven't been happy for a long while," he murmured.

"N-no," she said, her voice trembling. Not since Thaddeus had joined the King's Army. Oh, there'd been brief interludes here and there where she'd smiled or felt fleeting moments of happiness, but there'd never been the joy like she'd known with him.

In the reflective ice-flaked windows, she caught the way his throat bobbed. "I should have never let you marry Bourchier. I was so damned self-absorbed in my own misery: missing my wife, and too miserable to see that my own sister was hurting."

"Crispin, please, don't," she begged. He didn't bear the responsibility for her suffering. It had been their parents.

Drawing in an uneven breath, her brother dragged a hand through his hair. "Do you know the story of my marriage to Elizabeth?"

She hesitated, and then shook her head. She'd known of her brother's hasty marriage, and then Elizabeth had run off. But she'd never known the circumstances behind the split that had come before they'd found their way back together.

"I fell in love with her the moment I met her," he said wistfully. "Oh, I didn't realize until I was sixteen or so. Mother disapproved, but Father was unable to deny our mother anything."

"Of course he was," she said, not even bothering to conceal the disdain for the parents who'd separated her from Thaddeus. They'd both been guilty parties.

"Even after Elizabeth and I married, Mother sought to dissolve the union. She"—his eyes darkened— "orchestrated a meeting between Father and I. Elizabeth heard things I said...words I did not mean, meant to assuage our parents, and"—he grimaced and gave his head a shake— "they sent her away. They threatened to strip me of my fellowship at Oxford if she did not go."

Her heart twisted for the very pain she knew all too well. "Oh, Crispin." They'd both been manipulated by their parents. Before the dowager duchess had died, she'd begged Edie's forgiveness. She'd not been able to extend the same grace her brother had over the years to their mother.

"I never knew you had suffered in the same way, been manipulated by Mother." He paused. "Until earlier this afternoon."

Edie cocked her head. "I don't..."

"Someone has called on you," he said quietly, and looked to the entranceway of the parlor.

She followed his focus, and her breath caught on a soft gasp.

Thaddeus, alongside her sister-in-law, Elizabeth. Twisting a black hat in his hands, his dark hair tousled and windswept, his cheeks rough with a day's worth of stubble from not shaving.

She sat motionless. Afraid to move. Afraid to breathe. Afraid that if she did, he'd go, and this dream of him would leave her, too.

"Edie," he said thickly.

Only...he spoke, proving he was very much real, his being here. All of this.

All of this.

And then came rushing back...the reasons they could not be together.

She dimly registered Thaddeus stepping aside, and her brother moving past him, to join Elizabeth.

Crispin and Elizabeth closed the door behind them.

Edie found her legs and her voice. "Th-Thaddeus," she greeted, sailing to her feet.

CHRISTI CALDWELL

"You left," he said, his voice hoarse with emotion.

She took in a long, shaky breath. "Yes. It seemed for the best."

"It seemed for the best?" he echoed, and in one swift movement, he was across the room and before her, stopping a pace apart. "How could it be for the best when I love you as I do,"

"Thaddeus," she begged. "Please, don't do this."

"Do you love me?" he asked bluntly. "Because if you don't, I understand why. I certainly don't deserve your love for doubting you as I did." He dropped his voice. "But that night, before you left, you told me you loved me, and it made me hope that you might somehow, despite me being an enormous arse and undeserving bastard, love me still." Desperation bled from his eyes.

She bit her lip hard. Lie to him. Because that lie, hurting him this way, would be hurting him in the other way that would see them together, and him without the babes he should have. Only, she couldn't. There'd been enough misunderstandings between them. "Of course, I love you, Thaddeus," she whispered, her voice catching.

He closed his eyes, the small knob of his Adam's apple bobbing.

"But—"

"I don't care about any babes we might or might not ever have."

"We *won't*," she said, needing to be clear that he understood. "I cannot g-give you those children."

"There are other ways for us to have children in our lives, Edie," he said, stretching his fingers towards hers. "There are so many boys and girls in London, struggling on the streets, cold and without homes or families of their own. In need of parents." Children who'd lived a harsh life in East London, as Thaddeus and his family had. "But if you don't want that, and don't want any

226

child, then I'm fine with that, too. I just want *you*," he begged, adding several syllables to that word. "All of you. Only you."

Tears welled in her eyes.

He closed the rest of the space between them, and she had to tip her neck back to meet his gaze, blinking back the glimmering drops that blurred his face.

"I don't deserve you," he said, his voice husky with tears. "But I want you anyway. I want to spend every day pulling smiles and laughter from your lips." Edie caught a sob against her fist, and he caught a teardrop with the pad of his thumb, dusting that winding drop away. "I ask you to just take a chance on me and a new beginning together."

All these years she'd believed her chance at love and happiness gone.

Only to have Thaddeus here, before her now, offering her everything she'd ever wanted. All of it.

Accepting her as she was and offering her the decision on whether there'd be babes.

His face fell, and his quivering arm dropped to his side.

"Yes," she rasped.

Hope lit his eyes.

Edie threw her arms about him.

Bracing his legs to keep from toppling back, Thaddeus immediately brought his arms up, too, folding them around her, holding her close. "I want that," she managed between tears. "I want those children, and I want a life with you, forever."

"Oh, God, Edie." He dropped a kiss hard against her temple. "I love you so much."

"And I love you." She continued to weep. "And I never, ever want to be apart from you again." They'd lost so much time together. So much.

Thaddeus drew her closer. "And you won't. I was lost."

"We were lost."

"And now we're found," he finished.

And tipping her head back, she welcomed his kiss, and the future to come.

Together.

The End

More by Christi

The Read Family Saga

A Winter Wish

Regency Duets

Rogues Rush In: Tessa Dare and Christi Caldwell

Yuletide Wishes: Grace Burrowes and Christi Caldwell

Her Christmas Rogue

Standalone

Fighting for His Lady

Memoir: Non-Fiction

Uninterrupted Joy

with her own girls and courageous son. For more information visit www.christicaldwell.com

About the Author

Christi Caldwell is the USA Today bestselling author of eleven series, including Wantons of Waverton, Lost Lords of London, Sinful Brides, Wicked Wallflowers, and Heart of a Duke. She blames novelist Judith Mc-Naught for luring her into the world of historical romance. When Christi was at the University of Connecticut, she began writing her own tales of love—ones where even the most perfect heroes and heroines had imperfections. She learned to enjoy torturing her couples before they earned their well-deserved happily ever after. Christi lives in the Piedmont region of North Carolina, where she spends her time writing and baking with her twin girls and courageous son. For more information visit www.christicaldwell.com.

The Wolf of Westmore

AMALIE HOWARD

One

LADY JOCELYN CAPEHART, daughter of the dour Duke of Tyne, peered at her reflection and let out a pleased exhale. Covered in a crimson cloak, her sunset-red hair hidden under a dark wig, and her face painted in a way that accentuated her features, she was mostly unrecognizable. Because for what she intended to do tonight, she had to be.

No one could connect her back to her father. The duke was cruel enough to lock her in a convent and throw away the key until he could use her as a pawn in some marriage to bolster his influence or his holdings. Three daughters...and each one of them disposable. Two already married off and only she remained. Jocelyn was determined to avoid the same fate as her older sisters, though she knew her prospects were out of her hands.

Unless she did something about it first.

She wanted to live—to experience some of the world —before she was forced to marry a man three times her age and deliver his blue-blooded heirs for the sake of her father's ambition. And she knew that was what Tyne had planned. The Marquess of Perrin was an old lecher of a man whose property adjoined theirs to the east. The

237

thought of sharing a marriage bed with him made her want to retch.

Jocelyn bit her lip and balled her trembling hands. Inviting ruination was one thing, but scandal had a way of corrupting everything. She did love her family, despite her parents' iron fists where she, and her precious virtue, were concerned. While she craved escape from the chains of duty, she didn't want to bring shame down upon them. Hence all her subterfuge.

With luck, her daring adventure would remain a wonderful, enduring secret to tide her through an inevitably bleak future.

"You can do this," she said to herself, pursing crimson-stained lips that made them seem fuller, and reached for the reticule that lay on the top of the dresser. She pulled out a plain black, gold-dusted invitation and gulped. A scandalous invitation to an auction at the most notorious club in England, part owned by Wulfric Bane, the Duke of Westmore.

The name made a frisson course through her. Would she see him tonight?

She hadn't seen the master of the ducal estate across the river in years. Their properties were separated by the River Tyne—a wide swatch of dangerous water that embodied the churning relationship between their families, from their competing shipping and mining businesses to their lands and influence in Northumberland and Durham.

The family rivalry went as far back as the Middle Ages. If there was ever any peace between them, it was never recorded in any history books, to Jocelyn's knowledge. The Capeharts were always taught to loathe the Banes, and vice versa, and the contention had endured through the ages. If there was ever a dispute, they were always on opposing sides. If one liked oranges, the other would almost invariably like apples.

Although it was more about fortune and land than fruit these days.

Jocelyn had no idea what Westmore looked like now. She'd seen him from afar during her come-out in London years ago. He'd been rangy and formidable even then, a scowling presence in a corner of the ballroom, warning all and sundry away. And yet, she had been fascinated. The monster from all the stories her siblings told—the *Wolf* of Westmore.

It hadn't been fear that had tumbled through her as her eyes had greedily taken in the dark unruly hair, the thick layer of matching scruff on that hard jaw, and the glint in those predatory eyes, even from across an entire room...it had been a bolt of pure, unmitigated lust. And then, when that predacious gaze had met hers, spearing her like the trembling prey she was, Jocelyn hadn't been able to breathe.

That memory was engraved onto her brain.

Westmore had prowled toward her, lean and lithe, his piercing stare never wavering as he cut through the throng of guests. With each step, Jocelyn's body had locked, her knees wobbling beneath the sparkling new flounces of her gown, her pulse fluttering like a bird trapped in a bush, but she hadn't moved. She had remained still, held captive by a fiery orange-brown gaze that blazed with power and possession, until he stood a foot away.

"Who are you?" The demand had been uncouth, low and blunt, the sound of his voice like stones falling through silk. They had not even been introduced, but the Duke of Westmore obviously didn't care for social niceties, given the whispers and the gasps.

"Lady Jocelyn, Your Grace," she had replied.

His eyes had narrowed. "Tyne's girl?"

The hint of disgust had been plain as day to see, and Jocelyn had lifted her chin. "The Duke of Tyne's daughter, yes." She'd bristled with instant ire. He wasn't that much older than she, perhaps a little more than a handful of years, and yet he acted like she was a green miss fresh out of the schoolroom. "And perhaps you will find it polite to share who *you* are, considering that you stalked all the way over here and demanded my identity in such an unchivalrous manner?"

Heavy, dark slashes of eyebrows had climbed with each scathing word. "You already know who I am," he drawled. "You addressed me as Your Grace."

Blast it, she had. Heat had crept into her cheeks, but she refused to cower. "Clearly my error, sir. I mistook you for someone else. A *gentleman* to whom I'd already been introduced, perhaps."

The set-down hadn't gone unnoticed, but a pair of vexingly full lips had twitched with mild amusement, eyelids hooding in a way that made her pulse scatter. "Then allow me to correct my *faux-pas*. Duke of Westmore, mortal enemy of the Capeharts."

"Not *my* mortal enemy," she'd replied with a cool half-smile. "At least not yet. I allow a gentleman to prove himself before committing him to be hanged, drawn, and quartered."

A spark of interest had lit the stare that had dropped to her lips, but then her best friend Prudence had come back from the retiring room and barreled into the duke's arms with a very unladylike squeal. "Wulfric, you're here!"

Wulfric. His given name suited him, Jocelyn had thought.

Wolfish, deadly, and singular.

"Look at you, my lady," the duke had rumbled in a

light tone that had been a far cry from his previous hard one. "Roth didn't tell me you had grown this beautiful —for good reason, probably. Whom do I have to kill in this ballroom?"

Jocelyn's heart had shriveled at the obvious affection between them, while Prudence had made a scoffing noise. "No one." She'd grinned. "Have you met my dearest friend in the world? Lady Jocelyn and I went to finishing school together."

Thick-lashed tawny eyes had drilled into hers. "I'm well aware of exactly who she is."

"Goodness, Wulfric," Prudence had muttered. "Isn't it time you let all that hostility go? Jocelyn isn't like her papa or her cousin or any of them. Give it a rest."

"Old habits die hard."

It was true. Their families had waged wars over old habits.

Over old everything.

After he'd escorted Prudence to the next waltz, Jocelyn had watched them dance with no small amount of envy, even though her own partner was more than charming. That had been the last time she'd seen the snarling excuse for a duke. Prudence had confided sadly that he'd gone back to the Continent. That season had been a whirlwind, before tragedy had struck. Prudence's shocking death had sent Jocelyn into mourning after that, and she had never returned to London, preferring to stay in the country.

Sometimes she wondered if Prudence's death had hit Westmore as hard as it had hit her. They'd been close, perhaps even someone that her best friend might have carried a secret tendre for. Jocelyn had seen the duke briefly at the funeral—a stark shadow of a man looming on the periphery—but never anywhere in the years after. She'd heard talk of him, of course. The West-more name was synonymous with profanity in her household, especially when income and tenants were lost to her father because of him.

Scoundrel! Reprobate! Villain!

Westmore was everything her father hated...and everything she needed.

Nerves alight, Jocelyn turned over the invitation in her hand. It was addressed to her cousin Tybalt, and one he would never accept. She expected that it was sent as a barb—an invitation to a scandalous auction at the hottest social club in London, The Silver Scythe. Her cousin would never go, of course, not to a club owned by their family's most hated foe. But to her it was a ticket to freedom. At least for one night.

And if she only had one night, she intended to go out with a bang.

Quite literally.

AMALIE HOWARD

Two

WULFRIC BANE, the very smug Duke of Westmore, tugged his cravat off in the middle of The Silver Scythe as he came off the stage with a satisfied grin. It had already been scandalously untied to show more of his bared throat during the auction. The ladies had loved it—a little rule-breaking, for gents garbed in proper attire drove them wild and loosened the drawstrings on their reticules. Speaking of, he should probably locate the one who had won a night of his company to the tune of two-and-a-half thousand pounds.

Lady J.

He wondered who she was. Female guests used all kinds of names at the club for anonymity, especially when participating in an auction of the *ton's* most coveted gentlemen. At least it hadn't been Lady Darcy, a popular *nom de guerre*, thanks to an anonymous, irreverent periodical for ladies that was taking town by storm. He had his suspicions as to the identity of the outrageous author...but that mystery would be unraveled in its own time.

Matteo, the Marquess of Roth's man of affairs, attired in black trousers, a red banyan, and nothing but gold paint on his chest, had led the auction to delighted chaos. The rake loved the attention, not that Matteo cared at the moment. His interest was currently shared by a handsome young footman as well as a notorious widow who loved to draw nubile young men.

The last year, Roth, his business partner and half owner of The Silver Scythe, had won by a landslide to be a nude model for the very same dowager, Lady Hammerton. It had been hilarious in the extreme and Wulfric took great pleasure in ribbing the marquess about it. This time, however, Roth had been won by his wife, the dauntless marchioness who was intent on shaking up her husband's life. It was about time, Wulfric thought. Those two were perfect for each other—they simply needed to get out of their own way to realize it.

With any luck, they were doing just that in the offices upstairs.

Roth was hopelessly in love with his wife, though he couldn't see past his own nose when it came to her. But the bond between them was obvious, even to a man as jaded as Wulfric. Such a thing wasn't in the cards for him, however. Love was Pandora's box, which he intended to keep firmly shut. He was focused on his own lands and cheating the Duke of Tyne out of any opportunity. That reminded him. The dukedom was thriving in Durham, but it was about time Wulfric upped the stakes. He intended to drive the man to ruin.

For now, however, he had to find his auction winner.

Lady J. He'd been pleasantly surprised at the small fortune—two-and-a-half thousand pounds. Roth had looked astonished, too, eyes widening with what looked like recognition in the direction of the bidder, but Wulfric knew it was more likely due to the exorbitant amount. He'd thought he'd had the highest bid in the bag until Roth had been won by his wife for double that. The bastard had the devil's own luck.

Wulfric wondered if *his* winner was comely. The hint of a profile in the crowd had been enough to convince him that she might be. Not that it mattered. He enjoyed all females, especially ones with a little bit of wit and salt about them. Most of the female members of The Silver Scythe were smart and capable, and not afraid to let the world know it. While he was a dominant lover, he wasn't above letting a woman take the reins once in a while, if so inclined.

Though the club catered to more dissolute appetites, the famed bachelor auction wasn't only about sex, though carnal relations weren't off the table. If such desire was mutually consensual, and it had to be, the couple could avail themselves of one of the many private suites scattered throughout the labyrinthian space. While the auction itself flirted with scandal, all the proceeds went to charity. The latter was in Prue's name, no less. Wulfric let out a small chuckle. Prudence would have adored this hedonistic circus. It had been years since her death, and he still thought about her every day.

He suspected his best mate and Prue's brother, Roth, thought they had been involved, but his feelings for Prudence Vance went much deeper than anyone knew, even Roth. Some secrets belonged in the grave, and this was one of them. Wulfric rubbed at his aching chest, the hollow there taunting him of his own guilt. If only he could have saved Prudence from the fortune-hunting scum who had dragged her down with him in an opium den in Seven Dials, Prue might still be alive, but Wulfric hadn't been there.

He'd failed her. They'd all failed her.

And it was Tyne's fault.

Then again, Wulfric could have done a lot of things

differently himself. Taken her under his wing as he should have. Protected her. Cherished her. Kept her safe.

Clearing his tight throat, he let out an uneven breath. He could not change the past, no matter how much he might wish to. Burying the memories back where they belonged, Wulfric strode through the club, eyes panning the throng searching for a spot of scarlet. It was crowded, and he still needed to find his winner. God only knew what the lady would expect of him.

Some of them requested for him to escort them to various parties—to be seen on the arm of the Duke of Westmore sparked both interest and competition—and one or two had opted for other sensual comforts. Thankfully, unlike Roth, he was unmarried and not bound by wedlock. And anything went, as long as it was in safe, mutually agreeable, *consensual* fun.

Consent was sovereign within the walls of The Silver Scythe.

His breath stilled in his throat when a diminutive figure in a red cloak and a matching red mask that covered most of her face cut boldly into his path. "Looking for me, Your Grace?"

Good God, but her voice was husky and rich, the lush low sound of it arrowing straight to his groin. Wulfric wished he could see her face, but perhaps she could be coaxed to remove the mask once they were in private. "Lady J, I presume," he drawled, hiding his unexpected reaction behind cool ennui. "As a matter of fact, I was."

"Well, here I am," she said softly.

"Here you are indeed."

Bloody hell, he sounded like a simpleton. Wulfric blinked, taking her in. She was petite, barely reaching his chest, the wealth of midnight-black hair coiffed in intricate loops adding an inch or two to her diminutive stature. Her crimson cloak or cape, or perhaps it was a new kind of fashionable costume, was made of voluminous satin, teasing along the subtle curves of her body and falling to the floor.

Body heating, his very interested stare swept back up. Ribbons securing the cloak at her throat dropped down into her ample décolletage, the creamy skin there flushed. A pulse fluttered at the base of her neck, his gaze climbing to a pointed chin, parted red-stained lips, and a pair of glittering eyes of indeterminate color behind the mask.

"Do I pass muster, Your Grace?" she asked with a low throaty chuckle.

Wulfric faltered at the teasing, realizing that he'd been ogling her, but something about her ticked his brain. They'd met before—he was sure of it. But then again, he'd met many women over the years and at the club, especially. Normally, he was good with faces, but hers was well covered, so he would have to figure out the puzzle another way.

He gave an unabashed wink. "Would you like to return the favor, my lady? Evaluate and rank my individual assets?"

"Alas, Westmore, I already have the measure of you. The ladies call you the Duke of Bad Decisions, do you know? *Their* bad decisions." A pink tongue darted out to moisten her lips as more color climbed down the distractingly long column of her throat. He wondered how low that flush descended...whether it led to even rosier nipples. His mouth watered with a raw desire to taste them, to bite them until she whimpered. "It was why I bid on you, after all."

"What do you wish of me then? Dinner? A dance?" He paused for a beat. "More?"

The tempting little vixen tucked her arm in his, and

Wulfric couldn't help noticing how well her small body fit into his side, despite their marked difference in height. He was a tall man and she fit like she'd been made to be tucked into him. *Shielded* by him.

Wulfric frowned, confused by the arbitrary thought. Women who frequented The Silver Scythe didn't require protection—they were usually forces of nature, out for whatever bit of mischief they desired. He shook his head and discarded the random emotion. A lady who spent such a fortune on a gentleman's company wasn't looking for security; she was looking for something much more specific.

"I find myself suddenly interested in hearing what *more* entails," his companion said. "Perhaps you can give me a tour of your club and we can go from there?"

"As my lady wishes," he replied.

His companion might seem confident and bold, but he had a feeling that *Lady J* was playing a game meant for a more experienced woman. Or perhaps that was part of her allure...the innocent jade combination she had going for her. Dress and voice of a courtesan, eyes and mannerism of an ingenue. But Wulfric had learned over the years never to underestimate women, especially those who had the wherewithal to brave a club meant for vice and pleasure.

The Silver Scythe was an enormous maze, and it took them the better part of an hour before they'd ambled through it all, from the reception hall that led into the enormous gilded ballroom, to the gaming rooms with their felted tables and the dining rooms with rich, mahogany furniture and gold-framed paintings of bucolic scenes. They paused in the stocked library and writing rooms that had caught her fancy before moving on to the communal billiards and cigar lounges that welcomed both sexes, an art gallery that featured works of the club's members, the exercise and fitness center, and lastly,' a number of private parlors for quiet conversation.

"That was the first floor," Wulfric said, when they got back to where they had started near the grand, curving staircase. "Up there are additional salons, as well as suites and rooms for guests."

He summoned a footman with a glass of champagne. "The whole place is incredible," she said, after a cautious sip. "I admit, I've never been to a social club before, especially one that welcomes women. Do you have many female members?"

"Several dozen," he replied, cataloging the information she shared without meaning to. It was more apparent by the minute that she was a lady of quality. One couldn't be sure if guests were from the beau monde or the demimonde. Sometimes a woman claimed the title of lady when they weren't part of the peerage, but Wulfric suspected that Lady J might very well be an aristocrat. Her mannerisms were too precise, her diction too crisp. She was clearly accustomed to luxury as well as the deference those of elevated station enjoyed. "Most prefer anonymity, but some do not. We also do not differentiate by station. As long as you can afford the fee and accept the rules, the doors are open."

"Rules?"

"The hard and fast rules are permission and consent, especially in the more...risqué areas of the club."

She blinked up at him, nearly gasping as her sip went down the wrong way. Her eyes flicked to the upper rooms as though expecting to see something scandalous on the landing. "Risqué?"

"Not up there. Going down is much more fun." His grin was slow and dangerous, her eyes widening at his obvious innuendo, before he pointed to another staircase behind them that led downstairs. "There's a lot more to the club on the lower levels."

Her throat worked. "What is there?"

"It's not for the faint of heart."

The underlying meaning—*not for someone like you*—was more than obvious.

She swung back to glare at him, those eyes—a warm bottle green now that he could see them in the light of the nearest wall sconce—flashed with ire. "You do not know me so well, Your Grace, to make such a judgment about the proficiency of my heart. Trust me, I can take whatever your little den of pleasure has to spare."

Christ, every dominant part of him rose to the challenge; he wanted to crowd into her space, take those saucy lips with his, and give her a taste of the hazards that existed belowstairs. But he also sensed that beneath all that bravado was a thread of uncertainty. Wulfric frowned. How had she procured an invitation? It was something he would have to bring up with Roth. They did their best to monitor the exclusive invitations, especially to non-members for the auction, but a few often got out. Case in point.

"Do you have your invitation, Lady J?" he asked.

An unreadable stare met his. "The factotum took it when I arrived. Is there a problem?"

He knew for a fact that Matteo would not have, which made it all the more suspicious. But it was done now, and she *had* contributed an immense sum for him. The least he could do was oblige, but first he needed to be sure that no fathers or brothers were going to come bashing down his door. "The age of majority is one-and-twenty. Are you above that?"

That pointy chin hiked. "I am three-and-twenty. How old are *you*?"

"Older than that. Are you here of your own free will?"

"I am." Those pretty red lips compressed slightly, something shadowy like worry appearing in her gaze before it disappeared as quickly as it had arrived. Determination and renewed resolve swallowed her irises. *Curious.* She eyed him and drained the contents of her glass in one gulp. "Are you done with the questions or shall I ask for my generous settlement to be returned?"

"Buyer's remorse?" he drawled, leaning back onto the balustrade.

The imperious little minx turned the tables on him and tossed her head. "I did not pay a fortune to be coddled and talked to death."

"What, pray tell, were you expecting?"

Stormy green eyes crashed into his. "Less talk, more action, Your Grace. In other words, more prick and less prejudice."

His mouth went slack, even as he wanted to laugh at her wit. Whatever he'd expected her to say, it was not that, at least not uttered so baldly by a woman he was starting to realize wasn't at all what she seemed. Perhaps she *wasn't* such an ingenue. Because by God, she was turning him into a mincing prude and he owned the bloody place.

"I beg your pardon?" he grunted.

"That's more like it. The begging. I've heard rumors that you're quite marvelous on your knees." The unnerving temptress gave him a half-smile that tugged at his memory, but for the life of him he could not place it. He could not *think*! Her provocative words were scrambling his brain, and all the blood in his body was rushing to his cock. "Your reputation precedes you in these anointed circles, do you know? Your skills in bed sport. If we are plain-speaking, I wish for you to educate me thoroughly, Westmore. Now will you show me downstairs, or shall I request another, more enthusiastic partner?"

Stunned practically senseless, Wulfric stared at her. "Are you certain that this is what you want?"

"Don't ask me that again. Tonight is mine, and I intend to enjoy every second of it without reality crashing in. Allow me the fantasy, Your Grace. That is what I'm here for."

Wulfric understood that all too well...the need for escape.

"Very well, my lady. Your wish is my command. Welcome to the Underground."

DEAR LORD, she was going to lose her virginity in a dungeon.

With a very scary dungeon master.

A very sultry, muscular, virile specimen who made her body respond in ways she had not known it could. Jocelyn peered up at him. Goodness, he was huge, towering over her like a silent warrior god. She was certain he could pick her up with one hand. Her pulse streamed at the notion of being manhandled by him...of those huge palms fondling her overheated, untried body, placing her where he wanted, however he wanted.

Jocelyn went dizzy at the thought. She'd planned this meticulously for months. Years, if she was being honest with herself. Not the club, the *man*. By her choice, the Duke of Westmore was going to be her first. She was going to get him out of her head once and for all, and see if the reality matched up to the million-and-one fevered dreams she'd had of him in every imaginable sexual position. Because while she was an innocent in body, she was extraordinarily fertile of mind and she wanted to try everything she'd envisioned.

Every wicked thing.

Her core fluttered, adding to more warmth between her legs.

Her parents might have plans for her future, but her body was hers. When the opportunity at The Silver Scythe had presented itself, Jocelyn had not hesitated. She had hoarded her pin money for years, and when she learned of the auction and that Westmore was one of the gentlemen up for bids, she'd sold two sets of expensive parure that her parents had gifted her for her birthdays. She'd come to the club with three thousand pounds in the form of a promissory note and a mission to be deflowered by one man.

The Duke of Westmore.

"So what do you think?" his deep voice asked, breaking her from her thoughts.

Jocelyn blinked and took in the sumptuous space. Like the floor above, no expense was spared, though the ambiance was much darker and richer. This space was designed for carnal pleasure. The furniture was overstuffed and crafted for comfort, and the paintings on the walls of lewd, sensual scenes of cavorting nymphs and nude lovers made her blood run unspeakably hot. Everything in here was meant to seduce.

Flexible young ladies folded their beautiful bodies into impossible shapes from hoops dangling from the ceiling. Jocelyn gaped up at them, gasping when one completed a particularly daring twist, the scrap of gold fabric between her thighs hiding nothing. Shirtless servants in golden silk breeches carried gilded trays to the guests lounging in the corners, whose eyes were fixed upon the performance above.

Gentlemen had partners of any sex perched on their laps while ladies leaned against other women, fingers interwoven and lips touching. Cravats and bodices were askew. If Jocelyn looked or listened closely, she'd catch a glimpse of an exposed breast or the sound of a ragged moan and the rasp of skin on skin. She imagined more than one gloveless hand skating up bare legs. The idea excited her unbearably. Some of these guests here, unlike the ones upstairs, did not wear masks. Likely because they did not care or were longtime members.

Jocelyn reached up to tug on the lace edge of hers.

"Wish to remove that?" Westmore asked, a hint of humor in his tone.

She shook her head. "No."

His intake of breath was soft. She knew he wanted to know who she was, but she also knew that the moment he realized the truth, all of this would be over. Jocelyn intended to be well and truly ruined before he had any inkling of her identity, if at all. Her mouth firmed with renewed purpose. She was doing this for herself...to know the touch of a man she had chosen of her own free will *and* to reduce the ills of being traded off like a precious prize to the decrepit Marquess of Perrin.

If her virtue was lost, perhaps he wouldn't want her.

One could only hope.

"What are those rooms?" she asked, noticing a row of clear glass windows over what she realized was the far end of a massive foyer. All the other secret nooks and crannies led from this main entry room. This was quite beyond anything she'd ever imagined.

"Those are for the guests who wish to watch but not participate. Shall we?"

Nodding with eagerness, she took his arm. When they reached the closest of the glass panes, Jocelyn's breath caught in her throat. In the first section, a woman dressed in black leather breeches and a black lace corset, stood over a gentleman strapped to a wooden contraption. Arms were tied above his head and his legs were spread. It was the most shockingly erotic position

Jocelyn had ever seen, and for a heartbeat, it wasn't hard to imagine herself in the man's place.

She flinched when the leather fronds of the woman's whip whistled upward and hurtled down to mark his already reddened skin, though he did not look pained. In fact, he wore a look of intense euphoria. After a few well-placed strikes, the woman halted in her work, gloved fingers feathering down the man's sides and reaching around to the front of his hidden groin. A lewd moan escaped his lips as she caressed him, the pumping motion of her arm leaving no doubt as to what she was doing. A shiver of delight crept down Jocelyn's spine and spread into molten ripples between her hips. The scene was utterly wicked...and equally arousing.

"Come," Westmore commanded, and she wasn't sure whether it was an order for her body to release its maddeningly building tension or to follow him. She bit back a wild giggle and did the second.

In the next room, which featured a dais with an enormous bed, a woman lay on plump pillows and satin bedclothes while she was being tended to by four scantily dressed men, who rubbed her barely clothed body with oil. One pair smoothed slow glistening circles at her ankles and her knees, moving leisurely up her thighs, while the other two near her shoulders, kneaded her bare breasts. Jocelyn gasped and pinned her lips between her teeth. She was very aware of Westmore at her side, though she was sure that he was more than used to such scenes.

She glanced up, only to find him staring down at her with hooded, unreadable eyes. A muscle drummed in the hard line of his jaw, his full lips slightly parted. The tip of his tongue caressed his bottom lip, leaving a wet trail, the Adam's apple in his thick throat bobbing as he swallowed. Jocelyn stilled. It wasn't a stretch to let her mind envision that tongue leaving a similar glistening path on her skin...or what those lips would feel like licking and sucking their way down her body. Her nipples drew tight with need, breath catching in her lungs.

She cleared a dry throat. "I suppose none of this is new to you."

"Watching *you* watch is new to me."

"I'm not a prude," she said.

"Never said you were." His eyes flicked to the woman who had arched her back and was moaning when her attendants replaced their hands with their mouths. "Does this excite you?"

Jocelyn exhaled. "Yes."

"Being with multiple partners?" he prodded.

She shook her head—she couldn't even imagine being with one, much less four, though the *idea* of it was scintillating. All that sensation had to be overwhelming. She was only observing, and already her body felt coiled and ready to burst at the barest promise of touch.

"Being so exposed," she replied. "Does the lady not care that people are watching?" They weren't the only ones standing near the glass observing the show.

"She enjoys it," Westmore said. "To her, it's a performance. Sometimes it's a man in the place of the woman, surrounded by whoever brings him pleasure. We don't discriminate."

Jocelyn frowned. "Is she an actress?"

"A posture moll."

"What is that?"

The duke shrugged. "A performer of sorts. She poses, dances or does other things for entertainment. Anything she pleases, really. London isn't called the *wicked city* for nothing." He waved an arm. "In here, anything is permitted, as long as all parties agree. Our single golden rule, as you know by now." Westmore called over a gorgeous footman, and Jocelyn felt her cheeks warm at the man's shirtless gold-dusted muscles. "Drink?"

The duke was watching her when he handed her the glass filled with champagne. Only it wasn't an ordinary glass. No, this one was hand-blown into the curvaceous shape of a woman's breast, complete with shaded areola and distended nipple with a hole through it meant for sipping. Jocelyn sucked in a breath, hiding her appalled reaction. "Are you trying to shock me, Your Grace?"

"If I meant to shock you, my lady, I would have offered you this one." He smiled. "Though, in hindsight, you *did* demand it upstairs."

This time, she choked on her own spit. The one he held was blown in the shape of a man's sexual organ. Thank God it was dark because her cheeks felt like they were on fire, and down below, her core clenched on air. Over a sodding glass. "Lovely, though whoever the model must have been overcompensating for something. That thing is enormous."

A wicked smile crossed his face, making a shiver race through her. "I suppose you'll have to see for yourself."

"*You* were the model?" She gaped at him, eyes dashing back to the vessel, her tongue coming out to wet her dry lips.

"A gentleman never tells."

"If you are indeed telling the truth, isn't it a bit vainglorious to be drinking from a glass made in the mold of one's own genitals?"

"Perfection should be celebrated at all times," he replied succinctly.

Jocelyn couldn't help it, she laughed. She had never expected to experience this side of a man who was rumored to be fractious and cold, and ruthless in business, not this playful, charming version who didn't seem to take himself too seriously or who drank from a cock-shaped glass with aplomb. Which was the real version of him, she wondered. She'd be naïve to think the hard-nosed brutal duke wasn't in there somewhere.

He was not known as the Wolf of Westmore for nothing.

She needed the reminder that the more time she spent with him, *conversing* with him, the faster she would expose herself. Time was of the essence. Exhaling, Jocelyn turned to face him and ran one finger down his sleeve. "Are there private rooms down here?"

Hooded, gleaming eyes met hers. "Yes."

"Show me."

Four

POURING himself some expensive Scotch whisky from the stocked mantel in a plain tumbler, Wulfric watched her through a heavy-lidded gaze as she prowled the perimeter of the private apartments. He still could not shake the feeling that he recognized her from somewhere. But he met dozens of ladies in any given month at The Silver Scythe, not to mention the female aristocrats in London ballrooms. His lovely mistress of the hour could be anyone.

"Whisky?" he asked her.

She gave a short, decisive shake of her head, and then pinned her lips, changing the gesture to a nod. "Some sherry, if you have it."

"We do." He poured a glass, a much less obscene one this time, and handed it to her.

She arched a brow, several shades lighter than her dark hair. "No prick glass?"

His prick jumped as if it'd been personally addressed. "Alas, that's only in the main room. We're much more sedate in our dish choices behind closed doors."

That red mouth curled in a smile so sinful that he felt it in his ballocks. "Pity."

Wulfric had to admit that she'd taken the vulgar glasses in stride. Perhaps he'd been wrong in his estimation of her as well. Wouldn't be the first time. He'd had the sneaking suspicion for some time that Roth's own marchioness was the infamous Lady Darcy, author of the scandalous sex periodical, not that he would share that with his best friend, but Lady Roth was one of those women who had many, *many* secret layers. Perhaps this Lady J was the same.

A tempest behind a veneer of elegance.

"What makes this different to other bawdy clubs in London?" his guest asked, her steps taking her near to the enormous bed with its decadent wine-colored silk counterpane and frilled pillows. Once a room had been enjoyed, servants were very efficient in their duties, the entire space cleaned from top to bottom. It amounted to a mountain of laundry, but supplied jobs to those who wanted honest work...paid for by the very deep pockets of the members who kept them in business.

A win-win.

Her question took him by surprise because it was underscored by what sounded like true interest, not an attempt at small conversation. "It's not a brothel, my lady." When a skeptical gleam came into her expression with a pointed glance at the bed, he spread his hands wide. "Call it a social club with a twist. We cater to an exclusive, elegant clientele, and we're in the business of pleasure. Excellent food, games and revelry, and if that extends to a bedchamber or three, so be it. Our staff is free of disease, our spaces private and clean, and our patrons can enjoy themselves in any way they want, free of censure, judgment, and punishment. Life should be indulged, shouldn't it?"

'Isn't all this against the law?"

"Whose law? The church? The crown? Parliament? Men or women are their own governance when it comes to their own bodies. We might be the epitome of the civilized world in drawing rooms, at White's, or the Royal Opera, but here within these very private walls, you can choose to drink, smoke, consume, gamble, dance, watch, fuck."

She gasped at the last, her body giving a delicious sort of shiver, eyelashes dipping down to hide her reaction. Deep color distilled down the slim column of her throat to her collarbones, like ink through water. She was aroused—it was obvious in that telltale flush over her pretty skin, the shallowness of her breaths, and the constant way her tongue flicked out to wet her lips. God, she was lovely.

Who was she?

Why does it matter?

It didn't matter. It shouldn't matter, but the mystery was begging to be solved. Not to mention his cock was more eager than it had been in some time. As much as he played the rake in his position at the club, he preferred a quiet evening spent with his estate ledgers and a good Scottish whisky than the debauchery he was reputed for. He and Roth had shared a similar reputation for years. They were known as libertines of the first water, and people believed what they wanted to believe. In truth, Wulfric hadn't been with a woman in years.

Not since Prue's death.

Seeing her in that filthy opium den had cut something from him...any ability to feel had died with her that day. Oh, he continued to play the part of the dissolute rake that was expected of him, but it was all a performance.

"And what of adultery?" Lady J asked. "Men and women who break their vows?"

"Their decisions are on them." He gave a careless shrug. "And how do *you* know what goes on behind closed doors? We have many married couples who come here together, seeking adventure or to share mutual fantasies in a safe space. One can easily judge when one is on a high horse."

She snorted. "I assure you, Your Grace, if there is a steed involved, I'm being dragged behind it like chattel, not sitting atop it."

Cocking his head, Wulfric stared at her, his opinions shifting yet again. What did *that* mean? Was she a widow? A scorned wife? Or had he been wrong about her being a peeress and she was simply a high-class courtesan thrown aside by her lord and protector for a younger one? He couldn't countenance that—who would discard such a prize? The skin of her cheeks was smooth, the porcelain skin youthful. Her lips...his eyes fastened on that lush bow, painted in the same hue of her garments, and he felt his length stiffen more when he imagined that perfect pout leaving red smudges upon him.

Turning toward the adjoining antechamber, he discreetly adjusted himself and leaned against the wall, watching her finish the rest of her wandering exploration. He frowned, the possibilities narrowing, but still endless. Perhaps she was a fallen lady, a *former* aristocrat, who had been compromised in some way. Or better yet, an unmarried heiress out to make mischief. He snorted a laugh at that—sheltered misses would faster swoon before setting foot here.

Eventually, she stopped to perch on a gold-covered armchair, the scarlet folds of her cloak billowing about her.

"What do you do with the money?" she asked. "From the auction?" She wet her lips again and folded her hands in her lap. "Do you keep any of it?"

"No, all the proceeds are donated to charity. A women's shelter."

"That's commendable," she murmured.

Wulfric didn't know why the next words came out of his mouth. Maybe it was the dubious way she said it, as if she didn't quite believe they would send every penny made from an outrageous auction at an equally outrageous club to such a place. "I knew a girl once who needed help and didn't get it. She died. The charity is in her name."

A wide green stare collided with his. Her hands, so expressive, lifted from her lap to tug at a button on her cloak, a look of distress coming over her face that she tried to smooth away with a trembling smile. A muscle worked in her throat. Had she lost someone too? Not for the first time, Wulfric wished he could see the entirety of her face.

Oddly, the small thread of commonality between them meant something, even if she was a stranger he'd never see again. Wulfric downed the glass of whisky, relishing the burn...and the forced clarity it brought. It didn't matter who she was, only what she'd contributed. Setting down his tumbler, he cleared his throat. "What do you wish of me?"

More color suffused her skin before that chin of hers jutted upward, a sure sign that she was reaching for internal fortification. "Could you..." She let out a hiss of breath through her teeth and fisted her fingers in her skirts. "May I see what my charitable donation has bought me?"

"You want me to undress?"

A roll of that lower lip beneath the upper. "If you will."

Slowly, Wulfric shrugged out of his coat, and then his waistcoat. All the while, he felt her stare intent upon him, the shallow, quick rises of her chest, the only indication she was breathing. When he tugged his shirt over his head, leaving his upper body bare and on display, he met her gaze boldly. That bottom lip of hers was wedged between her teeth, posture rigid as if she didn't trust herself quite yet to relax.

"Shall I continue?" he asked.

"Yes," she replied hoarsely. "The rest, please."

If it wasn't for the slight quiver in her voice, Wulfric would have believed the convincing show of sangfroid. He sat on the bench at the end of the bed and removed his boots and stockings, until he was only clad in his trousers.

"You're not finished," she pointed out.

"The rest is for you to unwrap," he drawled, primal satisfaction building in him at the hiss of indrawn breath when that gaze fell to the obnoxious bulge at his groin that he made no move to hide.

He prowled toward her, stopping only when he was nearly on top of her. He leaned down and propped his hands on either side of the arm rests, caging her small body in. The pulse at her throat fluttered like a captive, panicked thing, but she met his look without hesitation.

"Don't be afraid," he whispered, bending even more to feather his mouth along one side of her temple before pulling back to do the same on the other side. She smelled of crushed lilacs.

"I am not."

That was true, he realized with delayed astonishment. In the spare candlelight, the green looked like molten jade, flecks of gold visible in their heated depths. She might have been nervous and excited, but there was no fear in that wide gaze. No, in her stare, he saw drive and resolve, and enough desire to match the tide teeming through his blood. Still watching him, she removed her gloves, exposing smooth skin and long elegant fingers.

Definitely the hands of a lady.

Surprising him, she slowly pushed her body upward, making him straighten, even as her breasts grazed his torso and chest. Wulfric found himself being the one to inhale, his lungs going tight when her sweet flowery fragrance wafted into his nostrils. *Fuuuuuck*. He had experienced physical attraction with women in the past, but nothing had ever quite been this sizzling. This raw. The level of arousal felt like he was going to peel out of his own skin, his cock so fucking hard, it hurt to even breathe.

And that was *before* her fingers went to the ties of that cloak, *before* they released the fastenings, and *before* the fabric descended into a scarlet pool at her heels, taking every goddamned ounce of his good sense with it. Because the bloody chit was wearing nothing but a tiny pair of cream-colored short stays, embroidered with pink flowers, over the filmiest chemise known to man.

Hell if she wasn't every erotic fantasy come to life.

Wulfric's throat went unspeakably dry while his cock tried to punch a hole in the fabric of his trousers. He didn't know where to look...at the lush expanse of her breasts, the curves of her small waist and generous hips flaring beneath the embroidered sateen panels of her stays, the long lines of her legs and the shadowed apex of her thighs just visible through the sheer lawn.

"Like what you see?" she whispered, lifting her face to his dazed one.

"You're bloody stunning."

Blushing, she smiled and twined her arms around

his nape. "I am here for your pleasure, Your Grace. And mine, of course."

THE DUKE OF WESTMORE

his nape, "I am here baby, my pleasure Your Grace. And bliss of course.

Five

WHERE SHE FOUND SUCH BOLDNESS,
Jocelyn would never know.

Inside, her body felt like a mass of jelly. Because, *heavens*, the sight of that man unclothed had turned every bone, every muscle, and every brain cell to complete mush. Had anyone ever been built so perfectly? So godlike in his masculine beauty?

The duke was not stocky, but he was tall and obviously strong. Shelves upon shelves of sleek, golden muscle, from his wiry shoulders to the deeply grooved abdomen to those ropy, veiny forearms dusted in dark hair, had made it utterly impossible to breathe. To move.

To *think*!

Because here was the Wolf of Westmore in all his predatory glory.

Those orange-hued eyes of his glowed, his black pupils huge, like a lunar eclipse with a darkened sun gilding its edges. His jaw was hard, full lips pulled taut. And his scent... God, she could bask in it. Rub herself in that warm leather-and-bergamot aroma like a shameless vixen in heat. Jocelyn bit back a snort. She'd be his lady wolf any day.

The space between her legs practically *throbbed* with want. She could feel her heartbeat echoing there like a drum, announcing to all and sundry that the enormous vessel in his pants was more than welcome into her empty harbor. Jocelyn nearly snorted again at the absurd metaphor, and then swallowed her mirth, as a pulse of anxiety surged. Her body felt wet and ready, but she'd never done this before. Would it hurt? Should she say anything? What if she bled?

No, no, no. Gentlemen did not like hearing such things...it would cause him to stop and question.

And she didn't want questions. She wanted action.

If there was blood, at least the dark red sheets would hide it. One of her older sisters had bled, though the other hadn't, and their experiences in the bedchamber had been wildly different. Jocelyn blinked rapidly, heart racing with excitement and panic. Excitement for what was to come, and panic that her greenness would be immediately apparent to a proficient lover like Westmore. Dear God, would he see right through her?

"I haven't done this many times," she admitted in a low whisper.

There, that would do.

"I'll be gentle." A palm banded around her back as another arm reached under her legs.

In the next breath, she was swooped up into his sinewy arms and ferried over to the bed. The mattress at her back was soft, not that she expected lumps since everything about The Silver Scythe was designed for luxury and comfort. Why would a bordello bed be any different?

Good gracious, are you really doing this?

Closing her eyes, Jocelyn shook away the prim voice

in her head. If her parents wanted to sell her to the Marquess of Perrin, she would damn well be sure he didn't get everything. This was for her, and so what if she had paid for the pleasure? Every penny went to charity. Heavens, she'd almost broken down when he'd confessed whom the shelter was for. She knew...Jocelyn *knew* it was for Prudence. It'd been no secret that the Duke of Westmore had loved Prue deeply.

A secret charity in her name was just like him.

Jocelyn bit her lip and tried to bring herself back to the moment—this chamber was no place for parents or the ghosts of dead friends. This chamber was for *her*, for the man about to receive the gift her body could only offer once, and for shared gratification.

She wrinkled her nose. She *hoped* it would be gratifying. She'd been an avid reader of the Lady Darcy periodicals, which touted that pleasure was to be had for both men and women during sexual congress. It was thanks to that racy publication that she had felt confident enough in her own power as a female to go after what she wanted. Specifically, the Duke of Westmore. At least, before she was bartered to a gout-ridden fossil for a parcel of land and a title.

"Where did you go just then?" the duke asked, watching her.

Jocelyn's eyes flicked open behind her mask. "Nowhere. I'm right here."

"Good girl." Those feral orange-lit eyes glittered with dominance, making her insides promptly turn to jelly again. Then he kissed her, his hard male lips taking hers in a kiss so tender her toes curled. Per the periodical, his tongue would come next. There *was* a thing as too much tongue, Lady Darcy had cautioned, and Jocelyn braced for entry, but all she felt was firm, soft pressure, followed by a sinful, velvet swipe over her bottom lip. She tasted whisky and a dark flavor that was all him, and she wanted more.

Playfully, he nibbled at her lips, drawing his tongue —*definitely not too much*—along the seam of her mouth before she opened for him in invitation. He swept in, a silken invasion as his tongue teased hers, coaxing it into his own mouth. She went greedily and was rewarded when he groaned and kissed her deeper, stealing the breath from her lungs.

"You do that well," she gasped, when he pulled away.

His eyes hooded. "So do you."

Delighted, she pressed her tingling lips together. If only he knew that Lady Darcy recommended practicing with one's hand curled into a loose fist, with the thumb and upper curve of the forefinger mimicking a pair of lips, as well as with a ripe apricot, he might be shocked. She couldn't believe the technique had actually worked.

All hail Lady Darcy, the devoted champion of female pleasure!

According to the publication, there was more to come, including kisses elsewhere. As in down *there*. That indecent throb at her core began anew. Would a man truly do such a thing? Kiss a lady between her thighs? Would Westmore? She had washed in lilac-scented water, even taken a pair of scissors to her maidenhair—grooming was more of a courtesan thing according to Lady Darcy—but she'd wanted to be perfect.

Jocelyn froze. Oh, *hell*. Her maidenhair!

She'd worn a dark wig, her wealth of red hair much too noticeable. Would the duke notice the difference? Remark upon it? And even more importantly, *could* a man recognize a woman by something like that? As much as she longed to discover whether the duke was proficient in the artistry of the tongue, per Lady Darcy, she could not risk it.

One warm hand slid up her leg, making her shiver and forget her momentary worry. When his mouth traveled to her neck, Jocelyn tried to relax, but her whole body felt as though it was on fire. His other hand was not idle as he unlaced the tie at the top of her chemise and stays, and nuzzled between her breasts.

"Do you like breast play?" he asked, his voice like gravel.

"I..." *Don't know.* Jocelyn clamped her lips together, just as his fingers brushed her nipple and her spine bowed.

"I'll take that as a yes." When his mouth dipped to take the aching peak into his mouth, Jocelyn's eyes nearly rolled back into her head as lightning tore through her entire body. His tongue swirled, his teeth scraped, and she writhed. By the time he moved down to remove her shoes and roll down her stockings, she was delirious with need. He bit at her knee, licked up the inside of her thigh and spread them wide. When she glanced down at the wanton picture his broad shoulders pushing her knees apart made, she trembled.

"I can't wait to taste you," he growled, nostril flaring as though he was ready to pounce.

Yes, for the love of all things wicked, yes!

Wait, no! Positively no.

"No, please stop," she said, reaching down to keep the hem of chemise over her groin. "I'm shy."

His eyes widened, even as a sultry smirk tugged the corner of his full lips upward. "Is that a fact?"

"Yes," she said on a ragged breath. Damn her disguise to purgatory!

"Fingers?" he asked.

She nodded mutely, that heated, hungry stare too

much to take. He didn't look upset at her refusal, only a speculative gleam appearing for a moment before it disappeared. Perhaps he'd chalk it down to her inexperience. Pushing up onto those lean forearms, he crawled up her body and she felt the bare heat of his hair-roughened legs against her skin. When had he discarded his trousers? It was on the tip of her tongue to demand her unwrapping rights, when two fingers slid through the copious amounts of wetness at the juncture of her thighs.

"Guh..."

"You're drenched," he said, lifting his fingers between them, glossed in the shine of her essence. Without releasing her gaze, he slid them into his mouth, a low groan of pleasure rumbling from him. Jocelyn stared in shock as he sucked them clean. "As I thought, delicious. Nothing at all to be shy about, I promise you."

The dark, indelicate rasp nearly made her shove him back down there and tell him to go to work, discovery be damned. "You're very wicked, Your Grace," she said.

"Wickedness is a matter of perspective, my lady." He lapped at her tight nipple and took it between his teeth, biting just hard enough for her to feel the edge of pain, before soothing it with his efficient tongue. She moaned as heat rushed into the smarting peak. "I could dine on you for hours, lick every crevice of this beautiful body." His palm reached behind to squeeze a full handful of her behind. "See *my* marks on this creamy skin."

Her brain went blank.

"You would spank me?" Her voice was so breathy she barely recognized it, even as her heartrate tripled behind her ribs as the image of the couple from the windowed room flashed into her brain. The man had seemed in raptures.

"Do you want me to?"

Did she? Biting her lip as her body scorched and burned, she gave one nod.

With barely any warning, he lifted them both up, sat himself on the edge of the bed and splayed her over his bent knees. Jocelyn could feel his hardened erection prodding into her stomach that was still guarded by the fabric of her stays. Cool air kissed her bottom, when he lifted the hem of her chemise over her cheeks.

"What a lovely canvas," he said, running a hand over her skin in a small circle.

He gave no warning other than the absence of his touch, the flat of his palm connecting with the fleshiest part of her. She gasped. The initial shock of it was worse than any actual pain. Three successive strikes followed to alternating sides, and her body tightened at each one. It hurt, as she'd expected it would. Jocelyn frowned. Where was the pleasure? Why had that man looked delirious with it, when his partner had been using a whip?

She opened her mouth about to tell him to stop, that this wasn't for her, when he completed two more, one on each cheek, followed by a soothing rub that ended with his fingers dipping between her legs. Two fingers grazed over the heart of her. Suddenly the heat spreading across her bottom from the strikes blended into warmth she felt everywhere. In her nipples, in her cheeks—upper and lower—and in her sex.

Jocelyn gasped when those probing fingers delved into her saturated core, a pleased rumble breaking from him at what he found. The amount of moisture leaking from her had to be indecent, and the vulgar sounds her body made around his fingers were mortifying, though shame was the least of the emotions barreling through her. Her core was tight and so hot, every part of her sex alive with sensation.

She almost cried when he withdrew, her body clenching on air. Jocelyn was so wound up, she knew it wouldn't take much to send her hurtling over the edge, and when two more strikes rained down on her over-heated, tender flesh, she bit into the bedclothes, her body so strained it felt as though she was going to explode out of her skin.

"Westmore," she begged, back arched helplessly up. "I can't."

"You can." A pair of successive strikes on each side and her bottom was officially on fire. *Everything* was on fire, but those flames were tempered in honeyed bliss.

Thick fingers sank into her passage again, scissoring slightly once or twice, then pulled out to graze lightly over the tight bundle of nerves at the top of her sex, and Jocelyn's back bowed with the force of her release. Ecstasy pounded through her in waves, her vision going white as her body convulsed around Westmore's fingers. She screamed into the bedclothes as her body detonated like a lit fuse, blowing every part of her into sublime rapture.

As she drifted, riding the waves of pleasure, he brought her upright with one arm, cradling her limp upper body to his chest, and took her lips with his in a drugging kiss. "You're so responsive," he told her while planting heated kisses to her jaw and her neck as he rolled her to her back and positioned himself between her legs. "So fucking beautiful when you come." Jocelyn could barely function, her mind lost in the aftermath of her orgasm. "You'll do it again, all over my cock."

Yes, please, Duke...

When he pushed carefully and slowly inside her, it was thanks to his extensive preparation that Jocelyn felt nothing but an intense kind of fullness. He wasn't done, her dull brain realized, as he eased gently backward only to push in further. It stung as he stretched her. *Oh*, that was a lot. She tensed around him with a frown, and he stilled. "Are you well?"

"You're big," she said with a breathless moan. The edge of pain was riding the edge of pleasure, and she needed the pleasure to take over. He was too large, his body pressing her and her sore bottom into the sheets. "And my behind stings."

Westmore chuckled. "I'll rub some salve in it after, I promise."

"Make me feel good again, Your Grace."

"Wulfric," he said, staring down at her, right before sliding his fingers to where they were joined, his thumb unerringly finding the needy spot that made her gasp and ripple around him. "That's it," he said, circling the area, while easing backward and stroking in, filling her more each time.

Pleasure coiled in languid ropes when his mouth latched on to her neck, nibbling up to her earlobe, before claiming her mouth in a kiss so fierce, all she could feel was him working her body at both ends...making her his. When he was fully seated, and so deep she didn't know where either of them began or ended, Westmore —no, Wulfric—started to move.

One powerful thrust, and dear Lord, if her body didn't seize and explode then and there.

"Wulfric!" she whimpered, stars bursting behind her eyes.

Jocelyn could only hold on as her second release catapulted her into space, her fingers digging into the tight meat of his shoulders as that strong body drilled into her, chasing his pleasure on the heels of hers. All she knew was that if she let go of him, she'd be torn away on the surge of pleasure taking her body in its unyielding grip.

But more than ever, all Jocelyn wanted to do was watch him. That handsome face was tight with strain, lips parted and eyes burning with lust. She'd never seen anything more incredible in her life than this man poised at the pinnacle of his passion. A formidable wolf between her legs. *Her* wolf...at least in this moment.

Powerful, magnificent, wild.

With a growl torn from the depths of him, that long, sinewy body stilled for one glorious moment, head thrown back and corded veins pulsing at his neck, he withdrew from her still quivering body to spend in the sheets between them. When he collapsed with a groan and took them both to their sides, Jocelyn had no words for what she'd just experienced.

She didn't care about Perrin. She didn't care about her parents. She didn't care about anything but the fact that she was wholly, divinely, *deliciously* replete.

WULFRIC PINCHED the bridge of his nose with his thumb and forefinger, and leaned back in his chair, the beginnings of a headache gnawing at the edges of his skull. The desk was covered with a mountain of papers. Normally, he loved poring over his estate accounts, financial investments, and making money hand over fist. Columns of numbers made sense to him, calmed him, but today he was distracted. The last *week* he'd been distracted.

All he could think about was a dark-haired minx who had invaded his mind.

Who was she?

After what had to be one of the most satisfying sexual encounters of his life, the woman he'd bedded had risen, presumably retied the fastenings of that voluminous cloak over nothing at all, and taken her leave. While he had been asleep...and all without saying one word.

Wulfric put his head in his hands and groaned. Sex of that nature was supposed to be detached. He shouldn't care for anything but how good it had been and leave the interlude where it belonged, but for the life of him, he couldn't stop thinking about her.

Obsessing about her.

Not to mention that he was the butt of all kind of jokes, ever since he'd bolted up from that empty bed and darted out into the foyer in nothing but a cushion to cover his half-masted cock, whereupon he had come face-to-face with none other than the Marquess of Roth, who had stared at him and lifted a brow in flagrant amusement.

"Do I even want to know?" he'd asked.

"Dark hair, red mask, red cloak. Did you see her?"

"Lady J, I presume?" Roth had asked and Wulfric had nodded. "No, I had my own female problems to contend with in the form of my willful wife. Did you find out who your mistress of the evening was?"

"No."

That brow had arched higher. "Will you?"

"She's gone, so no."

"Losing your touch, Westmore?" Roth had taunted. "Normally they're back here begging for seconds and thirds."

"You damn well know that was before..." He'd trailed off as a look of stark pain had come over Roth's face. He hadn't even had to finish the sentence. *Before Prue.* They both had their demons when it came to his sister.

Without waiting for a reply, Wulfric had stalked back into the chamber that had still smelled of crushed lilacs, irrationally angry. He'd wanted to sit in that room and breathe in the last of her. He'd also wanted to tear it apart so he could banish it from memory. In the end, he had dressed quietly, like a civilized man, and left to see to his many pressing ducal duties.

But honestly, what kind of woman ran out on a man?

The kind that didn't want to be identified, his brain supplied. He shouldn't be surprised. The Silver Scythe dealt in secrets, thousands of them. What was one more, with skin so soft, he stiffened thinking about that reddened arse and the copious amounts of arousal between those slender legs. What about her entranced him so?

Beyond the incredible physical connection, that was.

Wulfric snorted. He couldn't remember ever in his life spending so hard that his brain had blanked, and thank God, he'd had the wherewithal to withdraw. Normally, that was the sole thing on his mind—complete mastery over his body, to the end that he was used to finishing himself off in hand, just to be safe—but this time, he'd been so lost that he'd pulled out at the last possible moment. A half-second more, and he might have had a lot more to contend with than not knowing who she was.

And yet, even that thought wasn't as appalling as it should have been.

"Pull yourself together, damn it," he muttered, and then cursed as ink splattered over his fingers. He cursed even harder when he realized that he'd doodled the letter J in the margins of his ledgers like a besotted finishing-school miss.

"Begging your pardon, Your Grace!" His normally efficient butler knocked, looking like his hair was standing on end.

"What is it, Hall?"

"The Marquess of Roth sent a note with an address in Covent Garden. There's trouble. The marquess's brother, Lord Oliver, is here and he's got Runners with him."

Worried that it might be trouble at the women's

shelter, Wulfric didn't stop to think, he bolted to his feet. "Coat, hat, carriage."

"Already waiting, Your Grace."

"Good man."

Within short order, he was on his way to Seven Dials on the heels of Oliver, Roth's brother. What the devil had Roth gotten himself into now? Wulfric was in a state of dread, because the address on the note was right near Prue's shelter house. Were any of the women there in danger?

But when the carriage came to a stop, all he could see was Roth and his marchioness glaring at each other. The altercation, perhaps a mugging gone wrong, seemed to be over. The Runners were quick to take an irate but injured man—whom Wulfric belatedly recognized as the disgraced, former Earl of Beaumont, Edmund Cain —into custody, and the situation looked to be in hand, until it wasn't. Cain pulled a gun from nowhere and pointed at Roth's wife. "Shoot me, and she dies, too," he shouted.

Wulfric froze where he stood. Everyone did. "Put down the gun, Cain," he called out. "Even if you get the shot off, we both know what will happen." Cain mumbled something to Roth, and Wulfric saw his hand tighten on the weapon. "Don't try it!"

But it was too late. The sound of a gunshot renting the air made him jerk into action, but two men went down as Oliver crashed into his brother. By the time the Runners had restrained Cain, Wulfric was across the square to assess the damage. Oliver had taken the shot meant for the marchioness, while Roth had had the same idea to leap in front of his wife. Thankfully, Roth had only a shallow gash on his head, and they would both survive.

Something ached in Wulfric's chest as he watched

his best friend and his wife hold each other, their every emotion transparent. Suddenly, he wanted that. He wanted someone to give a shit whether he was dead or alive. An image of clear green eyes danced over his vision, and he shoved it away. *She* was no one to him. Nothing but a passing piece of muslin, and it was better that way.

And besides, he had other things to deal with before any thought of marriage.

Destroying the Duke of Tyne was paramount.

Jocelyn's eyes scanned her book as she munched on a half-eaten apple. She was pretending to read, but was straining her ears and avidly listening to the conversation between her papa and her cousin Tybalt, her father's heir, at the other end of the library. They had not seen her in her quiet, favorite little nook. Something about an attack on the Marquess of Roth and his wife in Covent Garden by some shoddy earl, over a fortnight past. Along with everyone in London, she'd heard the gossip, of course, of the despicable earl who had pursued both the Duchess of Beswick as well as her younger sister, the Marchioness of Roth, almost to ruin.

Jocelyn bit her lip. She was in a similar boat, about to be traded to a marriage prospect like the bartering tool she was. Unfortunately, unlike Isobel Everleigh, she did not have any intrepid older sisters looking out for her, or in the case of her elder sister Astrid, a powerful duke who'd wage wars for her. Exhaling, her thoughts drifted to Westmore, and she banished them as quickly as they'd come. If the duke truly knew who she was, he'd use her for the sport of it, probably to get at her father. No, it was better that he never knew.

'It says that devil Westmore was there as well," Tybalt said, drawing her instant attention. Her body jerked with alarm. Had the duke been hurt? "Too bad he didn't get shot," her cousin went on in a vicious tone.

"That would have solved our problems," her father agreed. 'It should be our good fortune that one day, some brave soul will call him out. For the honor of the Capehart name."

Jocelyn stiffened—was her father insinuating that *Tybalt* should call the duke out? She hoped her cousin wasn't that stupid. Her father hated Westmore with an unhealthy passion, but premeditated murder was a step too far.

The Duke of Westmore had made no secret of undermining any investment her father showed interest in—steamships, locomotive expansion, mining or manufacturing contracts, anything at all—he went over and above to snatch it from beneath her papa's nose. It drove her father mad, Jocelyn knew, but the bitter feud between their families had been ongoing for centuries. Stolen lands, stolen brides, stolen property. Back and forth like children bickering over toys. Jocelyn was sick of it.

It was the sole reason she was being married off to Perrin.

For land on the eastern coast, and an estate that included a portion of valuable shoreline. Her father had crowed that Westmore would have to marry Perrin himself to thwart the plans for enlargement of their family's shipping ports. Jocelyn sighed. There was to be a masked ball in a week for the purpose of introductions. Introductions, her eyeball! The betrothal agreement had practically already been inked and put to dry. The thought of being salivated over and touched by the old lecher made her feel ill.

Could she somehow escape the ball? Feign sickness? Feign *death*?

Come now, you're being melodramatic, Jocelyn! You're a clever girl, you'll think of something. Death is no answer to one's troubles.

But her usually wily mind came up blank. Her fate was sealed. Short of running away with the rest of her jewels, which wouldn't last more than a year, if that, since she'd sold most of them to pay for her evening of passionate ruination.

Jocelyn wrapped her arms about herself and took comfort in that. At least, she had the memory of what had been the best night of her life. Could *that* sustain her when the Marquess of Perrin heaved his old, gout-ridden body to rut into hers?

She shuddered. How did so many ladies put up with such marriages?

Lie there and think of England.

She'd rather eat gruel for the rest of her life. Jocelyn had no doubt she'd find a way to avoid her future husband somehow. And perhaps she might be lucky. Men his age died suddenly all the time. Perhaps fate would be kind and the marquess would drop dead in the next few weeks, right before the ball at which her father intended to announce their betrothal. And, well, if he didn't die, then she would simply have to make the best of it.

Lie back and think of every country in the world.

In alphabetical order.

Perhaps her costume for the masque should be an old crone covered in warts. Maybe if she disgusted him enough, Perrin might change his mind. Jocelyn giggled at the image of herself in the ugliest disguise she could muster. Her father would never allow it and would punish her severely, but heavens, the idea of it tickled her to no end. After her wedding vows, she would make herself so disagreeable that her husband would wince to come near her.

With that energizing thought, she closed her book and headed back to her chamber. Perhaps she'd go for a ride to curb the restlessness in her blood. It was the only thing she could do that tired her out enough so she stopped trying to find Westmore at every party she attended. Tonight was a ball at the Duchess of Beswick's and she knew he would not be there. The man simply did not do *ton* events.

Was he at The Silver Scythe? With other women? The thought wracked her. A man like him would not be without female company. He was too virile, too handsome, too *everything*.

One evening a week ago, she'd had to stop herself from sneaking off to the West End, just to see if she could catch a glimpse of him at the address she'd memorized from the invitation, but she wasn't a member and would not be allowed entry. Besides, there was the risk of exposure. Then she'd heard a few days later, via Tybalt's ranting, that Westmore was in the country with the Marquess of Roth in Chelmsford. That had cooled her heels somewhat.

Until of course, her mind had wondered if he'd been in Chelmsford for one of Roth's raunchy country parties with its equally raunchy guests, which had sent her off on yet another horseback ride to calm her emotions...and her hopeless jealousy.

Why the devil couldn't she stop fantasizing about him?

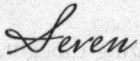

WULFRIC ADJUSTED HIS MASK—A
snarling wolf. Fitting for the occasion, since he was infil-
trating enemy territory. His man of business had reported that Tyne was on the cusp of obtaining access to
a tract of coastland that would fatten his coffers. Wulfric
frowned. The land in question was entailed, which
meant that Tyne, that devious bastard, was going to
marry his last remaining daughter off to get it.

He vaguely remembered being introduced to Lady
Jocelyn Capehart, Prue's best friend from finishing
school. A petite, demure, redheaded chit, if he recalled.
Perrin would destroy her. But it wasn't his concern
whether an old man debauched an innocent girl. He
needed to figure out how to stop Tyne from getting
what he wanted, and short of finding a replacement
bride or an offer that would turn Perrin's loyalty, he was
out of ideas.

Wulfric prowled the perimeter of the ballroom, and
then his heart jumped, caught by a figure at the top of
the stairs. A brunette in red. His breath hitched, every
part of him going on high alert, before disappointment
was quick to set in. It wasn't her.

He almost laughed at himself. Lady J would not be *here*.

Chances were that his lover wasn't even one of the aristocracy at all, at least not one to be invited to Tyne's affair. The man only associated with the *crème de la crème* of the *ton*. Not that Wulfric had been invited—he'd finagled his way in through a side entrance. Tyne would have conniptions if he knew his sworn enemy was in his house.

At least, he was sure Lady J hadn't been a courtesan, or at least an experienced one. One, no courtesan worth her salt would give up two-and-a-half thousand quid for charity. Two, her lack of proficiency had been obvious, though somewhere deep down, that had pleased him. Wulfric liked knowing she hadn't had many lovers before him. He hoped, whoever she was, that he'd ruined her for any other man. That she thought about him as often as he thought about her. Which was every hour of every damned day. He chuckled to himself.

If she hadn't left, would *he* have crept off in silence, as he usually did?

She'd beaten him to it, the minx.

Scanning the crowd, his eyes snagged on a young woman in a bright gold gown, a scarlet sash beneath her breasts as she danced with the Duke of Tyne. He could not see her face, but a head of shining red curls, twined through with diamonds and pearls, made him stare for a protracted moment. Christ, what was his preoccupation with that color? Everywhere he went, he found himself bludgeoned by it...as if red had suddenly become his nemesis.

More like his *weakness*.

His gaze settled on the couple, revulsion curling his stomach at the man who had sent his father to his death. Tyne might not have held the pistol, but he was responsible all the same for spreading the rumors of infidelity and bastard children that had sent his mother to Bedlam and his adulterous father to a cruel, if undeserved, fate.

Wulfric would not rest until Tyne had paid his pound of flesh.

You could ruin the daughter.

The thought slid into his head like silk, but he discarded it. His vengeance would be exacted on Tyne alone, not via underhanded means that would destroy an innocent girl. Wulfric had seen what Tyne's machinations had done to his mother—exposing her husband's latest lover, a married peeress, pregnant with his child—and the scandal had shattered the dowager. He would not wish such heartbreak on anyone, not even for revenge.

Besides, Tyne's chit had her own problems.

Wulfric directed his attention to where the Duke of Tyne was now in conversation with the Marquess of Perrin. The old man kept darting looks over to the duke's daughter and licking his chops like a man standing before his last supper. If he hadn't also been looking at the girl, Wulfric would have missed the shudder of revulsion that she didn't bother to hide, just before slipping out of sight behind a column and disappearing.

Good for her. He'd want to escape such a fate as well. Squinting at the two gentlemen, Wulfric moved closer to where the duke was standing. If he could hear what they were saying, perhaps he could come up with an alternate plan to weaken Tyne.

He spotted an alcove a shadowed balcony just above where the men were standing. That would do. Wulfric wasn't familiar with Tyne's home, but there had to be a servants' staircase somewhere about. He kept an eye on the moving footmen, serving drinks and carrying trays, and followed them. Hustling up some narrow stairs just before the kitchen, he made his way down a carpeted corridor that was lit with a single sconce.

Heading to where he remembered seeing the small Juliet balcony—the fancy indoor overhang, likely copied from Shakespeare's play of the same name, that served no purpose beyond ostentatious decoration. That was just like Tyne, to be so excessive. Who had inside balconies in their ballrooms? It was just pretentious. Wulfric pushed aside the curtain and eased his large frame into the narrow space.

Only to discover that he wasn't alone.

"Oh, my apologies," he said in surprise.

"Hush!" the crouching redhead in the gold gown scolded. The overpowering scent of rosewater hit him. "Get down before you're seen!" A furious flash of a gaze assessed him and then fell away as quickly as it had risen. A panicked sound escaped her lips—fear of discovery, perhaps?—but she remained silent, spine as stiff as a board in her stooped position.

Torn between backing away and doing what he'd come there to do, Wulfric ducked down beside Tyne's youngest daughter. "I do beg your pardon."

"What are you even doing up here?" she muttered. "This is the private family wing."

"What are *you* doing?" he countered in a low, matching tone.

"What does it look like?" she shot back. "Resting for a moment. And I live here, so this is allowed. *You're* not allowed."

"Shall I leave?" He made to stand, and an urgent hand, gloved in delicate white kidskin, pressed down on his arm, as the Duke of Tyne, who was right below them, looked upward with a frown on his face. The lady was surprisingly strong.

"Don't move," she commanded in a soft, imperious whisper. "For the love of God, I beg you."

"What are you really hiding from?" he asked.

She almost didn't answer, her fingers squeezing reflexively on his arm as if she'd forgotten it was there. "I'm to marry the man Tyne is talking to," she replied eventually.

"And you don't wish to?"

A suffocated laugh left her. "Who would?"

"I don't know," he whispered. "He's quite handsome from this angle."

"We can only see his hat."

Wulfric hid his smile. "Precisely."

~

Who knew that the Duke of Westmore had a sense of humor outside the bedroom?

Jocelyn had known it was him the moment he'd squatted down beside her. That smell of warm leather and bergamot was reminder enough. Why on earth was he here? And did her father know? Did Tybalt know? Her cousin was a hothead at the best of times—he would likely call the man out in the middle of the ball, or something worse, and get himself killed or arrested in the process.

The snarling wolf mask—fitting, if a bit on the nose, though that might be only to her—covered most of the duke's face, and he was dressed in formal black evening wear like most of the men in the room. For her part, and to the displeasure of her father, Jocelyn had refused to wear a mask at all. Let him see the daughter he was bargaining away for the sake of his precious fortune. And besides everyone knew who she was, so she hadn't made much effort to hide behind a disguise either. As much as she'd wanted to embody a crone, being herself had made more of a statement.

She hadn't expected to run into her former lover, however!

Not that Westmore would recognize her. She *hoped*.

Her breath had faltered when she'd looked up to see him, only to dip her chin in horror. Luckily, she'd worn a scent Perrin loathed, because it reminded him of his late marchioness—a small act of defiance to be perverse, she supposed. And she wasn't wearing a dark wig. She'd have to keep her voice to a whisper and hide her eyes. She wasn't taking any chances there. While a part of her would have loved to see the look of shock on his face, Jocelyn would not be held responsible for him facing down her father or her cousin.

Her body had gone molten, however, in pure muscle memory, heat firing over all her nerve endings. Gracious, it wasn't normal to feel so unsettled by a man, was it? Her nipples turned to stone beneath her bodice, every inch of skin tightening, and her core clenching at the visceral memory of him. What would it be like to be his permanent lover? To be taken every which way known to man, each night? A pulse of rabid envy shot through her.

They had only coupled once, before she'd lost her nerve and left while he was sleeping, but Jocelyn knew there were many other erotic positions. The minute she'd returned home from her racy adventure, she scoured her collection of Lady Darcy periodicals for any information she could find on the subject. According to the knowledgeable old biddy, there was quite a bit. A woman could ride a man. He could take her from be-hind—*that* particular designation had left her breathless —when the image of her wolf taking her like an animal made her fantasies run wild. Coitus could be had outside of a bed as well...standing up against a wall, sitting on a bench, crouched in a garden arbor. The possibilities were endless.

Jocelyn peeked over at him. Perhaps even on a *balcony* above hundreds of people.

Oh, dear God, her drawers would be ruined if she continued on this path.

"Why are you here, Westmore?" she asked curtly, trying to distract herself from mounting the man and having her wicked way with him. "Planning to destroy my father?"

If he was surprised that she had recognized him, he did not show it. "Is it that apparent?"

She didn't dare look at him. "This feud is ridiculous."

"Says the pampered princess who has never lost anything of value in her life," came his disparaging whisper.

An outraged Jocelyn nearly looked up then, and only kept her head down by pure force of will. "You know nothing about me, Your Grace. Nothing about this house or my situation, so don't presume to judge me. I cannot control my father's actions—I can only control my own."

Silence grew at the end of her whispered tirade, but then she felt him shift, his knee brushing the back of her gown. "Fair enough. How did you know who I am?"

"You could have chosen a less obvious mask for one," she said tartly. "A wolf, really?"

"What's wrong with a wolf?"

She let out a huff. "You do know that everyone calls you the *Wolf* of Westmore? Prudence started it back when she would regale me of tales of your many conquests, but then it turned into a descriptor of your ruthless nature in business—according to Tybalt anyway."

She felt him stiffen at the mention of their mutual

friend, and forced herself not to feel a sour prickle of jealousy at the fact that Westmore had likely returned Prue's tender feelings. Jocelyn didn't know what made her press on...maybe the fact that she could never speak of Prudence to anyone, not even her own family. The name was barred from their household.

"You were her favorite subject," she said, and felt him flinch. "I'm sorry. I just miss her."

The silence grew between them again, heavy and sticky. A shuddering breath filled the small space. "I miss her, too."

"You loved her," she whispered.

"I did." The duke had a compassionate streak beneath all the ruthlessness, she realized. It had to be painful for him to talk about Prudence, and yet he was doing so, and Jocelyn knew it was only for her sake. Or perhaps he needed to talk about her, too.

"She adored you," Jocelyn said, a melancholy lump filling her breast. "Thought the sun rose and fell with you. Sometimes you were all she could talk about. Before..." She trailed off. They both knew what she meant...before Prudence's rapid descent into addiction.

Westmore inhaled and shifted again. "I didn't find out how much trouble she was in until it was much too late. Roth had his own issues with his father, and Prue was alone, the illegitimate daughter of a woman who scorned her and a man who had claimed her as his own, despite her not being of his blood."

Jocelyn's eyes went wide with shock. "She was illegitimate?"

Westmore's jaw clamped shut and went tight as if he'd revealed too much. Out of her peripheral vision, she saw him give a short nod. "It was one of the reasons she declined the way she did, feeling lost and unloved and unworthy. What mother would do that to her own child? I could have been there for her. I *should* have. I could have saved her."

"You can't blame yourself," she whispered.

"I was so consumed by my own vengeance, by my own woes, that was all I could see. And now, I still am. Retribution is all I have. All I will ever have." His tone went dark. "Tyne has to pay for what he did."

Jocelyn shivered at the unguarded wrath in his voice, the primal growl of it so wolf-like, so raw, that her senses screamed for her to flee from danger. But she didn't. She sat there, blanketed in the shared pain that shrouded him.

"What did my father do?" she whispered.

A fist curled against his trouser leg. He was quiet for so long, she feared the duke wouldn't answer, but then he exhaled. "He tossed Prue to the wolves. Exposed she was a by-blow."

His reply hit like lead ballast, ripping through her soft, vulnerable insides. Jocelyn closed her eyes, her palm going to her chest, sorrow followed by pure, white-hot rage. And suddenly, she knew what she had to do.

What she *would* do. For Prudence. For herself.

Maybe even for him.

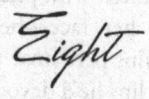

Eight

CHRIST, he was an imbecile!

What the devil was he doing pouring his secrets out to the offspring of the man he hated most in the world? Yes, she had been Prue's best friend and had loved her, which was the only reason he'd deigned to talk about what would always be a raw memory for him. But what if she ran off and informed her father or her loathsome cousin that he was here?

What then?

"My lady—" he began leaning down to whisper, but to his surprise...to his utter shock, she tilted her head up and kissed him, her lips soft on his and then harder, as if she needed fortification from the unexpected embrace. Without thinking, his lips parted when she licked across the seam of his mouth in a move that was unnervingly familiar.

Wait. He *knew* those lips. That teasing flick against his upper teeth.

The fucking *taste* of her.

What the *devil*?

Wulfric reared back, green eyes boring into him. Those pretty eyes, like bottle-green glass. He'd seen them dilated and molten with pleasure. Blinking in confusion, he studied her face—heart-shaped with that pointy stubborn chin, pert nose that had been hidden behind a lacy mask, lips he'd devoured over and over—it was her! Lady J was Lady *Jocelyn*.

His scarlet vixen.

More like his scarlet *virgin*.

In disbelief, his finger lifted to curl around one auburn strand. Of course, she'd worn a wig, she hadn't wanted to be recognized. She'd claimed to be experienced. He shook his head. No, she said she hadn't done the act many times, and he'd made the foolish leap of assumption as she'd no doubt intended.

Wulfric frowned at her. What was her game? Was this a ploy by Tyne? Had they been playing him like a hand of cards all along?

"All will be well," she whispered calmly, as if she could read the storm of wrath and doubt in his eyes. "Trust me."

"Trust you?" he bit out.

She swallowed. "You'll have what you want, I promise."

"Wait," he said.

But then she stood, drawing the attention of every eye in the ballroom, including her father's, to the small balcony that was lifted above them like a stage. "Lord Perrin," she announced in a clear voice. "I'm afraid I cannot marry you."

The gentleman in question spluttered, his face turning puce. Instead of the ballroom erupting in wild chatter, dead silence fell upon it. Even the music faded away, guests standing in mortified, stunned silence. Wulfric knew it was because everyone in attendance was aware of Tyne's temper. They were all waiting for the other shoe to drop.

The duke's thin face hardened with displeasure. "What is the meaning of this, Jocelyn?"

His daughter quailed, her small body shaking. Good God, she was bloody terrified, Wulfric noted. His brows pulled inward. Of her own father? That chin of hers jerked up, though he swore he saw it wobble, and the tell-tale sheen of moisture in her eyes. "On account that I've already pledged my hand."

That pronouncement started the blather as a wave of scandalized whispers rose to the rafters.

"Stop this farce, or so help me," the Duke of Tyne threatened in a voice that had the blood draining from her face. "Get down from there."

"It's not a farce. I went to an auction at The Silver Scythe." She forged forward, despite the irreparable damage to her own reputation she was intent on causing. "I bid on a prize there for charity." The slightest of smiles curved her quivering mouth. "The Duke of Westmore."

The noise in the ballroom was colossal, even as his own brain struggled to make sense of her confession. What would admitting that achieve?

"Westmore?" her cousin roared. "You vapid, useless twit. You've ruined yourself. Who will have you now?"

Wulfric didn't know what the lady had intended with her declaration. Perhaps she'd felt that it would give him the satisfaction he craved by denying her father of his prize. It did, but he wanted to be the one to deliver the killing blow.

"I can think of one person," she said, and her words registered like a hammer to an anvil.

Oh, fuck no. The little minx couldn't be thinking of...

Only then Wulfric realized that her shoulders hadn't been shaking with fear at all, they'd been shaking with amusement. Dancing green eyes lit with glee peered down at him. "Don't just kneel there, Your Grace," she said loudly. "Stand and let us announce our betrothal properly, as we came up here to do. Your idea of using this balcony was *so* romantic." A hand went to her breast and he could practically hear the swoons gathering in force below.

"What are you doing?" Wulfric said through clenched teeth as he rose to deafening shouts. He had no eyes for them, however, only the conniving virago at his side, who had trapped him so neatly, he hadn't even realized he was being spun into a clever web.

"Saving you. Saving me."

"What if I don't want you?"

Her eyes narrowed, glancing down to where his arousal was obvious just from the earlier touch of her lips. Her voice was low. "Your cock doesn't seem to think so."

"Luckily, that part of me doesn't rule my decisions."

"Thank me later, then. Vengeance is yours." She took his hand in hers, and gazed up at him with a fake besotted look that had him blinking, before she turned back to their avid audience and her furious father. "His Grace was courting me in secret for months. He asked me to marry him and I said yes. I choose him, Papa."

Wulfric, even in his ire, had to hand it to the little actress. She was magnificent.

"You were promised to Lord Perrin," he seethed. "Do you know what you have done?"

"Won a duke?" she said sweetly. She had him there, by some of the approving nods from the women in the ballroom. His title outranked Perrin's by a mile. It was not only higher, it was much older. And he was rich. The matchmaking mothers had been attempting to tie him down for years. Soon the sniff of scandal around their secret betrothal would fade by nature of what he was...a duke with a grand title and an even grander fortune.

"You won't marry him," Tyne bit out.

She fluttered her eyelashes. "Not even if I am—"

Wulfric cut her off then, knowing exactly where she was going. A secret courting was one thing, announcing sexual congress and possible pregnancy before wedlock was another. He lifted her knuckles and kissed them, drawing cooing noises from the ladies present. He wasn't a demonstrative man, so this performance would convince the hardest of hearts. "Completely, irrevocably in love," he finished for her.

The brightness of her smile took him by force. "Glad you've decided to play," she said out of the side of her mouth.

"This is a game you will lose, *Little Red*."

A shiver coursed over her, though her eyes sparked with interest at the nickname, considering the nature of his own. "Not if we're in it together."

He scowled. "There is no *us* in this scenario."

"You want to hurt my father? This is the way to do it. Don't pretend for one instant that you're the victim here, Your Grace. What hurts your precious pride is that I've used you for my own ends. Savor the triumph I've handed you. I assure you, if I know my father, it won't last."

Jocelyn descended the staircase with her reluctant new fiancé in hand. Lady Darcy would be proud of the way she'd cobbled together a series of events that hadn't led to her ruination or unhappiness. Had it? She glanced up at the silent duke at her side, the wolf mask making him seem even more menacing than normal. Or was that her imagination because of what he'd called her? Perrault's *Little Red Riding Hood* was a story about a girl who had been eaten by the big, bad wolf. Would she be?

Like the bone-deep shiver on the balcony, another stole through her. What *would* it be like to be devoured by him? Her body heated at the memory of him sucking her arousal off his fingers. Jocelyn had no idea what he would be like as a husband, though at least she knew they would be compatible in bed.

She wouldn't be thinking of England at all when he was on top of her.

Biting her lip to swallow the half-hysterical laugh that bubbled up into her throat, she shook her head. Instead of a randy goat, she was marrying a dominant wolf. More fool her, if she thought she hadn't gone from the fat straight into the fire.

She accepted the murmured congratulations as they made their way through the ballroom. They weren't in the clear yet. Tybalt looked like he was about to murder someone, and her father did not look any less angry. Nor did the Marquess of Perrin, though he probably couldn't belt a fly in a fight. He looked quite put out, as did her mother, whose disappointment was written all over her face.

"Papa," Jocelyn said with the demurest look she could muster.

"Study," he barked. "Now."

A low, foreboding growl stopped her in her tracks. "Don't speak to her like that."

"How dare you presume to tell me how to talk to my own daughter?" her father barked, stalking a path through the inquisitive guests, followed by Tybalt, her mother, and the Marquess of Perrin.

"Because I'm her future husband."

"We'll see about that."

In the study, her father took his place behind the enormous desk. Westmore had yet to release her hand, and while she knew it probably irked him to touch her thus, Jocelyn was grateful for the solid strength of him. As much as she'd stood up to her father earlier, she was nervous. The Duke of Tyne had never struck his children, but his punishments were creative.

When they were much younger, her middle sister, Juniper, had talked back to the duke and had been locked in her bedchamber for a week with barely any sustenance. Jocelyn and Jacinda had sneaked her food from the kitchens so she wouldn't starve. Later on, Juniper had been prohibited from going to London for an entire Season, because she had refused to wed the man their father had chosen for her. When threatened with missing a second Season and being sent to a nunnery, she had conceded.

Jocelyn, too, had faced the brunt of his temper when he'd forbidden her from seeing Prudence, barring her from leaving the house or her friend being welcomed. It had been his fault Prue had felt so abandoned and gotten so lost. Jocelyn would never forgive her father for that. And now that she knew of the hand he'd had in exposing Prudence's illegitimacy, because of this long-suffering, stupid feud, her heart was brimming with bitterness.

"You won't get a cent from me, if that's what you hope," her father hissed.

"I don't need her dowry," Westmore said.

"I'll disown the chit."

Westmore didn't move a muscle. "And how will that reflect upon you, do you think? Your daughter has made the match of the century."

"With a reprobate!" Tybalt spit out.

"There you are," Westmore said, with a sidelong glance to her cousin. "It would not have been the same without some asinine yelping from the ever-faithful hound."

"Name your second," Tybalt shouted. "I'm going to kill you for dishonoring my dear cousin. She was promised to another, to Perrin. Contracts have been signed."

Her father slammed his hand down on his desk. "Enough!"

"Careful, Tyne," Westmore said, not even rising to Tybalt's challenge as if it was beneath him to even respond. "Don't want to lose the only heir you can control, do you? I'd muzzle your dog before he makes any other threats that finds the two of us in a field at dawn."

"Tybalt is not wrong," her father said. "Contracts have already been signed by myself and Perrin."

"But I have not given my consent," Jocelyn said from between clenched teeth. "I won't marry him."

"I'm your father, I decide what's best for you."

"What's best for me?" she burst out. "Or what's best for *you*?"

He glared at her. "Who saw you with Westmore at this club? Perhaps we can manage this debacle you've gotten yourself into. No one will dispute my word. Perrin, what say you?"

"I'll take her," the marquess said, with a lascivious look that made bile sour her stomach.

Jocelyn's blood boiled. They were discussing her as if she were a cow to be handed over. She might as well be, for all the say she had in her own future. And if Westmore decided to take the easy way out and walk away, then what choice would she have? He'd taken her virginity, and that in itself was a perverse kind of vengeance. Perhaps that would be enough for him.

And while no one might dispute her father's word to his face, that did not mean she would not be inured from slanderous gossip. They would all speculate as to why the duke would cry off and let her go to someone like Perrin. She choked back a strangled sob. What did the gossip matter anyway? The loathsome marquess intended to force himself on her and keep her as a broodmare in the country somewhere.

"You will have to drag me kicking and screaming to the altar, I swear to you." She turned to her mother. "Do you not have anything to say, Mama? You would let him treat me thus? Marry me to that...man."

"It is your duty," she replied icily. "Perrin is a marquess."

Jocelyn sniffed, desolation welling in her throat at her mama's callous disregard for her feelings. "And it is your duty to protect your daughters! Not worry about whether your next set of jewels will be enough to gain you more influence as the Duchess of Tyne." Her mother glared, but she wasn't finished. "Your daughters' lives mean something. *Should* mean something beyond material possessions. My God, don't you have a heart?"

Her tirade drifted into silence, a single tear tracing down her cheek, even as her mother turned her head away, coldness and disapproval stamped in every line of her. Apparently, she did not, though her mother's heartlessness was something she'd known all along. After all, how could she endure life beside a man like the cold-blooded Duke of Tyne? Like attracted like.

Defeat swamping her, Jocelyn stepped away from Westmore, as if to unconsciously protect herself from his certain rejection. He hadn't wanted her—he'd said so himself up there on the balcony. It made sense that he would cry off, while still savoring the secret victory over his sworn enemy.

She felt his perusal over her person for a charged moment, and braced when his deep voice penetrated every corner of the room. "Lady Jocelyn stays with me."

Jaw agape, Jocelyn peered up at him, but the duke wasn't looking at her.

"Now see here, Westmore," Perrin blustered.

A burning stare silenced the man, before it was directed to her cousin, who paled at what he saw there. "Since you've issued your challenge, my second is the Marquess of Roth or the Duke of Beswick, take your pick."

Jocelyn didn't hear another word as she was ushered from the room in the arms of the duke who, astonishingly, had saved her from a fate worse than death, despite his avowals to the contrary. But blood would still be spilled, and from the victorious look on her father's face, that was *exactly* what he wanted.

Nine

"HAVE YOU SODDING LOST YOUR MIND?" Roth demanded. "Tell him, Beswick."

The marquess's brother-in-law, the Duke of Beswick, leaning against the wall with his arms folded, gave a nod. "Dueling is illegal, as you know."

Wulfric sighed. "That fool challenged me, and demanded satisfaction for dishonoring his cousin."

"Did you dishonor her?" Roth asked with a leer.

"What happens at The Silver Scythe stays at the Scythe, you know this," he replied. "The lady got what she wanted, and we shall leave it at that."

A scowling Roth shook his head. "You didn't have to accept the challenge. Isobel will geld me if I even *think* about showing up to a dawn duel. I've learned that it's in my best interests not to cross that woman for my own wellbeing."

There was a joke in there about being henpecked, but Wulfric was much too agitated at the prospect of taking a man's life for no good reason at all, and not having a trusted second with him. "You know very well I could not decline a challenge against my honor without being called a coward," he said. "Does that mean you won't be there?"

"No, you ass. Of course I will. You're my best mate, even if you make the stupidest decisions known to man, antagonizing that pompous boot-licker, Tybalt Capehart, of all people. The man is a hog-grubber who can't wait to inherit his uncle's estate and be duke."

"You can count on me to be there as well," Beswick said. "No doubt Tyne will try to be untoward, like hire some thug to shoot you from afar if his idiot nephew misses."

Relief sluiced through him. Wulfric wouldn't have wanted to trust his life to a man he couldn't depend on, and both men currently in his study had become more than brothers to him. He wasn't afraid of Tybalt or his uncle, or whether the latter would try something dishonorable. He was more worried about the woman ensconced with the Duchess of Beswick. He let out a breath. "How is she? Lady Jocelyn?"

"She is as well as can be expected," Beswick said. "Astrid says she is shaken and fearful because her cousin is an excellent shot."

Roth raked a hand over his scalp. "Honestly, how did this even happen? I thought you loathed anything to do with the Capeharts. And now you're to be married to one and dueling another. What's next? Holidays in Bath? Cozy family dinners? Wearing matching holiday vests?"

Wulfric ignored the man's caustic tone and debated how much to reveal. He pinched the bridge of his nose and exhaled. "She's Lady J."

Roth blinked. "Wait, Lady J? As in Lady J who bought you for two thousand quid? That Lady J?"

"Two-and-a-half thousand quid, and yes. Stop saying Lady J like it's a scandalous sobriquet."

"Fine." Roth's eyebrow shot skyward. "But for the record, let's not argue trifles, my friend. I'm still the king of the auction hall, remember that before you quibble over five hundred pounds."

"The five thousand that your *wife* bid for you doesn't count."

"And Lady Jocelyn is now your *wife*-to-be."

The Duke of Beswick cleared his throat with a rumble of vexation. "Children, please! Can we focus on the matter at hand instead of how much your pricks are worth? Like the fact that Westmore might get shot, die, and make his future duchess a widow before any vows are said, which means she will be right back in her father's clutches." Wulfric stared at him while Roth did the same, both wearing the same incredulous looks. Beswick spread his palms, his badly scarred face pulling in more of a grimace than a smile. "I'm not saying that you will, just that you *might*. And you may want to think about her in the eventuality that something unfortunate does happen."

Wulfric sobered. Fuck, the duke was right. He'd have to marry Jocelyn to make sure that she was protected from her father's machinations. As a widowed duchess, she would have more independence than she ever would under Tyne's hand. "I don't suppose either of you have an in with the Archbishop of Canterbury for a special license?" he asked.

"The man runs at the sight of me, and for once, it's not because of my face," Beswick muttered. "Considering how dreadfully I harangued him for Roth's after my own marriage license. But I suppose it won't hurt to ask. I'll be three for three."

"Thank you."

"Now what?" Roth asked.

"We go see a bishop about a horse." They both

gaped at Beswick. He grinned. "What? Can't a man make a joke?"

"Married life is turning you," Roth said, with a shake of his head. "You've gone from beast to biscuit."

Beswick's lip curled. "Call me 'biscuit' one more time and perhaps we can arrange a duel for you as well."

~

Jocelyn squinted down at the pressing note the messenger had delivered to the Duke of Beswick's London residence, her stomach swirling with indecision. How had her parents known she was here? Had someone followed her and Westmore the day before? She glanced at the two faces before her. The very kind but no-nonsense Duchess of Beswick, Astrid, who had taken her in, and her sister, Isobel, the disheveled, bright-eyed marchioness stood on either side of her, both somber of countenance.

"I don't like notes," Isobel said with a frown. "It could be a trick."

"This is written in my mama's hand," Jocelyn replied. "It says she's fallen gravely ill with fever. The coach is waiting outside for me."

Astrid let out an apprehensive sigh. "I think you should wait for Thane and Westmore to return."

"What if she's truly feverish?" Her mother might be cold-hearted, but she was the only mother Jocelyn had. She'd never forgive herself if something happened, but she also wasn't completely gullible that this could be a ruse to bring her home. "I have to go. Perhaps I could take one of your footmen with me?"

"I'll go with you," Isobel offered.

Jocelyn shook her head. "No, I'd be beside myself if anything happened to you. They're my parents. As horrid as they've been, I'm not in any danger from them."

Even as she said the words, her belly flipped. She *could* wait for Westmore, but she'd already involved him more than was needed. She'd come this far managing her parents, what was one small visit home if they were lying? She would go, check on her mother, and return. At least, these two women would know where she'd gone. Still, her nerves knotted, indecision plaguing her.

"Then take this," Isobel said, handing her what looked like a very sharp hairpin in the shape of a crimson rose. "Lady Darcy says a woman should always be prepared to defend her dignity and integrity."

"Do you read her?" she asked, and to her surprise, both women burst into laughter. The sisters exchanged a look, and then Isobel canted her head at Astrid, as if giving her permission for something.

"I'll let you in on a little secret," Astrid said. "Izzy is one half of the termagant that is Lady Darcy. The other is Clarissa Bell."

Jocelyn's jaw dropped open. "I did not see that coming."

"My sister is a master of subterfuge as well as the written word," Astrid said, pride in her voice. "Isobel, Lady Darcy, Izzy, Iz...she has many faces."

"Who is Iz?"

"Long story," Isobel said with a cheeky grin. "But I pretended to be a groom to get to know Winter a little better when I first came to London. It all went a bit sideways at first, I won't lie, but I'm working on it. My reformed rakehell is coming nicely to heel."

Jocelyn giggled, her smile growing as she shook her head in mild disbelief that this woman was one of her many heroes. "I have you to thank, then, for giving me the courage I needed to find my feet. For giving so many women the needed advice to be our true, strongest selves."

"I'm glad," Isobel said. Smoothing her skirts, Jocelyn tucked the hairpin into her bun and hugged the two ladies. Isobel gave her an earnest look. "If you're not back here by supper, I'm fetching the Runners and coming to get you."

If she wasn't back by then, Jocelyn had the feeling that something dreadful would have happened, but she didn't voice her qualms. This was London and her *parents*. Besides, there would be servants about and it was broad daylight. When she donned her cloak and walked outside, her father's coach was waiting. If she went home, it wasn't as though the Marquess of Perrin could abscond with her in front of witnesses, snatch her away to some secret place, and force her to marry him.

Then again, her *father* could.

Jocelyn's blood chilled in dismay at the thought. What if that was his plan? Panic riding her hard, her feet stalled on the cobblestones and then she felt a palm on her back. Her heart lifted, thinking it was Westmore, and then crashed when she recognized the dark scowl of her cousin. "Get in," Tybalt whispered in a sinister tone. "Don't make a scene, Jocelyn."

She flinched. "Take your hand off me."

"Oy! She doesn't look like she wants to go with you." Isobel stood at the top of the stairs, like an avenging angel about to swoop down.

Tybalt swore so ferociously that Jocelyn recoiled from the anger in his voice. His fingers slid to his waistcoat, and she quailed when she saw the pistol tucked into his belt. Why would he be carrying a *weapon*? Unless he'd been expecting trouble, or *planning* trouble, and now, Isobel would be caught in the crossfire.

"Don't hurt her," Jocelyn whispered urgently.

"Then get in the coach," he said. "And I won't have to." His voice shook slightly as if the very idea was repulsive to him, and that was the only thing that made her stop from yanking herself free of his grasp. Her cousin might be under her father's thumb, but he wasn't a murderer.

"Fine, Tybalt, I will," she said, and looked over her shoulder, forcing a smile to her face. "All is well, Iz. I'll be back by supper." The lady's eyes widened at the nickname, but it was the only thing Jocelyn could think of in the moment that wouldn't draw Tybalt's suspicion or make him do something stupid. She hoped Isobel was as clever as she seemed.

Once they were inside the coach, her cousin glared balefully at her. "Couldn't you have done what you were told? Don't you know how important this is? We've been chasing Perrin's coattails for years."

"Then *you* marry him," she shot back. "Why do you even have a gun?"

"For protection." Jocelyn blinked at the reply. From Westmore and his friends? None of those men were the dishonorable sort, unless Tybalt had other plans. She frowned at him and he met her expression with no small amount of bitterness. "Looks like you proved me right, that women are only good for one thing."

"At least that was my choice."

His jaw clenched. "So you did lie with him? You selfish girl. You've so very nearly ruined everything, but thankfully, Perrin doesn't care. He just wants you, and so he shall have you. Soon all of this will be water under the bridge." A scathing gaze traced her from head to toe, and Jocelyn's entire body stiffened at the inspection before his words sank in. She had the sudden urge to dive from the moving coach because Tybalt wasn't taking her home. They were leaving London!

"Where are we going?" she asked. "Is Mama even ill?"

"She's well enough."

Of course she was. Deep down, Jocelyn had known that, but as always, her trusting, gullible heart had ever been her downfall. "Tybalt, where are we going?"

His mouth firmed into a flat, stubborn line. "To your husband."

Ten

THE STUDY WAS IN SHAMBLES.

Wulfric had torn it apart with his bare hands the moment he'd returned with the license and seen the ashen look on his butler's face. "Lady Jocelyn is gone, Your Grace, Lady Roth sent a footman with the news. Her cousin collected her. They had a man follow, but he lost them on the way out of London."

The helpless rage had been instantaneous. "*Out* of London?"

He'd wanted to rip that sniveling coward Tybalt to pieces, but he'd settled on inanimate furniture instead. At least for the moment. He panted, sat on a chair, and promptly fell backward because one of its legs was broken. He deserved that. Wulfric hadn't lost his temper in years. Not since he'd found Prue in that hellhole. He rubbed at his chest, not stopping to think what that meant. The two weren't connected. He'd loved Prue. He was...fond of Jocelyn.

Whom was he fooling? It was more than fondness. Whatever it was, he didn't want to lose it. It felt precious, like the possibility of something more than he could have ever imagined. Hope, maybe, after so many years of feeling nothing. Jocelyn Capehart made him feel alive.

Hell, he never should have left her alone!

Think, Wulfric!

Where could they have gone?

"Hall," he commanded. "Get my pistols and my horse."

"Yes, Your Grace," the butler said, and hurried away.

Wulfric paced the study, avoiding chair legs and broken glass. Tybalt wouldn't take her to Tyne's ancestral seat in Northern England. It was much too far. His uncle likely had properties outside of London, though. But *where*? He needed something to go on, and there was only one place he could get answers.

When his horse was ready, he rode to Tyne's Mayfair residence, calming the rage seething beneath his skin. He was greeted by a butler as he stalked into the empty foyer. Starkly empty. There were no vases of flowers, as there had been for the ball, and he could see servants cleaning and putting dusting cloths over some of the furniture in the adjacent salon. "The Duke of Westmore to see Tyne this instant."

"His Grace is not at home to callers."

"Where is he?" Wulfric demanded.

"The duke and duchess departed this morning for Newcastle-Upon-Tyne, Your Grace," the butler said, with a fearful look as Wulfric faltered on his feet, fists clenching. Dear God, was he too late? Was Jocelyn with her parents? His brain worked furiously. He could catch up with them, switch out horse teams as often as he had to, but he had to leave *now*.

"You have the look of your mother, boy," a frail voice said, making him spin around on his heels. A tiny birdlike woman he recognized as the Dowager Duchess of Tyne, garbed in black bombazine that swallowed her small frame, peered at him over a pair of spectacles from the top of the staircase.

"Thank you," he said, anxious to leave. "Good day, Your Grace."

"I'm here until the end of the week, not much room in the cramped carriage, you see, for these old bones," she told him conversationally, making her slow way down. "You haven't seen that granddaughter of mine, have you?"

Wulfric froze. "She didn't go with Tyne?"

Green eyes, too much like Jocelyn's, pierced him when she finally reached the bottom. "Shouldn't she be with you? Heard about that hullabaloo during the ball, that my girl got herself leg-shackled to the Wolf of Westmore." The dowager cackled, and Wulfric wondered if her wits were all there. "Takes after me in spirit, she does."

"Do you know where she is, Your Grace?"

The old lady waved an arm. "Somewhere about with that snot-rag of my grand-nephew, I expect. Heard him ranting about duty and property and doing the right thing earlier. That boy wouldn't know the right thing if it bashed him in the *arse*."

If he wasn't so wound up, Wulfric would have laughed. Since Jocelyn hadn't left with her father, then that meant she might still be here, though she was with her cousin, which made things arguably worse. "Did Lord Tybalt say where he was going?"

"No," she said and cocked head, watching him with those too-familiar green eyes that made his chest twinge. Wulfric's hope faded, but then he gritted his teeth. He'd pay every Runner he had to and cover every route out of London. He'd find her, no matter what it took.

He bowed. "Thank you, Duchess. I bid you a safe journey."

"Do you care for my granddaughter, Westmore?" the old woman asked, squinting at him with an odd look on her face.

Wulfric didn't hesitate. He *did* care. And he wanted more. He wanted a *chance.* "I do."

"Enough to give up this vendetta you have against Tyne?"

That stumped him. Revenge had driven him for so long. Could he give it up for a woman who might not turn out to be whom he hoped? "I don't know."

"Well, at least you are honest," she murmured, a hint of regret crossing her weathered features. "At some point, you will have to decide whether chasing past demons will bring you the same fulfillment that looking to the future will. She's rather special, you know. My fool son never appreciated it, but Jocelyn's heart is as wide as it is deep."

"I know it is. Good day, Your Grace, and thank you."

She smiled. "You're welcome. Tyne maintains a hunting property in Dartford from my late husband. Check there."

Wulfric froze as his heart leaped behind his ribs. On impulse, he reached up to where she stood on the third step, grasped her hand, and kissed her lined knuckles. "I'll get her and bring her back."

"No, dear boy," she said, patting his cheek. "If you have any sense at all, you'll steal her far away from here."

~

Jocelyn struggled against the rope binding her hands. How dare Tybalt tie her up? It was a rhetorical question. She knew why. He'd told her, so she couldn't try anything stupid and escape, before leaving her trussed up in the study in her father's hunting lodge. The house was deserted, a thin layer of dust on all the furnishings. No one had been here in months. Her heart quivered... which meant no one would have reason to come find her here either.

Her lips were dry and she longed for a sip of water. Well, thirst or not, she wouldn't make this easy for her dolt of a cousin, and she *would* try to escape while he was gone. Tybalt hadn't tied her feet so she rose unsteadily and attempted to search the room. Surely there had to be a pair of scissors or a knife she could use to cut her bindings? At worst, she could break a vase or lantern and use that.

Jocelyn didn't find a knife or scissors, but she did discover a letter opener in the study drawer. The edges were dull, but it would do. Sitting down so she wouldn't trip and accidentally impale herself, she worked the tool between her fingers and started to saw. It was grueling work. Sweat dripped into her eyes, and she nearly lost her grip on the opener twice before she felt the rope start to fray. Encouraged, she worked harder and then the tie snapped.

Wincing, she rubbed her bruised wrists.

Bindings might be a fun adventure in the bedchamber, according to Lady Darcy, but not by a demented cousin who intended to keep her prisoner before handing her off to that lecher of a marquess. If she didn't find a way out of there soon, she would unquestionably see herself wedded and bedded to Perrin, and she doubted that Isobel's trusty hairpin could thwart two men at once. She tucked the letter opener into her pocket just in case.

As expected, the study door was locked. Damn Tybalt! The windows were old with iron casings and heavy diamond panes, but they were her best bet...at least until she tried them all and the bloody things wouldn't budge. The casements had rusted shut over the last winter. Jocelyn went back to the door and peeked through the keyhole. Curious, no light came through it, which meant the key on the other side was still in there.

Huzzah!

This would be a delicate operation, but her middle sister, Juniper, was particularly skilled at escaping locked bedroom doors and had taught her the trick of it. Tearing a piece of fabric from the hem of her skirts with the help of the letter opener, she slid the fabric under the door just beneath the keyhole. Luckily, there was enough of a gap from the bottom of the door to the wood floor.

Please don't bounce away!

Using the letter opener, she carefully pushed the key out, praying it wouldn't twist in the lock, until she heard it clank heavily down to the floor on the opposite side. Luck seemed to be in her favor. She tugged gently on the swatch of muslin, and lo and behold, the heavy key came with it. Jocelyn let out a relieved breath. Not willing to waste a second, she unlocked the door and grasped the letter opener in one hand and the hairpin in the other. A noise near the kitchen had her spinning, rage sloshing through her veins. Tybalt would get a rude awakening. She'd stab that sneaky cretin right in the crotch.

Holding her breath, she crept to the wainscoting and placed her ear to it. A floorboard creaked to her right, and she nearly leaped out of her skin as a shadow loomed. With a panicked shriek, Jocelyn lifted her weapons, only to be foiled by a tight grip on one wrist that made her drop the letter opener, and crushed by a huge body into the wall. She didn't think. She started to struggle for all she was worth, kicking out and trying to wriggle loose from what felt like an unbreakable hold. Her free hand snaked up with the hairpin in hand, ready to lodge it into the first soft body part she could find.

"Cease, you little hellcat, it's me!"

Heart in her throat, the owner of the voice registered. "Westmore?"

"Yes." A warm, orange-brown gaze peered down at her. "If I release your wrist, will you stab me?"

"Oh, Wulfric!" Loosening her death grip on the hairpin, she flung her arms about his neck. "How did you find me here?"

"Your grandmother led me to you," he said.

She blinked and then tried to calm the tornado of her emotions with deep, even breaths. Not many knew of this lodge, but it had belonged to her grandfather. "Tybalt is somewhere about, and I'm certain he'll have Perrin with him. Perhaps others. He's armed, too. I'm not sure what he intended, but it wasn't good."

"Your cousin has been detained by Beswick and Roth," he told her, gathering her in his arms. "I did not come alone."

"Oh, thank goodness." She bit her lip. "They won't kill him, will they?"

Jocelyn saw the puzzled look on his face—the fact that she cared what happened to her abductor—but the man was still her cousin and her father's heir. "I don't want blood on their hands. Your hands."

"You don't have to worry about that."

His nose bent to drag through the loose curls at her temple, and strangely, she felt a sensual heat lick through her. But then again, that could just be Westmore—proximity to the man made all her senses muddle and modesty fly out the window. He was just being considerate.

When his mouth trailed down to her ear and he bit

gently, making her whimper at the slight sting that was countered by a soft, wet suck, she reevaluated that assessment. Considerate rescuers did *not* nibble the earlobes of their charges. Her sense of self-preservation kicked in as his earlier words registered.

"*Do* I have something else to worry about?"

The Duke of Westmore scooped her up. "Yes, me."

By God, if that growled threat didn't set her off. Her nipples went instantly hard, her core liquefying. Heat blasted outward like a wildfire, consuming her thoughts and distilling her need down to one thing: *him*.

"And why is that, Your Grace?" Her voice was so husky she barely recognized it.

"You should have waited before getting into that coach." The duke stalked toward the study she'd just escaped, stopping only to lock the door she'd just unlocked and pocketing the key. Jocelyn gulped. Her frazzled senses warned that her person was in imminent danger, but a wicked thrill coursed through her blood, reveling in the excitement.

"You're not my husband, sir."

His body trembled at the pert intonation of the last word. He set her down in front of the enormous desk. "Not yet," he told her in a gravelly pitch that promised retribution. "But you will belong to me in every way that matters, Jocelyn. This body is precious, and you will not put it in harm's way."

His nose drew a line up her throat and across her jaw, his scent filling up her nostrils, as his big hand grasped her hip. The duke was shaking with suppressed emotion, muscles vibrating into her ribs, and coiled like a creature ready to strike, those tawny orange eyes of his glowing with purpose and dark passion. Jocelyn licked her lips and swallowed. He seemed on edge, holding on to his control by a thread.

The trembling of his thick muscles was warning enough in itself, but she couldn't help her mouth. "I'm not a thing to be owned."

Those lupine eyes flared. "You. Are. Mine."

The possessiveness of those three words echoed in the study, seeping under her skin and into her bones. Then he caught her by both hips and lifted her onto the desk, the hairpin she still held on to clattering to the floor. In mute shock, Jocelyn stared at him as he fisted handfuls of her already ruined muslin skirts and tore them straight up the center to her navel.

Oh. Dear. God.

The duke ran his lips up one knee to the edge of her drawers. His fingers kneaded a path forward up each leg, squeezing into the meat of her thighs, climbing higher and higher until she was dizzy with lust. Shoving the edge of her chemise up, his breath warmed her center through the narrow opening of her drawers, and when he eased his hands to the damp fabric there, he met her gaze. Slowly, *decisively*, he split her drawers right open, baring her intimate parts to him.

His eyes burned. Jocelyn didn't have time to be embarrassed before he leaned in with a groan and took the flat of his tongue to her heated flesh in one decadent, wanton swipe.

"Fucking delicious," he growled.

When he knelt and flung her legs over his shoulders, Jocelyn dug her nails into the edge of the desk and held on for dear life. Because he didn't just lick her. He *gorged* himself on her. His mouth worked every inch of her folds, nipping, sucking, thrusting. Even his tongue was inside of her! No part of her sex went undiscovered, and when two thick fingers intruded into her needy passage, she flung her head back and nearly suffocated him with the force of the release crashing through her.

Easing out from under her legs, he rose, and she saw her essence glistening on his swollen lips. His hands went to the fastenings at his tented riding breeches, a large wet spot on the buckskin evidence of his own plentiful need. Jocelyn tried to cover herself, only to be stopped by his hand and a noise of displeasure.

"I'm nowhere near done with you, Duchess."

She huffed out a useless breath. "I'm not your..."

Jocelyn had meant to say she wasn't his duchess, but the word stuck in her throat as he pulled himself from his pants and stroked his engorged length from root to tip. A bead of moisture glistened at the tip, making her sex hunger like a beggar awaiting a crust of bread.

"Are you arguing with me, Little Red?" A tremor ran through her at the name. He gave himself another stroke, harder this time, more need seeping out of him. "Because if you continue, I shall have no choice but to fuck the disobedience out of you."

The filthy promise tumbling from his lips was almost as hot as the sight of him stroking into his clenched fist. She *wanted* him to do that very thing—to dominate her into docility. Jocelyn wasn't altogether submissive by nature, but hell if this man didn't make her want to surrender everything to him.

"What if I am?" she managed, knowing she was provoking the beast and willing to take the consequences. Desperate for them, even. His head cocked to one side, lips baring in a predatory smirk, eyes shining with an unholy light.

"Jocelyn."

A clear warning. A last chance.

Here he was, the feared, revered Wolf of Westmore in all his savage, beastly glory.

She let her knees fall apart. "Punish me then."

Eleven

WULFRIC WAS GOING to fuck his brazen little vixen until she couldn't speak.

Punish me then.

He wanted to laugh at her audacity. Trying to exert her will. Christ, but she was made for him. Not just her stunning body, but the intelligent mind, her quick wit, her complete lack of fear...and most of all, her trust in him. Wulfric could see it in her eyes. She trusted him to take her outside her own boundaries...to break her apart and bring her back together.

He placed a hand behind her nape and brought her mouth to his. The kiss was sweet, tender, unlike his earlier filthier vow. As he caressed her mouth, Wulfric wanted her to know what she meant to him, even if he didn't have the words to describe what was blossoming between them. It was destined to be something more, given the chance, and he didn't want to ruin it. Sex was one thing; true intimacy was another.

It required *him* to trust her, too.

She kissed him back, tongue tangling with his and fingers winding into his hair and pulling enough to sting. Wulfric groaned at her willful behavior, his hands going to her bottom and squeezing. The memory of her last punishment had his cock going even harder. Breaking the kiss, Wulfric drew her close to the edge of the desk and rubbed his crown into her dripping center. She moaned and arched her back. Fuck, it felt as though he was coming undone, like all of his skin was going to shed and fall away, leaving nothing behind but raw sensation...and he hadn't even pressed himself into her.

As if she'd read his mind, she reached down between them and notched him to her entrance. Wulfric didn't release her eyes when he eased into her willing depths, the exquisite slide nearly making his knees buckle. He'd promised her a fucking, and it was turning into something entirely different. Something he'd never experienced with any woman. Not that he was complaining. Wulfric was discovering that everything with Lady Jocelyn seemed to become an extraordinary adventure.

An auction had led to the best sexual encounter of his life.

A masquerade had guided him to the one woman meant for him.

A foiled kidnapping had steered him to a connection he never thought he deserved.

Wulfric could only imagine what was next. A life with her, full of joy and unexpected exploits? He remembered her grandmother's soft words...would he be willing to let sleeping dogs lie for the sake of true happiness? Could he let himself live and be happy? To forget the feud with Tyne?

To *forgive*?

"Where did you go?" Jocelyn whispered, one hand moving to thread through the strands of hair that had fallen onto his brow. The gesture was so affectionate that something inside of him contracted. He remembered asking her the same thing the first time he'd joined with her. Oddly, it felt like they'd come full circle. He'd be a fool to ignore the significance, no matter how small.

"Nowhere. I'm here. With you."

"Then be with me." She pulled his lips to hers and wrapped her legs around his waist as if she felt it, too, both of them shying away from it, as if it was much too precious to touch.

Lovemaking, that was what this was. It wasn't just the sublime friction, the sultry drag of her body as they came together and withdrew in a motion that was as old as time. It was the look in her eyes, the feel of those fingers at his nape, the sensation of fullness and utter completion in his chest. He could make love to her for hours. Love her forever, if he had to.

Give up everything.

The realization scared the shit out of him.

It was too much, *too* fast. Too fucking soon. He needed to be in control...to regain the power he'd somehow misplaced along the way. His mind was whirling. Never had he felt so vulnerable, so *exposed*, and Wulfric wasn't sure he was ready for that.

"Harder," Jocelyn whimpered, her fingernails dragging over his scalp, hips tightening around his in wanton demand.

Sex, he could do. The rest would have to wait.

Wulfric felt her ripple all around him, the pressure of her inner walls gripping him as he stroked deeper, making her thrust upward for friction as her pleasure built. When he pulled from the clasp of her body, she let out a discontented protest, but he only lifted her to flip her around, her torso resting on the surface of the desk.

Palming her hips, he sank back into her warm, wet depths, and they both groaned at the fullness in this new position. He rode her body hard, coming through on his promise until she was a writhing, needy mess in his arms, the only sound in the room were her soft cries of passion, the sound of slapping flesh, and his own grunts.

Pressure built at the base of his spine, signaling that he was close to the precipice, but he wanted her to come again before he peaked. Reaching forward, he eased her upward so that her spine was flush to his chest. Wulfric delved his fingers into her bodice, rolling her taut nipple between his thumb and forefinger, and pinching just hard enough that she hissed before he released the compression.

"So good," she moaned coarsely. "Feels so good."

He was close, too. "I know."

Skating his palm up her throat, he squeezed. Not hard enough to constrict her airway completely, but enough for her body to go rigid.

"Wulfric." The airless sound had the beat of panic.

"Easy, I have you. Trust me."

She relaxed, marginally, though her panting was still frantic. His pelvis continued its onslaught, his thrusts slightly shallower, but hitting that front wall of hers that had her grinding back against him. He slid his other hand down and made a slow circle on the tight bud of nerves when he felt his ballocks tighten, his body surging into hers one last time as his release built like lightning in his veins. Jocelyn screamed, both their hearts thundering as they spun undone.

White light shooting through his vision, Wulfric bent and slanted her chin up to his so he could take her lips in a wet, open-mouthed, all-too-savage kiss, even as the pleasure barreled through his body in heated spurts. He'd swallow every sound, every cry from her. Take her pleasure as though it were his own. A sob broke from her at the intensity of her own orgasm, her walls wringing the last few frenzied pulses from him.

It was only when he'd collapsed against her limp,

sated form, still joined with her, Wulfric realized he'd finished inside her.

∼

Jocelyn floated slowly back down to earth, her body completely spent. She couldn't begin to make sense of what had just happened. Between his dirty, erotic oaths, the multiple, seemingly infinite orgasms she couldn't believe her body was even capable of, and the breath-stealing—*literally*!—dominance, she was in a boneless, utterly mindless state.

After a few minutes, she felt him lever off of her, but was unable to bring herself to move, confident that her rickety knees were in no shape to even support the rest of her. Too much pleasure had rendered them into noo-dles. Fused to the desk in a limp display and certain that her skirts—what had survived of them from Wulfric's manhandling—were in a tangled mess around her waist, Jocelyn sighed.

"You owe me a dress," she murmured. "And perhaps a new pair of knees."

He chuckled from somewhere behind her, and then she felt a warm hand pass over her posterior. A soft cloth stroked between her legs before her tattered, torn skirts were gently lowered. Wulfric peeled her off the desk and gathered her into his arms. With some mortifi-cation, she realized that the cloth he'd used to wipe them both clean had been his cravat.

"I'll get you anything you need," he whispered, pushing the hair out of her face, and kissing her on the lips. It was a soft kiss...a deeply meaningful one that left her mute. One that translated into emotions and words she wasn't sure either of them was ready for.

A beginning in a flashy club, followed by forced engagements, didn't exactly bode well for a happy-ever-after, and people were wont to say words in the heat of the moment that they didn't truly mean. Jocelyn remembered his growled *'you are mine'* and her breath hitched in her throat. How much of that had been because he'd been in the throes of lust? They'd both been. Because after the ordeal of being abducted, coming together had felt like a meshing of bodies and souls, guided by nothing but passion and primitive instincts.

Jocelyn bit her lip and placed a hand on his chest. "Wulfric. What are we doing here?"

A dark eyebrow quirked. "I should think that was obvious."

She blushed. "I meant you and me." Jocelyn released a breath and stepped out of his orbit so that she could pull her thoughts together. To give her hands something to do other than touch him, she reached up to smooth and re-pin the hair that had come loose from its confines, tucking the fallen hairpin back in place. She felt his eyes on her. "What happens now?"

"We will marry as soon as we get back to town," he said. "I managed to obtain a special license, and Beswick will have a vicar ready at his residence upon our return tonight." When she didn't speak, he went on. "Doing it quickly is best, in case Tyne or Tybalt tries something more to get you to wed Perrin again. I wouldn't put it past either of them."

Nor would she. But the reason for her hesitation wasn't the thought of her father, it was because of the man who stood a few feet away. "Why would you do this? I entrapped you."

Narrowed eyes met hers, as if he sensed the note of uncertainty in her voice. "You didn't trap me, Jocelyn. I could have said no."

"Why didn't you? That evening on the balcony?"

"Your reputation would have been torn to shreds had I denied your claim and refuted any agreement between us," he explained. "I couldn't let an innocent girl get demolished by the cruelty of the *ton*. Not again, not on my watch."

The warmth inside of her turned to ice. He meant Prudence. Of course he did.

Jocelyn inhaled, her heart feeling like it was being crushed under a giant weight of bittersweet envy and inexplicable sorrow. "Because you felt obligated to protect me as you could have done with Prudence?"

Confusion lit his expression. "This has nothing to do with her."

"You said yourself that you loved her." Jocelyn swallowed past the lump of pain thickening in her throat. As much as she missed her best friend, she would always be second-best when it came to the Duke of Westmore. It was quite obvious that his heart had been buried with Prudence long ago. "Prue would have married you, if she'd had the chance."

His laughter was low and cold, making her stare at him, despite being cautious in her reply. "No, Jocelyn, she would not have."

"You were in love with her!"

"I loved Prue like a sister," he whispered so softly, she barely heard it, and then dropped a bombshell that she'd never expected in a million years. "My half-sister."

Her mind went blank and sputtered back to life. "*What?*"

"My father broke his marriage vows with Roth's mother and Prue was the result of their indiscretion." Westmore's voice was toneless, that hard, vulturine gaze back in force, and for a moment, she cursed its return. "Tyne found out and exposed him to my mother, and well, I'm sure you know the story of how she found herself sent to Bedlam."

Jocelyn's blood chilled. She did know, but only from second-hand gossip from her sisters. The Dowager Duchess of Westmore had shown up to Tyne Manor screaming bloody murder and had had to be restrained. A stint in Bedlam had been the only way her philandering husband could save face, and the awful scandal had only become worse when the Duke of Westmore had died shortly thereafter. A breath shuddered out of her. Had her father been responsible for that? For the destruction of two lives?

She glanced at Wulfric in horror. *Three* lives. No wonder he was so hell-bent on revenge. His entire world had been shattered in one fell swoop.

"I'm so sorry, Wulfric."

"There's nothing you can do, it's done now," he said and then exhaled, scrubbing a palm over his face. "We need to leave to make it back to Beswick's residence for the vicar. Unless you've changed your mind. I won't force you into wedlock, Jocelyn."

Silence stretched between them, now that the haze of sensuality and desire had dissipated. Now that their very real future hung in the balance. A marriage would tie them together forever in the eyes of the church, the *ton*, their families.

They were from two different worlds...two different *feuding* worlds. Jocelyn had never condoned her father's vendetta against the Banes, never truly understood what drove men to such violent extremes. Whatever the cause of it, that was long forgotten now, but her father's choices were on him, and she could only stand by her own actions.

What if they weren't enough? If *she* wasn't enough? What if Wulfric valued retribution and revenge over anything he might ever feel for her? Jocelyn had to know. She'd much rather face the sword of truth with courage than feel it in her back because she'd been afraid.

"If we do this, will you promise to stop trying to destroy my family?" she asked in a soft whisper.

Wulfric went still. So preternaturally still, not even the air between them moved. It wasn't an ultimatum, but it felt like one. After what seemed like an eternity, Wulfric took the key to the study from his pocket and stared at the whorled metal as if it were some kind of talisman to the answer he was about to give.

Indecision etched his features, a muscle flexing in that hard, uncompromising jaw, those full lips she had felt graze over every inch of her skin pulling into a tight, ruthless line. Her heart sank, along with any hope for them, even before he spoke.

The duke unlocked the door, one hand on the jamb, head bowed. "No," he replied. "I can't promise you that."

Twelve

EACH TIME JOCELYN thought of Wulfric's parting words, her heart fractured a little more. A lifetime of bitterness and vengeance could not be abandoned so easily, but she had hoped beyond hope that it would. That whatever esteem the duke had held her in might have lessened the ills of the past and been enough to smooth a path forward for the future.

A future *together*, in which he'd choose her.

But he hadn't.

Jocelyn swallowed hard, rubbing a fist over the gnawing ache in her breast that hadn't abated in the past week. There was no visible injury, no mark that she'd been skewered through and through, but it felt like one, all the same. Like he'd reached in and wrenched her heart out while it was still beating and beseeching him to choose compassion instead of anger.

Perhaps they were fated to remain enemies—star-crossed lovers doomed to be kept apart by their own immovable pride. Because that was the problem with unseen wounds...sometimes they never healed. They festered into rot. Into *rage*. Into something that consumed people whole. And now the Duke of Westmore would have the perfect reprisal—an eye for an eye—and the chance to kill her foolhardy cousin in a duel.

Jocelyn let out a frustrated curse.

Tybalt might deserve punishment for his actions, but he did not deserve to die.

Not that Westmore cared. He wouldn't even give up his lifelong grudge for her sake. Though why would he have? His entire family had been destroyed by hers. As the Duke of Tyne's only remaining male heir, Tybalt was the end of the Capehart family line, and his death would be the ultimate *coup de grâce* for a man like Westmore.

A man she'd so very nearly let into her heart.

You're a fool if you think he's not inside already.

Gulping past the ugly knot in her throat, Jocelyn scrubbed hopelessly at her chest again, the hollow twinge there strong enough to make her eyes water. Screwing them shut, she clenched her jaw. She was *done* weeping over him; he had made his choice and it wasn't her. Now she had to focus on keeping her family from falling apart. From allowing her cousin to make a deadly mistake.

Exhaling her fears, Jocelyn narrowed her gaze on Tybalt, who was currently under house arrest at Tyne Manor, which had subsequently been restocked with provisions and staff, considering the abrupt change in plans. The head of the Runners had ordered him to stay put, pending an investigation of matters surrounding his conduct, launched by the influential Dukes of Beswick and Westmore as well as the Marquess of Roth.

Her grandmother had delayed her return as well, thank goodness, because Jocelyn could not deal with her bean-brained jackanapes of a cousin on her own. Tybalt was refusing to admit to any wrongdoing, arguing that it had been her duty to follow through on the agreement with Perrin. Her father would have already completed the three-day journey back to his ancestral seat, but there had been no word from him on what her cousin should do.

In hindsight, her rotten father had probably commanded the kidnapping.

"Tybalt," Jocelyn began. "Why do you want to see this betrothal with Perrin done so badly?"

His mouth pressed into a mulish line. "Tyne wanted the land."

"Why?"

"Because with a larger shipping port, it would give him an edge over Westmore. Everything was dependent upon it. I was the one who sold Perrin on the idea of combining our estates and resources."

Jocelyn blinked, hearing the desolation in his tone. "Tybalt, Papa is not going to think any less of you if he doesn't get this tract of land or a deal with the marquess. You're his heir, and nothing is going to change that."

"You're his *daughter*, of course you would say that."

"A daughter he was willing to trade to a man as old as Grandfather would be, if he were alive," she said, and glanced over at their grandmother. "No offense, Grams."

"None taken," the dowager said with a dramatic shudder. "I wouldn't want to marry that half-dead overgrown toad either, at *my* age. At least your grandfather was sprightly and could take me for a tumble in the sheets once in a while."

"Grams!" Jocelyn spluttered while Tybalt made a gagging noise. She pushed any thought of her grandmother's bedroom capers from her head, *far* away, and focused on her cousin. "It doesn't matter what my father says, Tybalt. You are next in line as the Capehart male heir. That's how primogeniture works. Unless Papa and Mama conceive a male child at this late stage, which is nigh impossible, there is no way for you to lose your position."

Tybalt flinched. "He said he'd disown me if I didn't see it through."

"He can only cut off your fortune, and even so, not any of the entailed properties of the dukedom or the title. There are laws in place to protect against such things. Papa is posturing to get you to do his dirty bidding." She drew in a breath. "Do you even know what caused the feud between the Banes and the Capeharts in the first place?"

Tybalt shook his head. Their grandmother lifted her hand. "I do!"

"Go on, Grams. Enlighten us."

The old dowager grinned. "My great-great-great-grandfather," she began, then stopped and wrinkled her nose. "Maybe one more great or one less, I'm not sure. Well, he was in love with a Capehart and stole her away from an arranged marriage. Took her right on his horse, like the marauding Viking he was, and rode away." Both Jocelyn and Tybalt waited for her to go on, but she winked and spread her hands wide. "That's it."

"That's *it*?" Tybalt echoed.

"There was a land dispute as part of the dowry, and we've squabbled and descended into revenge of the nitwits ever since. I do believe the infamous bard wrote a play about a similar disagreement two centuries ago."

Jocelyn's brows rose at that, but Tybalt frowned. "It's hardly the same."

"Isn't it?" Her grandmother squinted some more, tapping a wrinkled finger against her chin. "Someone died or got killed. Then it was always tit for tat over the many centuries, with no end in sight."

A bright gaze came to rest on Jocelyn, who shrugged. "Don't look at me for answers. Westmore is well within his rights to go ahead with the foolish duel that your grandson here issued. Tybalt has to apologize and call it off."

Her cousin's scowl returned. "He dishonored you by entertaining your capers, an unmarried daughter of a duke, at a club!"

"Tybalt, for the hundredth time, I went to that club on *my* own, of my own *free* will. That had nothing to do with the Duke of Westmore. Yes, I entered a charity auction for the sake of my long-lost best friend at said club, there's no crime in that." The white lie tasted bitter, but there was no point in admitting that she'd gone to The Silver Scythe for sex. Jocelyn held up a hand when he opened his mouth to quarrel. "And before you start in about my reputation, let me stop you there. I went, knowing all the risks. This is *my* body and I shall wield it how I see fit. Perhaps you should see fit to start doing the same with yours."

He gaped and blinked at her like an owl. "What do you mean?"

"Call off the duel."

"Then I'll be branded a coward."

Jocelyn paced, her tread nearly wearing a hole in the carpet. "Wouldn't you rather stand for something right? This vendetta isn't yours, Tybalt. Isn't *ours*, and yet we're constantly trapped in a cycle of who can outdo the other, who can kill the other. Frankly, I'm sick of it." She blew out a frustrated breath. "My father is wrong. Rise up, Cousin. Don't bend backward for someone who doesn't care if you take a bullet as long as it's to avenge the Capehart name." She moved to stand in front of him. "You deserve better than that."

"Even after all I've done?" Shame crossed his expression. "To you?"

She nodded. "Yes. We all make mistakes in the name of things we cherish and protect, but if we try to make amends, then we've learned something. You accused Westmore of dishonoring me, when there was no dishonor to be had. At least not from him."

Her cousin fidgeted but looked unconvinced. "He used you."

Jocelyn wanted to scream. That was the thing about dogmatism—sometimes a belief sank in so deeply that a person couldn't change or grow even if they wanted to. When fear and hate became innate and taught from a young age, they were insidious, dangerous things. Hard to challenge. Even harder to overcome.

But change started with one person.

Just one.

"I know you'll do the right thing, Tybalt. I believe in you."

~

Wulfric breathed out, the cloud of his breath forming a white mist in the early morning air. The shadows from the trees in Putney Heath made eerie shapes from the changing light, the dew along the grass soaking into the soles of his boots. He rubbed his gloved hands together and attempted to roll the kinks out of his neck. It wasn't ideal to start the day with a duel, but here he was, called out by Tyne's muleheaded nephew.

Jocelyn's cousin.

The thought of her made his chest ache. God, he missed her! Missed that ready smile, her sly humor, that generous heart, and her beautifully responsive body that he couldn't banish from his dreams no matter how hard he tried. She haunted him, day and night. He'd been a fool to let her go, Wulfric realized that now. Everything in the days following had felt hollow, as though life had been reduced to monotone, overcast shades. Jocelyn had brought color and sun into his life, and now that she was gone, it only made what she'd left behind even more stark.

Well, he'd made his bed and someone had to lie in it.

Pathetic and alone.

Christ, he was a sorry sack of shit. Shaking off his maudlin humors, he walked over to where Beswick and Roth stood with the boxes of dueling pistols. "Thank you for doing this," he told them.

Roth raised a hand to his ear. "What? I can't hear you because Isobel chewed my ear off last night. In truth, I'm surprised she hasn't followed by now, and isn't hiding somewhere in the bushes dressed like a bloody groom. I'll be groveling for months because of this."

Beswick rolled his eyes skyward at the marquess's theatrics. "Shall I do my gentlemanly duty and see if young Lord Tybalt will agree to reconciliation?"

"That would imply that I wish to apologize for my perceived dishonor to his cousin," Wulfric said. "He kidnapped Jocelyn and meant to force her to wed that old codger. I should trounce his arse."

Beswick nodded patiently. "Regardless, the code of honor states that the first offense merits the apology, which puts the responsibility squarely on you."

"Then no."

"Are you certain?" the duke asked.

Wulfric bared his teeth. "What would you have me do? Apologize, offer to be switched for an offense I did not commit? Any deflowering was consensual."

Roth, who was watching the verbal swordplay with

growing interest, cleared his throat. 'So you *did* deflower her?"

'Fuck off, Roth. That's not the point. There was no disgrace, no shame in what we did."

Beswick let out a breath. "That's where you are wrong, my friend. In the eyes of society, you are both unmarried, and regardless of consent, committed a cardinal sin." He lifted a palm at Wulfric's growl. 'I didn't say I agree, only what prevailing opinions are with respect to conduct and perceived honor." He lifted a shoulder in a shrug. 'If she were your wife or bride-to-be, this would mitigate most of the bad feelings."

'She's neither," Wulfric said, chest going tight. 'We've parted ways." It should not have hurt so much to say the words out loud, but it did. He felt it as acutely as though a lead ball had pierced his breast, shot by an unseen assailant. He nearly buckled from the force of it. 'Let's get this over with."

They marched over to where Tybalt stood with his second, a scrawny gentleman Wulfric did not recognize. He'd half expected it to be Tyne, even though the duke had gone back north a fortnight ago, but Tyne didn't like to get his hands dirty. He coerced others to do that for him. Case in point, his bullheaded, eager-to-please heir. With a curt nod to his challenger's second, the weapons were checked and chosen, time and paces agreed.

When the signal was given, Wulfric took his pistol, walked until they stood twelve yards apart but he didn't take aim. Even in the low light, he could see that Tybalt was sweating, his face ashen, his own gun lifted and cocked. Tybalt's arm trembled, and Wulfric braced for impact just as a feminine scream tore through the air.

"Tybalt, no!"

Two things happened simultaneously then. Both

men jerked in the direction of the voice, but Tybalt's finger was already on the trigger and the sound of a discharged gun blasted into the silence. Wulfric felt the heat of the ball as it tore past him and embedded in a nearby tree, much too close for comfort. Less than a handful of inches to the left and it might have torn through his skull. He watched through his shock as Roth kept Jocelyn back from running farther onto the field, and then turned his attention back to his opponent.

The young man looked fit to piss himself, the spent gun smoking in his fist. From the look on his face, it had been an accidental shot, even a fool could see it. But still, it was within Wulfric's right to take his satisfaction. Should he intend to do the young man harm, he would not miss. At twenty-five paces, he never missed a target and this was half of that. Perhaps a leg shot then. Or a shoulder. *Or* he could eliminate the Tyne ducal line forever.

Wipe them from the history books.

Claim vengeance for his broken mother, lost sister, and dead father.

Find fucking peace.

"Wulfric, please." The whisper was so soft, but he still turned, his eyes meeting wet green ones. "Don't do this."

The air hissed out of his lungs at the sight of Jocelyn. God, she was so beautiful, her sunset-colored hair loose around her shoulders as if she'd just tumbled out of bed, her eyes red-rimmed from weeping. He couldn't bear to think that he'd caused her any kind of pain, and yet he had. He'd ripped her heart out, because he'd been too selfish to see what was the true meaning of life.

Not an empty victory over an enemy.

A life built with someone he...loved.

The burden upon him suddenly felt different. Satisfaction was a strange thing. So was honor. One could be called a coward for not rising to a challenge of a duel to the death, but it was also honorable to do what was right. But would he be satisfied with that?

The answer was clear.

Wulfric took aim, heard the intake of breath as he did so, and fired into the air. When he saw her face, the light in those green, *green* eyes, he felt satisfaction down to the marrow of his bones. And then she was running toward him and crashing into his arms.

"I love you," she muttered into his neck, and burying his face with kisses, uncaring of their audience, not that any of the men were watching them. "You dratted man, scaring the life from me. You could have been shot and then I would have had to resurrect your ghost so I could shoot you myself."

"So bloodthirsty, my Little Red," he murmured, enjoying the deep flush blooming on her cheeks at the wicked nickname. He took her lips in a long, deep kiss, savoring the sweet taste of her and the delicious silkiness of her mouth.

"Were you going to delope from the start?" she asked, when they finally broke for breath.

He didn't want to lie. "I wasn't sure, but then I saw you, and in that moment, everything became so crystal clear—revenge compared to you suddenly seemed as insignificant as a pebble held up to the moon." Wulfric stared down into the eyes of the woman he loved so much it hurt to keep it all inside. "Ask me your question again, my love."

Confusion flitted across her face before understanding dawned. "Will you promise to stop trying to destroy my family?"

"Yes, I promise. I choose you, Jocelyn. I only need

you. Be my wife, please."

"Oh, Wulfric, of course I will."

"Good." He breathed her in, heart fit to bursting. "I'm glad, and now we can move on to things like your punishment."

Shining eyes flared with desire. "Punishment, Your Grace?"

He tutted, brushing her cold nose with his. "For running willy-nilly onto an open field when two men are about to shoot each other. I warned you about looking after this body. I'd say some atonement for such rash behavior was in order, wouldn't you?"

Rising to her tiptoes, she kissed him and nodded demurely, before clasping her hands behind her back and skipping backward just out of his reach. His eyes narrowed, instincts perking up at the idea of a chase.

"Do you think to run from me, Little Red?"

She grinned and stuck out her pretty pink tongue. "Come and get me, Wolf."

Epilogue

JOCELYN WAS WELL and truly trussed. Hogtied, as one would say, arms and legs bound behind her, with a cravat over her lips to silence her many whimpers as a powerful, dominant, sinfully wicked duke circled her with a riding crop in one hand and a feather in the other. Her body was awash with a riot of sensations, the alternation of texture enough to make her teeter on the blade-thin edge of pain and pleasure.

For what seemed like an eternity, her husband had seen fit to torment her with various stroking touches. He dragged the tip of the feather up the soles of her bare feet, the light touch only a precursor of what was to come, when the harder edge of the leather followed up one calf and then a quick lash against her bare bottom. She flinched and moaned, heat filling her when two more strokes followed. The flat of the crop slid against the seam between her legs and her entire body shook. It didn't even matter where he touched her anymore. The entire topography of her skin had become a pleasure center, her nerve endings all lit up. *Every* part of her burned.

"Wulfric," she mumbled through the cloth.

Lips chased over her cheek as he released the tie over her mouth. "Yes, Duchess?"

"I need you now. Please."

Jocelyn felt one of the restraints give, but she should have known better. The feather danced down the length of her spine making her back arch, even though her arms ached, hips rising in wanton appeal. He gave it to her, this time the sharp swat of his large hand making her gasp, right before he slid it between her legs to cup her mound in a possessive grip.

"You're not in control here, Little Red."

"I can't take it anymore, I want to come!" She writhed against the mattress, desperate for friction and his fingers to *move*. The blasted rotter wouldn't. Goodness, she was right bloody *there* and he was keeping it from her!

"You come when I tell you to," he whispered in a low commanding voice that urged obedience.

It was true. She did. Jocelyn had no idea how that was humanly possible...for a woman to have an orgasm on command. She'd laughed the first time he told her, saying that bodies didn't work like that. They released when kindled. Once more, her husband had proven her wrong, and now, it seemed she was attuned to him. Devoted to his demands. Compliant to his control. Ever at his complete mercy.

In full trust.

Usually.

Because now, she wanted to kick him, scream at him to touch her for the love of her dwindling sanity. Tantrums didn't work on him either. To punish her, he'd draw out her pleasure so much that she was a sobbing ball of need by the time he gave her what she wanted, so she'd learned to bite her tongue and let him have his way. It wasn't like she didn't enjoy it...

delayed gratification was its own brand of erotic torture.

The duke shifted again, blood rushing into her hands as they released and fell limply to her sides. The knots at her ankles were also loosened, but heaven help her, she couldn't move even if she tried. The feeling of blood flooding her arms and legs was almost too much to bear, the sensation stroked along her overstimulated veins and making her whimper with raw arousal.

Wulfric ran a hand down her back and moved to sit between her legs. He parted her knees, lifting her hips over his thighs. Jocelyn could feel him staring at her, exposed as she was, feeling those eyes burning into her, and sensing his utter masculine pride at the sodden mess he'd made of her.

"Fuck, I love when you're this soaked," he growled.

She arched in desperate invitation. "I need you."

With a grunt, he fit himself to her and drove inside in one hard thrust, the scream tearing from her lips as her entire body lit up like the lanterns at Vauxhall. The orgasm that had been hovering just out of her reach detonated as her husband broke the last of the threads holding her together. Jocelyn flew apart, bolts of lightning firing across her insides, bliss pouring through her like an uncontrollable, never-ending wave.

Wulfric kept thrusting, so hard that the bed frame shook, and her body shuddered anew, her brain falling into a welcome darkness of complete, exquisite bliss, even as her pleasure went on and on and on. Dimly, floating somewhere out of her own body, Jocelyn felt his hands tighten on her hips as he found his release, warmth filling her center in a gratifying gush. When his sweaty body collapsed on hers, she purred in cocooned bliss.

"Jocelyn," he purred into her ear. "Am I too heavy?"

"No," she murmured. "I love the feel of you like this."

A gentle hand swept from her shoulder, down her ribs, over her tingling buttocks to mid-thigh before he took them to their sides, warm palms stroking over her flanks in that soothing motion, fingers threading into her damp hair. After a minute, Wulfric left the bed and returned with a cool glass of water that he brought to her lips. Jocelyn drank thirstily.

"More?" he asked, gazing down at her with so much love, all she wanted was to curl up and bask in it. She shook her head. When he kissed her, drew the sheets over them, and tucked her backwards into the warm curve of his body, murmuring more words of praise, a languorous sigh left her. Her wolf was always so good to her when he took her on these passionate journeys—before, during, and after.

Much the same as he was outside the bedchamber.

Life as the Duchess of Westmore over the past year had been everything and more she could have expected. They had married. Her parents had shunned her, which came as no surprise to anyone. Tybalt had returned to the proverbial fold, but Jocelyn got the sense that he might have changed. He wasn't the same deferential creature he'd been before to her father, which was remarkable in itself. While he was still arrogant as all hell, he didn't cut her in London, and he was always unfailingly polite to her husband.

A thank-you, perhaps, that Westmore had let him live.

Or perhaps Tybalt was simply growing wiser.

Wulfric, her darling, wicked duke, was her match in every way; intellectually, emotionally, and physically. Especially the last. The man could look at her across a crowded ballroom and her knees would weaken.

Finding a deserted music room or a private arbor had become one of their favorite pastimes. Their friends poked fun at them when they disappeared and reappeared with rumpled ballgowns and disheveled hair, but it wasn't as if Beswick and his duchess or Roth and his marchioness didn't do the same—they were just as besotted with each other.

Jocelyn adored their sexual games, but most of all she treasured *this*. When he held her close to him, letting her know every night how very much he loved her.

"Wulfric?" she whispered.

"Yes, my love."

She bit her lip, suddenly nervous at what she had to tell him, though she had no reason to be. "I've missed my monthly courses for two cycles now."

The hand grazing down the side of her ribs stilled and slid around to the soft flatness of her belly. "Are you with child?"

"I think so. I know we haven't discussed children, but is this something you want?"

❧

Wulfric's chest suddenly felt ten sizes too small, a suspicious prickle stinging behind his eyelids. The idea of her carrying their child filled him with so much joy, he struggled to put his emotions into words. He scooped his hands beneath her and gently turned his wife to face him. "I love you. And I will love him or her with all my heart."

"I'm glad," she whispered.

He lifted his brows and formed a perplexed look. "Why are you so surprised though?"

"What do you mean?"

"With as much unprotected sex as we have been

347

having all over every garden in England, it was bound to happen." His chest puffed. "I am rather virile, and in possession of some excellent, intrepid seed, if I do say so myself. In fact, it should have happened sooner. I shall have to have a stern word to my soldiers."

A huff of laughter left her. "The enormous ego on you."

"Enormous in *all* things, yes." His knuckles grazed over her stomach, marveling at the fact that in a matter of months, her abdomen would be rounded, a tiny person growing inside of her. He gave a chest-beating grin. "Perhaps it will be twins."

"Do they run in your family?" she asked. "They don't in mine."

He shook his head and winked. "No, but super seed..."

"You are nonsensical."

Amused green eyes met his, a reluctant smile tugging at her lips. God, her face was so beloved to him. Each day that went by, he fell in love more deeply. How he had ever existed before she came into his life, Wulfric would never know. She was his whole world—his sun, his moon, all the bright stars in his universe. Her wily old grandmother had been right after all, because loving Jocelyn, and being loved in return by her, was everything he needed.

Until now.

Until there would be a new person to love.

"Definitely twins," he mused. "Maybe even triplets or more."

Her giggles rang out between them. "We are not having a litter, Your Grace, no matter your fearsome nickname. I would be happy with one, as long as he or she is healthy."

Wulfric kissed the happy sounds from her lips. "Me,

too." He wasn't done teasing her, however. He loved seeing the adorable flash of annoyance in her eyes when he irritated her on purpose. "Come to think of it, Wolverine is a good strong name."

"I do *not* think so!" she gasped in outrage, and then laughed when she realized he was provoking her. "Tybalt, then."

"Minx!" He tickled her. "We might as well name him after your father."

"Never," she said with a shudder. "I want him to have a name without any of the sins of the past. Any son of ours will forge a new future, a fresh start, free of any feud between our families." Jocelyn met his eyes, her heart in hers. "On the subject of names, I was thinking that if it is a girl, I'd like to name her Prudence, if that's all right with you."

His throat went instantly tight, emotion daggering him. "That's more than all right," he whispered hoarsely.

God, this woman. This beautiful, huge-hearted, incomparable woman. How had he found her? How on earth had a hardnosed, ruthless bastard like him even *won* her heart? Sometimes, he wondered if it was a cosmic joke, that fate would steal her away and cackle that she was much too good for the likes of him. Because Jocelyn was, he had no doubt of it.

"Prue would love that," he said softly.

"I think she would, too."

Wulfric drew her close, wrapping his arms around the two most precious things in his life. Their future was bright, and he intended to live up to the greatest gift he'd been given, every single day for the rest of his life. The Duchess of Westmore deserved to be worshipped like the queen she was. He would do everything in his power to make her happy, and that was his solemn, binding vow.

The Wolf of Westmore grinned. Minus a few punishments, of course.

He wasn't *that* tamed.

Author's Note

Just a quick note of reference regarding the aforementioned "prick glass" in my story. Yes, Dear Reader, the infamous dribble glass from one of Scotland's most notorious Eighteenth Century sex clubs, The Beggar's Benison, was a real thing. In an age when aristocratic gentlemen rebelled against the stringent morals of society and the church, they loved to flaunt their personal and sexual desires in private clubs where anything went. At The Beggar's Benison in Scotland in 1732, members would meet to celebrate all things bawdy and depraved, including art, books, poetry, songs, women, self-stimulation, and yes, sipping from the occasional dribble glass sculpture shaped like the male phallus. Per the Beggar's Benison's records and their initiation motto, *"May Prick and Purse never fail you."*

More by Amalie

The Taming of the Dukes series
Always Be My Duchess

The Daring Dukes series
The Princess Stakes
Rules for Heiresses
Wicked Beautiful Spy

The Regency Rogues series
The Beast of Beswick
The Rakehell of Roth
The Wolf of Westmore

Tartans & Titans series
Sweet Home Highlander
A Lord for the Lass
What a Scot Wants

Lords of Essex series
My Rogue, My Ruin
My Darling, My Disaster
My Hellion, My Heart
My Scot, My Surrender

About the Author

AMALIE HOWARD is a USA Today and Publishers Weekly bestselling novelist of "smart, sexy, deliciously feminist romance." *The Beast of Beswick* was one of Oprah Daily's Top 24 Best Historicals to Read and *Rules for Heiresses* was an Apple Best Books selection. She is also the author of several critically acclaimed, award-winning young adult novels. An AAPI, Caribbean-born writer, her interviews and articles on multicultural fiction have appeared in Entertainment Weekly, Ravishly Magazine, and Diversity in YA. When she's not writing, she can usually be found reading, being the president of her one-woman Harley Davidson motorcycle club #WriteOrDie, or power-napping. She currently lives in Colorado with her husband and three children.

Join Amalie's Newsletter.

Put Up Your Dukes

JANNA MACGREGOR

One

LONDON, 1819

**AMELIA RICHMOND WAS NO LONGER
WELCOMED** in society, but that same society still
managed to cross her threshold on a regular basis. The
viscount and his viscountess seated across from Amelia
were proof of that fact. Amazing that when the privileged in society wanted something, they could easily
find a way to visit her in her modest rooms at the boardinghouse.

Yet, they'd never invite her into *their* homes. They
saw her as a means to an end.

They wanted her influence with her estranged
husband.

All because Amelia had married Martin Richmond,
the owner and editor of *The Midnight Cryer,* the most
successful gossip pamphlet in all of London. When
they'd been newly married, Martin had written a
scathing article about the Marquess of Overton, the fiancé of Amelia's former friend Elizabeth Reynolds.
Amelia had begged and pleaded with Martin not to do
it. He had argued that it was his chance to make a name
for himself and *The Midnight Cryer.*

That had left her with no recourse. On that fateful

day, she walked out the door leaving her husband, her marriage, and her former life behind. It'd been like walking off a cliff. Without family or friends, her life had turned desolate. Now, she was accepting visits from the very people who spurned her.

"I'm afraid our poor Diana became a little overwrought with Mademoiselle Mignon." Lady Benchley batted her eyelashes while exhaling softly. "It could happen to anyone if the modiste doesn't listen to you."

"Overwrought?" Lord Benchley murmured. "Be truthful, dear. Your daughter was irate."

Lady Benchley dismissed her husband's comment with a wave of her hand. "A Season-opening event ballgown turns the strongest women into shrinking violets."

"Or into shrieking Valkyries." Lord Benchley shifted his gaze to Amelia. "I've spent a fortune on Diana's wardrobe for her introduction. If your husband publishes that episode with the modiste, all that money will be lost. It doesn't make any difference how beautiful our daughter is. Mademoiselle Mignon is so beloved by her powerful clients that an affront to her will mean all of society will turn their back on our daughter."

"Did your daughter insult Mademoiselle Mignon?" Amelia asked keeping her voice low.

The viscount and his wife shared a look, a guilty one at that. With a bowed head, the viscountess nodded slightly.

"What we need is for you to ask your husband not to print this unfortunate episode." Lady Benchley pleaded with her eyes. "We'll do anything you ask. Pay anything you ask."

"I'm sorry. If the story is factual, I have no influence with my husband," Amelia replied in her most sympathetic voice. "I can't help you. Nor accept payment."

However, she didn't belabor the point that Mrs.

Pauline Johnson, the headmaster's wife of the foundling home where Amelia volunteered, would send out a brief note to everyone who visited Amelia. The notes would gently remind the guests that the foundling home was the favorite charity of Martin Richmond's dearest wife.

Amelia didn't mind such a blatant request for money. The home always needed funds.

From their gaping mouths, Amelia had stunned the Benchleys. It couldn't be helped. She never approached her husband with matters that were ultimately truthful. However, if a story was based on rumor, Amelia would do her best to convince Martin not to publish it.

It was the morally right thing to do. Besides, Amelia hated gossip. She always had, especially when it ruined her life.

She hesitated for a moment as she considered how best to help the couple before her. Frankly, what the situation needed Amelia couldn't provide. Deportment lessons for Lady Diana would fix what ailed their family.

"I don't ask my husband to stop a story that's true. It's an unwritten rule between us." She sat on the edge of her seat and smiled courteously. "My advice? Have your daughter apologize to Mademoiselle Mignon and beg for her forgiveness," she said in her most soothing voice. "Take her home and explain that people are people, no matter whether they're in trade, the military, domestic service, or on the fringe of society. You'll be doing her a great service if you explain that."

"Can't you make an exception for our Diana? We came all the way to this godforsaken part of town to seek your assistance." Lady Benchley scowled.

Amelia let the insult hang in the air. There was little wonder whom Lady Diana took after.

"You still see *him* every Wednesday if rumor is correct." Lady Benchley curled her lip as she sat on the edge of the brocade chair facing Amelia's desk. "That's today."

Indeed, it was. Amelia quietly exhaled. Every Wednesday, she went to her estranged husband's apartments and spent the evening with him. They'd shared this peculiar ritual for almost five years now. And Amelia relished it. She had an opportunity to pretend she had a husband who cared about her. Though Amelia hated the articles that Martin published, she was still married to the editor and owner of *The Midnight Cryer,* and would be until death parted them. Amelia had always believed in her vows.

And there was a strange part of her that believed in her husband.

After Amelia had left Martin, everyone had forsaken her.

Except *him.* For that reason, he would always have a hold on her heart.

Every two weeks, Martin had traveled across town to her small room at the boardinghouse where she lived. He'd give her money for food, clothing, and lodging. He was always generous, and they learned not to discuss what had happened between the two of them, unlike the couple who sat before her now. Thankfully, four years ago their circumstances had changed. Martin had told her the pamphlet required more of his time and asked if she would consider moving closer to him. She'd done it in a heartbeat. It provided the opportunity to see him every week.

"You're the one who spoiled her and allowed her to have these fits of histrionics," Lord Benchley asserted in the direction of his wife. "Now, I've wasted a fortune."

The viscountess puffed up like a broody hen defending her chicks. "You waste a fortune every night you gamble."

Amelia studied a blank piece of parchment on her desk trying her best to ignore their bickering. Thankfully, she and Martin didn't quarrel. They expressed their anger and frustration with each other in different ways.

Like tearing each other's clothes off and making wild, passionate love as if the world was on fire.

Others might think her weak, and perhaps that was true. Yet she was in love with Martin and always had been. During their first kiss in their brief courtship, Martin's lips against hers had curled her toes. It was the first taste of passion she'd ever received. As their desire for each other ignited, his kisses had become her addiction. He'd shown her nothing but kindness and courtesy. But in the bedroom the hunger he had for her was almost barbaric and all-consuming.

And she suffered the same craving for him. The fact was she still loved sharing her body and herself with him. For those precious hours every Wednesday, he thought of nothing but her. He needed her, and she needed him. It was a way to believe in the façade that she was in the marriage of her dreams—a man completely devoted to her.

She enjoyed the marriage bed particularly with her virulent and handsome husband. He was the only person in the world she truly felt connected to.

If only he wasn't married to his gossip rag as well.

"Are you blaming me for raising her with a horrid disposition?" the viscountess's shrill voice broke in a sharp cry.

"Cordelia, *stop*," the viscount shouted.

As the couple's volume grew, Amelia winced. These two could wake the dead twice over with their tirade. She stood signaling their time was at an end. "I'm sorry but I have another appointment."

With that, the couple thankfully took their leave. As they went down the stairs, Amelia could still hear them arguing. She let out a breath and finally allowed her straightened back to slump. Thankfully, her appointment was at the foundling home around the corner. It was her salvation and oasis from the loneliness of her life.

Except for Wednesdays, when she'd see Martin.

~

After several hectic hours at the foundling home, Amelia managed to purge Lord and Lady Benchley's visit from her thoughts. She tried to dismiss the nervous energy that buzzed through her. Her skin was sensitive to every simple touch, as if jolted alive after being in a long slumber. It always happened on this day, an ordinary weekday. She could only attribute the anticipation to seeing *him*.

No, it was the simple pleasure of stroking him, sharing herself in the most intimate of ways with him. It's how they spent their precious little time together, and she adored it.

When it was time to leave the foundling home, she stood up from her desk and reached for her cloak. Her routine never varied. She cuddled the babies in the afternoons, read stories to little ones, and taught letters and numbers to the older children, who should have been in school but were sequestered in the foundling home because no one wanted them.

Amelia knew exactly how they felt.

She said a quick goodbye to the staff and Mrs. Johnson, then dashed outside. Walking the narrow pathway to the street, she stopped when she caught a glimpse of a man with an air of authority and incredible height. He stared at her from across the way. With a tall beaver hat sitting atop his blond locks and a black greatcoat billowing around his body, he possessed the looks of an archangel ready to relay a message from Heaven itself.

Her eyes widened as the man strode purposely straight towards her. It was the Duke of Southart, her husband's archnemesis.

Well, the duke wouldn't be an enemy if her husband hadn't started threatening to publish articles about the duke's duchess, the former Lady Daphne Hallworth.

"Mrs. Richmond?" the duke asked in a silky-smooth voice. "Might I have a moment of your time? I'm the Duke of Southart."

"I know." She dipped a curtsey, then tilted her head to meet his gaze. Unusual blue eyes met hers. There was no hint of desperation, but the outline of his hardened jaw indicated a steel determination. "How can I help you?"

"Is it that obvious that I need help?" he asked, while motioning her forward with his hand. His voice carried a hint of amusement.

"Most dukes don't wait for me outside the foundling home unless...they want something." She strolled in the direction of home, not minding that the duke had to slow his stride to walk comfortably with her.

"I'm not here as a duke," he said cautiously. "I'm here as a besotted husband desperate to keep my wife healthy and happy."

Amelia slowed her steps. "What's happened?"

Southart tucked an elegant walking stick beneath one arm and slowed to a stop. Both turned to face the other. It made scant difference that little heads were popping up in the windows of the foundling home, wondering what her business was with the tall man.

Let the little scamps speculate. She was pondering the same question.

The duke let out a pained breath. "I've discovered that *The Midnight Cryer* will report a false story about my wife."

Members of the *ton* visited Amelia quite regularly with requests such as these, but never had Southart or any of his family come to see her. They stayed above the fray when it came to her husband stirring trouble.

"Your husband's gossip rag will report that my wife has taken a lover and is carrying his unborn child." The frozen expression on the duke's face would intimidate a lesser man.

Thankfully, Amelia was immune to such looks. "Is it true?"

"Parts of it," the duke answered with one eyebrow perfectly arched. "She has no lover except for me, and she's carrying my child."

"Congratulations," Amelia said with a smile. Oh, she shouldn't be envious of the Southarts' good fortune, but she was only human. There was nothing Amelia wanted more in this world than to have a child of her own. That's why she spent so much time at the foundling home. But after five years of marriage, having a family wasn't her fate.

"Thank you," he said graciously. "But your husband will say my wife's lover is a Mr. Jasper Love from Essex."

"Jasper Love?" she asked incredulously. "I've known him since I was a little girl. He's a wonderful husband and completely devoted to his wife."

"He is," the duke said softly. "But one of your husband's henchmen saw my duchess climb into his carriage. When it began to rock from side to side, I'm afraid that your husband's employees came to the wrong conclusions." He sneered slightly. "Excuse my crassness. But those henchmen returned with a tale that my wife was in the throes of passion with Mr. Lane."

The expression did nothing to dim his appeal. But Amelia had always been attracted to men with darker features like her husband.

It was difficult, but she managed to keep from laughing at the image of a proper duchess entering a commoner's carriage and seeing it rocking from side to side. "What were they doing?"

"Wrestling with puppies." The seriousness in the duke's demeanor cracked, and a slight half-smile tugged at his lips. "She was purchasing two puppies from Mr. Love. He breeds the finest retrievers in all the British Isles. He came to London to meet with my duchess so she could pick out one. It was too difficult to choose, so she took two. They were jumping all around the carriage." He lowered his voice and leaned closer as if sharing a grand secret. "The pups are to be given to my three-year-old heir and me to celebrate our birthday month."

"Puppies," she said longingly as little soft fur bundles frolicked in her thoughts. Amelia's hand flew to her chest. "What a beautiful gift for the two of you."

"Indeed. But that's my wife. She's always generous and amazing." He studied the ground for a moment as if struggling with something. Finally, he lifted his gaze, and the glint in his eyes showed a new hardness. "I'd be obliged if you could keep your husband from printing such lies. I'll not see my wife or family suffer because of such nonsense. Her brother is livid and threatening to take matters into his own hands. It would be so much easier if we could stop the publication. Now, how can I entice you to see that your husband doesn't print such filth?"

She glanced back at the windows of the foundling

home. Still enthralled with the goings-on outside their window, her audience had grown. She faced the duke, and his gaze lowered from his perusal of the foundling home to her. He'd seen where her interests lie.

'I have a favorite charity myself," he said knowingly. 'If you'll help me, I'll give a thousand pounds annual donation to them as long as I'm alive. In your name, of course."

She stilled at the staggering amount of money. With a thousand pounds, the children could easily be clothed and fed for a year, and proper teachers hired. The foundling home was teetering on the brink of insolvency.

'You must understand. He doesn't always listen to me," she confided softly.

'Yet everyone in society knows that you see him weekly, and he welcomes your company." The duke studied the ground then lifted his gaze to hers. 'That's rare for Martin Richmond. You must have some type of power over him."

'You're mistaken."

Southart held up his hand at her look of disbelief. 'All I'm asking is if you'll try."

'I'll give it my best, but there are no promises."

It was another strange ritual for her and her husband. The first time Amelia had asked Martin not to print a story, he'd agreed. It was an olive branch of sorts between them. Since then, he'd hardly ever refused.

But this was the Duke of Southart.

Her husband hated him.

Two

"I HAVE to convince her to come home to me." Martin Richmond wouldn't say the word *need*. He fancied himself as not needing anyone.

"Well, Duke, that shouldn't be a problem. You're a wordsmith." Bowen Green smirked slightly.

Though Bowen was a friend and ran a weekly gossip rag named the *Daily Ton-Tales*, Martin gritted his teeth at the epithet of Duke. He despised the aristocracy and especially dukes. But there were more important things to consider.

"With your talent, you'll convince her," his friend added confidently.

"You don't know my wife," Martin quipped. Amelia would likely refuse his request to move home and play the happy couple, particularly since it was to help *The Midnight Cryer*.

"You're going to have to do something." Bowen said as he looked around the Greedy Vicar, their favorite pub. "Trimble is beside himself at the news. If your *Midnight Cryer* faces a fifty-percent increase in tax, then Trimble's *London-Town Tattler* does too. He writes everything you write."

Martin arched a brow. "Why can't the *London-Town Tattler* come up with their own stories?"

Edgar Graham, Martin's assistant editor and right-hand man, frowned. "Because he's not as clever as you. You write innuendos. He wouldn't recognize one if it bit him in the arse."

Bowen laughed then finished his ale. "I must be getting home to the wife."

"Tell her me and my missus send our best," Graham said. "I'll go look for Mrs. Richmond."

As both men took their leave, Martin sucked in a breath, trying to quell the envy that burned through him. His friends were fortunate. They'd found wives who tolerated what they did for a living.

Martin's wife hated his work. But there was little he could do about it.

He'd always considered himself a word provocateur; perhaps a better phrase was tittle-tattle artiste. It was his nature, and you couldn't change a leopard's spots.

Martin took a sip of brandy for fortitude as he waited for Graham's return. The pub was for the common class, the workers, the ones who kept London's commerce, mercantile, and underbelly alive. His father would have hated the place.

Martin's father respected the nobility and the privileged classes and everything they represented when he was alive. After all, such distinguished company had kept him and his son clothed and fed during their lean years. Unsurprisingly, the politics and mores of such an esteemed group were whole-heartedly embraced by his father.

With such a legacy, Martin had learned early on to despise the whole lot. But he did owe them a debt or two. He'd become wealthy and powerful because of his disdain.

With his cynicism and mistrust, he'd started *The Midnight Cryer*. When Martin's quill touched the paper, magic happened. He laid their privilege bare, stripped them of their cloak of advantages and status, much like a professor who handled a cadaver at one of those prestigious medical schools. The dissection of their weaknesses and frailties was Martin's gift to the masses. People were people no matter their class or positions.

A raucous cheer rang through the Greedy Vicar. He ignored it and traced his thumb around the rim of his glass, learning each groove where a chip or small crack lay.

Mayhap a better description of Martin's chosen profession was a *slayer of reputations*. A moniker he gladly accepted. Though he could speak and write in three languages, he still had trouble with a few words.

Fate and destiny.

And "forgive me."

Circumstance had led him to be standing in the kitchen of the Reynolds' home that lucky day he'd met his wife. After Amelia's parents had died, she'd moved into Mr. and Mrs. Reynolds' house, since she was best friends with their daughter, Elizabeth.

Martin had fallen for Amelia at first sight. She possessed an ethereal beauty that had stolen his breath. But her kindness had undone him. No one had ever treated him as their equal the way she did. Fate had kissed his cheek when they'd said their vows in a lonely church with only two witnesses and the vicar to celebrate their union. But then fate had slapped him with her other hand when his wife, the former Miss Amelia Wyndham, had left him after only a month when he refused to pull an article.

The disappointment in his wife's eyes could only be

attributed to destiny. It was Martin's providence that he'd procured the piece of gossip that Elizabeth's husband had a male lover. If Martin didn't publish it, then someone else would have, and reaped the financial windfall associated with the story. It had set Martin on a path of success and pecuniary security. It was everything he needed to provide a home for his wife, even though she didn't want it.

Or at least, she didn't want it with him.

"Duke, she's arrived." Graham had returned to Martin's side and was crumpling his hat in both hands as if nervous. "Good luck, sir."

"Excellent," Martin murmured sarcastically. "The very people I detest, you compare me to. For the love of God, man, why do you insist upon calling me that?" Martin's anger flared briefly. "It gives the impression that I have aristocratic airs."

Edgar chortled at his employer's annoyance. "It's a term of affection. Everyone goes silent as soon as they see you. Happens all the time." He pointed at the crowd behind him. "Just as it does with those real dukes, if one ever bothered to show their face around these parts." He rocked back on his heels. "That's why you're considered so rare. You stay and work in our areas of London that those other fops wouldn't dare step foot in."

Martin swallowed the rest of his brandy, then stood. Immediately, all the boisterous chatter at the Greedy Vicar halted.

"See what I mean?" Edgar waggled his eyebrows.

Martin ignored the affectionate prodding. Frankly, he was used to such treatment as the owner and editor of *The Midnight Cryer*. It happened at least five times daily. All conversation stopped when others sensed his presence.

When Martin slid a side-eyed glance in a man's direction, they'd squirm in their seats. Ladies and elderly matrons swooned when his attention turned their way. But today, the same sort of fear he invoked in others simmered in his belly. He smiled at the irony of it all. If people felt even a smidgen of the amount of his unease at facing his wife, then Martin had all the empathy in the world for the blighters.

How would his wife react when he made his appeal? With loving arms? Most likely, she'd throw rotten tomatoes at his face. He smoothed his hand down the black brocade waistcoat, then straightened his gray morning coat. Forgoing a greatcoat though the air flirted with winter, Martin exited the pub house and crossed the street to *The Midnight Cryer's* office. Above it was his living quarters. He'd spared no expense in outfitting his apartments. He'd done it in hopes of enticing Amelia to move home.

Alas, it hadn't worked.

Graham followed Martin across the street without speaking a word. When he opened the door, he murmured as if saying a prayer, "She looks exceedingly lovely today. Make certain you compliment her."

Martin lifted a brow at the advice.

Graham shrugged. "It's easier to catch a bee with honey than vinegar."

"Not a bee. A fly. It's easier to catch a fly with honey," Martin corrected, as he walked through the door to the printing room.

"Don't compare your wife to a fly," Graham admonished. "That won't earn you her good graces."

Martin rolled his eyes.

"A bee has a stinger, much like your wife. But they make the sweetest honey," Graham sighed.

Martin ignored the man and his nature lesson. His footsteps echoed down the wooden hallway announcing his presence. So much for surprising her. The printing presses were still. The evening edition had already been printed and distributed. He slowly came to a stop outside the room where she waited and contemplated what he'd say. For the last several lonely years, they hadn't spoken a word aloud about her living across the street from him. They always met here in his offices every Wednesday with polite, distant deference that the Prince Regent and his estranged princess would have admired.

Until they reached his private quarters when all hell would break loose.

As quickly as possible, he twisted the handle then opened the door to his office. For some odd reason, his heartbeat had accelerated. Perhaps the meeting was more monumental than he'd given it credit. After all, it wasn't every day that a man requested that his wife come home.

Amelia Richmond stood with her back to the window, waiting for him. His mouth grew dry at the sight of her brilliant evergreen-velvet walking gown. It didn't subdue the color of her dark red tresses. If anything, it stoked the fire in the gleaming strands. She gracefully turned to face him.

Her eyes never ceased to steal his breath, even though they blazed in defiance. Some would call them brown, but they were either color-blind or fools. The color matched the winter wheat ready for harvest in September. Gold that rivaled the finest regent's jewels in the Tower, surrounded by a ring of rich brandy brown. The cheeks of her heart-shaped face glowed at the sight of him. Her nostrils flared, and in answer, so did his.

He'd always been an optimist, so he considered it a good sign. She was affected as much by him as he was of her. It happened every single time they met.

"Hello, darling." He spoke the simple greeting in the

voice he frequently used when dealing with an informant, the one designed to alleviate any fears.

She continued to stare without answering. When Martin closed the distance between them, he reached to take her hand.

Instead of welcoming his touch, she turned on the ball of her foot, walked out of his office, and preceded up the steps to his living quarters. "I'm starving," she said over her shoulder.

So was he for her.

He blew out a breath. It always happened when he saw Amelia.

His wife was a beautiful, self-sufficient gentlewoman of impeccable manners and breeding. Her exquisite eyes didn't miss any detail. When the urge had slammed into him to take her in his arms and kiss her, he made a strategical error by starting forward. By the flash of her eyes, he'd realized that this wasn't one of their simple weekly meetings.

Uncertain of his next tactical move, he studied the mesmerizing sway of her hips as she preceded up the steps. She turned in profile, the stance reminding him of that fateful day when she'd swept out of their modest home never to return. Immediately, he remembered everything.

He always disappointed her.

Except on Wednesdays.

～

Amelia had fallen in love with Martin the first time she'd laid eyes on him. His black hair gleamed in the early morning sunlight when she'd met him in the kitchen at the Reynolds' home. Martin's sapphire-colored eyes matched the streaks of indigo that highlighted his long hair when the sun's rays graced him. Tall with athletic grace, he'd been whispering with a scullery maid. Once his gaze fell on Amelia, everything else melted into silence.

He'd nodded his acknowledgment at Amelia's entrance but didn't say a word. He'd given a small purse to the maid, who disappeared, leaving them alone. As if pushed by a guardian angel, she'd walked to his side.

In retrospect, it was the last time she would ever believe in anything as silly as angels.

After both of her parents had perished with a fever, Amelia found herself alone and without the finances to afford a Season. Thankfully, her best friend Elizabeth Reynolds had invited Amelia to live with her at her parents' home. There had been no other choice but to accept the generosity of Elizabeth and her family.

Perhaps that was the reason she'd married Martin Richmond after a month of courtship. He'd given her the opportunity to have her own home and family. Of course, it didn't hurt that he'd swept her off her feet. But as the old saying goes, "What goes up, must come down." Amelia finally found her footing after tripping a couple of times along the way. Soon thereafter—four years to be exact—she'd moved across the street from *The Midnight Cryer's* offices.

He stood before her now, more handsome than when they'd married. It didn't take a genius to realize that the years had been kind to him. Her hands tingled with the need to caress his angular cheeks. Her body heated at the vision who stood before her. It was simply sinful, the effect he had on her. Martin Richmond was pure male in the prime of life. His every breath possessed a power that reminded her of a hunter—tight, controlled, and oh so deadly to those who let their guard down.

It was hard to fathom that it had been five long lonely years since she'd left him. It wasn't because he dropped his clothes wherever he took them off. Truthfully, she'd never blushed so much as when she'd picked up his breeches, as it always reminded her what they'd done in bed.

Or in his study.

Or on the desk.

Or on the kitchen table.

Nor did it frustrate her that his right hand was always ink-stained. It didn't even bother her when he'd come home late at night, because she'd known from the onset that news waited for no one. Whoever posted the latest gossip first got the lion's share of pamphlet sales.

Any other woman in her shoes might have made another choice. Within a month of leaving him, Martin had started to accumulate wealth and status. It was everything a woman in Amelia's shoes should covet. But if anything, Amelia was rich in loyalty. When Martin had published the seething article about Elizabeth's husband, Amelia had walked out Martin's door and never returned, except for their ritual Wednesday meetings.

There was no use in reliving the past. Not when she had him in her future, and she could pretend again that she was happily married with a husband who adored her.

She walked into the entry of his expansive and elegant sitting room. The sound of his footsteps following her and the turn of the key in the lock stopped her in her tracks.

All other sounds grew silent. The bustle of the London street below them became non-existent. Even the flames in the fireplace seemed suspended in motion, just like her. But a wave grew, one that would rapidly envelop both her and Martin. Her skin prickled in recognition that soon her every desire would be satiated.

"What are you starving for, darling?" he asked softly.

Without hesitating, she turned. Martin was in the process of disrobing. First, his evening coat hit the floor, then his waistcoat fell next to it. He was panting as he looked at her. Her heart pounded in her chest, encouraging her not to prolong the torture and go to him, but this was her favorite part—watching him disrobe. It was a private performance just for her, and she didn't want to miss a single second of it. As he unbuttoned the falls of his breeches, he stared at her. The fire in his eyes had to match hers.

Without another thought, she closed the distance between them. Her gaze traveled down his shirt. The outline of his thickened cock bulged away from his body as if seeking her.

"You." She licked her lips at the sight of it. "I'm ravenous for you."

"I'm yours for the taking." He held out his arms as if offering her his whole body.

"Take it all off," she demanded softly.

"Your wish...is my—"

She didn't let him finish as she pressed her body against his then took him in a punishing kiss. He laughed softly at her boldness, but it had always been that way between them. They may not agree on their chosen professions or politics, but they were always each other's greatest temptation.

She took advantage of his laughter and swept her tongue between his lips. Immediately, his laughter turned into a moan. As she ravished his mouth, she cupped his cock. He jutted his hips as if offering her everything, and this time, she was the one to groan in return. Yes, she'd take everything he offered tonight and then more.

His arousal wet the fine linen of his shirt. Without taking her mouth from his, she pushed the material away and grasped his member. After a tug or two that elicited a groan, she rubbed her thumb over the crown. She was always amazed that something that hard could feel so silky and hot at the same time. It was velvet-covered steel, silken-iron. How she'd missed it, and if she were at all honest, she'd missed Martin, or at least she missed this intimacy. They could always share each other's bodies. They just couldn't share much in the way of conversation.

"Slow down, darling," he growled into her mouth, as he batted her hand away. "What is the rush?"

She moaned a protest, then took him in another punishing kiss.

With his chest heaving, he pulled away and sucked in a deep breath. "Christ, what has gotten into you?"

She answered by dropping to her knees, cupping his sac. "If I'm down here, you can't interfere."

His eyes closed as he hissed in a breath. Bunching the sides of his shirt in his hands, he whipped it off his head.

The sight stopped her frenzy for a moment so she could admire him. Slowly, she reached up and traced the graceful sculpture of his taut abdomen. Lines of muscle and sinew shivered beneath her touch. No matter how many times she saw him in a state of dishabille, it never ceased to steal her breath. Most would believe him to be a man of leisure, but they'd never seen him when he was trying to get the latest pamphlet printed and on the streets. He'd stand alongside his employees, pick up the twined bundles with his own hands, and load them onto the delivery carts.

He'd do anything to be the first on the street with the latest gossip available to the masses. Even though he wrote nothing but what she considered garbage, he was a hard worker.

Still stroking him, she latched her gaze to his. With each bold touch of hers, she could tell whether she pleased him by the way he breathed and the way his eyes flashed. She fisted his cock in her hand and slowly ran her tongue from the base to the crown. He leaned his head against the door behind him.

With shaking hands, he cupped her head. "You don't have to do this."

In answer, Amelia took the ruddy head of his cock inside her mouth and sucked. She'd do what she wanted, when she wanted, and at that moment, she wanted to suck him dry.

"Amelia," he sighed.

She closed her eyes. A prayer or a benediction never sounded as sweet as the sound of her name passing through his lips. She'd promised herself that she wouldn't allow romantic drivel to steer her away from her course.

And that was bringing Martin Richardson to climax.

So, she sucked harder. His hips jerked forward and backward, mimicking the movement he made when he was inside her about to come. Just thinking about his pleasure caused her own to take flight. Between her thighs, she was achingly wet. The need to rub her fingers against her cleft grew nigh impossible to ignore. But he had to find his release first.

She cupped his sac again and gently juggled as she fisted his cock. All the while sucking. The come that seeped from the head tasted of musk and Martin. She glanced at him and smiled slightly. He was the most delicious thing she'd had all week.

"Amelia," he warned as he gently tried to push her head away.

"No," she murmured. "I want this. And I know you want this."

He heaved a sighed signaling his resignation as his hips increased in their pace. With a guttural cry, he pushed deeper between her lips. The hot, salty come exploded in her mouth, and she moaned in triumph.

Like a cat with a bowl of cream, she swallowed every drop, then licked his entire cock and sucked the head once more, hungry for every single taste. Still semi-hard, he relaxed against the door, and a devilish smile tilted his lips.

Gently, he took her hands and helped her stand. He pulled her into his embrace and kissed the corner of her lips. Then he kissed the other side. At his touch and the brush of his warm breath against her skin, she shivered. As his hands skated across her back, he pulled her closer as if he'd never let her go. Selfish woman that she was, it wasn't close enough. If only she could find a way to crawl inside of him.

Perhaps then she could determine what made his heart beat. Perhaps she'd discover a shriveled prune where the organ should be. It was doubtful, as he was a passionate man—about his writings, his pamphlet, his Wednesdays.

If only he felt that about her.

His tongue swept across her lips begging entrance to her mouth. She moaned slightly, and his tongue slipped through, exploring hers as if it were the first passionate kiss they'd ever shared. It was sweet and gentle, then grew fierce, indicating the ever-present fire that smoldered between them threatened to combust.

He drew away and stared deep into her eyes. A hint of raw emotion crossed his face. For a moment, she considered if it was strong affection, then dismissed the ridiculous idea.

"Wife," he said softly. "After that performance, whatever you want, you can have."

She softly exhaled. He could always ruin a tender moment by speaking.

What she truly wanted, he wouldn't give her.

And that was giving up *The Midnight Cryer*.

Three

"GO TO THE BEDROOM." Martin cupped Amelia's cheeks with his hands and pressed a chaste kiss against her lips. "Do not undress until I get there."

For a moment, she appeared dazed as if awakening from a dream, then her eyes came into focus and narrowed. "You're a bit overbearing today, aren't you?"

"I'll make it worth your time," he said confidently.

As she sauntered out of the room with her hips swaying, he relished the view of her backside.

Amelia Richmond had never been more beautiful in all the years he'd known her. She was the type of woman who grew more exquisite with each day passing. Age was kind to her, and he was the only beneficiary of all that beauty. At least, he hoped he was the sole beneficiary. They never discussed fidelity. But once she moved back in, he'd insist upon it.

He shook his head at such a thought while buttoning his falls. He didn't look forward to that conversation. He made his way to the small kitchen, not bothering to pick up his clothes. His housekeeper was the wife of one of his employees. She would tidy up the place. She cleaned and cooked for him while he was busy working, so his apartment was always perfect when he arrived home, no matter how late.

Specifically, it was perfect in appearance. Sometimes, the loneliness became unbearable. On those nights, Martin would go to his bedroom, the one across the street from Amelia's rooms and stare out the window, hoping that she'd be looking for him at the same time he was looking for her. But it never occurred.

He picked up a black lacquered tray filled with succulent chicken, grapes, fresh bread and cheese, a bottle of fine French wine, glasses, and several raspberry tarts, which were Amelia's favorites.

When he entered his bedroom, Amelia looked up from her study of the floor. Her swollen lips and rosy cheeks almost brought him to his knees. He placed the tray on the side table next to the bed. Without his eyes leaving hers, his boots landed with a thud, followed by his stockings. With his gaze never leaving hers, Martin pulled a chair to the end of the bed and sat down, spreading his legs wide as if the king of all he surveyed. His cock was already thickening.

"Undress slowly," he commanded softly.

A genuine smile tugged on her lips. "There's no need. We must talk, then I'll be on my way."

The words slashed a piece of the organ in his chest, causing it to stumble. "That's not fair to either of us. You played with my cock, and now I'll play with your quim. Undress."

Slowly she stood, then unbuttoned her velvet gown. Her eyes didn't leave his as it dropped to the ground.

Her body was perfection. Her ripe breasts begged for attention as they threatened to burst free from the imprisonment of her front-tying stays. Never fear, he'd rescue them.

His cock jerked at the thought.

The dark rose of her nipples peeked over the satin boning, a wicked invitation for him to sample all her sweetness.

Clever wife. She knew how much he loved the unveiling of her feminine beauty. Tomorrow he would order her the most delicate lingerie in all of England, a set for every day.

"Now, your stays and chemise. Leave your stockings on. I want to see what color of pretty ribbons you chose to entice me."

She did as he asked. Standing nearly naked, she licked her lips as her gaze landed on his hands when he unbuttoned his falls. His thickened cock sprang free, the randy fellow ready for another round with her. He gave it a tug for good measure.

"Lie on the bed and spread your legs."

"Martin." The warning in her voice was unmistakable. "What game are you playing?"

"One that you'll enjoy, I promise."

A grin tugged at her mouth, and his heartbeat stuttered in his chest at the sight. She laid herself across the bed much like a bountiful feast that was all for him. Without him saying a word, she spread her legs until he could see the pink petals of her center. They glistened with her arousal, and he licked his lips, anxious to taste her.

"Touch yourself, but don't make yourself come."

"Martin," she said in mock outrage.

"Did I forget to say 'please' again?" he teased.

She ran her fingers through the light brownish-red curls that framed her center. "The same goes for you." She slowed her movements as her fingers reached her sensitive pearl. "Watch me," she said softly.

He gripped his cock tighter as her finger circled over and over. Her breathless moans made him groan in answer.

With her beautiful golden eyes flashing, she lifted a finger coated in her essence and brought it to her mouth. She painted her lips with that finger.

He practically came out of the chair at the sight. Amelia was a hellcat, determined to seduce him again. And he was the richer for it.

Without saying "please" or "thank you" or "I want to fuck you," he stood abruptly and shucked his breeches. Like a lion claiming his mate, he leaped on the bed and covered her body with his, then he kissed her mouth, his tongue swirling around hers. Desire coursed through his veins at the taste of her arousal. It wasn't enough.

He rested his weight on his elbows and stared down at her. Both of their chests rose and fell in a tumultuous rhythm as if they'd raced up a mountain.

"You're such a naughty woman to tease me like that."

She stroked his cock in answer, and he hissed. Grabbing her hands, he entwined their fingers and placed them above her head. She moaned low in her throat. She loved it when he did that.

He tongued one of her nipples, and she arched her back wanting more. He ground his erection against her mound as he sucked the rosy peak into his mouth.

"Please, Martin," she whimpered.

"Hush. I'll take care of you," he soothed. With care, he gave the same amount of attention to the other perfectly shaped mound. It was heaven.

No, she was heaven.

When she canted her hips against his cock, he released her hands. He slowly kissed his way down her body, leaving no inch of skin untouched. When he came to her center, he inhaled deeply, her scent marking him. Unable to tease her anymore, he ran his tongue in between the soft petals. She mewled in pleasure, and he couldn't help but smile.

His wife had always been responsive to his touch. Once she agreed to move back in with him, they could do this every night.

'I ache...for...' she said softly.

'I know, darling,' he answered, then he licked her again before turning his attention to her precious pearl. With a swirl of his tongue, he could feel how swollen it was. She was on the verge of her climax, if the way she was bucking against his mouth was any indication. Her fingers slid into his hair, holding him in position. He sucked the nub carefully as he pushed two fingers into her center.

He loved that she'd always been a woman who knew what she wanted. He sucked again, and it was enough to take her over the edge. She bucked wildly against his mouth as her internal muscles squeezed his fingers, almost as if milking him. She cried out his name.

At the sound of her voice, he pulled out his fingers, then entered her. Her legs encircled his waist as he ground his hips against hers. He would retreat, then slowly enter her again. Her nails raked against his back as she softly said his name, repeatedly.

The sound of it was like an aphrodisiac. He couldn't get enough of her as desire hummed through every inch of his body. As his bollocks tightened, his hips became pistons. In and out. In and out. Again and again. Sensation, much like lightning, lit up every part of him—from his spine to his head until it settled in his cock. He closed his eyes when he climaxed, filling her with his seed. An image of her was seared upon his eyelids. And one truth stole his breath.

He'd never satisfy this hunger for her.

When he regained his senses, he forced his gaze to hers. Amelia smiled slightly but didn't stop running her fingers through his hair.

"I think we should talk," she said quietly.

He grunted, pressed a swift kiss to her cheek, then reluctantly pulled away. He stood and, for the oddest moment, felt a slight shift in balance as if his world tilted.

What nonsense.

Grabbing a fresh piece of linen, he dunked it in the basin of water that stood on a table nearby, then came back to her side and sat on the edge of the bed. Without a word, he gently cleaned her. Thankfully, she didn't protest when he took care of her. For some unexplainable reason, he found immense pleasure in such a simple task. For tonight, they could pretend that the last five years hadn't happened, and they were still a happily married couple.

However, that might be too much pretending for both of them.

He stood and returned the linen to the basin, where he rinsed the linen out and cleaned himself.

Amelia had sat up in bed and prepared a plate of food. Two glasses of wine sat on the tray. She patted the edge of the bed closest to her. "Come."

It was a one-word command, and he didn't hesitate. But he didn't sit next to Amelia. He pulled the chair he'd sat in earlier to her side of the bed.

"Amelia, this is difficult." He leaned backed in the chair and regarded her. "I can't do this anymore. The cost is too high."

~

Amelia sucked in a silent breath. Carefully, she placed her glass of wine on the table, then regarded him with a face she'd hoped didn't betray her shock. "Pardon me?"

Martin leaned forward, resting his elbows on his parted thighs and clasped his hands while studying her. Somehow, she'd missed him donning his breeches once again. For one absurd moment, she felt at a disadvantage as she was still naked. His posture emphasized his broad shoulders and well-defined legs.

"We can't continue like this," he said gently.

Indeed, they couldn't. Martin's body still mesmerized her. She was afraid that her ability to hold a conversation had flown out the window the same as her self-control. She'd demonstrated that when they'd entered his apartments. But she strongly suspected that wasn't what he meant. Her traitorous eyes swept down the length of his long thighs. She swallowed her unease, which had risen like a murmur of starlings. She'd shouldn't allow his huge body or his statement, which he'd thrown out much like a gauntlet, unsettle her so.

In defiance, she tilted her chin in the air. "Our arrangement doesn't please you anymore? I admit it's unusual. But not difficult." She waved a hand between the two of them. "No more difficult as it is for me to be sitting here naked while you're partially dressed."

He chuckled under his breath. "My word, you're in a mood." His gaze swept across the room. "There's a bottle of whisky here somewhere."

"Wine suits me. Just say what you have to say. Then you and I can depart and hopefully salvage the rest of this miserable day." For a moment, she wanted to withdraw the words. It wasn't a miserable day. It was her favorite day. She sounded defensive and bitter. This wasn't her, but she dreaded what would come next. He'd tell her that he had found someone else. Someone prettier, younger, nicer. She closed her eyes to tame the tears that threatened.

"Amelia." The whisper of her name sounded like a plea of some sort. "Don't make this any harder for me than it already is."

Prickles of unease raced across her arms. In a hopeless effort to protect herself from any more of his trickery, she huffed a breath. "I'm listening. Just tell me."

He leaned forward and placed a hand over hers. "I *need* you to come home."

For an eternity, she sat there speechless. Thoughts and reasons whirled in her mind like leaves whipped in a frenzy by the North Wind's fury. Never in her wildest dreams did she ever think she'd hear those words from him.

Finally, he squeezed her fingers, stealing her away from her thoughts.

"I've shocked you," he said.

She blinked again, as if trying to awaken from a dream or, God forbid, a nightmare. "Shocked me," she repeated. "Yes, you have. I thought you were going to say you had a lover and wanted me to leave England."

"What kind of a man do you think I am?" His cheeks reddened with aggravation. He ran a hand through his hair, setting the black locks akimbo. "Don't answer that." He slid her a side-eyed glance, then stood and paced the room like a caged animal. "I'd never ask something that insulting of you. We're married, for God's sake. Is it so outrageous that I want you home?"

"I don't know. You've not asked me before." Amelia had never seen him in such an uproar. Usually, her estranged husband was everything polite, courteous, and charming, especially when he wanted something. But now, he looked like the world was splitting in two before their very eyes. "We've been living in separate residences for years. Why are you asking me to come home now? Are you ill?"

"No, I'm not ill. But I might be." He exhaled and studied the ceiling as if searching for the answers in the paint. "Tomorrow, a new law will be introduced in the House of Lords. They're targeting *The Midnight Cryer* with a fifty percent tax increase. Instead of the pamphlet costing seven pence, I'll have to charge ten pence just to break even. I can't afford it. Neither can the coffee houses or the tea shops, who are some of my biggest customers. Even my wealthier readers won't be able to afford this. Which means..." He bent his head and stared at the uneven grooves between the wooden slates. "I can no longer afford to support you in a separate residence."

The evening had turned into night. Moonlight streamed through the lone window in the room as if trying to reach Martin. The soft blue rays caressed his midnight black hair. She'd never been jealous of the moon until tonight. It would be so easy to say yes. But then she'd be in the same position she was before she left him.

Without any distance from Martin, she'd be trapped in *The Midnight Cryer's* web once again.

"You don't have to support me anymore." Though her voice had softened, her words rang clear. "I've saved enough for a rainy day. I'll cut back my hours at the foundling home and find work." Then she remembered the one-thousand-pound donation the Duke of Southart offered. With that, she could seek employment at the foundling home as a teacher or perhaps assistant headmistress. She had volunteered there for years. The experience gave her knowledge about the institution that no new employee would possess. "In fact, a new opportunity presented itself today. It's one I would need your help with."

He narrowed his eyes. "Ah, I see now why you were so amorous when you saw me today."

"Stop it," she hissed softly. "This could help you save money."

"Lucky me." He lifted his gaze to hers, and the knowing smile on his face stole her breath for a moment. "Tell me what you want."

"Do not run the story about the Duchess of Southart having a liaison with Mr. Jasper Love."

"Did this Jasper Love come to see you?" A slight growl escaped as he lifted an arrogant brow.

A ripple of something, perhaps a thrill, shot through her veins. Could her husband be a tad jealous?

"No," she said calmly. "However, I know Jasper. He's a kind man and wouldn't hurt a soul."

His shoulders relaxed. "The duchess?"

She shook her head.

He sat on the edge of his seat. "If the duchess didn't come to you, then who did?"

"The duke."

He leaned back in his chair with a nonchalance that might convince others that he'd agree, but she could tell by the set of his jaw that he wouldn't grant her request.

"Martin..." His face melted into a smug look that didn't bode well for her plans. What in the devil game was he playing? "What is it?"

"It's too late. The pamphlet was published this afternoon after I'd teased my readership about it yesterday. I expect to make a tidy profit off it."

Anger hotter than a farrier's fire blazed through her,

leaving nothing but charred remains of her idea in its wake. She clenched her teeth so hard that her jaw ached.

Yet, she dared not move. Otherwise, she was afraid she was about to commit murder.

And the victim would be her husband.

Estranged husband, that is.

Four

AT THE UNBRIDLED glistening in Amelia's eyes, Martin jerked back in his chair. "You're angry with me? I should be the one angry with you. You know how much I loathe Southart."

She flung the covers off her body and stood.

When he saw that she was about to dress, he stood and retrieved his banyan. "Wait. Put this on."

Hesitating for a second, she donned it. As if she'd done it a thousand times, she rolled up the sleeves. It pleased him immensely that she wore something of his. He could easily become accustomed to such a sight every day. It would take so little to untie it, then slip his hands inside and cup her magnificent breasts. He shook his head slightly. This wasn't like him. He had a job to do, and only afterward would he think of pleasure.

Such was the power of Amelia.

She settled back on the bed and regarded him. "Why would you train your sights on the duchess? Because she's Southart's wife?"

"It could be my own mother...if she's a hypocrite, I'm going to expose her," he said defensively. Martin didn't care for the look of censure on his wife's face. "His duchess was seen getting into a carriage with another man."

"She was acquiring puppies," Amelia said, clearly exasperated.

"A five-year-old could come up with a better excuse." He lifted an eyebrow in challenge. "You know why I detest the man." He practically spit his displeasure. "I blame Southart for the fire that nearly closed me down."

"One of your employees caused that fire by knocking over a lamp."

"Semantics," he replied. "Southart was there breaking into my offices. He had Lord William Cavensham help him escape. Both reeked of their sacrosanct privilege that night. If it had been any other man breaking into my shop, they'd have been sent to twiddle their thumbs in Newgate with their only company the resident fleas, lice, and bedbugs."

"You are so coarse," Amelia replied rolling her eyes. "That may have been the case with the duke before he married, but not now." In an act of placation, she leaned forward and smiled. "If you could have seen the look on his face. He loves her, and by his expression, he is worried. Like he had the entire world resting on his shoulders."

"Hmm," he said noncommittedly. "I suppose marriage does put the weight of the world on a man."

Her eyes widened. "Did it do that to you when you married me?"

"What do you think?" Immediately, he regretted his tone when she increased the distance between them. "It's not right that you live across the street when you're married to me."

A look of contriteness fell across her face. "How

sweet, but you know why I choose to live apart. I can't condone the stories you write. You hurt people. Good people."

"Explain the concept of 'good.'" When her lips pursed in exasperation, he continued, "The people I write about deserve it. They're the privileged, aristocratic snobs who believe that through their inbreeding, they've become intellectually superior to the rest of us plebeians. They actually think they're the only ones who have the divine right to decide what is in our best interests."

He shook his head so vehemently it was a wonder it didn't fly across the room.

"It takes two types of people to make the *Cryer* a success." He held up his forefinger. "A person like me who is willing to ferret out the truth about the aristocracy, particularly the stories that they don't want to be exposed." He lifted a second finger and arched an eyebrow. "The other is the reader, who shares the stories with others. We're all willing participants in this dance. Besides, three-quarters of the aristocracy have the pamphlets delivered every day. Do not lay the entire blame at my feet." His chest rose and fell with his justified ire.

"I know men have hurt you in the past when you were at Eton." She smoothed a hand across the coverlet, eliminating all the wrinkles.

Perhaps she thought she could do the same with him—eliminate all his flaws. He clenched one hand into a fist, desperate to forget the agony of his younger years. But he never forgot when he was the subject of ridicule because of his secondhand clothes and lack of funds to purchase expensive texts. Nor did he forget the snub of not being recognized and rewarded for earning the highest marks of his class. It was also a judgment about his father, a loyal tutor for the institution. Martin had miraculously attained the highest marks in all the major subjects. His father had shared the happy news with him. It was the proudest moment of his life as it meant he'd have a scholarship to study at Oxford.

But the Don never called him to his office to receive his due. Instead, they'd given the honor to a young aristocratic man whose father gambled heavily.

Every time he thought back to those times, it left a bitter taste in his mouth. He'd made it his life's mission to point out every conceivable weakness the aristocracy had. If the stories he printed stretched the truth, his readers didn't care. They embraced it.

"But I'm afraid you've gone too far this time, Husband." She sighed.

His pulse accelerated every time she referred to him as her husband. *Perhaps the weakened matrimonial bonds aren't as frayed as he once thought.*

"I never go too far." He smiled. "Back to the original subject. Please move home. See, I used the word please." He waggled his eyebrows. "All we have to do is appear in public as a reunited happy couple. I'll not lie to you. Besides money, there is another reason I want you to return to me."

She blinked slowly. "You must be joking."

"No darling, I'm not. I never joke about the *Cryer*. The sponsor of the new law is Lord Pembroke, the Duke of Southart's brother by marriage." When she stiffened, he held up his hand. "Please, don't make any judgments"—his gaze locked with hers— "at least until you hear me out."

She nodded once, signaling for him to continue.

"I have an informant inside the House of Lords..."

"Naturally," she murmured.

He gave her his best wicked smile. "Part of the language of the bill is that I'm a philander, libertine, a scandalmonger...and other choice descriptions. I won't bore you. But basically, it will say that I'm immoral, as can be attested to by my marriage state. Meaning...that you left me." He widened his stance and dropped his hands between his thighs. "If you don't come home, all will be lost."

She worried her bottom lip with her teeth.

Desire hummed in his veins at her gesture. Was it a mere hour ago that he'd nibbled those same lips demanding, then begging for more of her kisses, more of her passion, and more of her? It felt like years since he'd held her supple body close to his while making love to her.

He cleared his throat in a mad attempt to keep his sanity. Perhaps it was beyond foolish to convince Amelia to come home. What did he have to offer her except the floor above *The Midnight Cryer* offices? Granted, they were richly appointed in terms of design and comfort; the printing press below could awaken the dead, particularly when a late edition had to hit the streets. How would his fair wife tolerate such noise and commerce in the early hours of the morning, with the boys crying out that the latest scandal was available for reading? Yet, it was his livelihood. He needed her to come home to hopefully stop Pembrooke's law from passing. Otherwise, his ruination would be guaranteed.

He'd never considered himself a man who knew desperation, but tonight proved him wrong.

"Amelia, I'm a proud man. I'll give you anything if you'll just say yes." He cleared his throat and did the unthinkable. He lowered himself to his knees and took her hand in his. Slowly, he brought it to his lips. "I'm begging you. Please come home."

Amelia's free hand flew to her chest. Martin Richmond had never fallen to his knees for anyone, including her, even when he proposed they marry. Real trepidation had turned his ruddy cheeks pale.

If she agreed to do as he asked, she'd be surrendering the remaining scraps of her reputation. Truthfully, those scraps hadn't helped her much over the last several years. Her visitors weren't contributing much to the foundling home if it was facing insolvency. If she moved in with Martin, it could mean an entire new life for her. She could work at the foundling home and help the Duke and Duchess of Southart.

She made the only decision she could in this bizarre situation.

"On one condition." She squeezed his hand in reassurance.

"Name it," he said softly.

The relief in his eyes made her even more determined to set things right with the Duke of Southart. What she planned to do would be good for Martin also. Sometimes, you had to take a bitter medicine before you could start feeling better. "I'd like to write an article or two for the paper."

His face lit up in a smile, and he clasped her hand. "Anything you want. A column on housekeeping, the foundling home, decorating. For the first time in the history of the *Cryer*, we'll have a feminine perspective. We'll double our readership, I wager."

"I was thinking more along the lines of the articles that you write."

He sat back on his heels, his earlier euphoria melting into a scowl. "You want to write gossip? I thought you hated it."

"I do hate it." She nodded, not tearing her gaze from his. "Maybe I'll write about the people who work at the foundling home. They're good, honest, and kind. They're inspiring examples of mankind. I'd like to share their stories and how they see the world differently."

"Honoring the common man?"

"Something along those lines," she said.

"Yes. Of course. Excellent idea, darling."

"I need your promise that they won't be edited or changed." She smiled sweetly.

"I agree. However, good editing can do wonders for a sensational piece." He waggled his eyebrows. "Shall we move you in tonight? Several of the lads are waiting for another batch of the papers to distribute. They can fetch your things for you while Graham bundles the sheets." He stood and pressed his lips against hers, then whispered, "I'm pleased you're returning home."

"I hope I won't interrupt your routine." She laced her arms around his neck and pulled him to her until she lay beneath him. With one hand, she played with his silky black locks. With the other hand, she traced the supple outline of his lips.

"You won't." Resting his weight on his elbows, he stared down into her eyes. "There's one more request."

"Hmm," she said non-committedly.

"I demand fidelity," he said softly.

An undeniable hint of vulnerability and hurt flashed in his face. She stroked his hair again in comfort. "I've never been unfaithful." She'd heard rumors about him with other women, and she'd never asked outright. She hadn't the heart to know the truth, but now it seemed paramount. "Have you?"

"I've never," he said softly. "I'm married to you."

A new peace descended between them. They were quiet for a moment.

"You know there is another solution to this tax business." What she would say next would darken the mood faster than a cloud covering the summer sun. Yet, it had to be said.

He kissed her again, then nipped at her lower lip. "You have the most fuckable mouth, and you know how to use it."

"Is that a compliment?" She laughed huskily. "Did you hear what I said earlier?" Now, he was trailing his lips down her neck, using his teeth to take quick nips along the way. It felt divine, and she arched her neck and back like a kitten awakening from a nap.

"Yes, it's a compliment. And yes, I heard what you said earlier." He trailed his lips up her neck again, then tongued the shell of her ear. "But I have more important things to do right now, such as exploring this freckle on the side of your neck." He sucked gently.

"You'll leave a mark," she said distractedly. His kisses should be outlawed.

"What's the other solution?" he asked softly.

"Ahh, you were listening."

"I hear every word you say." He pulled back, and his gaze searched hers. He smiled and pressed a kiss on the tip of her nose.

Good heavens, he was distracting with that mouth of his. She cleared her throat, hoping it would help clear her muddled mind. "You could write a retraction," she murmured.

He broke away from her with such speed that she thought she'd scalded him with her words.

"Are you daft?" He stared down at her with his arms crossed. His nostrils flared much like a bull before it charged. "If I write that, then everyone will be knocking on my door demanding one. It'd be akin to sending every member of the *ton* an engraved invitation to call on me, so I'll apologize in print."

She sat up in bed and crossed her arms the same as

his. "If you apologize promptly, then perhaps Lord Pembrooke would see that you are sorry and not introduce his legislation. You'd save yourself from being taxed."

"That's pure fantasy." His gaze shot to her breasts, and his eyes narrowed. "I know what I'm about even if you're offering up a proverbial feast on a platter. You'll not distract me with your tits or convince me otherwise," he said matter-of-factly.

"You are so crude," she answered.

"Just stating the obvious," he replied.

"And I remember why I left you in the first place."

The words stood suspended in the air between them. Amelia glanced down at the coverlet, desperate to keep her emotions in control. It was difficult as all those old hurts came to the surface. All those nights when they argued and fought over what he was writing. Why had she agreed to move in and subject herself to it all again?

Then she remembered. One thousand pounds a year.

And not to be alone.

"Forgive me," he said softly. "You're a lady, and I *was* trying to shock you to put you on your defensive. I shan't do it again."

"Why, Martin Richmond," she said, surprised by the admission. "I've never heard you apologize before."

"I know when I'm wrong," he said. "Fortunately for me, such an occasion is as rare as a solar eclipse."

"I see you haven't lost your modesty," she teased.

"Indeed." He slipped his linen shirt over his head and started to tuck it into his breeches.

"Where are you going?" she asked.

"I'm going to direct the lads to bring your things over, then I have another column to write." He slipped into his black evening coat. The cut and fit of the garment fit him perfectly. It was simply sinful how handsome he was. "And it won't be a retraction about Southart. I'll not apologize for that. What I reported is correct. My man saw the duchess enter Love's carriage. I simply asked the readers if they thought the duchess had been enjoying another man's company. Someone other than her husband. Readers are smart. They draw their own conclusions." He motioned to the tray of food and wine. "Eat. I don't know when I'll be back."

Without a goodbye, he swung open the door then closed it. His footsteps grew fainter by the second. Even after all these years, his bravado hadn't diminished. Amelia still found it as thrilling and confounding as when she first met him.

She rested against the silk brocade headboard and closed her eyes for a moment, thinking of all the things her husband had said this evening.

Why were apologies so hard for him? Was it hard for all men or just her husband? Perhaps she needed to write an article about why men should apologize, including a section on why words were important.

Then the perfect solution presented itself to her. She opened the drawer of the nightstand where Martin always kept paper and a sharpened pencil.

Like any good wife, it was her duty to help her husband.

Even if it meant finding a way for him to apologize without having to do it himself.

Five

IT WAS close to midnight when Martin walked into his apartment and stood still for a moment. His wife, his Amelia, slept in his bed. The place possessed a different energy, if you will, because she was here. That had to explain the unrelenting desire that seemed to dog him with every step since he'd left her.

It made tomorrow's edition preparation a little complicated. Martin could not have cared less if the Earl of Tremayne and the Marquess of Rydervale were about to come to blows over a woman. Typical ridiculous conduct of people with too much privilege, money, and wasteful time at their leisure.

If one of the laggards had challenged the other to a duel, that might have brought some much-needed excitement to the story. Since they were like two alley cats hissing over territory but terrified to approach the other, Martin had to season the story in his usual manner.

He simply put another man into it. Only this time, he had the woman in question leaving with an identified peer in a black carriage with four perfectly matched grays.

Such a nonsensical description fit practically every lord in the British Isles. They all possessed black carriages and matching grays. He sighed. Already Amelia was having an impact on his writing.

Perhaps if he fucked her a few more times, he could return to his usual routine.

He cringed at using such a vulgar word. Damnation, she was his wife, not some pleasure transaction.

Without further delay, he made his way to the bedroom. Silently, he slid open the door. Amelia lay in the bed with the covers drawn to her chest. His heartbeat accelerated at the sight that she still wore his banyan. The moonlight fell across the bed surrounding her body almost as if embracing every inch of her. Her red locks curled around her head like a halo of fire, and his fingers itched to luxuriate in the softness once again.

Oh, but he was a besotted fool.

It foretold trouble ahead. If Martin allowed himself to believe that Amelia was here for anything other than a "mutual convenience," he'd be crushed when she left again.

And he did not doubt that she'd leave him again in the future. He couldn't stop writing his stories. But she was here now, and he wasn't going to waste this precious time with her.

It had to be close to midnight, and he would soon have to go out again. But for an hour or so, he'd hold her. Quickly, he undressed, then slipped under the covers beside her.

The moonlight drifted away, chased by a cloud or two. So, Martin took the moon's place and enveloped his wife in his arms.

Amelia stirred. then turned to face him. "Hello," she said huskily as her hands trailed down his chest.

"Imagine meeting you here. My name is Mrs. Richmond. And who might you be?"

The seductive huskiness in her voice caused him to harden instantly. There was nothing to compare to a sleepy but playful Amelia. "I'm the man who's going to make love to you."

He pressed a kiss to her lips, and she moaned in encouragement.

"I don't think I've ever had someone make love to me. My husband only wants to...fuck me." She cupped his erection in her hand.

He hissed in a breath. Amelia's hands were like magic with her tugs and pulls. His cock was already leaking. "Your husband is a fool."

"But he's a handsome one."

As she kissed him, he unfastened the banyan and slipped his hand under the folds finding warm, soft skin that begged for his attention. Her lips sought his, and when her tongue begged for entry, he opened for her. He cupped her breast and squeezed. She sucked in a breath at his touch.

"Too much?" he asked.

"Not enough," she replied against his lips. "Touch me lower."

"Saucy wench." He laughed softly. "Mrs. Richmond, those are my favorite types."

He skated his hand down her chest and across her belly until he met her curls. He slipped a finger between her folds. For a moment, he couldn't move. She was drenched.

With a moan, she bucked her hips to meet him. Her heat enveloped his hand as he slid a finger across her clitoris.

"I *need* you," she said softly.

And he didn't *need* any encouragement.

She pulled him on top of her, and he braced his weight on his arms not to crush her. Instantly, her hips pressed against his, and her legs encircled him. Without fanfare, he entered her.

"Yes," she hissed. "I'm close."

"You're close to coming?" He pulled away until only an inch of his cock remained inside her, then pushed even further inside until he was completely seated. He stared down at her, marveling at her beauty. Her eyes glittered from the fireplace's soft glow. It reminded him of her—warmth, fire, passion, and endless heat.

"I've been thinking about you all night."

"Touching yourself?" he said as he pulled out then pushed back in. With the movement, Amelia groaned.

"Yes," she said without hesitation.

The image of her with her hand between her thigh, stroking her fingers against her slick skin, made his mind nearly explode along with his cock. "Did you have your hand on your tit?"

"Yes."

"You're trying to kill me," he whispered, stroking in and out of her. He slipped his hand between their bodies and caressed her nub. She whimpered, and the soft sound sent waves through him.

Suddenly, the bells rang midnight, and he stroked harder and harder.

"Come with me," she pleaded.

"I'm there," he reassured her as his climax hit with the force of a rogue wave. His seed filled her, and she cried out as she reached her pleasure.

Consumed by their lovemaking, Martin collapsed beside her. The euphoria overwhelmed him, and he tucked her close to his body. Her mouth met his in a sweet kiss that laid him bare before her. Never had he felt such contentment and peace.

"I like making love," Amelia whispered against his lips.

"I think I like it too." Martin ran his lips over her soft hair and pulled her closer. By then, the midnight bells had quieted. "Have I ever told you how *The Midnight Cryer* name came about?"

He tilted his head and looked down on her, and his heart stopped for a moment. It was the most breathtaking scene he'd ever witnessed in his life.

His wife was sound asleep. Her hand rested against the middle of his chest as if claiming every beat as her own. He wanted nothing more than to stay there with her warm body curled around his, but gossip had to be collected because it never, ever waited for morning.

The following day, Martin swept into his offices at half-past nine. He looked longingly toward the stairs to his apartments. He'd give his right hand for a bath and a shave, but there was a scandal rag to print. The salacious tidbit he picked up last night would not keep. They never did. Everyone loved to hear when a peer too deep in his cups wagers an estate and loses. Of course, it wasn't an entailed property of Lord Peters, but this estate just happened to house his estranged wife—which meant she would have to move in with Lord Peters and his mistress.

Oh, what a tangled web his lordship wove last night, and Martin had a front-row view of the carnage.

Martin held up the article he'd written and waved it toward Graham. "Let's get this set up to print."

Graham scowled slightly. "Is it a special edition? Is the Prince Regent divorcing Princess Caroline?"

"What the devil are you talking about?" He threw

the piece of parchment on the man's desk. "This is for the morning edition of *The Cryer*."

"What the devil are *you* talking about?" Graham perched his glasses on his nose and peered at the paper. "The morning edition went out hours ago, Duke." He reclined in his seat. "Best writing you've ever done. Heartfelt and succinct. Bravo, man."

"I didn't write a column." Martin shook his head to cast away the remnants of his tiredness from staying up all night. He didn't remember composing a single word. But he did remember that his wife slept in his bed while he watched Lord Peters create a mess for himself.

"Did someone hit you on your head?" Graham narrowed his eyes. "Have you lost your memory? Your wife gave it to me this morning and said you wanted the edition out first thing." He chuckled slightly. "I never thought I'd see the day you apologize. But you made it sound like pure poetry."

"She told you about the apology?" It wasn't like his wife to share the intimate details of their marriage or their conversations with anyone. If Amelia heard a piece of gossip, it stopped with her, as she never shared anything, much to Martin's chagrin.

Graham nodded. "She didn't have to. I read it." He pulled out a fresh copy of *The Midnight Cryer* and held it out for Martin to take. "Pure genius. Charming. Jovial even. Didn't know you had it in you."

No edition left the office unless Martin proofread it first. Something was wrong.

Very wrong.

A deep sense of foreboding churned in his stomach. With a surprisingly steady hand, he took the paper and lowered his eyes to the headline.

The Midnight Cryer prides itself on the accuracy

of its content.

Yet, its editor is only human, a humble man who knows when to print a retraction.

Our Utmost Apologies to Her Grace, the Duchess of Southart.

Dear readers, there were no carriage trysts or shenanigans involved here, only adorable puppies for the Duke of Southart and his heir.

May the duke and his son have the merriest of celebrations in honor of their birthdays.

The Midnight Cryer

"Who wrote this?" Martin knew but wanted confirmation before he went and strangled his wife's beautiful neck.

"You did," Graham offered. He pulled out another piece of parchment and handed it to Martin. "Here's the original. Your wife said you were anxious to get it out on the streets early this morning. She said you wrote it last night." He laughed again. "We've sold more papers than the Duke of Southart scandal from years ago. I've printed off more."

Martin studied the penmanship, then ground his teeth together. It looked like his writing except for the S's. They were much too frilly. The urge to crumple the paper in his hand and sling it across the room became overpowering. How could she do this to him?

"Do not sell any more copies." The words were remarkably calm, even if his blood was practically boiling in anger.

"Why not?" Graham asked, scratching his head.

"I didn't write it," he seethed. "Is my wife upstairs?"

Graham shook his head. "No, Duke. She went to her old residence. Said she needed to be available if there were any callers. Then she's going to the foundling home." He studied Martin's face for a moment, then lowered his voice. "You don't look well. You should go to the Greedy Vicar and get something to eat and drink."

"Thank you for the kind advice," Martin said sarcastically. "From now on, you're only to print what I personally place in your hands. Understood?" Without waiting for an answer, he turned on his heel and walked out the door. Before he confronted her, he would find a stiff drink. It would allow him the opportunity to plot his revenge.

He crossed the street without regard to the traffic. It wouldn't have made any difference if there was a carriage or not. With his fury fueling his thoughts, nothing would stop him. He turned at the street corner, then made his way into the Greedy Vicar. When a serving girl saw him and his dark mood, she scampered out of his way.

He slid into his usual seat at the old wooden table centered in front of the tavern's bay windows. In seconds, the owner was before him and set down a cup. "Usual?"

Martin nodded, inhaling the dark aroma of the coffee. "Add a whisky to it."

"Richmond," a voice called from behind him.

Martin turned to discover a few of his fellow gossip writers. They all congregated at the Greedy Vicar in the morning for breakfast while rehashing the news of the evening.

He wanted to bury his head in his hands when his gaze landed on John Trimble, the owner of the *London-Town Tattler*, the largest competitor to *The Midnight Cryer*.

"What in the devil has gotten into you, Richmond?" Bowen Green, one of his friends, called out. "A retraction?"

"Never thought I'd see the day," another announced as he slapped the paper on his table. "*Our Utmost Humble Apologies*?" he chortled. "What does the Duke of Southart have hanging over you to write something so insipid?"

The owner brought a plate of boiled eggs, crispy bacon, and toasted bread. He placed the whisky next to Martin's plate. Ignoring the others, Martin offered his thanks, then proceeded to eat.

A shadow crossed his plate, then slid into the chair opposite of him. Martin didn't have to look up to know that it was Trimble.

"What do you want?" he growled as he picked up his whisky, already regretting that he hadn't ordered another.

"A word," the man answered. He pushed a plate filled with some type of meat pie in Martin's direction. "Since you have an appetite, I thought you'd enjoy a humble pie because you're a *humble* man."

Martin lifted the glass to his mouth and downed the contents. The liquid burned his throat, but he didn't care. "Make this brief. I'm eating."

"Nasty business you printed this morning," Trimble looked at the table then shifted his gaze to Martin.

His blue eyes always reminded Martin of an icy river. Rough around the edges, hard as a rock, and colder than a witch's tit. He leaned back in his chair and proceeded to crack open an egg without taking his gaze from Trimble. "Why do you care?"

"It's bad precedent and bad business. Does this have anything to do with the missus moving into your apartments?" Trimble scowled slightly. "I heard about the tax Pembrooke wants to impose upon *The Midnight Cryer*." He leaned back in his chair with that ice-cold glare never wavering from Martin's. "Better you than me. You could afford it."

"My wife is none of your concern," Martin said lazily. "Neither is *The Midnight Cryer*."

"We'll see," Trimble slowly rose from the table. "When you publish filth like you did today, it becomes my business. You're opening yourself up to those nobs taking legal action. If any are successful, then they'll be coming after *London-Town Tattler* and me." He waved his hand around the near-empty tavern. "They'll be coming after all of us."

"They wouldn't bother you if you'd stop regurgitating every single story I write in your pamphlet. If you can't compose an original article without libel or slander being bandied about, then I suggest you retain a good editor... and a solicitor." He set down his fork, then pressed the linen napkin against his mouth. "Or get out of the business."

"You always did consider yourself above everyone else," Trimble growled. "Trust me. You're like the rest of us. Bottom dwellers."

"Speak for yourself." Martin wanted to roar, but with miraculous restraint, he kept his voice even. "I don't piss where I sleep."

"By the looks of this morning's *The Midnight Cryer*, you do. You and your fancy airs," Trimble growled. "Like you're a duke yourself." Bits of spittle flew. "You'll fall just like they do."

Thankfully, Martin was far enough away from the deluge not to be in the direct line of fire.

"This is your only warning." Trimble stood abruptly, then practically marched out of the tavern.

Martin proceeded to finish his meal and coffee, then pressed his hands on the table and stood. He threw a guinea on the table, nodded to the owner, then his friends. There was no time to waste. He had a very important date with his outrageous, meddling, gorgeous wife.

AS AMELIA CHANGED THE DIAPER, she softly sang to the baby girl as the precious bundle cooed in return. Her days assigned to the nursery were what she loved best. The little one before her had been named Ivy after she arrived at the foundling home. One of the attendants had found the baby partially hidden behind a wall of ivy in the garden. Hence the name.

Amelia picked her up and walked to the window. Several children of various ages were playing out front when one of the older boys with a nasty reputation for bullying pushed a younger boy who fell on his backside. The older boy started to laugh but stopped abruptly when a man approached.

Heaven help her. It was Martin, and by the look of his countenance, he was angry. He never came to the foundling home. She huffed out a breath. What did she expect?

Thankfully, he wasn't one to raise his voice when he was angry. Amelia prayed this time wasn't an exception.

Martin glared at the older boy and said something. Amelia cradled Ivy closer and gently rocked her as she watched the events outside.

415

The older boy hung his head and said something to the younger one, then extended his hand. When the younger lad took it, the older one helped him stand. Martin nodded, then sent the older lad away with a sweep of his hand.

Her heart swelled when Martin lowered himself to his haunches. He put his hand on the lad's shoulder and started to speak.

The caring look on her husband's face stole her breath. The young boy wiped his eyes as Martin patted him lightly on the back, comforting while consoling the lad.

She'd never seen him so gentle with a child. Against all her best senses, she fell in love with her husband once again. Did he even want children? They'd never discussed it, as the subject never came up. After all these years of coming together once a week, she'd never once found herself carrying a child.

He reached into his pocket and gave the boy a coin.

A knock sounded on the door, and she turned away from the window to find Mrs. Johnson entering the room.

"It's time for the wee little one's nap," Mrs. Johnson said softly as she smiled.

Amelia nodded, then pressed a kiss to Ivy's temple. She inhaled the sweet fragrance of the baby, then tried to push the sudden feeling of longing aside. She had other matters to attend to, namely her husband.

"If anyone needs me..." She didn't finish her sentence as her husband stood in the doorway with an enigmatic smile directed her way.

"I need you, Mrs. Richmond," he said flatly, then turned a brilliant smile to Mrs. Johnson. "If you'll excuse my wife and me? She'll be leaving and won't be returning this afternoon."

Mrs. Johnson's eyebrows almost hit the ceiling.

"Ma'am, if that's acceptable?" Martin asked.

"Of course," Mrs. Johnson answered.

He turned his smile Amelia's way. Its earlier brilliance had turned dark and daunting as if she would soon be facing her judgment day. "If you'll come with me?" He held out his arm for her.

She studied his outstretched arm as a lump of dread lodged in her throat. For a moment, she grew dizzy and tried to take a deep breath for fortification. She smoothed a hand down her skirt while regaining the ability to swallow.

"How delightful you came to see me," she answered and strolled his way. She latched her arm around his and smiled reassuringly to Mrs. Johnson. With her head held high, she walked alongside her husband while saying her goodbyes to the other staff.

Once outside, unease crept through her with the stealth a pickpocket would envy. Amelia had never seen Martin so relaxed, and confidence seemed to ooze around him. His customary élan, always a part of his persona, was gone. This was a Martin Richmond whom she'd never seen before.

She shivered slightly imagining this was what others felt when they were escorted to their doom by their executioner. With a trembling sigh, she tilted her chin and faced forward as they walked toward his office. Now was not the time to weaken, and she had to have all her wits about her.

She had little trouble keeping up with her husband's brisk pace. "Where are we going?"

He didn't look at her. "Where did you write it?"

She drew to a halt in front of her rooms, directly across the street from *The Midnight Cryer* offices. "I started in your bedroom then finished in your study."

'Our bedroom," he corrected.

His unshaven face with all those beautiful angles and hardlines lacked any emotion except for the flex of muscle in his square jaw.

'I thought we were supposed to be the happy couple. Marching me down the London streets hardly projects happiness." She was deliberately provoking him, as she knew how to spar with him. But she didn't know how to be quiet with an angry husband by her side.

He stopped and moved closer, facing her. By his stance and the smile on his face, anyone would think they were sharing a romantic interlude. He could fool others, but the chilling glare of his eyes turned her blood into sludge as if overcome with a sudden burst of hoarfrost.

'Cold, darling?" he said with a lift of an arrogant brow.

She shook her head and swallowed. 'Nor am I frightened."

His brow creased into neat rows. 'Why would you be? It's just you and me." He tugged her across the street. 'Come, let's get you inside."

Edgar Graham leaned in his chair with his feet resting upon his desk, reading a broadsheet. When he glanced their way, he nodded. 'Duke. Mrs. Richmond." He turned his attention back to his paper.

She opened her mouth to return the greeting, but Martin leaned close. 'He won't help you," he whispered, then led her up the stairs to his private quarters and escorted her down a short hall to his study. The elegantly furnished room offered an excellent view of the street. On several occasions, Martin had brought her here to conduct their business after they'd shared the bed.

For a moment, she couldn't breathe. Last night when he'd come to her, he'd said he was making love to her. His tenderness toward her last night reminded her of when they'd made love all those years ago during their first month of marriage. They were discovering who they were together, and those days held a sweetness she regretted losing when she'd left him to start her own life.

She always had. But things were different now.

She squared her shoulders, then turned from the windows. "Are you going to lock the door?"

"There's no need. You're free to leave any time." He strolled to his desk and took out a sheet of parchment.

She chewed her lip for a moment. What exactly did that mean? Perhaps it was a just punishment for writing the retraction. "Is that what you want? For me to leave."

Without looking at her, he took out a knife and started to sharpen the quill. "I wouldn't have brought you here if I wanted you to leave."

Her chest loosened, and Amelia released the breath she was holding. She'd been waiting for Martin's order to move back to her rooms across the street. Surprisingly, she didn't want to leave. She hadn't as soon as he'd ask her to move back in with him. Perhaps it was the first time that she felt as if he needed her.

In turn, she'd realized how much she needed him. Since last night, the constant feeling of emptiness and the accompanying loneliness had vanished. But the truth was, they still hadn't come to a resolution as to how he chose to live his life.

"I know you're angry," she said softly. "But I did what I thought I had to do. For you and me."

"I think angry is the wrong word." He flipped the lid on the inkpot and held out the quill to her. "Come."

She walked to his side and took the quill. "What's the correct word?"

He tapped one finger to his chin and gazed off into the distance. "For a man who considers himself a wordsmith, I'm having the hardest time describing it. Somewhere between incensed and irate." A half-smile tugged at his mouth. "We can discuss that later. This first." He pushed the paper in front of her.

She turned to face the desk and looked at the parchment. It was completely blank. "What is this for?"

By then, he stood with his front to her back, almost as if embracing her from behind. "Bend over," he growled softly.

She bit her lip to keep from moaning. The seductive tone of his voice laced with anger melded into something foreign, and immediately, she felt that always-present undercurrent of desire struggling to emerge. Why did such need consume her at this moment?

Because he was here. Even if he was dismayed, he was feeling something for her.

"What are you doing?" An airy breathlessness escaped as she spoke.

He pushed forward, leaning over her slightly. His erection dug into her backside. "Helping you do the right thing."

She pushed against him. Whether it was to feel the heat of his cock or in rebellion, she couldn't decide. With one touch, he could easily disassemble her into nothing.

"I want you..." He nipped at her neck, then trailed his mouth to her ear. "God, I want you."

It was the words that a lover would say to another. Instantly, he pushed his hardened cock against her and then began to grind. This time, a deep moan escaped.

She grew increasingly wet at the motion. Her husband could take her across his desk, and she would welcome his hard heat plunging into her, relieving the newfound achiness.

"To write a retraction of your retraction." He bit her earlobe then soothed it with his tongue.

She stilled much like a deer caught in the sights of a predator.

In response, he placed his hand over hers that held the quill. Gently, he picked up her hand, and with an innate elegance, he dipped the sharpened point into the bottle of ink. "Let me help you start." He drew her hand away, careful not to allow a drop of ink to spill. "Graham said your column was charming and pure genius." He placed her hand on the paper. "I can hardly stand the excitement of what you're going to compose next."

"No." She dropped the quill, then twisted around, finding herself pressed against his chest with his arms wrapped around her. She tamped the urge to kiss him senseless. "You told me I could write whatever I wanted. I encouraged you to write the retraction, and you failed to do it. I was merely assisting you. I won't retract that apology."

He pulled her closer, and his arms tightened as if he couldn't help himself. "Oh, my darling wife." He kissed the middle of her forehead. "Yes, you will."

With any other couple, it would be a sign of affection. With Martin, the gauntlet had been thrown to the ground and then stomped. But she couldn't let it stand. Not now. Not if they had a chance to reconcile their marriage.

He stared at her face, and his eyes narrowed slightly. "My God, you grow more beautiful every day, but it will not work to diffuse my anger."

"Don't you see?" She put her arms around his neck. "I couldn't let the poor woman suffer." She dipped her eyes and straightened his cravat, then lifted her gaze to his. "The Duchess of Southart wanted to surprise her husband and her son with a puppy, because they shared the same birthday month. But when she met Jasper Love to pick one, she couldn't do it. They were too adorable, so she picked two."

"And why are you telling me such rot?" The curtness in his tone unleashed a bit of his anger. Yet, he began to slide one hand up and down her back.

If he was trying to reassure her, it was working.

"The duchess adores her husband and her son. To see her love for her family tarnished and turned into some untrue, prurient, sordid tale is a tragedy." She smiled slightly. "It was a simple act of love and kindness on her part." She placed her hand over his heart. "Just like it was an act of kindness and love when you stopped your determined march to waylay me, to help that lad Benjamin when Whitcomb pushed him down."

"You saw that?" He stiffened slightly.

She nodded once. "It's important that there's kindness in our world. Life is already hard enough trying to survive. You're capable of great kindness and civility."

His hand slowed to a stop on her spine. "Turn around."

"I'm not going to write that." She protested, but his hands were on her arms, lending assistance.

As she faced the desk, he leaned over her, then closed the inkwell. He opened a drawer from the front of the desk and placed the crystal decanter inside, then shut it.

But he didn't move away. Instead, he gripped her hips and pressed his erect cock against her backside. "Life is hard in *so many ways*. Since you've pointed out I'm capable of great kindness, I'll show you the sort of kindness that I deliver. Now, lift your skirts. We'll forgo the civility part."

When she turned to stare at him, a sly smile greeted her.

"I'm going to *kindly* tup you," he answered.

"Oh." That was all she could say with the press of his solid length against her backside.

"Now, lie face down on the desk." His gravelly voice indicated that he would brook no argument. "I'm going to fill you with my cock. Then I'm going to make you come so hard, you'll beg me for mercy."

Martin didn't have to ask twice. She hoisted her skirts, leaned over the oak desk, then gripped the other side with both hands. Just listening to him made her desperate for just what he described. "Is that a promise?" she asked, knowing she was taunting the beast.

Good heavens, she was already achy and wet for him. She pushed against him at the sound of him flicking the buttons on the flap fall of his breeches.

"Quit making it difficult," he said softly.

"I can't help..." She groaned as she felt his fingers separate her folds.

"Christ," he murmured under his breath. "You're already soaked for me. I need to take you to task more often." He grabbed one hip.

He entered her. With a groan, she tilted her bottom toward him. In response, he pushed in again, seating himself fully within her wet, aching core. She gripped the desk even tighter at the delicious feel of him so deep within her.

"If this is your idea of punishment, then I'll misbehave more often." Before she could say another word, he started moving.

"Let this be a lesson," he said, grasping her hip to keep her stationary as he began to thrust his cock in and out of her. With each stroke, he uttered a word. "Never. Interfere. With. My. Work. Again."

"I was helping you," she gasped as he continued his relentless pounding of her backside. With her hips perched on the desk and feet dangling off the ground, she wouldn't give this up for anything. She'd never experienced the rich fullness of her husband like this before when they'd been together.

"Help someone else," he panted as he sank to the hilt, then ground his hips against her bottom. "You help me just like this. By letting me fuck you." He withdrew, then thrust inside again.

She wanted to cry out as pleasure unfurled in her lower belly. It was starting to radiate outwards, the sign that she was about to climax. "Please." She was panting now at the incredible sensation rolling through her.

"Is this what you're begging for?" He reached around her hips to her quim.

As soon as his finger touched her clitoris, she whimpered. "I'm going to come."

"Not without me," he hissed.

Then his hips became pistons pounding her backside as his cock moved inside her. Her muscles contracted, trying to keep him close. She sucked in a breath and closed her eyes as her orgasm pushed endless waves of pleasure through her body. A million stars seemed to explode behind her eyes as her heart accelerated. She couldn't breathe or move.

Martin roared her name as his seed filled her. He collapsed, holding her tightly to him.

She didn't mind his weight on her back. It was lovely. In broad daylight, they'd come together just like animals mating. A giggle escaped at the very thought, and she could feel her cheeks heating.

"Why are you laughing?" Martin's voice was gruff as he pushed aside her locks of hair that had escaped from her simple chignon. His fingers lingered on Amelia's skin as if relishing her softness in the aftermath of the storm they'd created.

"We've never done anything like this before."

Martin released her, then helped her stand. "Well, I've never had anyone try to correct my work before."

"Perhaps you need an editor," she quipped.

He lifted one arrogant brow as if the last minutes were a distant dream and let go of her hand. "You try me. Don't do it again, Wife. I still don't understand what possessed you to act. What did Southart promise you?"

At the loss of his touch and the dull heat in his eyes, she felt awkward, like an adolescent trying to find her place while the rest of the world danced around her. "What?" she asked hesitantly.

"Tell me what caused you to intervene on their behalf. Always before, we've come to an agreement on which stories I'd let pass. You've never, ever done something like this."

It was wrong of her to have interfered. She knew that now. Martin had built *The Midnight Cryer* with his own hands and pen. It was his livelihood, and she profited from his effort. But for the sake of the foundling home, she'd had to do it.

"The allowance I give you is generous, but you never seem to spend it. It doesn't take a genius to figure out your finances." He smoothed her dress, then proceeded to put himself to rights. "Are you charmed by the duke like every other female on the planet?"

"Are you jealous?"

The banked fire in his eyes suddenly blazed. He was jealous. A thrill shot through Amelia. Her husband was feeling something for her again.

"Why would I be charmed by the duke? You are my

husband. I want to help the home. I give as much as I can to them."

"What did the duke promise you?" He swept around the desk. After he sat, he placed his elbows on the oak top and regarded her.

"A contribution to the foundling home," she said. She leaned over the desk to capture his gaze. "When I saw the depth of emotion on the duke's face for his wife, I was in awe. I wanted to help them. It's wrong of me to be jealous of what the duke and duchess have." She dropped her voice. "But I want it, just the same. I want a love like that." Tears threatened, and she repeatedly swallowed to tame this wave of emotion that wouldn't leave her be. She'd never told him any of this. She'd never let herself be this vulnerable in front of him before. But this was her future with her husband, even if he was the despised editor of *The Midnight Cryer*. "I want that with you. But we can't have it if you continue to leave chaos in your wake without a care in the world."

"Who says I want that?" He leaned back in his chair and stared straight through her.

The silence in the room stole her confidence right out from under her.

His words gutted her. For all those years they'd met on Wednesday nights, she believed he had some affection for her. Now she'd exposed all the wants and desires she ever wanted with him, and it was all wasted. "I'm lonely," she confessed and looked down at her clasped hands. "I...I thought you might feel the same. It's conceivable that you might have wanted a family, the same as me..."

"If you wanted a family, you shouldn't have left." He looked down at the desk and pulled out the inkpot. "You're the staunchest advocate for causes I've ever seen. Your friend Elizabeth, the foundling home, and even the duke and his family." He dipped the quill in the pot and regarded her. "Your passion, the undeniable fire that burns deep within you, is a thing of beauty."

"I care about them." For a moment, she didn't know how to respond to his kind words.

"How does a person earn such a sacred position with you?" The disinterest in his voice felt like a slap against her cheek.

"Don't mock me." She turned to leave and dashed away a renegade tear.

"Amelia," he called out.

She stopped but didn't turn around in fear she'd reveal her devastation.

"Why do you spend so much time at the foundling home?" he asked.

"No one ever comes for them, so I do...by visiting. Those children matter, Martin. We all do." She cleared her throat slightly. "Since you and I have never been blessed..." Her words sounded like babbling nonsense. "They're running out of money. I try to help."

"I see why you're their greatest champion," he said gently. "You care about them. But do you know what I find ironic?" He started to write on the parchment in front of him, the scratching sound sending unexpected chills down her spine. He stopped writing.

Slowly, she turned around to face him. "What do you find ironic?"

"You believe the best in all of them, but you have never believed in our marriage or *me*."

At his accusation, she was momentarily speechless. "I...I care about you. I always have."

He grunted softly as if in disbelief.

"Did you care about me?" she asked in a soft whisper. Without waiting for his answer, she gathered the remnants of her dignity and closed the door silently behind her. She closed her eyes at the sound of his chair scraping across the floor.

He was coming after her. Quickly, she wiped her eyes again and waited for some sign that she mattered to him. If he'd open the door and said he understood, she could forgive him. If he offered to take her into his arms, she'd never leave his side again. *If he'd just show a hint that what she wanted mattered.*

But he never opened the door. Perhaps Martin was like her. He couldn't let go of their past transgressions either.

She straightened her shoulders, then headed downstairs. She prayed no one stood in the offices, as her nose was running. At least her tears had stopped. It was painful holding them in, but if she could just make it to her rooms across the street, then she could wallow in her grief in private.

Her luck apparently had taken an unexcused holiday as Mr. Graham stood in front of the printing press, laying out the evening edition.

"Mrs. Richmond, a young woman is waiting for you across the street at your place." Graham nodded briefly, then returned to the task at hand. "She says she's Lady Overton."

"Thank you," she said, rushing out the door as she pushed aside her heartbreak. She hadn't seen Elizabeth since Martin had published the story about Lord Overton. Their friendship had ended years ago. Something was wrong if Elizabeth would dare to travel to see her.

Seven

MARTIN FISTED one hand as he gazed at the center of his desk. What had he been thinking taking his wife across a piece of furniture like a rutting animal? He closed his eyes as the memory of her rosewater scent mixed with her feminine fragrance that had wafted toward him. Of course, like the beast he was, as soon as he felt her firm bum meet his groin, he'd lost all sense of decorum then taken her.

Martin would never walk into this room again without remembering what they had done. Her sweet moans and cries were a serenade.

Damnation. The more he allowed Amelia into his world—his home, his work, and his life—the greater the chance that it would eventually lead to heartache for both. He could never forsake *The Midnight Cryer*. It was the only way to exact his revenge and prove his contempt for the fops who parade around the British Isles under the disguise as the so-called *nobles of the aristocracy*.

But she would never agree to it. She was too kindhearted. When she'd said she was lonely, it took everything within Martin not to take her into his arms and confess he felt the same.

He let out a long, slow sigh. The purpose of Amelia moving in here was to prove that he was a man of morals with a wife. He'd accomplish this by attending a few social engagements and showing London he was a devoted married man. Now, such a ruse wasn't as easy as he thought.

He didn't want their appearance at the theatre or opera house to be some nugget of titillating gossip that would become the hallmark of the next day's social calls. When he escorted Amelia into society, it would be for her own sake, so she might experience some enjoyment in her life, instead of receiving callers who were not there to enjoy her wonderful company. Those parasites of the *ton* were only there because they wanted something from her. They wanted her to calm the scandal that surrounded them.

No wonder she spent all her free time at the foundling home.

His gut clenched at the vision of her cuddling the baby. He hadn't even been aware that she felt so strongly about wanting a family.

The truth was he'd like nothing more than to see her belly round with his child. For the love of everything, what was happening to him? He was losing all control.

But what caused his gut to clench was the devastation on her face when he'd asked why she hadn't made him and their marriage a priority. The words had slipped from his mouth before he could bite his tongue. He knew the answer but wanted to hear it from her own lips. She might care for him, but she didn't want anything to do with his work.

He exhaled, then took out a piece of parchment. His work was his mistress, and she waited for no one. The first to publish the stories won the lion's share of coins from the coffee shops, the tea shops, and the other readers. Everyone wanted to be first with the news, including Martin.

It took him several minutes to compose the articles for the afternoon edition of *The Midnight Cryer*. He almost wrote a retraction of Amelia's retraction. He could easily claim a high fever caused him to act so irrationally.

Yet, it would be best to let it lie. By tomorrow, no one would remember the apology. He quickly sanded the parchment, cleaned his desk, then headed for the printing room. He'd give the edition to Graham, then head out to find Amelia.

As soon as he entered the printing room, Edgar Graham stopped unbundling the clean paper that would be used for the printing press later in the day. The man's gray eyes narrowed.

Martin ignored the look of censure on his assistant editor's face and handed him the paper. "Here's the evening edition."

"Anything newsworthy?" Graham asked. As an afterthought, he added, "*Your Grace.*"

"What the devil, man?" Martin leaned back as if slapped in the face and challenged to a duel. "It's just the two of us."

Graham raised an eyebrow. "Dukes who insist upon being referred to by their titles or correct form of address are stuffy and inconsiderate." He looked at Martin from head to toe. "I think I'm seeing one of those types now."

"Meaning?" Martin calmly regarded his associate editor. Graham was usually quite jovial, but there was a distinct disapproval coloring his face.

Graham threw a thumb behind his shoulder,

pointing to the exit. "Your wife was distraught when she left here."

Martin bit his lip to keep from snarling. "It's none of your business."

Graham's face turned to granite. "It became my business when I see you rush upstairs every Wednesday to be with her. She always leaves in the most pleasant of moods. A kind word for every single employee." He smiled, and his gray eyes flashed like steel. "But I've never seen her so upset." He glanced at the paper, then lifted that same eyebrow again. "This doesn't appear to be much news." He waved the parchment under Martin's nose. "Lady Fredrickson's cat is missing?"

"It's a full-grown tiger that escaped and is now prowling Mayfair." Martin snatched the parchment from his assistant editor's hand and corrected his error.

"I see. Funny how we lose our concentration when all isn't right with the missus. Happens to me from time to time." He placed a hand on Martin's shoulder. "The truth is that if she'd come to you before you'd published that story about the Duchess of Southart, you'd have pulled it. You've always pulled the stories that she's requested, haven't you?"

"I must have told her *no* at some point," Martin argued, then stopped. Perhaps his assistant editor had the right of it. Martin couldn't recall ever not agreeing to her requests.

"I'm old enough to be your da, and that means I've lived enough to have more life experiences than you do." When Martin was about to protest, Graham squeezed his shoulder affectionately, then dropped his hand. "How are you going to make her happy?"

Martin nodded in understanding. "I'm going to tell her she's beautiful every day."

"Is that your only plan to convince her to stay?" Graham tilted his head.

Martin narrowed his eyes. His assistant editor only did the head tilt when he thought Martin had either not been listening or had missed the convoluted point the man was trying to make. "I suppose you have some sage piece of wisdom you'd like to impart?" His sarcasm cut the air like a newly sharpened sword.

"You're the man with all the intelligence. Eton and all, with the highest marks."

"Oh, please." Martin rolled his eyes. "That was ages ago."

"Exactly. You're in a different world now. Use this," Graham said as he tapped the side of his head. "You have a nimble mind. Figure it out."

"I don't have time for your convoluted Socratic lecture," he growled. "Where is my wife?"

"Interesting. Lady Overton was also looking for your wife. The woman looked like she'd seen a ghost. Came right through that door, *The Midnight Cryer*'s main entrance, and asked if Mrs. Richmond was available. Imagine the fortitude to walk through those doors after what we printed about her husband." The older man looked down to the floor and shook his head.

Martin schooled his features so he wouldn't betray his unease. Elizabeth, the Marchioness of Overton, had once been Amelia's closest friend and confidant until he broke them apart by posting that story. There was always a niggle of guilt that bandied about Martin's chest when he thought of it. Printing the article wasn't a personal vendetta against Overton. Martin really didn't care about the marquess. His concern was being the first to print a story.

And he'd hurt Amelia in the process.

"What did you tell her?"

"I told Lady Overton to wait for Mrs. Richmond

across the street," Graham answered as he took another gander at the parchment in his hands.

"So, that's where my wife is?" Martin ran his fingers through his hair. Deuced bad timing for Lady Overton to appear out of the blue, particularly after his argument with Amelia.

It was like pouring salt on an open wound.

To make matters worse, why was he writing about cats instead of tigers?

Because he couldn't keep his head clear when Amelia was near.

~

Amelia straightened her hair in a hallway mirror outside her rooms. Without wasting another thought on her recalcitrant husband, Amelia pushed open the door to her rooms. She entered a lovely sitting area that doubled as a study where she met with her callers. If it were a single gentleman, then she met with him downstairs. But if it were a couple or a wife, she'd meet with them in her rooms.

Sitting on the edge of a pink brocade chair facing Amelia's Louis XV desk, her dear friend Elizabeth, the Marchioness of Overton, sat staring out the window. In the five years that they hadn't seen each other, Elizabeth hadn't aged a bit. Her hair still glistened like a river of brown silk.

"Elizabeth?" Amelia said softly.

The marchioness jumped out of her chair and slapped her hand over her heart. "You took me by surprise. I didn't hear you come in. The proprietor said it was all right if I waited here."

Without a word, they fell into each other's arms.

"I've missed you," Amelia said softly, pulling her friend tighter against her chest.

"The same for me," Elizabeth confided.

"Come, sit down." Amelia took Elizabeth's hand and led her to the brocade chair. "I'll make us some tea."

"Please don't bother on my account," the marchioness said. "I need to be returning home to Robert. He doesn't know that I'm calling on you, and it would displease him frightfully." Her voice broke on the last word.

Instantly, Amelia pulled the chair closer to her friend's side. "It must be important if you're here to see me."

The marchioness nodded then studied her reticule, the one she clasped tightly in her hands. Taking a deep breath, she forced her gaze to Elizabeth's. "I'm sorry I haven't seen you. After that article in *The Midnight*—"

Amelia put her hand over Elizabeth's hand. "I understand, and I'm sorry it put us at odds."

"It's not your fault," she said softly. Elizabeth's mouth tugged into a sad smile. "You didn't marry the paper."

"I married the editor." Amelia shifted so she could see Elizabeth's face. Lines of worry framed her friend's bloodshot eyes.

"But you separated from him." Elizabeth waved a hand around the rooms. "Yet, you moved across the street from him. Why?"

"He's still my husband, and the only one who welcomes my company." Amelia wrestled with how much to share, but the truth had always served her well. "I love him." She pursed her lips to tame her unwieldy emotions.

Elizabeth nodded once as if accepting Amelia's answer. "I've even heard from a few of my friends that they've visited you to seek your help with your husband." She cocked her head and examined Amelia. "They say you convince him to cull stories." She drew a breath as if seeking courage. "Is that true?"

"Sometimes," Amelia answered vaguely. For an awkward moment, silence reigned over them.

"Why didn't you do that for me and Robert?" Elizabeth asked sharply, breaking the stillness that hung heavy in the air. "Was I not your friend?"

Amelia's eyes widened. "I did ask my husband not to print the story. We argued about it for weeks. Did you not know?"

Elizabeth ducked her head and shook it slightly.

"My God," Amelia said in a low whisper. "You didn't read my letters."

"Letters?" Elizabeth gaze shot to Amelia's. "What letters?"

"I must have sent you at least a half dozen explaining my actions." All her pent-up sorrow at Elizabeth's years of silence deflated to nothing.

"My parents," Elizabeth murmured, then she closed her eyes. "They are the type of people who would burn my correspondence if they thought they were protecting me." She let out a soulful sigh. "I'm sorry, Amelia."

"I'm sorry, too." She didn't have the energy to elaborate, but she had a hunch that Elizabeth finally realized that the hurt she'd carried over the years mirrored Amelia's anguish.

Elizabeth stared at her hands as she tangled her fingers together. "I wish I would have called on you sooner. This makes everything inelegantly gauche."

"It's fine. You're here now." Amelia reached over and patted her friend's hand.

"Thank you." Tears welled in Elizabeth's eyes. "I know this sounds trite, but I wish..."

Amelia ducked her head until she could look her

friend in the eye. "I wish we could reclaim all those years too."

Elizabeth smiled sheepishly. "If I ever...by chance...needed your help?" Her voice was barely above a whisper.

"Anything," Amelia answered.

Elizabeth laughed, but her eyes were drowning in sorrow. "Ironic, I would come to you after all these years and find out the truth." She shook her head in disbelief. "Heaven help me, but I hope I never have to seek help from Martin Richmond, the very one who printed that story about my Robert." She brought a handkerchief to her mouth, struggling to rein in her emotion. "Some scandal is swirling around Robert. He hasn't confided in me, but it's serious. Once he does, I might call on you for assistance." She opened her reticule and pulled out a small pouch of coins. "I'd like to pay you for your time today."

Amelia's throat tightened at the heavy clink of the coins. She could no more accept money from Elizabeth than she could jump to the moon. Though they hadn't been a part of each other's lives for years, Amelia still considered her a friend.

"No." At the look of confusion on Elizabeth's face, she smiled. "Your visit is payment enough."

The relief on her friend's face was palpable. "Thank you." Her brow furrowed into neat lines as she replaced the coin pouch. "How much does something like this cost?"

Amelia shrugged slightly. "I truthfully don't know. I don't ask for payment, but sometimes people contribute to the foundling home where I spend much of my time. I only have what Martin provides. I contribute most of it to the home."

"That sounds like you." Elizabeth smiled slightly. "I could contribute too."

"Only if that's your desire." Amelia caught Elizabeth's gaze. "Not for payment."

"Robert and I have two boys. I spend most of my days with them. They're growing up so fast. Another year or so they'll have a tutor, then off to school." She sighed. "Perhaps I'll become a patron of your foundling home. I miss holding babies."

Amelia laughed. "We always need volunteers for that."

Elizabeth stood, and she followed.

"I must be going," her friend said softly. "Thank you."

Amelia didn't hesitate and took her friend into her arms. "Thank you for coming to see me. Whatever I can do to help, please let me know."

"I'd ask you to call upon me, but..." Her friend's chin trembled slightly.

"It's all right," Amelia rushed to reassure her, as a bit of her heart crumbled to nothing. Her friend was still ashamed to be seen with her.

Elizabeth shook her head. "It's not that I don't want to see you. But it would be best for Robert and me if everything settles before we start socializing again."

"Of course." Amelia hugged her friend once again. This time, she held on to Elizabeth a bit longer than necessary. "Any time you need me, just send word. We can meet here."

After Elizabeth took her leave, Amelia stood by the window and watched. A footman jumped down from the waiting carriage and lowered the carriage steps. Elizabeth looked up in Amelia's direction and waved.

After her friend's carriage lumbered down the street, Amelia stayed by the window. Lost in her thoughts, she didn't focus on anything as she tried to imagine her next conversation with Martin. She rested her head against the windowpane, the cool glass refreshing against her brow. Her shoulders curled as she exhaled.

After she'd laid her feelings bare before him, he'd rebuffed her. And why shouldn't he? He was correct when he'd said she'd not made him a priority. She'd chosen to defend the ones who had wanted nothing to do with her.

Yet, Martin had never thought about a family. Perhaps she should have told him in those first days of her marriage that she wanted one. Perhaps he would have given up *The Midnight Cryer.*

What balderdash.

She blew out a breath.

She'd written the retraction for them and their future together. But her future really hadn't changed. People still didn't want to be associated with her for fear they would become the next target of *The Midnight Cryer's* quill.

Unfortunately, her heart had completely ignored the dire warnings not to fall in love again with her husband.

Her heart always did what it wanted.

Now, the foolish organ had broken, and once again, she would have to mend the pieces together.

Alone.

MARTIN HAD LAID his satchel with his journal and pencils on the desk in his study. It was the exact same spot that Amelia had writhed beneath him just hours ago. Slowly, he picked up the leather bag and lowered it to the floor. His attention needed to be on her, not his work. People had to see that he was devoted to her.

Most importantly, she had to see that as well.

Trying to protect himself, he'd hurt her. He'd never forgive himself if he didn't make this right. As he glanced around the room and thought about their love-making, a startling truth came to light. He more than enjoyed having her live with him. He craved it.

With a deep breath, he turned to the window and studied the second floor of her building. She was staring out the window. The forlornness she wore caused his gut to tie itself into knots. Martin wouldn't be responsible for his actions if Lady Overton had added more heartache to Amelia's burden.

She wrapped her arms around her waist, then rested her head against the windowpane. She looked tired and as if she'd lost everything that mattered to her in the world.

Without second-guessing his decision, he bounded down the steps and quickly took the exit to the street. In mere seconds, he was inside Amelia's building and taking the steps two at a time to reach her.

Outside her door, he knocked. As he waited, he tried to think of what would be appropriate to say. *Forgive me. I apologize. I wasn't thinking clearly.* It sounded like rot.

Because he was all rot.

He'd promised himself on the way over that he'd be honest with her and himself. He lifted his hand to knock again when the door opened.

They stared at each other for several moments, neither of them saying a word.

The silence foretold things he didn't want to face. An even worse thought sent an icy river careening through his veins. What if this divide between them was too great to cross? What if the pain inflicted was too deep?

In that instant, he wanted to be the man that could give her everything she wanted—a family and a husband who would forever be committed fully to her.

Struggling with how to start, he cleared his throat. "Amelia..."

"Not in the hall." She retreated into her rooms and waved a hand, inviting him in. As soon as he stepped inside, she shut the door.

"I saw Overton's wife had called on you." He glanced around the room. His wife's tastes were imprinted on every spec of furniture and decoration. He felt that same mark on his lips, his arms, the rest of his body, and especially inside his chest.

She nodded slightly. "She and I cleared the air in a

manner of speaking. I think it's possible we might re-sume our friendship. But trouble is brewing for her husband. She might need me in the future...with you. I told her I'd help her in any way I could." Her eyes locked with his. "She offered to donate to the foundling home, and I said she shouldn't do it for payment."

"You should make her contribute double." He smiled slightly, trying to release some of the tension that vibrated between them. "You're worth every penny and more. You know that."

"Don't hand out false flattery like it's candy." She turned and walked farther into the room.

He followed and reached for her arm. "Darling, please."

When she turned around to face him, she would have hurt him less if she'd stabbed him in the chest. Abject misery made her eyes well with tears. Instantly, he swept her into his embrace. Thankfully for him, she accepted his touch. If she'd have walked away from him, he'd have been reduced to nothing, no longer of this world.

"It's all right," he crooned softly.

"Is it?" she asked, breaking away from him.

Instantly, the lack of her familiar warmth seared him with a sudden chill. "What does that mean?" he asked cautiously. "Was Lady Overton offensive?"

She wiped her eyes, then shook her head. "She was everything gracious."

"Then it's because I hurt you," he said softly. "I'm sorry."

She nodded once, then strolled away to look out the window again. "Sometimes, the truth injures. I'm discovering it might be better to face it rather than pretend or live a lie." She swung her gaze to his. "We had an arrangement that appeared on the outside to be to our

PUT UP YOUR DUKES

mutual benefit. I slept in your bed every Wednesday to honor our vows and hopefully create a child. Everyone thinks it's so you won't print articles that I object to. I'd always thought I'd kept my heart from becoming too entangled."

As did he.

"Over the last several days, I foolishly had hoped that we were rebuilding something between us." She shook her head as if in disbelief. "I assumed you thought the same."

When she sat down behind her desk, it was as if she'd raised a shield between them. Her earlier sadness had dissipated much like summer rain. In its place was... nothing. There was no emotion in her eyes, no smile or frown on her lips.

"But you don't care for me the way I care for you, so I'll resume staying at my residence during the days. Once I finish at the foundling home, I'll come to your quarters for the sake of saving your paper from the additional tax. However"—she placed her palms on the desk, then stood to meet him eye to eye— "I'll not sleep with you again until Elizabeth needs me. If that makes our marriage transactional and me a mercenary, then so be it."

"What?" Incredulous, he ran a hand through his hair. The magnitude of the disaster unfolding around him seemed to triple every second.

"Please, try to understand," she said calmly. "It's the only way I can help without destroying myself. You can say we're together. Hopefully, it'll ensure that the tax isn't approved. I predict that it won't be, if you leave the retraction as is. Once that threat is eliminated, and Elizabeth and Overton's crisis is finished, I'll move out for good." She shrugged her shoulders. "Perhaps we'll never have to sleep with one another again."

"How can you presume..." He let the words slip into silence. He'd been the one to say that she couldn't presume that he wanted the same as her—the respectability of being a family. So, she was making a logical conclusion that his earlier declaration meant he wanted none of that. He'd practically put the words into her mouth.

"I shouldn't presume anything about you, and I had no right to do so earlier when I thought we wanted the same thing," she answered softly. "You'll never give up *The Midnight Cryer*, and I can't live with that pamphlet. Now if you'll excuse me, I'm going to the foundling home."

She gathered her cloak and bonnet, then left him to stew in his own juices.

Or, as Chaucer had so famously said, "Let him to fry in his own grease."

Which he certainly was.

~

After spending the rest of the day in his study, Martin went downstairs to dispatch an errand boy to the foundling home. He gave the lad a coin and told him to pick up a meat pie or two for him and his mother.

When he started for the upstairs, Graham raised both eyebrows as if in shock. "You're having her followed?"

"If you mean my wife, no," he said with his chin high. "I want to have everything ready for her when she comes home. She spent the afternoon at the foundling home."

"As she does most days," Graham nodded in agreement. "What are you having made ready?"

'I'll have a light repast and a hot bath waiting for her. I'm preparing it myself."

"An excellent start to a cozy night at home," Graham smiled in approval as he leaned back in his chair.

'I'm so relieved I have your blessing for my evening plans," he said sardonically. There was nothing worse than a busybody, and Graham excelled at it. That's why he was such an excellent assistant editor of *The Midnight Cryer*. But it was unwanted when he turned his curiosity Martin's way.

"The evening edition is out on the street. I thought I'd take a stroll through some of the posher gambling hells. See what information I can glean. You and the missus enjoy yourself this evening."

"Take your time," Martin answered.

Without acknowledging Martin's disgruntlement, Graham sauntered out the door into the fog and chill of a typical London night.

Not more than a minute later, the errand boy Tom returned with news that Amelia was on her way.

"Thank you, Tom." Martin threw a coin, and the boy's arm shot out and caught it in mid-air. "Take the pies home and sleep well. We'll have a busy day tomorrow."

It wasn't too long until she stepped through the door. Amelia halted in her steps.

"Hello, darling," he said softly and held out his hand for her to take.

'I thought you'd be working." Amelia examined his fingers as if they might bite her. "What is this about?"

He nodded his head toward the stairs. 'I thought we could spend the evening together in each other's company. I'm taking the evening off so I can be with you."

Before he had finished, she was shaking her head. 'I'll not bed you."

"I'm not asking for that." Though he might be begging for her before the night is over. She was utterly delectable with the pink in her cheeks and reddened lips from the brisk walk home. He'd like nothing more than to warm her up himself.

But even he wasn't that selfish. It wasn't about the sensual adventures that they undertook together. He needed to convince Amelia how much he reveled in her and her company.

Her eyes narrowed as if she could hear aloud his thoughts and didn't believe him.

"Come, darling." He closed the distance between them and took her hand. "I'm going to take care of *you* this evening." Gently, he tugged her to follow him, and soon they were in their apartments where a cheerful fire greeted them in the salon.

Amelia took off her cloak and hung it on the hook beside the door. "I'm tired. I want a bath and something to eat. That's all."

"Great minds think alike, then." He strolled to the side table and poured her a glass of wine. When he turned to hand it to her, her eyes had softened, and she visibly relaxed.

"Thank you." When she took the glass, their fingers touched. It took every ounce of restraint he possessed not to take her hand in his.

"If you'll excuse me?" he said with his most affectionate smile.

Her eyes widened. "I thought you weren't working?"

"I'm not working for *The Midnight Cryer*. I'm working for you. I'm preparing hot water for your tub. Then, while you relax and bathe, I'll prepare something for you to eat."

She finished her wine, then sat down her glass. "This

is highly unusual. What have you done with my husband?"

A laugh escaped at the saucy smile and the defiant tilt of her chin. She joined in, and for a moment, it felt as if they were newlyweds again, enjoying and teasing each other endlessly. They'd been so innocent all those years ago. Tonight he'd do his damnedest to entertain her while making her feel safe with him once again.

"Your husband is right here." He held up his arms wide as if offering proof. "A selfish lout as usual."

A becoming blush marched up her chest and neck, then conquered her cheeks with bright pink flags. For a moment, Martin forgot about teasing and simply memorized the sight of her.

"When you blush like that, I can't move," he confided softly. "Sometimes, I wonder how I became so fortunate to have you as my wife."

She dipped her head for a moment, then lifted her gaze to his. The brilliant sheen of her eyes blinded him. "If you keep saying such things, I'll start craving them."

"I'm merely speaking the truth." He bowed slightly. From now on, he'd say something like that at least once a day just to see her expression melt into affection.

Within a half-hour, Martin had the water prepared for a hip bath that he'd placed in their bedroom. Then he laid out his banyan for Amelia to wear at her convenience, along with fresh linen toweling. Earlier, he'd built up a fire to keep her warm. Finishing his preparation, he placed a small folding screen around the tub.

When he went to tell Amelia her bath was ready, he found her asleep on the chaise longue in front of the fire in the salon. He crouched in front of her and pressed his hand to her cheek. She murmured something and pressed her face closer to his palm. Without hesitation, he lifted her in his arms, then took her into the bedroom.

Carefully undressing her down to her chemise, Martin tucked her into bed. It was a shame to waste the water, so he stripped naked and bathed. Afterward, he dried himself and didn't bother with his banyan. He crossed the distance to the bed and slipped between the covers. Amelia hadn't moved from where he'd left her. Careful not to wake her, he pulled her close. Immediately, she snuggled closer.

He released a deep sigh. For someone who never considered himself an optimist or even a romantic, there was no place he'd rather be than holding his wife as she slept. His only regret was that he didn't have a chance to feed her. But morning would bring another opportunity, and he'd not start his day until he served her.

She burrowed her head into his chest as if seeking his warmth. He pulled her tighter and pressed a kiss to the top of her head.

'Do you know why I changed the name of my publication to *The Midnight Cryer*?"

She mumbled something, and he chuckled.

'I take that as a *no*." He rubbed his lips against her hair, inhaling the unique scent that was hers. It always reminded him of sunshine, flowers, and honey. Perhaps he was a romantic. 'I'll tell you sometime."

He looked at her sleeping form. A sudden rush of warmth spread throughout his chest at the sight of his precious wife in his arms. Whether it was love or some other emotion, he didn't want to examine it too closely. Everything would be fine between them. He was sure of it.

But he'd not waste tonight. He had more important things to attend to than trying to discover what he was feeling, such as holding his lovely wife within his arms.

Nine

AMELIA GROANED as she forced her eyes open, which was difficult, as they felt glued shut. A weak ray of sunshine greeted her, and she knew exactly how it felt —faint and not all that interested in starting the day. Slowly, Amelia rolled to a sitting position. The urge to collapse back onto the warm covers hit her with the power of a swinging hammer, but she fought against it.

"There's my slug-a-bed," Martin said a bit too cheerfully as he strolled into the room with a tray.

Immediately, her stomach revolted at the smell of food. When he put the tray beside her, she took one look and knew that she was about to be ill. Without fanfare, she jumped from the bed and grabbed the clean chamber pot under her bed, then proceeded to cast up her accounts.

Instantly, Martin was beside her, pulling her hair back and offering words of comfort. She retched once more, but thankfully there was nothing left since she hadn't eaten last night. He helped her back into bed.

"Take it away," she said weakly and waved a hand at the food.

Martin did as asked. In a thoughtful gesture, he took

449

the chamber pot from the room as well. Though Amelia's stomach still roiled slightly, she smiled when her husband returned. Gently, he sat on the edge of the bed, then wiped a cool cloth dipped in water over her brow.

"Thank you." Her voice sounded weak to her ears.

"Are you feeling better?" he asked, still tending to her.

"I am." She closed her eyes and forced herself to take a deep, calming breath. That small action made her feel better. She did it again. She opened her eyes and found him studying her. "I appreciate the offer but don't bring me any food for a while."

He nodded, still regarding her with concern.

"It's nothing," she said. "Someone is always sick at the foundling home, it seems. There are so many of them." By now, the tidal wave of nausea had receded. "That must be the reason." She scooted back toward the headboard.

Instantly, he had a hand under her elbow, helping her up. "You must be careful."

"I'm not breakable," she protested.

"I'm aware of that, but you are precious," he murmured as he helped her sit up. "Shall I call a doctor?"

Just by sitting up, Amelia was feeling better by the moment. "There's no need. Whatever it was has passed."

"All right," he nodded, then left the room.

She'd obviously convinced him, as her husband's thoughts were already on his work. He was probably halfway down the stairs by now, which was probably for the best as she needed to start her day. Before she swung her legs off the bed, Martin entered the bedroom with his lap desk. He pulled up a chair.

"What are you doing?" she asked in bewilderment.

"I'm spending my day with you," he answered, then

sat next to her side of the bed and proceeded to unpack his lap desk. There was a quill, fresh parchment, a small journal of sorts, a pencil, and an inkpot.

"What about your work?" She rose to stand.

"Careful," he exclaimed, as he grabbed her by the waist. "You should be in bed."

"*You* should be at work." Unable to resist, she cupped his cheeks with her hands. He was being extremely kind and courteous this morning after she'd been unwell. The warmth of his hands on her waist sent little frissons of sensations careening through her.

"I'm not going to work if you're ill," he argued. He placed the lap desk on the bed, then stood beside her. He was so tall that she had to tilt her head to see his face. His thick, perfectly arched eyebrows drew together in worry.

"I'm not ill now. I'm going to work, and so should you." She skated around his chair and proceeded to the washbasin. Quickly, she brushed her teeth with her tooth powder and toothbrush. Once finished, she turned to reach for fresh toweling and suddenly found herself in her husband's arms. His look of concern had lessened, but it was still there.

"I'm your husband. It's my duty and pleasure to take care of you." He kissed her gently on the lips.

It wasn't a kiss of passion or possession but a pledge of something that she desperately wanted—a vow of togetherness.

When he pulled away, she stumbled, slightly off-kilter. Whether it was from the kiss or her wayward thoughts, she didn't want to hazard a guess. However, she wasn't fool enough to allow herself to think that there was any possibility of them being together in the future.

The Midnight Cryer still stood tall between them, looming as large as Hadrian's Wall.

~

Four slow, agonizing weeks had passed, and Martin was about to pull his hair out. Each day was absolute torture. His routine with Amelia never varied. She came home in the evenings, usually tired and sometimes hungry. Martin would meet her each evening and try to feed and pamper her. Sometimes, it succeeded, and sometimes it didn't.

The rumors of Lord Pembrooke introducing a special tax on *The Midnight Cryer* had faded since Amelia's apology to the Duchess of Southart and her family. Now and then, Martin would pull it out and read her original composition. The anger he'd first experienced when she'd interfered had disappeared, and now, he could find the humor in such a bold and audacious move by her to write a column and sign his name to it. His wife was a spitfire, minx, and the most desirable woman that inhabited the British Isles.

At least in his opinion. Hence, the absolute misery he was experiencing. They hadn't made love since that time he'd taken her on his desk. Now he couldn't even work in the room. Every blasted time he entered, his cock went on alert as if remembering the experience, and instantly hardened. It was becoming so commonplace that he walked around at half-mast practically every single day.

But the nights were the worst. Amelia would attend to her evening ablutions, and Martin would follow. He'd lie awake for hours holding her, while his aching cock protested every minute of it. Then the torture grew more intense when they ended up in bed entangled together in each other's arms, with her soft, supple breasts pressed against his chest.

But he endured, because he wanted her to know that he wasn't just interested in her body, but in her and everything she found interesting. The nights when she shared her time at the foundling home were endearing. She'd tell him little stories about the children, and which ones had twisted themselves around her heart. He could empathize, as his was entangled with his wife, particularly when her soft, lyrical voice chuckled softly at some silly tidbit she'd shared. Several times she'd shed tears over the new babies abandoned in the middle of the night. She shed tears for their parents as well. It was those times he wanted to comfort her the most. His wife's heart could bear undeniable pain, yet her perseverance kept her going back to the foundling home every single day, except for Sunday. It was the one day that she gave entirely to him.

But after all these weeks, they'd become accustomed to a routine, and they never veered from it. After Amelia left in the morning, Martin would go down to the offices and prepare the articles for that day's editions. All the while, his mind and heart were across the street with Amelia.

Today was no different except Graham stood at the bottom of the steps waiting for him with a broadsheet in his hand.

"Here, Duke," he said gruffly. "Before you say a word, you need to read this." He stuffed the morning's copy of the *London-Town Tattler* into Martin's hand.

There was one column. A print of a stopped coach and four appeared at the top of the page. Drawn lines surrounded the carriage to mimic a rocking back and forth movement. Two pairs of feet, one male and one female, were tangled together and hanging outside the coach's window. The horses stood still looking bored. It was evident that whoever was in the carriage was involved in a tryst.

He took a moment to calm the riot of apprehension that flooded his body. Whatever was printed wouldn't affect him. He was above reacting to any twaddle that John Trimble would dare publish.

What the Self-Proclaimed "Duke" Won't Confess

He's a cuckold with an egg in the nest that's not his. How does the London-Town Tattler know such a fact? A witness happened upon a midwife leaving Martin Richmond's wife's residence, I personally observed the "little woman" with the same lover as the Duchess of "opposite direction of north-heart."

In a carriage, no less.

What makes it more intriguing, reader? The Duke of "opposite direction of north-heart" paid the Duke of Apology's wife a thousand pounds. Rumor has it that he'll continue that every year. Could it possibly be for her services? She must be quite the paramour to charge such rates.

Who will claim her bellyful?

Not a word from The Midnight Cryer or its Duke.

When you seek the truth, buy the London-Town Tattler.

We don't ignore the news.

The urge to destroy the filthy and foul broadsheet made his fingers itch. He stumbled a step and raised his hand to his aching chest. "Christ," he whispered.

"Now, Duke," Graham comforted.

"Don't call me that." Martin's voice sounded like he was speaking from the bottom of a barrel.

Graham ignored him. "You can't possibly believe it's true. Have you looked at your wife? Really taken a hard gander at her?"

Martin repeatedly blinked, trying to capture the essence of his assistant editor's nonsensical words that seem to float through the air in no particular order.

"Martin," the man said kindly. "Listen to me. Your wife only has eyes for you. Every Wednesday for the last five years, she's called on you. She stays close to the office. It's a testament to her feelings for you. She's committed to *you*."

"No." Martin shook his head in disbelief.

Graham pursed his lips. "You can see all the dirt that no one else sees. But you're blind to the things that are right in front of you. She loves only *you*, you daft man."

Martin collapsed in a chair. "That's not what I'm upset about."

"You don't believe his lies? You're finally listening to me?" Graham asked incredulously.

"Of course, I don't believe it. But that doesn't negate the harm done." He braced his elbows on his knees, then held his head in his hands as the abject feeling of powerlessness overcame him. "How in the devil could she love me now? John Trimble attacked her because of me. He told me to get her under control, or he'd deal with it. He was concerned that if a tax were levied against *The Midnight Cryer*, then the House of Lords would come after him." Martin forced his gaze to Graham's stern countenance. "I ignored his threat, and now my wife is the headline for the week." He grabbed a handful of hair and pulled, hoping the pain would dull the ache in his chest.

One of the reasons Amelia met him on Wednesdays was hopefully to have a child. If she was carrying, there was no way in hell he could let her go. This was his family.

His wife and his child. He wanted them. He wanted that life.

Then the truth practically knocked him to the floor.

If Amelia was pregnant, she had even less reason to try and make a life with him. She wouldn't be lonely anymore.

"I'm going to lose her."

"Go find her," Graham said. "This very instant. Do not let her read this before you tell her how you're going to fix this mess."

"*Good God, I don't know how to fix it.* What have I done?" he murmured to himself. This was exactly what Southart had dealt with. Martin had known the truth, had known the claims against the duchess had a simple explanation, and had known that any other interpretation was absurd. He blew out a breath to relieve the pressure that threatened to burst his heart in two.

He deserved every speck of pain he suffered. He'd known that his readership would prefer to believe a more salacious version, and he'd fueled that fire. Now he faced the same situation with his wife.

No wonder Southart went to see Amelia so he could protect his wife. This was beyond maddening, to be in a situation where simple facts were purposely misunderstood for entertainment purposes and profit. All the filth that had been written about Amelia was false and the *London-Town Tattler* had profited.

Martin's lip lifted in a sneer. For the first time in his life, he experienced the smutty and indescribable havoc and despair when a loved one became a victim of gossips. John Trimble and the *London-Town Tattler* were dirtier than the filthy sewers of the city.

Slowly, he sank into the chair. He closed his eyes as

the truth burned like an uncontrollable wildfire inside him.

He was no better. He'd help create this monster of insatiable gossip. When Martin was a young lad, he'd been bullied and overlooked by the rich and powerful heirs of the aristocracy. As an adult, he'd turned the tables on them when he'd started *The Midnight Cryer*.

Now his own success at bullying threatened the only thing he truly valued in this world—his marriage.

And the only person he'd ever fallen in love with—his wife.

Ten

AMELIA FINISHED WRITING in her journal all the instructions she'd received from the midwife yesterday. She had rushed home to tell Martin, but he'd been out all night. Mr. Graham had said that a big news story was about to break, which was keeping her husband busy. When she started her morning, she'd been disappointed to discover that Martin still hadn't come home. However, tonight couldn't come fast enough. No matter what, she'd wait up for him and share their good fortune. She had no idea how he'd receive the news, but she was beside herself with happiness.

She smoothed the gown over her still-flat midsection. Whether her husband wanted the baby or not wasn't something she would worry about now. Yet, the sweet care and concern he'd shown her over the last month made her optimistic that he'd be thrilled with the idea of being a father.

Amelia looked at the ormolu clock that stood on the fireplace mantel when a knock sounded on the door. It was almost time for her to walk to the foundling home. She didn't want to be a minute late, as today she was assigned to the nursery.

When she answered the door, Pauline Johnson stood on the other side. Mrs. Johnson had welcomed her with open arms when she asked if she could volunteer. That had been four years ago, and she credited the woman with keeping her from drowning in her grief over her troubled marriage.

Mrs. Johnson met her with a sad smile. Her usual cheerful attitude and warmth were completely missing.

"Mrs. Johnson." Amelia swept open the door. "Please come in."

"I won't take up much of your time," the kind woman said. Slightly older than Amelia, she wore her dark hair pulled back in a neat chignon. Her remarkable blue eyes always mirrored the woman's unique joie de vivre. But today, something was terribly wrong. "There's some unfortunate business to discuss."

Amelia led her to her Louis XV desk and matching chairs. Instead of sitting behind the desk, she took the chair next to Mrs. Johnson. The gloom that surrounded them reminded her of the day that Elizabeth came to see her. "Is it the monthly budget?" she asked. "The Duke of Southart said the funds were to be paid by the end of the week."

Mrs. Johnson reached across the distance and placed one gloved hand over Amelia's. "That's not it." She exhaled slowly, never taking her gaze from hers. "Have you seen the *London-Town Tattler*?"

Amelia shook her head so hard that several of her locks fell askew. "No. I don't read it—or any of the pamphlets or broadsheets, for that matter." She lowered her voice. "Including *The Midnight Cryer*."

Wordlessly, Mrs. Johnson handed her a pamphlet. Bile rose in her throat. She swallowed, then forced her eyes to the morning edition of Trimble's *London-Town Tattler*.

As she read the words, she released a long, controlled exhale. There was no sense in upsetting herself. "I suppose you want to know if it's true," she said after a moment.

Mrs. Johnson squeezed her hand. "No. That's business between you and your husband. I came by to share this with you so you'd understand why I can't allow you to work at the home today."

"Why?" Her voice softened to a whisper. She stood abruptly and started to pace. "Are you afraid my reputation hurts the foundling—"

Mrs. Johnson came to her side and took both of her hands in hers. "Not at all. I don't even want you thinking that." She narrowed her eyes as if in pain. "John Trimble called on me this morning, looking for you. I told him that I had no idea when I'd see you next." She pulled her into a hug. "Amelia, I don't want you to be hounded by that man when you're with us. Give it a few days to die down. These stories always do, you know."

"They manipulate the truth for their own benefit without a care for any of the consequences." Heat bludgeoned her cheeks. She didn't say any more, as her husband was as guilty as John Trimble.

"You bring love and happiness to the children." Mrs. Johnson leaned back and cupped Amelia's hands with her cheeks. "I know it's upsetting. But remember, you're very important to us."

Another knock sounded, and when she looked to see who it was, it was Martin. "Mrs. Johnson, you've perfectly described my exact feelings about my wife."

At the sight of him, she felt a wave of emotion roll through her. When her eyes grew blurry with tears, that's when she knew she was in trouble. Her life, namely her marriage, was such a blasted mess.

"Mr. Richmond," Mrs. Johnson said politely. She turned to Amelia. "I'll come by later on this week, and we shall reassess the situation."

She glided out of the room, leaving Martin and Amelia alone. Without a sound, Martin closed the door and started toward her.

Instantly, she held up her hand to ward him away, but he kept on coming. His square jaw set in determination.

"Don't come any closer." Not only was her husband advancing closer, but tears swelled, making everything blurry, including him.

"Let me." He stopped suddenly as his voice broke. "I'm in desperate need to comfort you right now."

She had never heard him so frantic, and for a moment, she couldn't think of a response. But with everything that had happened to her in the last twenty-four hours, she had to say her piece.

"I take it that you saw the *London-Town Tattler*." She blinked enough of her tears to see that his face had turned ashen. "It's true that Southart promised if I kept you from printing that salacious story about his duchess, he'd give the foundling home one thousand pounds a year. That's why I wrote the retraction. Afterward, I went to see him, and he agreed to continue our bargain. The foundling home needs the money. It's also true that I'm carrying."

If possible, his face had grown even grayer.

As her tears fell in rivulets, she wiped them as best she could. She sucked in a breath and regarded him. "Don't *you* dare ask who this baby belongs to. If you believe what Trimble published, it'll destroy everything I've ever felt for you. I love you, but I can't live with you any longer. I've tried my best to find a way to be your wife." She sliced her hand through the air as her tears began anew. "I cannot compete with *The Midnight Cryer*, and I won't."

She bowed her head, struggling to regain her composure but lost the fight. All the sadness, heartache, and anguish that she'd tried to contain over the years washed over her. Her entire body felt as if she were mired in knee-deep mud and unable to move. What was supposed to be the happiest day of her life had been destroyed, wholly eviscerated, by a scandal sheet. But what was ironic? By some cruel fate of chance, it happened to have guessed the truth about her condition.

She straightened her shoulders and stared into Martin's gaze. "I'm so sorry that I didn't fight harder for us. I should have stayed with you in the beginning and explained my hatred for gossip. Convinced you to use your brilliance in another way. But I didn't. Now the *Cryer* has taken my place, and it's too powerful to stop."

"What do you mean that it's taken your place?" he asked hesitantly.

"You said you were faithful in your marriage. I assumed you meant to me. But you meant the *Cryer*." She laughed, but there was no humor behind her words. She'd created this life for herself by not fighting for her husband.

"Oh God, Amelia. Do not say that." His whisky-dark voice turned gravelly. "I never meant for you to compete with my work. I was trying to create a life for us, one filled with financial security. I thought the *Cryer* was the answer." He rubbed the back of his neck.

Another tear fell. This time she didn't wipe it away.

Martin stood before her and slid one hand around her waist. "You are *The Midnight Cryer*. The reason for the name is that whenever I came home at night, you'd be waiting for me, and we'd make love. It seemed as if every single time the church would toll the midnight bells, we were in each other's arms. You'd always cry out and scream my name."

Amelia didn't move.

"There's not a single day when I don't hear the name of *The Midnight Cryer* that I don't think of you. It reminds me of our first month of marriage. I've never been happier in my life."

"How can that be?" Suddenly, her world was up-ended as Martin swept her into his arms. She latched on to his shoulders. It was the sweetest story, but how could she forget all her convictions? It couldn't change a thing.

Martin pulled her tighter to his body, then took her into the bedroom. "I shall prove it to you."

"I'm not doing that." She sniffed as she waved a hand toward the bed. If he thought now was the perfect time to make love, he wasn't as brilliant as she'd thought.

"Resting?" He gently sat her on the bed, then proceeded to undress her.

She batted his hands away. "I'm not tired."

"Fine." He cupped her cheeks in his hand. "Then let me kiss you."

"Why?" She sounded like an argumentative shrew, but she didn't care.

As he drew nearer, his breath fanned over her cheek. The divine scent of cinnamon and coffee wafted toward her.

"I haven't kissed you in eighteen hours, four minutes, and thirteen seconds." He brushed his thumbs over her cheeks. "We're long overdue."

"Pfft." Amelia didn't even realize it, but somehow, she'd reached out to touch him in return. Her hand rested over his heart. The steady pounding of his heartbeat reminded her that her husband was a constant force in her life. How would she fill the emptiness when she left him? She swallowed to keep another round of tears from erupting.

"Pfft, yourself," he retorted. His countenance lost all humor. "Are you really carrying?" He shook his head. "That was a ridiculous question. Of course you are. How are you feeling?"

"Like my whole world has turned upside down," she said softly. "But in a good way, until I read that horrific column."

"Wretched business." He reverently pressed a kiss to her forehead. "Trimble was furious about the retraction. He wanted me to stop you from influencing my columns, but I told him no. I should have expected something like this. It's my fault he wrote that."

When he was arrogant, he was aggravating. When he was happy, his smile could light up a room. No matter what, he was devastatingly handsome. However, the look of dejection that currently marred his face couldn't stand. He wasn't the one who wrote the article.

Lord help her, she was making excuses for him.

"Mrs. Johnson told me that he visited the foundling home asking for me. That's why she was here. To tell me to stay away." She took one of his hands and pressed it against her stomach. "But it all pales to this."

He surprised her when he leaned down and pressed a kiss to her middle. "Whatever it takes to make you happy, I'm prepared to do."

"Martin, I meant what I said earlier about *The Midnight Cryer*." When he rested his forehead against her stomach, she stroked her fingers through the silken strands of his hair. "I'll not be a part of it anymore. Not now."

"Are you saying you're leaving me again?" His eyes flashed like streaks of blue lightning in a midnight sky.

'It's for the best." Her throat swelled with emotion making it difficult to breathe, let alone talk. 'I don't want the baby subjected to scandals. I'll ask Mrs. Johnson if she could hire me. You won't have to be responsible for me anymore."

He leaned back and sat on his haunches. The stubborn tilt of his chin meant he didn't like her plans. But it was the best for all of them.

'Are you just going to cut me out of his or her life?" The vibrance in his softened voice, a harbinger of his anger, rang through the room.

'I would never do that. But raising a child above the office of *The Midnight Cryer* would make me miserable. We'll work out something. You'll see the baby—"

He pressed his fingers to her lips. 'Don't, Amelia. I beg of you. Give me a week to get my affairs in order. If they do not please you, then I'll capitulate to your demands."

'We're still negotiating, I see." She smiled slightly.

'All marriages require work. Allow me an opportunity to show you what I'm capable of doing." He slowly rose to his feet, then leaned down and pressed his lips against hers. 'If we're still negotiating, what would it take for you to come home to me?"

'A miracle," she replied.

"That's quite a demand." He pressed his lips to hers again, his manner reverent. 'I believe I'm up to the task. Give me a week." He stood and walked to the door. Before he opened it, he turned and regarded her once more. 'I've been remiss in not telling you this sooner. I love you Amelia Richmond. I always have."

With that, her aloof husband did what he always did best.

Left her speechless.

Eleven

THE LAST PIECE of the puzzle Martin needed to fit all his plans together was finally in place. With some luck, he could prove to Amelia that he loved her more than anything else in this world. Otherwise, the idea of apologizing to Southart would be a wasted effort.

And Martin hated wasted efforts almost as much as he hated Southart.

He sucked in a breath as the truth punched him in the stomach. He didn't necessarily hate Southart. In years past, he'd always found the duke to be a wastrel. But once he found his wife, his life changed for the better—much the same for Martin.

Because of Amelia.

How could he hate the duke when their paths to happiness were so similar?

Martin hated the men and the women of the aristocracy who thought they were better than others. That certainly wasn't the case with this duke or his duchess. Their charitable efforts demonstrated the couple's generosity and compassion for helping others, particularly unwed mothers and people suffering from rheumatic fever.

He couldn't delay any longer. He entered the gate, then took the pathway to the duke's home. At the grand entrance, he knocked on the door.

A dour elderly butler answered. "How may I help you?"

"Martin Richmond to see the Duke of Southart." His voice confident, Martin pulled a calling card from his morning jacket and handed it to the butler.

The man lifted an eyebrow when he read the card. "I shall see if His Grace is receiving." The man looked down at Martin as if he were something the house cat had dragged in from its midnight hunts. "But if I were you, I wouldn't get my hopes up." With surprising energy in his step, the butler turned and walked down a hallway.

Within minutes, the butler was back. "The duke would be *delighted* to see you. His words, not mine." The butler turned, and Martin followed.

Soon they stood outside a massive study. The door stood open, and Southart sat at his desk reading something. He was an imposing figure, with his height and his perfect aristocratic features. No wonder women made fools of themselves around him.

His Amelia had met with him, but she didn't seem at all taken with him. Her only interest was helping the man with his marriage and securing funds for the foundling home. Something that Martin would contribute to, also.

But first, he had to write his column for tomorrow's *Cryer*.

"Your Grace, the editor of *The Midnight Cryer*," the butler said, sticking his nose in the air as if Martin reeked of manure.

"Thank you, Ives," the duke said as he stood in welcome. "Richmond, come in."

As Martin approached, the duke walked around his desk and extended his hand. Martin hesitated for a moment, thinking how he'd once threatened to ruin the man's duchess. He swallowed his unease, then clasped the offered hand.

At the memory, guilt rose from every conceivable part of him. He now understood how such a thing would drive a husband to do anything if it protected his beloved.

The duke shook his hand as if old friends. "Come sit down," Southart offered, completely unaware of Martin's shame. "I finished reading the astonishing report you wrote."

Martin took his seat in front of the massive burlwood desk, as the duke sat across from him. "What do you think?"

"Pardon me for asking but is it true?" the duke asked, narrowing his gaze. "These are inflammatory claims." Southart chuckled. "We both know that you like to be...how shall I say...sensational?" He quirked a brow.

Martin grinned at the humor in the duke's voice. It was a relief after the hectic week he'd had.

"Every word, Your Grace. My wife is friends with Lady Overton, who came to see my wife about a delicate matter. Lady Overton didn't confide in her that day. But my wife said the woman was upset, so I took it upon myself to call upon her. After I assured her ladyship that I wasn't there to destroy her or her husband, she told me the story. I went to see Overton for verification, and he confirmed it."

The duke relaxed in his chair, but there was a restless energy that hovered around him. "The Marquess of Hazelthorpe took bribes from officers looking for promotions so he could keep his mistress in new gowns? It sounds like something *The Midnight Cryer* would print."

"Indeed." Martin leaned forward a tad. "And the marquess signed them with Lord Overton's name. Once Lord Overton discovered it, he grew worried about how to confront the marquess. Overton was concerned that since he was new in the House of Lords, everyone would believe Hazelthorpe."

"Why did you think of me?" the duke asked while resting his ankle on the opposite knee.

"I told Overton that I'd take it to someone with the gravitas to see that the wrong was righted."

The duke nodded, then pulled the piece of parchment nearer. "I've some allies, family mostly, that will help set this matter straight. Thank you for sending it to me."

"I'm sure Lord and Lady Overton will be relieved." Martin stood. "I won't take up any more of your time. I have a column to write and publish about Lord Hazelthorpe."

"Leave that to me. I want to discuss something else," the duke instructed.

Immediately, Martin sat down.

"It's out of character for you to help someone, isn't it?" Southart narrowed his eyes as he surveyed Martin.

It was eerily like the way Southart's snooty butler evaluated him. "Well, you'll be pleased to know that *The Midnight Cryer* is retiring," he said, and the duke laughed. The strange feeling of camaraderie with the duke sitting across from him made him confess. "I'm going to lose my wife otherwise. The *London-Town Tattler* spread a tale which hurt her deeply."

"What's it like to be on the other side of the gossip?" the duke asked innocently, but his barb hit its target.

Right in the middle of Martin's chest. How fitting that it was coming from the Duke of Southart.

"It hurts like hell." Martin rubbed his chest where the imaginary barb seemed to have landed. "But the worst part? It was seeing the devastation on my wife's face. I knew then that the scandal sheets and the coffee house gossip prints weren't for me anymore." He dropped his hand and held the duke's gaze. "One more thing. I've come here today to apologize for the pain and heartache I've caused your family and you."

"It takes a good man and a good heart to learn the error of his ways." The duke said sympathetically.

"I'm not that benevolent, Your Grace. It's more than that." He fisted his hand, hoping to control the agony that resided in his heart. He had to believe that he'd win her back. "I love my wife."

"I wish you luck, Richmond," the duke said sincerely. "I almost lost my wife once. I've never felt so desolate in my life."

"A helpless and horrible feeling," Martin confided and bent his head to quell the emotion that threatened to turn him into a blathering idiot. "I'll be lost if I lose her."

"Richmond," the duke said softly. "We come from different places, but I know your pain. Don't allow that to happen. Fight for her."

Martin nodded. "You're being extremely kind."

"Like you, I'm not so altruistic either." The duke waggled his eyebrows. "What about your work?"

It was a question Martin had been asking himself all week. While he had enough money saved to support himself and Amelia for the rest of their lives, he still had to work. *Needed* to work. It was part of who he was. "I don't have any plans outside of shutting down *The Midnight Cryer*."

The duke nodded knowingly. "How would you feel about seeing me every day?"

Martin scowled slightly, then grinned. "Sounds like torture, but I'm intrigued. Tell me more, Your Grace."

~

"Ma'am?" One of *The Midnight Cryer* errand boys approached Amelia as she returned from her day at the foundling home. "Mr. Graham says I'm to give this to you. It's the first page printed of Mr. Richmond's column today."

Amelia took the paper and folded it under her arm. She opened her reticule and fished out a coin for him. The boy grinned from ear to ear then scampered off into the traffic that lined the busy street. No doubt he was headed to complete another errand. She sighed heavily and glanced up at Martin's study window. He stood on the other side, watching her. She lifted a hand to wave, then thought better of it. She must not react whenever she saw him.

Heavens, it was a hard thing to accomplish. Anything interesting that happened in her day, she wanted to share with him. Any small tidbit she heard, she wanted to share with him. But it would come to naught. Today was day seven of their week apart, and he still hadn't come to see her.

Perhaps he'd decided not to win her regard. With a sigh, she headed upstairs and entered her rooms. Taking a seat by the window, she unfolded the sheet.

She blinked once. Then again.

The Last and Final Edition of The Midnight Cryer

Alas, gentle reader, the time has come to retire this noble endeavor. Thank you for your patronage, but there are more meaningful ways for all of us to spend our time. I will use my retirement wisely by wooing my wife, whom I love madly.

You see, reader, when you have someone who makes you whole physically, spiritually, and in every other sense, you've uncovered something magical.

That's not to say there aren't ordinary days in our lives. But with her by my side, those simple days mystically turn into an extraordinary, singular life. I plan to continue that with her if she'll allow it.

It's shallow, but the first thing that drew me to her was her beauty. Yet, underneath her attraction is something far more alluring. Her inherent goodness and kindness are the food that enriches my soul.

Yes, I love her completely.

Adieu, gentle reader. My parting wish is that you nurture any love that comes your way. Let it grow, and you'll soon see the fruits of your endeavors blossoming into a well-lived life.

Wish me luck.

Amelia didn't trust her eyes. Not only were they in the nasty habit of weeping at the drop of a hat, but they were making her see things that couldn't possibly be. She had to reread the parchment in her hands at least twice to ensure that she wasn't misreading it.

Today, she'd shed a few tears while holding Ivy in her arms. The child was so innocent. Amelia had been like that once. But not anymore. Yet, she'd learned an important lesson. Sometimes you need to walk through fire to forge a strong and resilient love.

Without wasting another moment, she ran downstairs, crossed the street, rushed into *The Midnight Cryer*'s office. She didn't spare a glance at Mr. Graham, but she heard him chuckle at her entrance.

In seconds, she was up the steps and in their apartments.

Martin stood in the middle of the room waiting for her. The apprehension on his face melted when he saw her smile.

"What did you do?" she asked.

"I take it that you read the last column I wrote." His smile turned tender. "I meant every word I said. I love you. I want you to stay with me. As my wife. As my lover."

She leaped into his arms. "My foolish, irresistible husband. Of *course* I will."

"I gave it all up and am glad for it. You're my everything, my Midnight Cryer." He cupped her cheeks, bent his head, and kissed her. When their lips met, the earth didn't shatter, but she felt her heart start mending all the broken pieces, becoming stronger with every beat.

She groaned as that familiar fire surged between them. It happened whenever they unleashed their undeniable desire for each other. Breathless, she pulled away. "I don't know what to say."

"I do. Let me say it." He kissed her again soundly on the lips. "I have nothing without you." He dipped his gaze to hers, then slid it down to her belly. "And our family."

Everything inside her melted at the sight of love shining bright in his eyes.

This moment was everything she ever wanted. This man was everything she wanted.

She tugged his hand, leading him toward the bedroom. "Let's not waste another moment."

"Wife, you are a wicked woman." Once across the

threshold, he closed the door. "And I wouldn't change a single thing about you."

"Nor I you," she said.

Clothes flew as they undressed. Their gazes never parted from each other. Martin was naked first, then helped her with her dress and chemise.

Her heart jolted at the sight of his evident desire for her. His gaze slid slowly and seductively down her body as if trying to memorize every part of her. The sight made her want him even more.

"My God, you steal my breath. But there's no need. I'd gladly give it to you." He kissed her with his eyes as he stood before her and cupped her breasts. "You're larger. Fuller."

"So are you, I see." She laughed as she squeezed her eyes shut. A riot of sensation careened through her body, lighting a blaze of desire that only her husband could satisfy. "Please," she whimpered.

He took her in his arms, and his warmth enveloped her. Claiming her mouth, he crushed her to him. His lips met hers in a kiss of possession. When his tongue pressed against the seam of her lips, she groaned, letting him in.

As he stroked hers, no inch of her mouth was left untouched. It was a reclaiming of their love, their marriage, and each other. The sweet taste of him never ceased to make her ravenous for him. My God, she loved this man with her entire being.

When they broke apart, they were both panting, exhilarated by their touch. He whipped the coverlet back and helped her settle into bed. When he slid in next to her, she pulled him closer.

She had missed his smell, the cedar fragrance mixed with his musk scent. In an instant, he covered her, resting his body weight on his elbows.

"Do you know how many times I fantasized about this moment with you?" He pressed his lips to her cheek, then trailed them to the tender spot beneath her ear. His tongue licked her skin. Softly, she mewled as she pulled him tighter against her. "Over this last week, I've taken myself in hand at least a dozen times, thinking of holding you as I pumped into you again and again. Fantasies are nothing like real life."

She whimpered as his warm breath tickled the whorls surrounding her ear. He chuckled, then nibbled on her earlobe. Her body was on fire for him. If he didn't take her soon, she feared she'd combust on the spot. She arched, pressing her aching breasts against his chest.

"Minx," he growled.

She captured his mouth with her own and caressed her tongue against his. A low moan vibrated in his chest as he pulled her closer.

Using his mouth, he seared a path down her neck, her shoulders, but it wasn't enough. She wrapped her legs around his waist, then rubbed herself against him. His cock creased her wet folds, and she moaned at the heavenly rapture of feeling his hard length against her. "If you're going to tease me, then I'll find relief myself," she teased as she reached a hand between them.

Before she could touch herself, he grabbed it and interlaced their fingers. He pulled her arm above her head, pinning it in place. "Don't you dare." Then he tsked playfully, shaking his head. "Your pleasure is mine."

She canted her hips. "Do it before I perish."

With a sly smile, he nudged his cock at her entrance. They both hissed at the exquisite touch of their bodies joining. In one slow, punishing, sweet push, he entered her. Her muscles throbbed and contracted at his entrance.

"Heaven," she said softly. "That's what this feels like."

"We're just beginning." He established a slow rhythm of moving in and out. She lifted her hips to meet each thrust. He hitched her leg over his shoulder, making each penetration deeper and more intimate. Her body quivered, and she concentrated on his face as her climax was just within reach.

"I'm close," she whispered.

He pulled her body close as his hips hammered against hers. His cock was hitting a place inside of her that sent her over the edge. She cried out his name and closed her eyes as the sensation flooded her. It was as if a dam of pleasure had broken within her.

When she opened her eyes, there was a slight grimace on his face. In seconds, he closed his eyes, and with a final thrust, his seed filled her. Her muscles clenched against his cock.

He groaned in approval, then buried his head in the crook of her neck. "My God. I'll never have enough of you."

She combed her fingers through his midnight locks. "I feel the same. I love you."

He slid his body to the side of hers and brought her into his embrace. He pressed his lips against hers. "I love you. Never did I think I'd feel this way about another person until I married you."

"You loved me when we married?"

"Of course." He pressed a kiss to her nose. "It's another reason why I named my pamphlet *The Midnight Cryer*?"

Heat singed her cheeks.

"It's our secret." He smiled wickedly. "No one knows why. They think it's a name after the old-time criers who used to spread the news through the streets."

"Thank you." She nestled into the contours of his body. "What shall you do after giving up the *Cryer*?"

He bent his elbow and rested his head on his palm. "I've much to tell you. I went to see your friend Lady Overton. She told me a horrific story about how the Marquess of Hazelthorpe had signed Lord Overton's name to dozens of promotions in the army in exchange for bribes. She was concerned for her husband's reputation even though he was completely innocent. I verified her story with the marquess's disgruntled secretary. Hazelthorpe isn't timely with his wages, thus the need for money."

"What?" she asked, stunned at the news.

"There's more, darling." He trailed a finger down her cheek. "I called upon the Duke of Southart to apologize. After I saw what Trimble's ugly insinuations had done to you, I had to make things right with the duke. I finally understood the true costs of my work."

"What did Southart say?" It was unfathomable to believe that her husband, the one who never had a kind word to say about the duke or any duke for that matter, had called upon him.

"He was gracious. When I told him that I had two final columns to write, I meant to spread the news about Hazelthorpe, but the duke wanted to handle the matter personally. Yet, he offered me a new position."

"What kind of position?" She sat up and stared at her husband.

"I'll be reporting all the legislative news to the public. Southart believes that the House of Lords needs to be more forthcoming with their actions and offer an objective outlook on the issues presented for legislation. With my ability to ferret out gossip and write succulently, he said I'd be perfect for it."

He waggled his eyebrows playfully, and she sucked in a breath. How could a man elicit such intense feelings? He was a banquet for a starving woman, and she was hungry for the life he promised. He wasn't simply handsome. He was like an ethereal creature sent from Heaven only for her.

Was there any wonder why she was completely and utterly mad for the man?

"I have money saved," she said. "We can use it for your employees."

He pressed his lips against hers, then pulled away. The love on his face practically blinded her.

"No, darling. Save your money for the foundling home or however you want to use it. My employees will continue to work for me." He ran his hand down her belly. "Plus, I have plenty of money from all my years of running *The Midnight Cryer*. I've saved it for my family."

"I thought you didn't want a family."

He shook his head. "I lied to you. I said that trying to protect myself and prepare for the day you'd ultimately leave me. The truth is that I've wanted you from the first time I saw you. All these years, I'd prayed you'd come to me with news that we were going to have a baby. I thought you'd move home then." He lowered his head until he could gaze into her eyes. "I want our family. I want you." He looked to the ceiling briefly, then turned his gaze back to hers, where tears reflected in his eyes. "I regret...so much...that it took me so long to see the damage I caused. You are a saint to have stayed with me for so many years."

She closed the distance between them, wrapping her arms around him. It wasn't just an embrace. It was a fresh start for them as a couple.

The love they shared would ensure their life would

be a bounty of riches, filled with love, laughter, and family. But most important was their marriage.

"You've given me all I've ever wanted," she said softly. "A family. A loving—"

"A Duke?"

They both laughed at such nonsense.

"A loving husband. I only want you," she answered.

"Hmm," he said thoughtfully. "That's good to hear." Martin presented her with his endearing, cocky half-smile, the one she never could resist, then pressed his lips to hers. "You're my everything. My very own midnight cryer."

Epilogue

LONDON, *six years later*

"Momma, am I doing it right?" Ivy's green-eyed gaze met Amelia's as they sat on the brocade sofa in the sitting room. Ivy's fingers tangled with the strings of her half-boots as she tried to learn the intricacies of tying her shoes.

"Yes, darling," Amelia leaned over and pressed a kiss on the top of Ivy's golden locks. It was the fourth anniversary of their darling daughter coming to live with them. When Martin had suggested they raise her as their own, Amelia had cried with joy.

She pulled Ivy tight against her and hugged her with all her might. Sometimes, her love couldn't be contained. Her daughter looked up at her with a curious grin.

"What was that for?" Ivy giggled with pleasure.

"It's a 'because' hug. I did it because I love you." Amelia pressed another kiss to Ivy's button nose.

The little girl wrapped her arms around Amelia and squeezed in return. "Here's one for you, Momma."

"How does one garner a 'because' hug?" A whisky-dark voice rumbled from the doorway. "I want one."

Amelia's breath caught as she looked up to see the two dashing men in her life strolling toward her. Even after eleven years of marriage, she felt the thrill of seeing her husband after a long absence, even if that long period was only an hour.

"Eww," Graham, their precocious five-year-old son, never failed to offer his low opinion of hugs, girls, or baths. Of course, his big sister Ivy was the exception to the girl part.

Amelia considered herself very fortunate to be classified by Graham as "not a girl" since her title was "Mother." Yet, their son was an affectionate fellow and thankfully allowed Amelia to kiss and hug him.

By then, Graham had come to her side and kissed her cheek. He'd done the same to his big sister, whom he considered the most intelligent person on the planet. Martin leaned forward and kissed Ivy's cheek, then turned his attention to Amelia.

"Hullo, darling." He pressed a kiss to her lips, then whispered for her ears only, "It's such a shame that they don't nap anymore. I feel like I'm quite in need of one...with you." He waggled his brows with a wry grin.

"I miss those, too," she confided, then stole a peek at their children. When her gaze returned to Martin, his eyes were blazing, sending a shiver skating down her back. She would never tire of seeing him thus—happy, content, and desirous of her. If any of her friends, especially Elizabeth and Daphne, the Duchess of Southart, felt the same for their husbands, they were lucky indeed. "Are you done for the day?"

Before her husband could say a word, Graham piped up. "We are."

Today, Graham had accompanied Martin to the House of Lords. Whenever Martin had a short day of work, he always took Graham with him. Their son opened his satchel and pulled out a piece of parchment. "Behold, *The Midday Cryer*," he said proudly.

"What on earth?" Amelia took the paper and saw a drawing of a stick couple in an embrace with their lips touching. Underneath the drawing were the scribbled words, "The lord and lady performing the ugly." Her eyes widened, and she turned to Martin.

He shrugged slightly and delivered a roughish grin. "I was just like him at that age. He's a man who recognizes news when he sees it."

She shouldn't ask, but she couldn't help herself. "Who are they?"

Graham rocked back on his heels, entirely too pleased with himself. "Lord and Lady Overton."

"That's so naughty," Ivy exclaimed as she took the paper from Amelia's hands and studied it with acute interest. "That's gossip, and Momma says that we shouldn't encourage it," she said, tipping her nose with an air of authority that only an older sister could deliver.

Graham hmphed. "Then why are you studying it so hard?"

Ivy ignored him. She pointed to another stick figure on the paper. "Who's that?"

"I don't know," Graham answered thoughtfully. "But he seemed kind of sad when he saw the couple kissing."

Amelia and Martin looked at each other.

Her husband leaned close and pressed a kiss to the tender skin beneath her ear, then whispered, "Our son is just like me. He never misses a detail."

While Ivy and Graham were trying to ferret out who the man might be, Amelia swiveled her head and pressed a kiss to his lips. "And I love both of you for it. But you can't encourage him in reporting gossip."

Martin chuckled as he put his arm around her and

pulled her close. "It's not me. It's his namesake. Edgar Graham is showing him how to start his own pamphlet business. I expect by the time he's at Eton, he'll be quiet the popular fellow."

"Martin," she scolded.

He held up a hand to stave off any of her objections. "Now, before you say any more, hear me out. My old assistant is teaching our son the family business. While Graham keeps our son entertained, I finish my work as quickly as possible so I can return home to you." He raised a hand and cupped her cheek. "Look at the benefits. He'll be able to ferret out who the scalawags are for Ivy's benefit. When she has her first Season, she'll know whom to stay away from. Plus, that gives us time for more kisses."

The laughter shining bright in her husband's eyes ruined the earnest look on his face.

"Such poor advice," Amelia chided. "If I'd had such insight about *your* behavior early on, I might not have given you a second look."

"Even if I had been a duke?" he asked, then pressed his nose to hers.

"Da," Graham scolded at the sign of affection.

"Well, that might have changed things." Amelia pressed a kiss to his lips and wanted to melt into his arms. "Everyone wants a duke. But there's only one for me."

"That's a relief," Martin sighed softly.

Amelia pressed her head into his chest and laughed softly. "You're the duke of my dreams. I love you."

Martin tilted her chin until their gazes met. The endearing affection in his eyes reflected her own. "I love you. Always have. Always will."

More by Janna

The Widow Rules Series
A DUKE IN TIME
RULES FOR ENGAGING THE EARL
WHERE THERE'S A WILL

The Cavensham Heiresses Series
THE BAD LUCK BRIDE
THE BRIDE WHO GOT LUCKY
THE LUCK OF THE BRIDE
THE GOOD, THE BAD, AND THE DUKE

ROGUE MOST WANTED
WILD, WILD RAKE

Christmas Anthology
MISTLETOE CHRISTMAS

About the Author

Janna MacGregor was born and raised in the bootheel of Missouri. She credits her darling mom for introducing her to the happily-ever-after world of romance novels. Janna writes stories where compelling and powerful heroines meet and fall in love with their equally matched heroes. She is the mother of triplets and splits her time between Kansas City and Minneapolis with her very own dashing rogue, and one smug, but not surprisingly, perfect pug. She loves to hear from readers.

Join the Ladies of Langham Hall Facebook Group
Sign up Janna's Newsletter
Visit Janna's Website: jannamacgregor.com

Duke of Every Sin

STACY REID

One

HAMPSHIRE, KELLITCH HALL

THE GENTLEMAN who opened the door could only be the duke himself. His bearing was that of a man confident of his consequence and influence in the world. He wore a charcoal frockcoat and icy-blue waistcoat that fit flawlessly on his lean, muscular frame. His midnight-black hair needed a trim, and the angles of his jaw were savage and elegant. This gentleman could only be Ethan Benedict, Duke of Bainbridge, a man who has been an object of fear, fascination, and salacious gossip in high society for several years. He appeared younger than she had imagined, less dissipated, but hauntingly lonely. Lady Verity Stanton couldn't say what gave her that impression. Perhaps it was the rigid set of his shoulders or the flat, unsmiling mouth.

Or probably it was the way his figure framed the doorway of the fine house before her. It was constructed of stone of pale ochre, with a double frontage enclosing the main entrance. The three stories were lined with high windows and topped with a decorate railing, interspersed with small pillars. The central façade was classical in white marble with four large, smooth pillars and a triangular tympanum above, also in white. Three classical statues were at the corners of the triangle and looked down on the duke and the basket beneath them. Verity felt their stone gaze upon her, and for a few moments considered whether they wanted to point out the interlopers to their rake of an owner.

Gripping the jacket of her small friend, she pulled him in a crouch to hide from the chilling gaze that swept across the forecourt and into the woodlands. From where she hid, Verity could not discern the color of his eyes, but she felt the piercing depth of them intently when his gaze caught sight of the carriage that rattled down the gravel paved road, clearly running away from whatever they had laid at his front door. His eyes followed the passage of the hurtling carriage.

Verity and Artie had been too late. After seeing her sister's letter, Verity had mounted her horse and rode with Artie like the hounds of Hell chased them, and they still had been too late. Catherine had abandoned little Thomas in a basket on the devil's doorstep and run away.

"He looks like the bloody devil," Artie murmured.

Worrying minds do think alike.

"I read in a few scandal sheets that they called him the Devil Duke," she whispered.

"Wot was Catherine thinking?" Artie asked in a furious whisper, crouched at her side behind a large willow tree near the forecourt of the manor. "How could she do this to our family?"

Or what is left of our family, Verity thought, an ache gripping her throat in an awful hold. "She believes this is what is best for little Thomas." Or so the very silly, selfish letter she left behind claimed.

"Nonsense," Artie hissed, his voice wobbling with his tears. "What would this bleedin' nob know about taking care of a *baby*?"

'I am a nob," she whispered.

He squared his bony shoulders and lifted his chin. "You are different. Yer a *disgraced* nob, with no fine reputation. As you normally say, Lady Verity, "tis a fine distinction indeed."'

She turned her thoughts to Artie's remark and her heart felt a measure of amusement to hear her own words tossed back at her, but Verity could not smile. In truth, not even the fiercest of storms could have ripped her attention from the man standing in the open doorway, staring down at the basket on the ground as if it held the rarest of creatures. And perhaps to him, the little baby boy swaddled in several layers of blanket was a creature.

"Why is he just staring at little Thomas?" Artie fretted a bit too loudly.

"Do speak softer," she whispered, rubbing her thighs through her cloak. Her legs ached from crouching and holding herself still, lest she command the duke's attention. "Once he closes the door, run as fast as you can and take Thomas from the basket and bring him to me. We will make our way home as fast as we can."

"Are yer so certain he'll leave Thomas?"

Verity froze. "Of course. What would a duke want with a baby left on his doorstep?"

"He would be bloody cold-hearted to close the door on little Thomas."

"Perhaps he will return inside and send out one of his servants to take him. We will use that window of opportunity to grab Thomas and be away as quickly as possible."

"What if he takes 'im up 'imself?"

"The duke has a reputation of being cold and indifferent to others' pain," Verity said. "Why would he deign to do something servants can do?"

That was surely crediting the dissolute duke, whom they claimed indulged in every manner of sin, with too much kindness. Verity felt an odd pinch of guilt to think so little of a man she only knew by reputation.

"Is he little Thomas's father?"

No, that honor belonged to the dead Earl of Preston. "He is not."

Verity's blood turned icy in her veins when the duke stooped down and picked up the basket before standing. The duke stood there for a long time, just staring at the baby in his arms. His dark head lifted, and once more he stared after the carriage that had long disappeared around the twisting bend in the mud-logged country road. He reached for something in the basket, and her breath hitched to see that it was a note of some sort. After reading, the duke flicked it away, and the wind tossed it far from his reach.

"Do not take your eyes from that note, Artie," she whispered. "Once the duke leaves, follow it and retrieve it for me."

"Yes."

There was no hesitation from her fierce and loyal companion. The duke turned around and disappeared into his mansion. Verity lurched to her feet, and instantly groaned at the sharp cramp which shot through her hips and legs. A slight panic gripped her chest.

"He took little Thomas," Artie said, appearing stunned and a bit lost. Then he darted away, running after the note that danced to the tune of the wind. He caught it and brought it over to Verity. With trembling fingers, she opened it.

He is your problem now.

She recognized her sister's handwriting, and a tortured sound escaped Verity. Catherine had called her own sweet baby a problem and discarded him as if he were trash, on the doorstep of a duke.

"I've never seen you cry," Artie softly said.

It was then she realized hot tears coursed down her cheeks. Verity furiously swiped away the telling weakness. Little Thomas was her nephew, her family, a baby she had been caring for since he had existed in Catherine's womb. It was Verity who had seen him first, who had held him when he took his first cry, as Catherine had fainted from exhaustion. Verity had bathed him for the past year and three months; she had read to him at nights when he woke the small cottage with his mighty and beautiful bellow. It was only Verity who had loved and cared for him with her whole heart. Catherine had always been an indifferent mother, but there were lovely times when she had shown that she loved him in the way she smiled at him and kissed his brows and inhaled his baby scent. But there had always been pain and sadness in her smile, and the melancholy she had fallen into after birthing Thomas had never left.

Still, Verity never thought Catherine would have taken Thomas from his home, from those who loved him and left him with a stranger. Verity glanced down at the note once more, sorrow slapping her body with harsh pounds. It hurt. Everywhere. Catherine had not even referred to little Thomas by name and listed out what he enjoyed, like taking long baths while Verity sang and played with him.

He is your problem now.

"Artie," she said hoarsely.

"Yes, Verity."

"We are not leaving without little Thomas."

He lifted his chin and squared his bony shoulders. "Wot is the plan? I carried me dagger."

So loyal and brave. She wanted to hug him; instead, she ruffled his ginger hair. At ten years of age, he already fancied himself a man. "Perhaps we should ring the doorbell first. Then if we meet a wall, we might bring out the dagger," she said with a teasing smile. He was a fighter, and that was the reason he had survived harsh winters and life until she had stumbled upon him stealing from their small gardens. Despite Catherine's worry, he might rob them of the little they owned, Verity had taken Artie in their lives and her heart. She had not regretted it once.

"Wot are we going to do?"

"It is very simple, Artie. Little Thomas does not belong to the duke. I will ask him for my nephew, and he shall hand him over."

"Wot if he says no?"

"He has no reason to."

He had no reason to take him up either. She shrugged aside that worrying thought. The duke was a human being, and it was a kindness not previously attributed to him that he had taken up the baby. That was it, a simple kindness. There was no reason for her to fret so. Still, her belly quivered, and nerves rioted inside. Smoothing down the skirts of her gown and hating that the hem had been muddied, Verity squared her shoulders and marched from behind the large willow tree toward the forecourt of the imposing mansion.

Two

ETHAN HAD no notion of how long he stood in the drawing room staring down at the wriggling thing swaddled in the bassinet. He was vaguely aware of the housekeeper hovering somewhere behind him.

He is your problem now.

That cold, succinct note that had been etched in his mind had not revealed anything about the sender. Yet assessing the child, it was evident why the author thought Ethan's home the perfect place to dump this particular problem. The child was the piercing image of Oscar Thornhill, Earl of Preston, his best friend since their days at Eton.

A best friend I killed.

Ethan closed a mental fist around that crippling thought with ruthless will, and squeezed it until the echoes of torment died away.

"I beg your pardon, Your Grace," Mrs. Groves said, "A young lady is begging an audience."

"I am not at home to callers, Mrs. Groves. I have not been for over two years."

"I told the young miss, Your Grace, and she *insisted*

it was an urgent matter, that something that belongs to her was left quite by accident on your doorstep."

That arrested Ethan's attention, and he shifted his regard from the child to his portly housekeeper. It seemed the second part of the game was about to unfold. He was but mildly stirred, and with a lift of his chin indicated the lady was to be shown inside. Ethan was still standing by the bassinet when the soft scent of lavender invaded his senses. He faced the intruder, ensuring that his body hid the baby from her view.

A sense of shock filled him to see the young, flushed face of the girl who entered his domain. Surely this chit was not a day over seventeen years. Then he noted the lushness and the gentle curves of her breasts, belly, and hips. She wore no bonnet, and her rich auburn hair was caught in a loose chignon with several tendrils framing her gently sloped cheekbones. The young girl was not a great beauty, but she was uncommonly pretty. Her bright blue gaze darted about the room, and there was an air of anxiousness about her.

"Who are you?" he mildly asked.

Finally, she looked at him, and then she just stopped, as if she had slammed into a wall. Ethan reflexively closed his hand over the head of his cane, belatedly aware that his heart had taken on a peculiar thumping. A rhythm which he was wholly unfamiliar with.

"I...I am the guardian of little Thomas. He is in the bassinet behind you, Your Grace. I have come to retrieve him. Please forgive the intrusion of having him left on your doorstep. He was meant to be left on mine," she said crisply, meeting his regard unflinching.

"I see."

She held out her arms. "Yes. If you will hand him over to me, please."

"No."

"I beg your pardon, Your Grace."

"As you said, he was left on my doorstep."

"I assure you, that was a mistake."

He arched a brow. "Kellitch Hall sits on over fifty acres of land, and the closest neighbor is several miles away. It is a rather interesting mistake."

She gripped the edges of her riding habit, her gloved finger tightly twisting the material. "Little Thomas is my nephew," the girl said softly. "I have cared for him since his birth."

"Yet his mother left him here," he said smoothly, presuming it was she who had taken such drastic actions.

Wild grief flashed in the girl's eyes, with a look he recognized for he had been bound with the chains of grief and guilt for unending months. "I cannot presume to understand what my sister thought to act in this manner. I do know, Your Grace, it was a mistake. A dreadful one. Please, hand him to me, and I implore you once again to forgive the intrusion in your day."

"No."

"No," she parroted, a frown marring her brow. "I... what do you mean, Your Grace?"

"I will not hand him over, and you may leave."

The young girl gasped, her hand fluttering to her throat as she stared at him with dawning horror. "You mean to keep Thomas?"

"Yes."

"You cannot," she said, stricken. "You *cannot*."

"Yet I intend to do so."

She shook her head as if in a daze. "But why?"

"I owe you no reason."

"You are not his father," she snapped, balling her fist at her side. "You have no reason to be...to want to keep him! I am his aunt, I—"

She deflated, and tears pooled in her eyes, but she lifted her chin and attempted to stare him down, despite standing several inches shorter than Ethan.

"I will fight you," she promised, with a dark glint in her eyes.

"With what power?" he meant no mockery. He was genuinely curious. Though she flinched, there was an air of undefeatable energy about her. There it was, in the slant of that lush, berry-red mouth...the lift of her chest, and how she braced her feet apart. She appeared young, yet Ethan inexplicably sensed she had been wounded, but had somehow emerged stronger. And that strength could stand toe-to-toe with him without cowering.

"I do not know how," she whispered, "But I will. I make a mean enemy, Your Grace."

He released a long breath. Something that had been silenced a long time inside him, so much so, that it now felt unfamiliar, stirred. He mildly recognized it as interest, and with a flick of a mental hand, he slapped it aside.

"You will leave my home this instant, or I will have you tossed from it."

Admiration rose inside him when she held onto her temper, turned, and walked away with a dignified air. Ethan summoned his housekeeper, who promptly arrived.

"Has she left?"

"Yes, Your Grace."

"She is never to be allowed entrance again." Ruthless and pragmatic, but that was the kind of man he had become, and he did not shy away from it. Still, he became conscious of a curious sensation in his stomach. It tasted like regret that he might never see her again. Another casual flick and Ethan closed the door on that inane thought. "I have a few letters to write that must be sent to my man of affairs and solicitor in London right away. Hire a nursemaid for the child, and prepare something that he might eat right away."

Little Thomas.

"Yes, Your Grace."

He could feel his housekeeper's curiosity, and wisely she knew better than to probe into his affairs. Still, he expected the rumors to spread through the town soon that he had a child, and the scandal sheets would add having a bastard to his many sins. Ethan could have asked the young girl who was the child's mother, but he would not trust anything that came from her. He would have his man of affairs conduct a thorough investigation in the matter.

The child pumped its legs and made a warbling sound that tugged at a cold place deep inside Ethan. He reached down and took him from the bassinet, awkwardly holding him. As if he sensed someone new about him, the child stopped, and piercing gray eyes met Ethan's gaze.

Thud. Thud. Thud. Thud.

It took him several moments to realize that the rushing sound in his ears was his own heartbeat. There was an odd weakness in his knees, and with almost jerky movements, he stumbled over to the large wingback chair by the fire and sat, holding the child in his arms.

"Thomas," he said gruffly.

Clearly knowing his name, the boy twisted on his chest and peered up at Ethan.

A raw hiss slipped from him when he felt the burn at the back of his throat. He felt his lips twist, and that hollow place inside him yearned to reach for the decanter of brandy. With a sense of shock, Ethan realized the hovering burn must be tears. He had not cried when he had crawled, broken and bloodied, through the wreckage of the carriages and horses to find his friend amongst the rubble. He had not cried when he had found him and dragged him into his arms, holding him as he took his last breath. Nor had Ethan cried when his friend had been buried in his family's crypt.

Yet seeing the silver-gray eyes, the bright blond hair, and that smile that belonged to Oscar, emotions Ethan had never felt before, careened through his soul with forceful intensity. Only last week, as he had snarled at the empty bottle of whisky, breathed through the sweet curling smoke-scent of opium, he had opened his bedroom window to let the rain lash at his skin, and to feel the energy of the storm raging around him. Ethan had lifted his head to the sky and snarled, '*Redeem me of this endless guilt and pain.*'

'I knew your father," he said gruffly down at the boy. 'I vow you will be given the best life that he would have given you had he lived."

The child smiled, and in its gentleness, Ethan spied redemption. He shifted, holding the boy to his chest, allowing a feeling of peace to steal through his heart and calm the tempest that had haunted him for two years and eleven days.

I have your son, Oscar, and I will help him grow into a man of whom you would be proud.

Three

"A BLOODY KNAVE, a villain of the worst order. It is too kind to call him a devil," Verity cried, balling her hands at her side and staring up at the imposing mansion in a fury.

"Wot happened?" Artie said, running over to her, leading the mare by the reins. "Where is little Thomas?"

"The duke has him."

"*Why?*"

The pure bewilderment in Artie's tone pierced her. They had all been a family for the last two years. An odd set, but they'd found happiness and comfort with each other in a bond that had felt unbreakable. How easily it had shattered with just a few scrawled lines. Dipping into the pocket of her riding habit, she withdrew the note her sister had left.

Dearest Verity,

I have left for Paris by way of Dover. I am unhappy in this life my foolish passion trapped me into. I have found a kind, charming soul in a gentleman I have exchanged letters with for the past several months. I cannot take Thomas with me, for every time I look at him, I am reminded of the pain and the dashed expectations. I am taking Thomas to the Duke of Bainbridge. He will not be your burden anymore. Now that I am gone from Benbow, the scandal and the whisperings will lessen. Verity, see if Papa will once again welcome you home, and perhaps in time, you might find your own happiness.

Catherine

"He was never my burden, Catherine. He was our little love," Verity whispered. "I am going to steal into that house and rescue Thomas."

Artie's eyes widened. *"Wot?"*

"You heard me," she said grimly.

Artie looked back at the mansion and the rolling lawns and gardens surrounding the dwelling. "I don't think he needs rescuing."

"Little Thomas is clearly in the clutches of a villain. One who hardly cares about our bond, and one who most certainly will not allow me a space in his life."

Artie appeared dubious as he mulled this over. "He is a bleedin' *duke*. We don't want to offend a duke." He mimicked the dreadful notion of a noose around his neck.

With a sniff, she tossed her head. "I am Lady Verity, the daughter of an earl. What can a duke do to me?"

"Yer the *disgraced* daughter of the earl," Artie pragmatically pointed out. "Methinks the duke can do a lot."

Noting that he was worried, she hugged him toward her. "I will be careful. I promise. The house seemed understaffed. The housekeeper allowed me inside, and I perceived no footmen or maids about. I shall wait until it is dark, slip inside and take Thomas out. We'll take my horse and ride to Meadowvale Inn, rent a coach and a driver, and return here at about midnight. Catherine did not name herself in the note she left to the duke, and today he asked my name. I do not believe he knows who we are and that I am thankful for. Once we are away, he will not know where to look. May I rest my hopes on you to help me in this, Artie?"

His chest puffed out. "Yes."

"Thank you, Artie. I could not do this without you."

His brown eyes showed pride and the fierce resolve she felt brewing in her heart. One did not abandon family to strangers, especially one called the Devil Duke with a salacious and rather dubious and dangerous reputation. Her pulse pounded with a bit of fear and some exhilaration. The idea of seeing the duke again sent the startling reaction through her.

"I'll not be seeing him," she muttered under her breath, staring up at the only window that shone with light.

Outside, in the dimming twilight, the rest of the mansion loomed dark and ominous. It was that room that might be important, and she walked back and forth on the lawn, trying to understand its position inside the house. A figure walked up to the window, and she recognized the imposing frame of the duke. Verity gasped, and before she could dash away and hide, his gaze snared hers. She found herself rooted to the spot, her heart a frantic pulse, simply staring up at him.

He stood before the windows, one of his hands behind his back and the other holding a cane, his booted feet slightly apart, his expression haughty and cold. He was tall and broad-shouldered. That he used a cane did not diminish the duke at all. Somehow it added to the impression of formidable will and strength. Earlier, she had been secretly awed at the stunning beauty of his mocking green eyes, which were as the lush forest itself. With his sensually cruel mouth, the duke gave the overall impression of cunning and beauty, a kind of gentleman she would never dream of walking too close to, two years ago, when she'd debuted in London for her first Season.

There was such power and surety in that stare that pinned Verity in place. How wretched it made her feel. As if she were a mouse challenging a hawk. The awareness shook her resolve, only for a second. She lifted her chin, and his mouth curved in a barely-there smile.

Verity waited for the midnight hour to sneak into the duke's mansion. The small coach and the driver waited down the lane, but Artie moved stealthily beside her as they tested the terraced windows. The night was silent and still, and she resented the terrible uncertainty that prickled over her skin.

"This one is open," Artie whispered.

Relief hit her, and with it a lifting of her spirits. "I will go inside alone, Artie."

He nodded his head, and her heart pinched to see the worry on his face.

"I'll be careful, and I promise I will come back with Thomas."

With a soft grunt, she tossed her foot over the window, bent her back low and slithered inside. The room was dark, and she knocked her elbow onto something hard. Pain shot up her arm, but she bit her lip to stem the cry of agony. The silence outside permeated the mansion. The house was unfamiliar, and it would be a challenge to locate that room with the sole light. If it was impossible to find, she would stealthily check every room in the house. Verity had craftily procured the apparel of a maid, a black bombazine dress with a white apron, and a white cap covering her curls. Maids often crept around their masters' homes, ensuring windows were closed, the fireplace lit, and the house comfortable. Should anyone discover her, Verity hoped they thought that she went about her duties. Should it be the duke who discovered her, the aim was to keep her head lowered, mumble some nonsense, and make her escape.

It took a long time for her to navigate from the room in the dark. Thankfully once she was into the hallway, a few sconces on the walls provided a measure of light. Verity carefully made her way down the hallway, keenly listening to the noises of the house and those she made herself.

The silence itself felt intimidating, but should anyone stir, surely she would hear it. Knowing if she made any mistake, it would resound in the quietude, Verity crept up the winding staircase, thinking on the positioning of the house, the floor the duke had stood on, and tried to determine where Thomas might be. Over an hour passed with her testing cold knobs that opened without a squeak under her palm. More than seven rooms on the second floor, including a library and a music room, were cold and empty. Hurrying down the hallway, her steps faltered by a wall sconce. The door beside it shone no light beneath it, but surely it meant something that the only wall sconce in the long hallway was here.

Taking a deep breath, she opened the door. It slid noiselessly ajar, and she almost cried out to see a large crib by a low burning fire. There was no nursemaid in the room or any other servant. She shut the door behind her with a small snick, and a few cautious steps took her closer to the crib. Peering down, relief assailed her. She had found Thomas. Verity reached into the crib when a feeling of being watched trembled over her body.

Her belly knotted, and the breath inside her chest stilled. Surely she was mistaken. The thump of a cane sounded, and she almost fainted. *Oh God!* Verity straightened from the crib and slowly turned around.

"I wonder, can you truly bear the consequences?" the duke's low voice said from somewhere in the large room. "It is not every day a tempting morsel hands herself over into my care."

His wicked, dissolute emphasis on *care* sent a cascade of fright over her body. Her frantic gaze skipped around the nursery. Where was he? The door remained shut. That meant the duke had been in this room all along, and she had not sensed his presence. She allowed her gaze to sweep the darkened corners of the room, wondering where the devil lurked. It sank into her bones that she had been discovered, stealing into his home.

"I have a dagger," she said huskily.

"Ah, you mean to skewer me with it in a bid to escape?"

The dark humor in his tone rattled her, and she lifted her chin. "If I must."

"I believe I just might keep you for a few days. You are interesting," he drawled in a lazy tone.

A low, incredulous laugh slipped from her before she quickly caught it. "Keep me?"

"Yes. To do whatever I will."

She stared hard into the shadows. The duke of every sin they said. She paused for a moment to draw a few steadying breaths, then Verity allowed her mouth to curve as if she were amused by him. "Are you promising kidnapping and debauchery? How...dissipated and quite unoriginal, Your Grace. You do not disappoint your reputation."

A soft laugh answered her. Odd that earlier, she'd had the thought that he did not seem to be a man who laughed with any measure of frequency. He made no other reply, but she could feel the force of his contemplation and his eyes as they skipped over her body. Each unseen lingering of those green eyes felt like a caress of ice. Though she was tempted to fill the space with nervous chatter, Verity remained silent and swallowed down the chaotic mix of emotions tangling inside her heart—loss, fear, anger.

Four

"YOU HAVE ME AT A SLIGHT DISADVANTAGE," Ethan said, stepping from the shadows into the meager light of the nursery. "What is your name, and why have you concerned yourself in my business?"

"A question one should have insisted upon earlier, instead of threatening me from your home."

Ethan tasted the acid in her remark. And he found her inexplicably lovely. It meant she was not afraid to cross wits with him, or perhaps she was just the foolish sort. By chance, he had entered the nursery to keep the boy company. If he had left a few minutes earlier, the boy could have been lost to him. His gut knotted, and a sliver of unfathomable emotion wafted through him. That she could place it there felt unforgivable. "This child is mine," he said with icy precision.

"You are unbelievably shameless. He is not yours."

"Neither is he yours," he said, though he recalled her earlier claim of being the boy's aunt.

Her eyes sparked with her anger. "This babe is the child of the Earl of Preston and Lady Catherine Stanton."

The name sounded familiar. He vaguely recalled the scandal around the time of Oscar's death. Ethan closed his eyes, pained as he recalled the last name his friend had breathed. *Catherine.* "A rare beauty who fell from grace for having a child out of wedlock. The whispers chased her from town to some obscure part of the countryside."

The girl's expression brightened with tentative hope. "You admit the child is not yours, and you have no right to keep him here?"

"I admit you are a thief who broke into my home. I can see you off to prison by the morning."

The eager step she had taken toward him faltered. "*You* are the thief, Your Grace. As I told you, little Thomas is my nephew."

Lady Catherine's sister. "Ah," he said just as softly, studying her. "To your left, there is a lamp. Turn it on."

Surprisingly she complied, and it was a good thing he was a man in command of himself and his reactions. The lady was stunning, even dressed in servant garb. "What was your goal, to steal him from under my nose?"

"Yes," she said tersely.

A faint smile curved his mouth. "How fearless you are, Lady...?"

"Lady Verity," she said, and he noted that her lips trembled. "Should you not hand over Thomas, I will be a pest in your life, I vow it. Your enemy until the end of time."

He was tempted to smile at that fierceness. "How do you plan to do that from prison?"

She held herself still, and he watched as the implications sank into her bones. The little lady narrowed her eyes on him, clearly assessing how much of a threat his words promised.

"I have the sense I would regret it keenly to have you as my enemy," Ethan said, taking a few steps closer to her. "I believe I have a solution that will suit both our purposes."

"You are giving me Thomas?"

The bright light of hope that entered her blue eyes was painful to see. "In a sense."

She gave him a wary look. "I do not understand. Please explain it well, Your Grace."

"It is simple. Marry me."

❧

Marry me.

"I...*what*?" Verity's words escaped like an inelegant squeak. There was no excuse for it, but she never anticipated those words from the duke. She was certain there was some misunderstanding.

"No need to look so horrified," he said. "You'll be a duchess."

This was so unexpected she felt faint. "A *duchess*?"

"Yes."

Remarkably she felt like laughing. "This is a poor jest, Your Grace. A poor jest indeed, and one I cannot fathom at the moment."

Another one of those smiles touched his mouth, the one that suggested he was amused with her and possibly the entire world. The man was truly perfectly and ruthlessly handsome. Verity did not trust him. It was even painful to admit she found him a bit intimidating, even though she had lifted her chin and faced society without an ounce of fear or trepidation for the last several months. *Damn* this duke for making her feel this confused mess of sensation.

"It is no jest. As I sat in this chair earlier and planned

the boy's future, I realized he would need a mother. A nursemaid alone will never do," he clipped. "I already gathered it was his mother—who knew of my connection to his father—who left the boy on my doorstep, and you are in earnest disagreement with her actions. Given that you might do something even more rash than breaking into my home, a marriage between the two parties who have a vested interest in the boy is the best solution."

He was entirely serious. The realization set her heart to hammering.

The duke continued, "You will understand this is an offer for a marriage of convenience. I can see you will be a nuisance regarding little Thomas, and since I might be forced to do away with you, I must make you a part of my plans."

"Do away with me," she said faintly, her heart starting to pound.

That cunning gleam once more brightened his eyes. "Yes. I could see you transported to another country with no hopes of returning to England's shore."

She cleared her throat. "And making me a part of your plan is to take me as your wife, your duchess?"

"Thomas will need a mother, one who will love him and does not treat him like a bastard. I believe you qualify for the position."

"You do mean it," she said, still astonished and grappling with the implications.

"Yes."

Perhaps there was more to it than he was letting on. "I suppose you will be wanting an heir and a spare..." she began, only to pause when his lips twisted in a cruel, dark smile.

"There will be no need for that," he said.

"For what?"

He prowled closer, his expression was inscrutable. "For an heir or a spare."

She dropped her gaze to the front fall of his pant.

"You're a brazen one, aren't you?"

For a moment, she could only stare at him and then her cheeks heated. Verity hated that she blushed. A woman known in the country and London as a scandalous, ruinous disgrace should not know how to blush. "Are you impotent?" she asked in a choked voice.

He stared at her for a long moment. "No."

"Then..." Oh, perhaps he was not at all attracted to her. The idea was mortifying, especially when she found him so remarkably appealing. "I..."

He pierced her with his intense gaze and merely waited for her scattered thoughts to make sense of his extraordinary offer. To be a duchess would mean so much to her family. The family had been cast into fiery ruin with their eldest daughter falling with a child out of wedlock. Then their youngest had abandoned her attachment and run off to support her sister when the family cut Catherine from their ranks.

"The disgraced daughters," the scandal sheets had called them for weeks, and then the foul air of their scandal had chased them all the way back to the country, where they had met the ruthless will of their father, who turned his back on Catherine and put her away from their home.

Her heart lodged in her throat. *And now Catherine has run away and left us, leaving me alone to decide our future.*

Five

VERITY FELT FRIGHTENED AND HOPEFUL. The bewildering duality of the emotions clashing inside her set her teeth to aching. To be this man's...this stranger's duchess. His wife. Perhaps never his lover. But this might be what she and Artie needed to turn the tide of everything wrong and desperate and uncertain for the last two years.

"I cannot believe the woman who broke into my home with the plan to steal a child has been rendered speechless. Or does she plot?"

She flushed. The duke thought her a diabolical cretin. "I...I am uncertain what to say."

"Say you'll be my duchess."

Verity swallowed. This was madness. "If you knew the true measure of my public standing, you would not have so casually offered me any sort of attachment." *Oh, Verity, what are you doing?* Still, she continued, "My reputation is...is rather dubious."

"That is how I like them," he said mildly. "A perfect match to mine."

The retort strangled in her throat. Verity closed her eyes briefly before she met his regard. "While you are called the Devil Duke in some circles, no one blocks you from drawing rooms or chases you from shops. You are still invited to all *ton* events; men bow when you walk past them, and ladies dip into respectful curtsies. Some even drop their handkerchief at your feet, and some climb into your bed at house parties. You, my good duke, are not shunned, and despite your notoriety of being a duke who is intimately familiar with all sins, many families secretly dream of being aligned with yours. I have been to church with little Thomas and was asked to leave while the entire congregation, including my parents, stared us down with rebuke and condemnation. I have been denied the simple pleasure of buying laces and hats from the town's milliner, and even had an egg tossed at me."

Her voice cracked on those last words, and she squared her shoulders.

'Do you regret it?" he asked with chilling indifference.

'No," she said tightly, even though her heart ached something fierce. 'I made a decision, and I understood then I would live with the consequences."

Though she had been a naïve seventeen-year-old, she was appalled at her mother and father turning their backs on their daughter. Verity had been affianced within six weeks of her coming-out, and all those hopes and silly dreams were dashed when the swollen state of her sister's belly had been revealed. Verity had chosen to be in exile with her sister, living in a modest cottage in Hertfordshire. She had chosen to stand by Catherine when their fabricated tale that she was a widow had crumbled, and not even the local butcher would sell meat to their household. She had stood firm because little Thomas was a sweet, beautiful blessing that must be protected at all costs.

'I do not regret it," Verity said, some of that ache traveling from her throat to burn behind her eyes.

Oh, God, do not cry, Verity!

"Good," he said flatly.

"So I do not mistake the matter, this will be a marriage of convenience with no children."

"Yes."

She hated how dispassionate he sounded, as if they did not discuss a matter most important, a joining of life until death. "If I should refuse?"

"You will be a part of Thomas's life as my wife. Let me be clear, Lady Verity, that is the only way you will see him."

The cruel words were like a harsh blow that pushed her back a step. "He is my nephew," she said, her voice hoarse. "You have no right to keep me from him."

"Wrong," he said with something akin to icy contempt. "*You* have nothing to offer him."

"I love him and—"

"*Love*! What utter nonsense."

This time there was no mistaking the contempt.

"Can love clothe and feed him? Can it send him to the best schools and provide him with a decent living when he is of age? What can your love and a reputation that will ensure he has no place in the world serve him? Do you have money for yourself? A way out for him? What will your love do, other than ruin him further? What power do you have of your own to see him have a good life?"

He took a step toward her, his walking stick tapping the ground with jarring menace. He brought with him an air of icy indifference until she looked at his eyes. They burned with a fire of purpose she did not understand, and with an awful sinking feeling low in her stomach, Verity realized she would never be able to wrest Thomas from his grasp.

'I offer him a life of dignity and wealth. He will be my son in every way that is possible. He will inherit my dukedom and all my wealth."

"That is not possible," she said, 'He...there are no records he is yours or any of his birth..."

'I am the Duke of Bainbridge," he said icily. 'I will create the records."

The ruthless power it implied shocked her. 'And what of your own sons?"

His lips twisted. 'I already told you there will be no heir."

She took a steady breath. 'So our marriage will be purely in name, with no consummation and—"

A low, rough noise came from him, a sound of amusement perhaps.

"There *will* be bedding," he said. 'Over and over and over."

A hot, confusing feeling shivered low in her belly. 'Between us?" she asked dumbly.

He tipped her chin with a single fingertip. 'Yes."

'I...I do not understand."

'Odd, I had perceived you to be a lady of quick wit."

'It is childish, but I am tempted to kick your shin."

He laughed, the sound low and rough, a deep masculine pitch that reached in cold places and warmed her. She suspected his laugh had nothing to do with the chaotic sensations fluttering in her belly, but perhaps, it was the tip of his finger still lingering on her chin, and the look of banked heat in his eyes.

'Let me be blunt."

She cast him a peculiar look. 'Please, Your Grace."

'You will be in my bed and underneath me at least

every night for the first few months. Once I get used to the idea of you in my bed, it might lessen, hmm?"

She pressed her thighs together against a sudden lick of heat. Verity could not believe he would be so wickedly brazen with her. They stared at each other, unmoving, yet there was a challenging gleam in his eyes. She delicately cleared her throat. "I believe bedding and children are related, Your Grace."

He looked diverted. "There are ways to prevent it."

Oh God. "No agreement," she whispered. "Unless..."

"You are not in a position to negotiate," he said with an icy bite, that sensual gleam taking on a cunning cast.

"I have always wanted children of my own," she said on a tremulous breath. "I cannot enter a marriage that would deny me that joy."

"Joy?"

"Yes."

"What do I care about your joy?"

"That is how a marriage works, even the ones that are convenient. It is a *mutual* convenience and benefit."

His expression shadowed. "You are ruined. Without any prospect. Should I retract my offer, your life will remain as it is now, empty and hollow with little to fill it up. What children are these that you fantasize about?"

She flinched. "You are cruel."

"I am a realist, and given your situation, so should you be."

"You care about Thomas," she said, boldly taking a step toward him. They stood so close the hem of her dress brushed against his bare feet, reminding her that she was alone, in the dead of night, with a gentleman many called the Devil Duke because of his many illicit, sinful pursuits. She recalled reading about him in the scandal sheets and with a sense of awe, wondering what it would be like to be that free, to live life without any fear of consequences or condemnation.

'I care," he said flatly.

"Whether your caring is because of the bonds of love or guilt...you *care*." Verity could not say why, but she lifted a hand to cup his jaw. The duke faltered into remarkable stillness, those vivid green eyes flaring in shock for the briefest moment. Yet he did not pull away from her touch, and she wondered if he realized he tilted his face more into her palm.

"You asked me to be your duchess for a reason. And that is because you know I love Thomas and will be a mother to him. I am the easy choice, the wise choice, the *only* choice. You know this, and I suspect you are unwilling to wade through the marriage mart to select a diamond who will have my compassion and love for little Thomas. You know I might be the only lady willing to accept him in your life, our life, despite his illegitimacy, and help him grow with love and respect, and dare not blame this sweet boy for his parents' failings or stupidity. While your diamond may not gainsay your choice, she could make Thomas's life miserable— and yours. As the saying goes, 'It is better to dwell in the wilderness, than with a contentious and angry woman.'"

She gently rubbed her thumb across his cheekbone and over the elegant ridge of his jaw, feeling through her gloves the puckered ridges of a scar.

'I will say *yes* to be your duchess if you can assure me a bit of my own happiness, Duke."

A frown split his brows, and she continued before he could interject. 'I will love him as if he is my son. I *love* little Thomas. I will raise him with every respect as if he is my son. However, I will need my own children, sons and daughters, one day. I want them. *Please*."

A perilous stillness fell between them.

"Is that your only counter-bargain?" His eyes narrowed on her face. "Ah, there it is, what did you think of just now to merit that flash of raw hunger in your beautiful eyes? What else do you want, hmm?"

Love, she wanted to cry, then felt extraordinarily foolish. Had there ever been a marriage of convenience that led to actual love, where they cherished and trusted each other? Even if there were, staring into the duke's indifferent eyes, Verity couldn't imagine such a fate possible for her with this man. The sense of loss was jarring and unexpected, for she had been living a life of exile from social graces and acceptance, with little hopes of a contented future with a husband and children to call her own. She would be exceedingly foolish to give up on this chance. Here he offered a shelter of sort from the harsh, cruel world to which she had been exposed to, and she still got to keep her sweet little Thomas. "I want nothing else," she whispered.

She had the curious sensation that she had startled him.

"Ruthless pragmatism. I like it," he drawled, dipping his head a little bit lower. "You will understand I value pragmatism and logic in my duchess."

Verity allowed her hand to fall away from his jaw. "That is all you will get from me." As if she would ever be so foolish to entangle her heart with a man so icily indifferent.

That smile—there it went again, in the barely-there curve of his mouth.

"I require faithfulness and loyalty."

"Good," she whispered, frightened and out of sorts, wondering if she was making a terrible mistake. "I require the same."

"You shall have it."

She took a deep breath and plunged ahead. "There is

a rumor that you have a mistress back in town who routinely sends you letters professing her love."

He jolted, then swiftly masked his reaction. "I gather you are an avid listener to gossiping."

Verity smiled at him, and she gathered it was fierce given that his eyes gleamed. "I admit my weakness, and that I read the scandal sheets."

"Yes. I have a mistress."

The slow thud of her heart was painful. They stared at each other for a long moment, his gaze icily calculating and Verity hoping hers showed her aghast resolve. "See that you end it, Your Grace."

Silence fell as they studied each other. "Done."

The ache in her belly soothed. "Good," she once again whispered.

Unexpectedly he smiled, and it lent him a wicked, sensual air. "Very well, Lady Verity. Let us seal our bargain with a kiss."

ETHAN ALMOST CHUCKLED at the look of astonishment and alarm on Lady Verity's face. A well-deserved shock for acting in such a reckless manner, with her already tenuous place in society. Not that he should give a damn. He did not know her character, nor was he truly interested in getting to know her.

Yet she will be my wife.

She shook her head as if in a daze. "*Kiss* you?"

The devil in him urged Ethan to taunt her, to bring more blushes on those lovely cheeks. "Yes, only a kiss would do," he murmured, a bit surprised that he even felt the need to tease her.

For so long had he existed in the deep mire of guilt and emptiness, that her bright light felt suspect.

"You are being a right rogue," she said in a fiery hiss.

"Hmm," he agreed. "A scoundrel of the worst kind."

"Have you no shame, Duke?"

"None. It is best you learn that now."

Their back and forth felt unexpectedly, maddeningly wonderful. She sniffed and her teeth sank into her lush lower lip. Ethan had the sudden, inexplicable urge to kiss her, hotly and deeply. It was no longer about teasing her. Once, he would have acted on those urges without thoughts of consequences. Now, he hesitated. Examined the desire from every angle, wondering at the danger of ever giving in to it.

She straightened her back and hesitantly shifted toward him. He waited to see what Lady Verity would do as she moved closer. His pulse was rising as he anticipated the sensations of taking this enigma of a young lady in his arms. It had been an impetuous decision to propose to her, but her breeding was acceptable, and she was an attractive prospect to warm his bed for the rest of his life. She had enough determination and fire not to bore him. He wondered how much his desire to bed her and the need for a loving mother to tend to Thomas had influenced his resolution to take her as his wife. Both had greatly contributed, but possibly stealing a kiss before they were married was currently foremost in his mind.

Odd that he should feel this anticipation at the idea of a mere kiss when little had roused his for several months.

"Very well, a kiss to seal our bargain," she said.

A heady rush of anticipation rushed through Ethan, and he bent down slightly to kiss her, and she stretched up and quickly brushed her mouth against his jawline. He closed his eyes, reveling in the sweet whispers of sensation wafting over his jaw, savoring the fleeting touch. The damn minx had kissed him on the cheek. She then quickly whirled away and stepped back. Ethan laughed then, and she turned and glared at him, it appeared she did not like being the source of his amusement.

"What is your age?" he asked, truly mystified by the manner in which she delighted his senses.

"Nineteen," she said huskily.

That jolted him. "You are a mere babe."

She tossed her head, and those beautiful blue eyes sparkled with an irresistible inner fire. "I am a woman."

He found himself suddenly, darkly amused. Ethan strode forward and gripped her wrists, not tightly but allowing no resistance. He hauled her to him, so her body was pressed close to his. Then he nudged her head back and took her mouth, forcing a gasp from her. Her gasp was his opportunity to deepen the kiss, and for his tongue to flick into the depths of her sweet mouth. He could feel his visceral reaction to her proximity, and how it startled him. His cock twitched, his heart raced, and hot and urgent desire coiled in his gut.

Ethan breathed in the scent of lavender which flowed through him. She fitted to him just right, with her breasts and quim tightly against his body. It was a pity that several layers of clothing were between them, but her lips were luscious as he ran his tongue over them.

An alarmed whimper pulled from her throat. Breathing slowly, he calmed himself, willing his body to relax. Ethan released her wrists and draped them around his neck, then he pulled her closer, one hand clasping a pert globe of her rump and the other to stroke the nape of her neck, as he employed his mouth in learning hers.

Verity moaned softly into his embrace and a shiver cascaded through her. His little lady's hands twined around his neck, threading her fingers delicately into the dark curls of his hair, and she did not resist his kiss, her face flushed with emotion, and he watched her eyes as he pleasured her mouth.

He was ruthless but gentle, realizing that despite her sister's wantonness, Verity had never been kissed in this manner before. She sighed and he nipped her lower lip, urging her to open her mouth wider so he could deepen the kiss. He allowed his tongue to stroke inside of her mouth, to twine with hers as he slanted her head, deepening an already far too intimate kiss. She was a passionate creature, and with a muffled moan she tangled her tongue with his as she was returning his actions, lick for lick.

The taste of her was indescribably sweet and carnal. Her fingers were now tugging at his hair as she was breathing into his mouth. Then her hands moved to caress his neck and cling onto his shoulders, as their embrace became all Ethan could wish for. Eventually he broke the kiss, his pulse racing and his loins aching with desire.

Ethan did not slacken his embrace, holding her imprisoned in the cradle of his arms. He did not want to let her go, but eventually their ragged breathing returned to something approximately normal. Her skin was deliciously flushed, the blush diving deep into her gown's neck. He wished that she was more fashionably gowned, as he could reach more skin, but he rubbed his thumb over one hardened bud of a nipple, and she inhaled deeply and drew away, staring at him with widened eyes, her hand pressed to her mouth.

Who could imagine that under this innocent exterior, such a passionate woman was hidden away? He would anticipate exploring her lush curves on their wedding night. "Do not look so shocked," he murmured. "It is good to have passion between us. Most marriages are cold and empty."

A soft cry came from the cot, and they rushed to check on little Thomas. Verity reached the crib first and picked up her nephew. Thomas snuggled into her neck as she crooned to the little boy. Soon, the child was falling asleep in her arms, and a most contented expression settled on her face.

She met his eyes over the baby's head, and Ethan's

heart twisted. He was uncomfortable with the emotions he saw in the depth of her gaze. That gratefulness when he did not deserve it.

"Do not delude yourself about me," he warned. "I am the villain of the story. It suits my purpose to marry you, as it makes life easier. Do not read more into it than there is, Lady Verity."

Her expression did not change. "I shall not forget that you value pragmatism," she murmured. "Still, I thank you for giving me this life with Thomas. I will endeavor to make you a good duchess."

He made no reply to that. "I will see you in the drawing room when you have finished attending to him." Then he turned around and walked away. Ethan opened the door and paused when she called out to him.

"Are you not worried I will steal him away so soon?"

"Only a fool would act against her own self-interest, and I can tell you are no fool."

"Why are you the villain in the story?"

His gut tightened and those black, dangerous emotions knotted through him. Ethan did not answer, merely stepped through the door into the hallway and closed it behind him.

Seven

VERITY TUCKED baby Thomas back in his crib but refused Ethan's offer of having a bed made up for her. She knew from one glance at the duke, that if she accepted that suggestion, that she would not be sleeping alone. There was Artie to think of, and it was not so far to the inn, and from there to the cottage was only another fifteen minutes. The moon was full and high, and they could ride that distance before it set. Ethan demanded the directions to the small cottage they lived in, which she provided. He then let her out the front door of the house and watched her go.

She walked down the drive under his burning stare. When she reached the main gates, she waited for Ethan to go inside and the door to close before whistling the call of a curlew, hoping that Artie would hear. Shortly after, running crouched, Artie appeared from the cover of some trees.

"Ye do not have little Thomas," he said.

"No," Verity replied with a sigh. "For reasons I do not as yet understand, the duke is determined to keep him."

"Wot are we going to do?"

She inhaled softly. "The duke asked me to marry him. That way I will get to be a mother to little Thomas."

Artie stumbled. "Wot! You'll be a bleedin' *duchess*?"

"Are you so certain I said yes?"

"Of course—you love little Thomas."

Verity smiled and slung a hand around Artie's shoulder. "It will take some adjustment on our parts, but I am not worried."

"*Our* parts?"

It was then she heard the tremble in his voice. "Yes, we are not to be parted."

A big sigh of relief came from his small body. "Wot if the duke says me cannot come with you?"

She had come across Artie stealing from their small gardens. He had appeared half starved, and so desperate Verity's heart had softened, and he had stayed with Verity ever since. "You are my family, Artie. He will not say so," she promised. "I suspect the duke to be kinder that we might have anticipated."

"The Devil Duke?" he asked skeptically. "Kind?"

Verity chuckled, resenting that she still had that nervous energy coursing through her veins. "We shall see, won't we?"

They walked to where they had left the horses and then set off for the cottage together. She tried her very best to dismiss the wicked kiss from her awareness, but found herself anticipating this next chapter in her life. Only a few weeks ago she had sat under a beech tree, staring at the lowering sun, and wondered what the future might hold for their family. Everything had felt frightful and uncertain, as their money dwindled and Catherine sank deeper into her melancholy.

And now tonight...

Her recklessness had opened a door not anticipated;

however, Verity would do her best to ensure she succeed at her new role, while she protected her pride and heart. She had understood what the duke meant when he said he valued pragmatism and logic, the antithesis of love and romantic notions. The *ton* tended to mock any hint of tender emotions between man and wife, thinking it very unfashionable, and the duke appeared to be like-minded.

Pragmatism and logic.

I'll not be a fool, she silently vowed, *but I will be a good duchess and mother to Thomas.*

Ethan slept restlessly, his dreams fitful nightmares of a mangled carriage and a man dying in his arms. At some time throughout the night, those terrible dreams transformed into ones of Lady Verity splayed naked on his bed, while he showed her the delights of carnal pleasure. When he rose at dawn, he washed and shaved in cold water, but even the chill of the water did not reduce the desire for his newly affianced bride that his body wanted to make apparent.

"Bloody rubbish," he muttered. "As if I am a lad unable to contain my passions."

Ethan dressed and headed for his library. It looked a little dusty and he admitted that they would need more servants now that he was bringing a bride to his main country home. He interviewed a young nursemaid from the village, and after finding her suited for the task, hired her to care for Thomas. He then composed a letter to the Bishop of London, with whom he was acquainted. The Bishop was an amiable old man with a fine palate for good claret and setting a fine table. Ethan could imagine the bishop's chuckles as he read his imperative demand for a special license for the duke to marry one Lady Verity Stanton.

A lady I owe, even if I had not known it when I made my initial offer.

His letter would need to be taken directly to the old man, with orders to wait for a reply. Ethan wrote a more polite note to the Prince Regent to inform him of his impending marriage, although he doubted that gentleman would care. Technically, he could refuse to permit the marriage, but Ethan was a long way from the line of succession, and as Verity was an earl's daughter, unmarried and not a Catholic, he doubted that Prinny would make trouble.

See that you end it.

Recalling those impassioned words from Verity, Ethan withdrew another sheaf of paper. He had not seen his mistress in over a year, and his visits to her boudoir had become infrequent and hurried. As a point of courtesy, and that she had been a friend in his darkest moments, he did, however, owe her an explanation before the news of his marriage reached the newspapers. Ethan wrote to thank her, terminating their arrangement and enclosed a generous bank draft as her congé. He had considered that he would write another letter to Verity's parents, but as their seat was not far away, it would be more correct to call on them and inform them of his intentions. He doubted they would object either. Few fathers would sniff at marrying off their disgraced daughter to a duke, any duke, no matter how old or eccentric.

His housekeeper ferried in his breakfast. He was not really a good trencherman, which his cook despaired of, but the toast, preserves, sliced cold beef, deviled kidneys, and strong black coffee were today consumed without any hesitation. He asked his housekeeper to call for his stallion to be saddled, and went upstairs to change into riding clothes.

A little over two hours later, despite it still being early hours, Lord Stanton was indeed prepared to welcome the duke to his study to talk about a matter of business with him. In fact, the earl was gushingly pleased to see him, and offered him a glass of some very fine brandy. Brandy which Ethan suspected he had not paid any duty on.

"Now, what can I do for Your Grace?" he eventually asked.

"You can give me permission to marry your second daughter, Lady Verity, who has accepted a proposal of marriage from me, with the proviso that I adopt her sister's son, Thomas," Ethan drawled.

He did not think much of a man who would discard both his daughters as if they had no value at all, because the elder had borne a child out of wedlock. Ethan believed that Oscar would have eventually done the honorable thing and married Verity's sister if he had lived long enough to deal with the matter. But that disastrous drunken carriage race had taken his friend's life, and left him with only a slight limp and a few scars.

If only I had not bloody interfered.

He knew there was no legal way that Thomas could inherit his title or his main estates, but he could educate him at the finest institutions and settle a smaller unentailed estate on him, provide him with a generous allowance, and buy him a commission if he was militarily inclined. If Thomas should prefer a Parliamentary seat, or a parish, then he had both in his gift that could suit him when he was old enough.

Finished with his shocked spluttering, the earl straightened. "You wish to *marry* Verity?"

'I have said so," Ethan said, with polite indifference. 'Is there a problem?"

The earl grimaced. 'I...you might not be aware of it given that you have stayed away from the social scene for a couple of years, Your Grace, but...I..." he tugged on his cravat. 'My daughter's reputation—"

'I am aware of her selfless bravery and loyalty," he said, 'It has much bearing on my offer. It is rare to find such qualities in a lady of the *ton*."

Ethan knew the force of his personality, and that many were easily intimidated by him. Verity had been so brave to stand up to him and refuse to abandon Thomas, and also insist on progeny from their marriage. And she had been totally correct in both matters, even if they had not been what Ethan had wanted to hear. He had been captivated by her strength of character, and intrigued to feel her willing response in his arms, even returning his kisses and caresses. To his mind, she would make a most suitable wife.

The earl, as if still in a daze, drank another glass of brandy before answering, but was very fulsome in his agreement to the marriage, and promised to attend the parish church with his countess at eleven o'clock in three days' time.

Exiting from the earl's home shortly after, he mounted his horse and trotted along the country road. There was much to be dealt with, given the unexpectedness of Thomas and Lady Verity. Not for the first time since daybreak, he glanced at the overcast sky.

Are they my redemption?

No mystical voice answered him, and a rough sound of amusement escaped Ethan.

The next thing he needed to do was to send extra help to get Kellitch Hall ready for his bride. His housekeeper had only kept on a skeleton staff, and much of the house was shut up. After his injuries and Oscar's tragic death, he had kept to the country and only ventured to Town for sessions in the House of Lords. He had not stayed long, and had refused any society invitations, exiling himself to the hall.

He could not expect Lady Verity to come to a manor this severely understaffed. Cleaning maids and temporary waiters and men of all work could be obtained from the nearby town, at a price. They would not be very skilled, but the harvest was in, and there was little work for those casually employed. Many would jump at the opportunity in the hopes of being taken on permanently.

So, to the small town he headed next. He expected that the mayor would be just finishing his second breakfast, and possibly attending to some minor matters. He would know who might be available, and send them up to the housekeeper. The matter was quickly resolved with promises for workers to be sent to his hall immediately.

Ethan remembered that the town had an excellent dressmaker, and he made it his business to send a letter for her and her assistants to visit Lady Verity's cottage so that she could have something suitable to wear for her wedding day. From what he recalled of her first appearance at the hall, her riding habit had been rather dour and shabby, and from what he knew of women—and he had a lot of experience with them, he admitted—they liked to look nice for special occasions.

His last visit of the day was to the vicar. He could have decided to drag that invertebrate to his chapel and force him to perform their marriage there. That would necessitate considerable cleaning and decoration to make it fit for the wedding. It could be done, but he thought that hypocrite should be obliged to marry Lady Verity to the highest noble in the county in his own church. The very church that she had been driven from, with Thomas in her arms. And if the vicar choked on his words, then the curate could marry them, but married they would be, and if it could be done sooner than three days, he would wish it so.

Ethan resisted visiting Verity in her cottage; she needed some time to come to terms with the idea of marriage and all it would entail. That was best done alone. He returned to the hall and went to the nursery to visit Thomas. The boy was creeping around on the floor, and at times he would grab onto the edges of the small chaise and try to stand. The nursemaid used words to encourage him, and as Ethan watched he felt a deep agony inside his heart.

It is you, Oscar, who should be seeing this.

Walking away from the boy's chortling, Ethan went downstairs and outside to the lake, stripping from his jacket and shirt as he went. Tugging off his boots, he dived deep into the waters of his lake, drowning away the guilt and pain stirring deep inside.

While he would move onto the next chapter in his life—an unexpected chapter—he would never allow himself to forget his best friend had died and the reason for it.

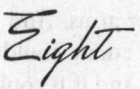

VERITY WAS BEMUSED by the arrival of Mistress Burbridge and her assistants, who delivered a note from the duke. The duke's note, while perfunctory, reassured her. She did not like to accept presents from a man, but she would have to get used to not being so independent, and as a duke, he would expect for her to be well turned-out. It would reflect on his standing if his bride dressed like a pauper.

The seamstress had been one of the sisters' most vocal critics, and her having to curtsy and treat her with the deference due to the duke's bride, tickled Verity's sense of humor. She was at her most dignified as she looked down her nose at the dressmaker, while that lady was most apologetic and obsequious in her manner. Verity admitted that she found the humbling of the old besom very satisfying. Then she rebuked herself for being so vengeful in taking pleasure in her humiliation. The woman was an excellent seamstress and could not refuse the duke's bride. Verity was sure she would do her very best to please her, now that her status in society had so suddenly been elevated.

So she submitted to having her measurements

taken, and selected fabrics and laces to produce a gown in the palest of blues, which would be correctly modest and moderately fashionable. She chose the most expensive of their lengths of lace for a veil, and selected some fabrics for a simple wardrobe to replace the shabbiest of her costumes. There would be no great urgency for the other gowns to be made, but at least she could choose brighter colors—blues, greens, amber, and gold—which would flatter her coloring more than the pastels suited to a young lady.

When she finally managed to get rid of the dressmaker and her entourage, a lad rode up with a huge bouquet of flowers for her. It surprised her and she shared a grin with Artie.

'Is he courtin' ye?' Artie sniffed.

'I think he might want to appear to do things properly,' she said, struck by the awareness he did so because of her already tainted reputation. A smile bloomed on her lips, and she found herself, not for the first time, exceedingly curious about the man she was about to marry.

The note attached said,

Dearest Lady Verity,

I will send my carriage to transport you to St Lawrence's parish church at half past ten this Thursday for the celebration of our nuptials. The vicar expects us at eleven o'clock. I look forward to being bound in marriage to you.

It was not very romantic, but she could picture the duke's dark and mocking smile as he scrawled it upon the paper for her. He had signed it, *Your most avid fiancé,* which she admitted seemed infused with dry amusement.

'Who are you really?' she asked softly, tracing his

elegant scrawl with the tip of her fingers. "And why am I now so eager to discover it?"

The very next day, Verity visited the lady from whom she and her sister rented. She had been one of the few people who had not turned against the sisters when Catherine's disgrace was revealed to all and sundry around. Mrs. Andrews was a widow, having lost her husband, a ship's captain, at Trafalgar, and had chosen to move in with her sister in the town, and so be able to rent out her cottage for a little extra income. It was on the outskirts of the town and very well maintained, even if it only boasted three bedrooms.

It was no hovel, but was the humblest dwelling that Verity and Catherine had ever resided in. Catherine had deeply felt the shame and mortification at the lowering of her status. Verity paid the rent to the end of the month and thanked her for benevolence in accepting them as tenants.

"I will be sorry to see you go—I heard that your sister had moved out."

Her heart ached inside her chest, and despite herself, Verity desperately wondered where Catherine was, and with whom she had exchanged letters. "Yes, she has."

Mrs. Andrews nodded. "I suppose you are moving to somewhere smaller, now she is gone?"

Verity was not sure what to say, but the news would be around the town, as Mistress Burbridge was sure to have revealed to all her cronies already that Lady Verity was to marry the Devil Duke. She was notorious as a gossip with a mean tongue. Verity thought she might have tempered her vitriol a little, with puffing herself up over having made the gown Verity was to be married in.

"I am sure it is no longer a secret, because Mistress Burbridge, as she likes to call herself, will have spread the news far and wide. But I have accepted a proposal of marriage from the duke, and we are to be married on Thursday morning at St Lawrence's. The service will be held at eleven. Mistress Burbridge is making me a new gown for the ceremony."

Mrs. Andrews chortled. 'Oh, that is wonderful, my dear. I hope you will be very happy, and that is thumbing your nose at that old termagant. She will be boasting of her handiwork for the next decade. *Did you know I was honored to dress the new duchess for her wedding to the duke—charming couple and so very handsome.*" She said, mimicking the dressmaker's shrill quavering tones.

Mrs. Andrews went on in her normal voice, 'Her tongue is sharper than her shears. You do know the 'Mistress' part is a falsehood. No man would have a shrew with a tongue like hers. Still, she needed to pretend to marriage, with her bearing that drunken sot of a son of hers. No one knows who his father is! Talk about the pot calling the kettle black! Such canting insincerity to denigrate you and your sister. The only reason she is tolerated at all is because she is the best seamstress for miles around. Many people can put up with a lot for a decently sewn gown."

Verity smiled and shared a pot of tea with her and some of Mrs. Andrews's best fruit cake. Then she went to the cottage and started packing all her belongings with Artie's help. Then they scrubbed and polished everything in the cottage until it shone. The gown arrived the night before her wedding, along with Mistress Burbridge, who fussed as Verity tried it on and made a few minor adjustments. It was a beautiful gown, and the old besom and her assistants must have worked hard to get it finished in time. She thanked her and tipped her a half guinea for her speedy work, but first asked if she would sew one strand of her long auburn hair into the hem of the dress.

She was a virgin bride, and traditions were important to keep.

~

Verity hardly slept the night before her wedding. She was frightened and a bit unsure about marrying the duke. She knew what he was and had been, and hoped that he would keep his word and try to be a faithful husband. Rolling onto her stomach, she thumped the pillow.

"What does it matter if he keeps his word or not?"

Her heart twisted upon itself, and though she had long given up the fanciful girlish dreams she'd owned about the ideal kind of husband, if she could not have the duke's eventual love, she would want his faithfulness.

But how can a man with a moniker as wicked as Duke of Every Sin confine himself to one woman?

"Perhaps the rumors are exaggerated," she said into the softness of her pillows. "There was that one that said he was caught in bed with a countess and her footman. Surely such licentiousness simply cannot be true."

Verity knew the duke desired her, and that he had promised to be loyal. And she admitted to herself, he made her heart flutter, her toes curl, and her knees go weak. Just kissing him had turned her into a wanton. It had been so hard to return to the cottage, when she had wanted to beg for more of his reprehensible advances.

A soft thud landed on the bed, and she rolled over to scoop one of her charming companions into her arms. Verity smiled and almost purred as she stroked

Columbine, her white cat with the comical black face markings.

Life will not be boring as the duke's wife.

As her mind veered off into shocking imaginations of her wedding night, and his salacious promise that he would bed her over and over and over, she forcefully dragged herself back to practicality and whispered to her cat, "The most important thing is that Thomas will be brought up in a family, as he deserves. So I should quit my worrying and remember all brides are jittery the night before their wedding."

Nine

COLUMBINE WAS HELD onto tightly as Artie brought in the basket, and Verity ruthlessly thrust her inside with her two kittens that Artie had been desperately searching for. The kittens, a ginger-and-white tom, was named Pantaloon, and his tabby-and-white sister was Pierette. Columbine had turned up, given birth, and had been part of their little household ever since.

Verity had been heating water, because whether he liked it or not, Artie was going to the church with her, and he would be clean. Artie was not fond of bathing, but Verity suspected he tolerated it because he loved her and knew she could not stand ingrained dirt. So he allowed her to scrub him in the tin bath, and to wash and tie back his hair. Then he dressed in his Sunday best, which was a concept Verity had introduced him to. More water was heated, and the cats yowled, complaining of being shut in the basket and being unable to get out.

Matilda, her little maid-of-all-work, who lived a few cottages away, arrived to help her mistress get ready for the ceremony. She had brought her own clothes packed with her to change into before the wedding, as

542

she would be Lady Verity's only bridal attendant. Verity planned to ask the duke if Matilda could have a place at the hall, as she was desperate to escape her home and most especially her brutish stepfather. Matilda stoked up the stove and got her mistress's bath ready.

When Verity had been buttoned into her new gown, Matilda arranged her hair and affixed the lace veil, then quickly changed into her best dress and tidied her own hair, with Verity's help, as they heard the carriage pull up outside.

The driver seemed somewhat bemused to find Artie loading up the boot of the carriage with a variety of luggage. Verity was too on-edge and nervous to tell him to leave it alone. A liveried footman assisted Artie in his endeavor. Then the basket of cats was placed inside, and Artie took in the bouquet, posy, and garland of flowers that he had made for Verity.

"These are for you," he said softly.

"Thank you, Artie."

Stooping, she kissed his cheek and he blushed.

"Are you nervous?"

"A bit," she admitted.

"Me too. I have me dagger," he said a bit fretfully.

Verity laughed, dispelling some of the tension that had knotted her belly. With the garland carefully pinned atop her veil and carrying her bouquet, she was handed into the carriage. Matilda followed carefully, clutching her posy as Artie added her bundle of clothing to the luggage in the boot, along with Verity's and his own. Then he scampered up on the box beside the carriage driver.

If only you could have seen this Catherine. Yet she was aware had her sister not abandoned little Thomas, Verity would not be becoming a duchess now.

Many people had come out of the nearby cottages to gawp at the carriage, which had been decorated with bunches of white ribbon, and Verity dressed in her finery and heading for the church. Some of the children waved and whistled, and Verity waved graciously back. The drive through the town brought out more onlookers, as the duke's carriage with his escutcheon had not been seen around for a long time. When they realized Artie was on the box and Lady Verity within the coach, they stared and doffed their caps. The carriage driver slowed, clearly enjoying being part of the spectacle.

They climbed the small incline to the parish church, where several other carriages and conveyances had been parked. The sun came out from behind the clouds, and Verity gasped, realizing that the church was not empty and that her father's carriage was prominent amongst those parked.

"Oh, Papa," she whispered. Of course, they would have come. Given that she was not yet one-and-twenty, her father's consent was needed. She breathed in deeply, hoping that her father was pleased with the news and would not try and stop the wedding.

Then the carriage came to a halt and the footman descended to let her down. Verity elegantly exited and straightened her back—she would face whatever was ahead with a smile on her face, and she would not show anxiety even to her father. Artie jumped down and followed her into the church carrying the basket of cats, who seemed to have accepted their lot and were now quiet, perhaps asleep.

As she neared the steps to the church, the bells rang out, announcing her arrival to the small town. And there, standing on the porch looking smug and beaming at her, was her father. Verity was secretly amused. One would think that he had never said all those harsh words to her for standing by her sister. Her father was holding out his arm for her to take, and she smiled and took his arm.

He hesitated a bit then said, "You look beautiful, my dear, and have made your mother and me so proud."

"Are you?" she murmured, biting back the harsher reply.

"Yes." Her father inhaled. "The duke is already waiting and prowling the church," he said, patting her hand.

Then the organ struck up a march, and her father led her in a stately stroll up the aisle to where her husband-to-be awaited her. The duke fairly stole her breath with his handsomeness. He surveyed the crowded church, a cold disinterest in his eyes, his manner of an overlord watching his subjects. Then his gaze touched upon her and she almost faltered. Verity most certainly blushed. The duke's regard was carnal and thorough. His sensuality was a palpable force for everyone to see and speculate. His regard was rousing and provoking.

Please do not look at me so, she silently cried.

Her breath rasped and her heart pounded. Beside her, her father, who must have correctly interpreted the duke's scandalous stare, cleared his throat a bit nervously. Her cheeks heated even more, and then to her surprise, she found her mouth curving into a smile.

The duke was shameless.

Ethan swallowed as he stared at the beautiful, dignified woman parading down the aisle on her father's arm. A peculiar longing rose inside of him, shocking him with its intensity. He had never been more certain that his hasty decision to marry Lady Verity was the only logical thing to do. His reaction to her was rather interesting. His bloody heart damn well pounded, as sensations never before felt whispered through it.

She looked away from him, and her gaze touched upon the decorations and several people crammed into the pews. His mother, who had almost fainted at the news he was to be married, sat in the front seats, next to Verity's mother and the nursemaid holding Thomas. The baby was beautifully arrayed in the family's Bruges lace and embroidered satin christening gown that Ethan himself had worn.

Despite the small representation of their families, the church was full. It seemed that everyone who thought they were anyone in the area had turned out to witness the wedding of the duke and one of the earl's disgraced daughters. Ethan had thrown money about, as the church was bestowed with flowers of all kinds and colors in a riotous display of affluence and nature's glory. The sweet fragrances of the flowers blended with the wafted incense that the bishop's acolytes had been swinging around the church. Ethan considered it excessive, but the bishop was convinced that the duke's marriage should have all the pomp and circumstance he could provide. Ethan believed the wicked old man enjoyed himself and played his part to the rafters.

Ethan's intentions had been two-fold with his preparation. Despite the suddenness of their marriage, the world would know he was not ashamed to be married to Lady Verity Stanton, and the lady herself would know of it.

As Verity reached the altar to stand beside him, the satisfaction worming itself through him made him unaccountably wary, for the simple reason he did not understand his reaction to her. Still, he sensed her nervousness, and Ethan smiled reassuringly, and she smiled back. The vicar in his best vestments did not have to strangle his throat by taking back his unkind words. The bishop had decided to take the marriage ceremony himself and was beaming at Ethan and Verity under his full panoply of purple, his mitre slightly askew on his balding head, and his crosier held by one of his junior priests. The music came to an end, and the bishop intoned the words of the service.

"Dearly beloved, we are gathered together here in the sight of God, and in the face of this congregation, to join together this man and this woman in holy matrimony, which is an honorable estate..."

Ethan and Verity made their responses clearly as required, and he could feel her amusement as soft, wondering gasps echoed from the onlookers, as if they had not really believed the duke and the disgrace would exchange vows. This was the vindication of her suffering for her sister and the uncharitable way she had been treated. And from the glimmer of tears in her eyes as the ceremony continued, Ethan was damn glad he had made all these preparations.

When the words, "You may kiss the bride," were solemnly intoned, he lifted Verity's veil, surprised to feel his hands tremble. Ethan frowned at the anomaly. He dipped slightly and pressed a chaste kiss on her lips.

"Not much of a kiss, Your Grace," Verity whispered teasingly.

"I promise to do much better when we are alone, Your Grace," he whispered back, and then lifted the hand now wearing his ring and brought it to his lips.

A cheer went up from the congregation and the organ struck up another march as the bishop intoned a hurried dismissal blessing on them all. Ethan offered his arm to his wife, and they sauntered back down the aisle,

STACY REID

graciously accepting the compliments of those assembled as they passed their pews.

They emerged from the church and the bellringers struck up again to celebrate the marriage of the duke and his duchess. Ethan handed her up into the waiting carriage and then joined her. It lurched away into motion, taking them back to Kellitch Hall and the new and unexpected future they would now share.

"I..." her words tapered off, and she flushed. "I am your *duchess*."

There went that primal slither of satisfaction once again. "Yes, you are."

Her throat worked on a swallow, and she briefly glanced away from his regard. "I saw little Thomas in the church."

"I have no plans to hide him."

Her teeth sank into her bottom lips. A nervous gesture, he realized.

"Thank you for planning the wedding in that manner." This time she smiled, and he perceived her smug satisfaction.

"I recalled your vengeful heart and thought it would make you happy, since they must be your enemy until the end of time and whatnot." *I also owe you, my duchess, more than you will ever know.*

She laughed, and the sweet sound of it pierced him deeply. *What the hell was this?*

"So what next, Your Grace?"

A week ago, he had no knowledge of this woman, and now everything was different. Ethan supposed the entire thing must be unnerving for her as well. He found it interesting he wanted to offer some sort of reassurance though he was at a loss at what to say. Before he could say anything, with a frustrated groan, she pushed from her seat and dumped herself onto his lap.

Well, hell. Ethan had thought he was incapable of being surprised.

"Is there something wrong with your seat, duchess?"

A muffled sound came from her, and her shoulders shook. "I *am* nervous. When I am nervous, I act."

"And the action you took was to cast yourself onto my lap," he said slowly.

Still, he gripped her hips and pulled her hard against his chest and more onto his lap. She gasped, and he smiled. "Not what you hoped for?"

"No," she gasped. "But it is not unpleasant."

She cupped his jaw, searching his face, looking for what answers he had no notion. But he liked the feel on his face of her hands, the softness of which he could feel through the gloves. Ethan felt like he wanted to nuzzle into that touch. It struck him then that her every motion aroused him, made him yearn for something unknown, tugged back in to a place he had long eschewed. A place of feeling. Of hope. A place he did not deserve to be. That raw sorrow rose inside once more, threatening to choke him, and he ruthlessly reined it in. He traced her bottom lip with his thumb. He was still amazed by the effect she had on him.

She made to get off his lap, and he tightened his grip. "You've already acted," he said with dark humor, thinking her nature contrary. "Commit to it."

The pulse at her throat fluttered wildly, tugging his gaze to the soft flesh there.

"You are nervous."

"I already said so."

"What is the point of it? We are already married."

Her finger clutched at the hair at his nape. "We do not know each other."

"This is a marriage, duchess—there is nothing complex about it. People do it all the time."

"I am aware of that."

Ethan considered the way she worried her lip until it turned red. "What is this 'getting to know each other' about?"

"Are you not at all curious about me?"

"Nay."

"Never say," she gasped, affronted.

Ethan chuckled. "I suppose you are curious about me?"

Those beautiful blue eyes met his. "There are things I have wondered about, and perhaps worry about their future occurrence."

He lifted a brow in question, and when she remained silent, he said, "Such as?"

"Rumors say you were caught in a particular countess's bed by her husband."

Bloody hell. It was his past reputation that concerned her? "There is some truth to the matter."

Her eyes took on a gleam. "Those rumors also said her footman was there."

Who the hell told an innocent debutante those things? Ethan hesitated slightly.

"In a marriage, there must always be honesty," she said pertly. "I want to get to know you...to trust you."

He heard the ache for something more, but he did not question it. Still, Ethan smiled inside, surprised at how her simple words tugged at something deep and unknown. He vowed to himself then he would never lie to her once she asked him a question. Yet there was knowledge he held deep inside that he would never willingly share with her, for they would expose his guilt, pain, and shame.

"The countess and I were already having an affair when I sneaked into her chamber unexpectedly. It seems she extended her charming favors to one of her footmen and had not anticipated my arrival that evening."

His wife pondered on his words. "Was she very shocked you had caught them?"

"Very."

"What did you do?"

He deliberately paused. "Took off my clothes and joined them."

His duchess's mouth parted, but no words came out, and then her cheeks pinkened. "And after such wicked adventures, will you be contented with a simple wife?"

He briefly kissed the corner of her mouth. "There is nothing simple about you, and I will be contented."

She narrowed her eyes at him. Ethan thought she might want to appear threatening, but his little wife only looked lovely.

"I am a crack shot," she said. "And I know how to use a rapier."

He mulled this over for a few seconds, secretly filled with humor. Given the fierceness of her expression, Ethan felt he dared not show his amusement. "Why must I be aware of this, Wife?"

"Should you dishonor our vows," she sweetly said, "I will challenge both parties to a duel."

Ethan laughed, thoroughly charmed by this bit of possessiveness.

"I am the jealous sort as well," he drawled. "I would kill any man who dares even to *think* to touch you. Dear Wife, I believe we have found common grounds."

A strangled sound came from her, and he kissed her, unable to stop the desire. Burning hunger licked through Ethan's body like a living flame, and he nipped her lips, almost in punishment for eliciting such raw hunger in a normally disciplined body.

"Thank you," she whispered, breaking their passionate kiss. "For what you did today. Though we marry in haste, I can always look back and say my wedding day was beautiful."

That gratitude sat heavily on his chest, and he rejected it, for it was wholly undeserved. "I did nothing," he said flatly. Then he kissed her again, robbing them both of thoughts as they rumbled toward their new fates.

Ten

THE FIRE on the hearth had burned down to orange embers, and there was a distinct chill in the air. She was no longer Verity Stanton, but Duchess of Bainbridge. In truth, she had been the duchess for the last three days and fourteen hours. Verity stared at the dark ceiling of her bedchamber, wondering why the duke had not consummated their marriage. And she had to accept that all her preparation was for naught. Verity had bathed in rose-scented water, her long, wavy auburn hair brushed with over a hundred strokes, and had put on a silky emerald shift that revealed more than it covered.

The duke would not be visiting her chambers. Despite being exhausted from the events of the day—the wedding breakfast, meeting the few staff on the property, and then a tour of the grand estate, Verity had waited for him that night, her entire body tight with nerves and anticipation. However, the connecting door had remained closed. She had been both mortified and relieved.

The very next morning, she had joined him for breakfast, and they had exchanged only mild pleasantries before he had disappeared for the day to his study to meet with his steward and a solicitor. Verity had happily spent the day with Thomas, Artie, and their three cats. Of course, she had left them for a good part of it to see to her duty of staffing the palatial house, to the happiness of the housekeeper. That task that had blessedly kept her busy for the last three days, but there would now be enough maids, footmen, a butler, and groundsman serving the needs of a ducal home. Many of the wealthy, titled neighbors and landowners had also come to leave their cards, hoping for an audience with the new duchess. Verity had not seen anyone, wanting the house to be fully staffed before she asked Ethan if he wanted to accept callers.

With a groan, she dropped back against the well-padded mattress, tossing an arm across her forehead. Acting on the impulse driving her, she parted the sheer canopied curtains over the large four-poster bed, clambered off, and padded over to the connecting door. Reaching for the latch, she hesitated.

Oh, what am I truly thinking?

Verity stared at the connecting door in seething frustration, knowing her stretched nerves could no longer take the anticipation. Each night she waited for the door to open and for the duke to frame the doorway and demand she take off her clothes. Then he would proceed to debauch her. She wasn't sure of the exact method of debauchery, but Verity knew enough to know it might be enjoyable. That would be the only reason so many women would cast themselves to ruin. Bedding *was* agreeable.

She opened the door to be met with a cold room and an empty bed. Curiosity driving her, for it was well after midnight, Verity first checked the nursery, to find it pleasantly warm and both Thomas and the nursemaid peacefully sleeping. Verity went downstairs, following the odd grunts that echoed in the stillness of the hallway. It took her to a room that had a fire burning low and the duke methodically punching what appeared to be a mounted punching bag with brutal strength.

Whack. Whack. Whack.

He was naked. Well, at least his shoulders and chest were, and they were roped with twisting muscles. Sweat slicked his skin, and the muscles of his arms bunched and contracted each time his fist slammed into the sandbag.

With a jolt, she realized he did this without protection on his hands. Surely the skin would break, and he would bleed and hurt. He paused, prowled over to a decanter, lifted it directly to his head, and took several swallows. When he lowered his head, it was almost the stance of a man defeated.

It was hard to see him so, when before, he had seemed too powerful and dominant. His chest lifted on a harsh breath, and the image of defeat melted away as he raised his head.

What drove him from his bed to...her thoughts careened when with a snarl, he shattered the decanter into the wall. Verity gasped, and her reaction informed Ethan he was no longer alone. Slower than she expected after that raw violence, he turned to face her.

Good heavens, he was beautiful. Her throat dried, and her belly went frightfully hot as she ran her gaze over his body. She felt his gaze on her, cool and prickling, and she lifted her regard to his. Ethan's eyes gleamed with something that seemed almost savage. As he walked toward her, he brought with him an air of pain and torment and desperation. It frightened her. Suddenly she sensed it had been a mistake to seek him out. "I am sorry to intrude," she gasped, whirled around, and ran away.

Verity dashed down the hallway and up the stairs as fast as she could when a sharp cramp in her leg hobbled her. She cried out and stumbled, and strong arms caught her.

Oh! She had not realized the duke chased her.

"Ethan, I..." With a sense of shock, Verity realized she trembled. She remained silent as he sat her on one of the steps and sat below her on another. He clasped her leg, and she cried out sharply at the awful pain. "It hurts," she gasped.

"Shh," he soothed, "the muscles are cramping. Let me knead out the knots."

His fingers worked the twisting and contracting muscles of her calf until the pain eased. When her whimpering died down, his ministrations slowed. The sense of intimacy was immediately startling.

"It is better?" he murmured.

"Yes," she whispered, painfully aware they were sitting on the wide stairs with only a few wall sconces to relieve the darkness. She could hardly discern their bodies, and that they could barely see each other somehow heightened the odd sensations crashing over Verity's senses.

"Why did you run?"

"I do not know," she whispered.

His fingers sank into her flesh again, then he rubbed her shin in a soothing motion. It was as if his touch singed her flesh. Just that slight contact set her whole body humming

"Why are you not sleeping?"

"I...I was looking for you."

"Why?"

Her entire body blushed, and she was suddenly grateful for the darkness. Swallowing hard and drawing a slow, deep breath, she whispered, "You know why."

His finger stilled, and she waited for his response, acutely aware of his masculine scent, the possessive yet gentle way he started massaging her calf, slowly sliding his hands down to her ankles and then up to her knees in a languorous glide. Not a whisper of sound passed between them as he continued touching her like that.

Finally, he replied, "I had a nightmare. Sometimes I find that I have to...I need the outlet."

She felt for one of his hands and raised it up. Lightly she trailed a finger over his bruised knuckles, feeling that his hand was swollen. "Does it hurt?"

"Yes."

"What chases you that you punish yourself so?"

"Dreams of the past," he murmured. "A carriage accident."

"The one that took Lord Preston's life," she said, recalling Catherine's wild grief and desperation. "You were with him, and you were also hurt."

His hands tightened on her shin. "Would that I could only take his place."

Verity gasped at that harsh whisper. "Do not say it," she hissed, startling him with her fierceness.

"The fault does lie with me," he said, his tone suddenly chilled and indifferent.

"Were you the driver of the carriage?"

"No, however—"

"Were you the creature that reportedly ran across the road causing the carriage to career?"

"No."

"Are you God himself, to determine who lives and who dies?" she asked in a softer tone. "Accidents happen every day, Your Grace. Should we carry the burden for

557

them, we would have no peace. I do not know your feelings fully, but I am here."

Verity recalled the guilt and pain she had felt, thinking she had not done enough to stop Catherine from sneaking off to meet a known rake and libertine.

Silence fell, and it shocked her when his head dropped to her knees. Ethan shifted, and a sigh filled the air, a sound that echoed with peace inside of it. Verity smiled and gently traced her fingers through his damp hair. "You were hurt as well, I am sorry for it."

"Just a few small scars."

"I notice that sometimes you walk with a cane. Will you tell me about it please?"

"My left leg had broken in three places. Though those bones were healed, some days they hurt and using a cane help relieves it. The physicians said eventually I will not need it anymore," he said gruffly.

Verity was glad he had not been hurt more seriously, but she did not tell him so, sensing he would not want to hear such words. Instead she asked,

"What else do you like, Ethan, other than boxing bare knuckles?"

"Riding at the crack of dawn, feeling the coldness of the day and racing across the lanes as if I am chasing the sun. Then I watch as it comes up over the horizon, painting the land in that vibrant cold, destroying the chill, and piercing me with...heat. It is a thing I enjoy, and I ride many early mornings."

"I would like to accompany you," she said softly.

She felt the curve of his mouth against her knees. Her duke smiled.

"You sleep late, Duchess, and do not seem to be a morning person."

She wrinkled her nose. "How observant of you."

'I have watched you splayed quite inelegantly over your bed. Surely you cannot have a bed companion. They will suffer."

Everything inside Verity stilled, and sensual awareness tingled over every inch of her skin.

DUKE OF EVERY SIN

"I have watched you sleep quite frequently over
your bed, surely you cannot since a bed companion.
They will either."

Something made Verity stilled and spread over
her, dripped over even flush of her skin.

Eleven

VERITY'S BODY'S reaction was immediate,
intense. Her heart fluttered, and a whisper of want
hooked into her heart and stayed. "How would you
know of my terrible sleeping habits?"

"I watched you this morning, tempted beyond measure to slide between the sheets and take you into my
arms."

Verity made a small, indelicate noise. "Why didn't
you?"

"You looked quite lovely sleeping. Peaceful. That
should not be so easily disturbed."

Her heart swelled with a peculiar tenderness. "You
could have simply slept beside me."

"A diverting thought, I have never slept beside
another."

"Never? You've had lovers."

A rough chuckle escaped him. "Yes. Always mutual
rough-and-tumble fun, but nothing where...we lingered, simply to be in each other's presence."

"Not even with your mistress?" she asked, a devilish
urge riding her.

"A duke does not talk to his duchess about past or present mistresses."

She grabbed tuffs of his hair and pulled. "I beg your pardon, Your Grace, past and what?"

He chuckled. "I assure you, my duchess, only past."

She smoothed her fingers in his hair and dipped her head slightly. "Verity and Ethan can talk about anything."

Another smile formed against her knee, and she wished she could see the curve of his mouth and the beauty of his smile.

"Very well. I never spent the night with my mistress. I was always too eager to paint the night on the town in my illicit pursuits with my cronies. I was the consummate rakehell, an heir to a wealthy dukedom. I had power and friends who seemed to admire me because of my status. I had courtesans, married ladies, and debutantes falling at my feet and climbing into my bed. Life was alive with frivolity and little purpose, and no diversion could capture my attention for very long."

He spoke without emotions, almost with boredom.

"Do you miss that life?"

"Never."

His voice echoed with an implacability that ensured she believed him.

His fingers tightened briefly on her knees. "I am no longer that man, and have not been since my father died and I claimed the title."

"When did he die?" Verity was curious, for even now, the scandal sheets thought it fit to remind the *ton* they had a Devil Duke, and reminisce on his past escapades.

"Three days after Lord Preston."

Good heavens. Having dealt such severe blows in days would have altered even the most reckless soul.

Grief and pain had reshaped him, and with an aching heart, Verity wished to know every aspect of the man before her. "I am so very sorry, Ethan."

"You had no hand in it. There is no reason to be sorry," he said, with a touch of icy disdain.

He was retreating, and not wanting him to go, she cupped his jaw and brushed her mouth against it. It was a kiss, if this mere touch could be called so, but they both froze at the contact, and, Verity swore she felt his heartbeat as her own.

"I will insist you start sleeping beside me," she said, kissing the corner of his mouth. "Every night. When you feel restless and then need to...beat your sandbag, perhaps you might wake me, and I shall keep your company."

"Are you offering to beat the bag with me, Wife?"

She laughed. "No. But perhaps we might retire to the library, read together, play chess, or this..." This time she pressed her mouth more firmly to his.

His lips were warm and firm, dissolving her hesitancy in a wave of honeyed heat. She flicked her tongue out, teasing the edges of his mouth. He growled his approval and parted his lips slightly. Verity slid her tongue into his mouth, a shallow, teasing glide. She gasped, surprised by the sudden pleasure. His groan trembled through her body, and her nipples beaded into tight, aching knots.

Her duke took her mouth in a deep, passionate kiss. Their tongues danced together in an evocative duel, one that was slow and sensuous.

"Open up," he murmured, biting her lower lip.

Verity almost fainted, but she complied, her heart thundering when he pushed the nightgown high up above her knees and thighs. He ran his palm along the length of her leg, a light stroke, from her ankle to her knee. She drew in a sharp breath and caught her lower lip in her teeth as a hot ache rolled through her body. He repeated the motion, lingering high on her inner thigh but never reaching to where she ached, at her center. Verity gripped the edge of the stair she sat on, conscious of where they were, yet emboldened and inflamed in the darkness which cocooned them in the carnality of the moment.

His fingers inched higher, and a whimper whispered on the night air when he slipped those fingers through the slit of her drawers. Her legs instinctively fell open, and he pressed a tender kiss to her knees as if to reassure her.

He slid a finger between her slippery folds, rubbing up and down her sex. *Oh, God!* Her breath quickened and her belly knotted, as he stroked those fingers up to that nub of pleasure and pressed. She felt herself getting wetter, and did not understand what was happening. Verity panted, wanting to squeeze her legs shut against the hot feelings stirring low in her belly and in that nub that he pressed, pinched, and rubbed. Unknown sensations erupted below her navel, making her weak with want. "Ethan," she cried softly. "I...should it feel so?"

"Yes," he said, his voice rough with arousal. "You are getting so wet, Verity."

Her cheeks heated. "Is that good?"

"Yes, and I want more. I want you to flow your passion over my fingers, and I want to feel the tightness of your cunny and anticipate how you will grip my cock."

The unknown words felt wicked, and somehow her body responded, flaming with wanton heat. He pushed a finger inside her body. The pleasure was so sharp, she gasped.

"Shh," he sensually crooned. "We must be quiet."

He moved his finger back and forth, dragging more wetness from her. He hissed his approval, and her hips arched into his touch. A second finger joined the first, and she felt a pinch of pain at the stretch, yet Verity wanted more. A sob came from her as those fingers plunged and retreated, filling her with pained bliss. A third finger joined, and when she whimpered, he kissed her and used his thumb to press and rub her clitoris. Verity almost arched off the steps, and she gripped his shoulders so tightly, she feared there would be an evident mark in the morning.

He stretched her, worked her with his fingers until she was a trembling mess. Sweat slicked her skin, and a dark wanton pleasure swelled inside her. Verity vaguely realized she had opened her legs wider, until Ethan rose so that he came over her, pressing her back into the steps of the stairs, slipping those fingers deep to rasp against nerves that felt as if they were being tortured with ecstasy.

His fingers stroked her sex, the pleasure an almost unbearable intensity until the aching pressure shattered, and she grew so wet she flowed over his fingers as he'd wanted, as bliss speared her. Her heart was beating too fast, too hard, her entire body trembling. Ethan withdrew his diabolical fingers from her body and swept her up into his arms. The casual strength only heightened her arousal, and she hooked her legs around his hips as he walked with her up the rest of the stairs.

His breath fell hot and rough on her neck, and a moan of anticipation left her. They reached her chamber, and he shoved open the door, and before it closed properly behind him, Ethan was kissing her, stroking his tongue inside her mouth and tasting her with carnal greed. A sweet shock of delight shivered through her, and she helplessly clung to him as he aroused her body to a feverish pitch.

She dropped her legs to the ground, and he allowed her, yet he never stopped kissing her. He cupped her breast through the nightgown and thumbed her nipple to a stiff, aching peak. He plucked her nipples between his fingers until they were so sensitive she could scarcely bear the pressure. Breaking from her lips, Ethan kissed a path down to her neck, her shoulders, and to the mounds of her quivering breasts.

"I need to feel you naked," he growled.

He whisked the nightgown over her head in a move of almost violent tenderness, and pooled it at their feet. Then her drawers and chemise followed until she was gloriously naked. She watched as he shoved from his trousers. His male beauty was...captivating. Muscles corded his shoulders, chest, and thighs. His manhood jutted thick and long, and something hot clenched low in her belly, and she ached between her legs in a way she struggled to understand. Verity dazedly wondered where had her maidenly nerves vanished. Ethan did not hesitate but lifted her into his arms, and in a few strides, he bore her down onto the bed. Then he crawled down her body, slid his hands beneath her buttocks and lifted her to his mouth.

Verity screamed at the shocking pleasure. He licked over her aching sex, parting her folds with his tongue, and then he covered her nub with his lips, sucking it delicately, then with piercing intensity. Frightfully hot, needy...almost desperately painful sensations crawled through her.

Ethan released her from the tormenting bliss of his tongue and blanketed her with his body.

"You must have bewitched me," he groaned. "I want you so damn much I fucking ache."

The sound of his voice was a whisper of velvet across her skin. He nudged her legs to open wider with his, lifted her slightly, and a hard pressure was notched at her entrance. He held her eyes as he inexorably pressed forward into her body. The pressure felt immense, and Verity gripped his shoulders, panting slightly.

When the pressure verged toward pain, she sobbed his name, suddenly uncertain. He tenderly caught her mouth with his, kissing her deeply, as he reached between them to stroke that nub of pleasure. There was the smallest of pauses, then his hips plunged, pushing him deep.

She cried out into his kiss as her quim strained and quivered around his invading length, but he did not let up on his ministrations. The pain ebbed, the pressure became tolerable, and the heat rekindled. Verity grew restless and lifted her legs to anchor at his hips. Only then did he move, thrusting his hardness in and out of her aching sex.

The sensations were exquisite. She dropped her forehead on his shoulder, gasping with each sensual yet forceful stroke inside her body. He slid one hand beneath her bottom, lifting her up and against him as he thrust deeper.

"Oh, Ethan. It's so good."

Tension peaked in her belly as he rode her with increasing depth and strength.

Don't stop. Please, don't ever stop, Ethan.

Sweat slicked their skins as they slid together, and she cried out in the crook of his neck as pleasure shattered and left her trembling. Ethan's hands gripped her tighter, and after several deep plunges, he groaned as he emptied his release deep in her body. She stroked his back as his breathing eased.

"Ethan?"

"Hmm," he murmured, sounding dazed.

"I agree. We must do this every night."

He laughed, and for some reason, she laughed along with him. This felt...perfect, and with the sweet sensation filling her heart, Verity hoped it would never go away.

ETHAN WAS UNABLE TO SLEEP, but tonight, the feeling of being wide awake was welcomed. The practical and logical heart of him had always known that he was mired in the complex cycle of grief for two of the most important men in his life, losing them days apart. While he had accepted his father's death as an inevitable part of the life cycle, with Oscar, Ethan felt he would forever wonder—if he had made other choices, would his friend still be alive today? He knew in time the pained guilt would fade like ashes in the wind, but he would always know that if not for his rakish, irresponsible ways of the past, Oscar might not have climbed up on that carriage, drunk as a lord, and driven the carriage to his demise.

Ethan closed his eyes, slicing away the images and memories from his thoughts. He did not want them to intrude at this moment, not when his wife lay in his arms. He did not want to miss Verity. The thought brought him some measure of amusement, for he had never been a man with a great sentimentality, but for the first time in his life, he admitted that Verity was a woman that wreaked havoc upon his heart and thoughts. She was a rare creature, with her sweet kindness and the way she listened without rushing in to fill the silence with noise. He liked that about her.

"Ethan?" she mumbled drowsily, snuggling into the crook of his arms. Almost idly the delicate tips of a single finger skimmed over his naked chest, dipping low, skimming over his abdomen to linger there.

"Yes?"

"How old are you?"

"Eight-and-twenty," he murmured.

She twisted so that she reposed on her back, her head resting on the lower part of his chest. He could only imagine where she had flung her feet. The lady had no grace when she slept.

"Bedding is very satisfying," she murmured huskily. "I see the appeal of doing this every chance we get. Is it always like this?"

He smiled in the dark, thinking how much he had been doing that of late. *Smiling*. Why was the notion so perplexing? "I can say I have never felt pleasure this intense in my life. It is disconcerting."

"Why should it be disconcerting?" she demanded pertly.

"What reason is there for it to be this good?" he growled. What damn reason was there for simple tupping and companionship to twist him into such a shambles of emotion, and fill him with hunger, to want her again within minutes of having tupped her?

"I am simply incredible all around," she said with a pleased laugh.

His duchess was indeed incredible. Something elusive stirred inside him, a whisper of pleasure and contentment. The feeling disturbed Ethan. He glanced down at her to find her peering up at him, a smile on her mouth, her cheeks rosy, and her eyes glittering with pleasure and good humor. "You are my wife," a bit of wonder in his voice, realizing how much he liked her.

An unreadable emotion touched her gaze for a fleeting moment, then her lips sweetly curved. "Aye, and I am glad that I am."

Fucking hell. Guilt pierced his chest, and with an inner snarl he tamped it down. *Not now.* He did not want to ruin this feeling of perfect peace. Yet he suspected guilt and regret would stab and wound him each time he looked into her blue eyes and saw laughter and happiness, for his little duchess did not know the hand he had in Oscar not marrying her sister.

Perhaps marrying her had been damned foolish after all. His heart rejected the notion with stunning violence. As if she sensed his sudden unrest, Verity turned onto her belly and crawled up his chest, and stroked a finger over his brow, soothing the beast that wanted to rise inside him, to fill him with a different kind of pain, one that could only be soothed inside her welcoming body. Ethan rolled with her until he cradled his weight through her spread legs, dipping his head to capture her mouth with his.

God, she tasted incredible. When last had he felt such pleasure from a mere kiss?

Her eager response enflamed his hunger even more, and he reached between them to fist his cock and fitted himself against her wet quim.

"Hold me, Verity," he murmured against her lips.

With a sweet, soft sigh she wrapped her hands around his neck and opened herself more to his ravishment. She was already soft and wet. Her instinctive response swelled his cock with pulsating need. With a groan, he sank his cock deep inside her cunny to the hilt. Pleasure rippled up his spine and settled into his balls.

Hell. He already wanted to spend inside her body. Ruthlessly pushing down the urge, he loved her slowly, wringing soft gasps and cries from her, waiting until she released three times before he took his own pleasure inside her welcoming body.

Several minutes later Ethan ensured his duchess was clean and snuggled against him as he sat up against the large carved headboard.

"You are unable to sleep," she whispered.

"It is the newness of sleeping beside another," he admitted brusquely.

It was little more than an exhalation of breath that escaped her, but it sliced through his heart. "You should return to your room, Ethan. The door between our rooms will always remain open."

He dragged her up so that she sat between the open V of his legs, her back flush against his chest. He tugged the sheets about them, wrapping them into a warm cocoon. She giggled at his actions, and he pressed a kiss to the corner of her forehead. "I am not leaving, Verity. We are going to sleep together until we are old and wizened."

"That is a lovely thought," she said with a happy sigh. "However *I* will be old and graceful."

"Tell me," he murmured, "What do you like to do?"

"Finally curious about me?" she asked archly.

"Yes."

"Your wife is frightfully simple. I like to read and draw and paint. I even enjoy needlework. I have always wanted to learn to swim," she said unexpectedly.

"I will teach you."

He felt her smile, and he said, "My wife also has a courage like none I have ever seen before. You are an extraordinary woman."

Her gasp was soft and shocked. "Is that how you see

me, Ethan?"

Something unexpectedly tender clutched at his heart. "Yes. You married me, a stranger with a dastardly reputation, for the sake of being there for a babe that is not your own. That is a risk many would not take."

"Rubbish," she said, "You are a duke. Many would marry you if you drooled while you spoke."

Ethan laughed, bemused by her sense of humor. He tightened his arms around her. "You willingly gave up your reputation and any chance of a future of your own, to accompany your sister through her disgrace. You lost your family...your friends...your hopes, and I suspect that even knowing the hardship that you endured, if given the chance, you would make the same choice. You are kind and loving, with a strength I admire," he said gruffly.

A nervous laugh rose in her throat. "I always thought I was selfish for allowing my parents to lose both their daughters to scandal. I know I did not deserve my father's ire; I just could not desert Catherine in her time of need."

"Wrong," he grounded out. "No father should ever abandon their child. *Ever*. He should have used his power and influence and closed ranks around Lady Catherine. She is hardly the first lady to have a child out of wedlock."

His wife sighed, took his hand, and kissed his knuckles. "You are kind and sweet, thank you."

Ethan dared not laugh. Only his duchess would call him kind and sweet.

"I was very anxious before, afraid that we might not have a good marriage because in truth, we are strangers still. But it is astonishing how...wonderful it feels being with you." She perked up as if struck by an incredible notion. "Perhaps we knew each other in a former life."

"You believe humans to have several lifetimes?"

"I own to it being a possibility. Don't you?"

"I am not so whimsical."

"I forgot you value logic and pragmatism," she said with a sniff.

"I find it wonderful being with you too, Verity," he said.

From his assessment of most *ton* marriages, they were cold and impersonal, with many gentleman having mistresses, and then ladies seeking other lovers to soothe the heartache of loneliness. Ethan had never thought much about marriage before little Thomas and Verity came into his life. He had known he would eventually get married, for he would fulfill his duties and responsibilities to the dukedom. But he had never once imagined what his duchess might be like, for the idea of marriage had not felt important, something to be cherished. It had simply been a duty.

Now he felt different, and it was because of the woman in his arms. He did not want to disappoint her. Ever. Ethan wondered how his little duchess would react should she know of the knowledge he held in his heart. Something ugly and dark crawled through his heart, and with a sense of shock he realized it to be discomfort that he might lose her regard, and the softness in her gaze whenever she looked upon him.

Rubbish, he silently snapped. There was no damn need to be discomfited. They spoke no more, and he stayed like that, with his duchess wrapped into his arms, and fell into slumber.

~

A few hours later, Verity stirred sleepily as Ethan slid from her restraining languorous limbs. He leaned over her, magnificent in his nakedness. She burrowed into the coverlet, intending to sleep, and smiled when he kissed her forehead and the lids of her closed eyes, and then more passionately her mouth, swollen from their night's adventures in marital bliss.

'Uh, what time is it, Ethan," Verity murmured, her eyes flickering open to a dark chamber.

'Nearly dawn, I'm going riding, are you getting up, or shall I leave you to slumber on?"

Verity propped herself up on her elbows and squinted in the dark at her husband as he lit a lamp. As the light glowed out, she enjoyed a long look of his naked back, buttocks, and thighs. It was a view she found classically splendid, and she frowned, slowly going through what her husband had told her.

Oh, he's going riding. He's had another nightmare. She sat up in the center of the bed. 'I'm getting up, but I need some help with my new riding habit, the buttons are at the back. I don't want to wake Matilda so early..."

'I can act as your dresser," he said, leering at her, and she giggled as she slid out of bed and into her duke's arms.

'I'll go and dress and then come and help you, can you find everything you need?"

'Yes, Matilda is very tidy, and we put everything away together." Verity felt stiff and sore, but she would keep him company. She washed her face and hands and brushed her hair into a queue. Then she donned her undergarments and got out her riding habit. It had been made a little loose for more ease of movement, so Verity did not think she needed to wear her stays underneath. She slipped into her new bright-blue riding habit and fastened the buttons at her cuffs. Verity felt rather than saw Ethan come up behind her and his hands reaching

574

inside the habit to cup her breasts, as his thumbs stroked her nipples into peaks.

Oh God. The pleasure was searing. "Um, that's nice, but if you continue, I'll have you back in that bed. Perhaps I might even ride *you* instead of my mare," she teased, not even certain if such a thing was possible.

"Now that's an interesting proposition, I should quite enjoy watching your breasts jiggle while you ride me. But I think perhaps I should fasten your habit so we can get out and enjoy what looks to become a fine day," he said, reluctantly releasing her breasts and concentrating on the many tiny buttons that held the habit in place.

Verity enjoyed the feel of his fingers dexterously fastening the back of her habit, and stood still to make the job easier. The house's staff would be rousing and getting everything that needed to be done for the morning. But they tiptoed down the stairs and out to the stables before anyone caught them sneaking out like naughty children.

Ethan's chestnut stallion was already saddled and pawing at the ground eager to be off. The stableboy rushed to saddle her piebald mare and soon led her out. Ethan moved to boost Verity up, and when she was firmly seated, the duke mounted his own horse, and they set off down the lane leading to a small copse of trees.

"Are you a good rider?" he asked, his tone a bit tight.

"Yes."

"Good, let's race."

They shot off together, trusting their horses. It was glorious, and they rode, galloping at top speed, other times trotting in companionable silence for several minutes. Ethan slowed his horse and she followed suit, staring in awe as the tiniest light appeared on the far horizon, then crept brighter and higher in the sky, painting the meadows and woodlands in bright hues of orange and yellow. Verity could not recall ever appreciating the beauty and peace of watching the sunrise, and a glance at Ethan showed his contentment.

Her heart stirred to know he shared this perfect peace with her, and the hopes she had felt for their marriage burned even brighter. He glanced at her, and he smiled. It wasn't mocking or laced with sensuality. It was a simple smile, and her heart gave a violent tug toward him. She sensed something had formed between them, a unique thread of connection perhaps. They watched the sunrise, and then trotted back to the main house without speaking, and Verity would not have it any other way.

I am falling in love with you, Ethan. Will you love me back?

Thirteen

THE NEXT TWO weeks passed in radiant bliss for Verity. Each day with Ethan, little Thomas, and Artie proved to be a wonder. After loving her most thoroughly, her duke slept with her every night, and got up fewer and fewer times to visit that sandbag. Even yesterday, they had possibly shocked the housekeeper by cavorting in the library during the day. How Verity had blushed and hidden her face in his jacket while the devil had laughed. Ethan had his duties, and while hers were less strenuous, for she had been trained in managing a large household, they filled some part of her days.

Verity consulted with the housekeeper and butler every day. She had made sure to learn the names of all the staff and what their duties should involve. She checked menus with the cook, and made sure there was not too much wastage. She also enquired about the poor of the area who would be considered in the duke's remit, and checked on any pensioners of the estate who had previously been employed there. Some of these matters she brought to Ethan or his steward's notice, but she arranged for baskets of food to be sent to those who suffered the most from their poverty.

Because of the neglect to the hall suffered since the death of the late duke, Ethan's father, she went through all the hall's linens with the housekeeper and one of her new laundry maids. Badly worn or stained linens were replaced, or cut to be used for other purposes. The cellars had been much depleted, and fresh supplies were ordered with the assistance of her new butler. Every room was cleaned thoroughly and checked for any repairs or replacements that needed to be made, so bedraggled hangings and drapes were repaired and gradually replaced.

Windows were cleaned, and a carpenter and a builder called in to deal with some minor problems. She inventoried the silverware, had the stillroom cleared out and made sure it was properly stocked, and then set about personally to classify the documents and maps which had been tumbled into a small room, instead of carefully archived. Although the hall had been built by the late duke, the family records went far back, and referred to other properties and land as well as the hall. In these ways, Verity spent her time making the house more comfortable and running more smoothly.

Little Thomas was contented, and even Artie had taken greatly to the daily lessons she gave him, already making a great stride in reading, and even in his comportment. A modiste and tailor from London had come down to Kellitch Hall at the duke's behest, and Verity, Thomas, and Artie's new and quite fashionable wardrobes should arrive soon. Artie did refuse to relinquish his dagger, which had only amused her, and Verity had reassured him he could keep it. But she arranged for the local cobbler to take a paper outline of the knife, and asked him to make a proper sheath and belt so he could wear it safely. The worries of the past had melted away, and she could not even regret or resent the hardship of the last two years, for they had led her little family to this contentment. Even her parents had called upon them, and after the first few minutes, the tension had disappeared, and her mama and papa had expressed an interest in knowing Thomas.

Verity had cried that night, knowing it was all Catherine had hoped for, but she was gone and might never return. Verity missed her sister and ached to know if she had arrived in Paris safely, or even if Catherine thought of little Thomas, Artie, and her.

With a sigh, Verity brushed aside that worry, and handed over this week's menu to the cook, who bobbed a quick curtsy and headed for the kitchen. She then hurried up the winding stairs to find Ethan for their swimming lessons, which were coming along quite splendidly. Verity found him in the nursery, standing by the window with a chortling Thomas in his arms. She paused, listening to his deep, soothing voice, and the tale he told the baby.

"Your father was brave and never hesitated to go on an adventure," Ethan said. "When we were lads of thirteen, we fancied we found a treasure trove as we explored some caves in Somerset."

Thomas babbled as if he understood the tale, and certainly listened with rapt attention not often seen in babies of his age. She listened for several minutes to the adventures he painted for Thomas of himself and Oscar, walking deep in the caves for miles, or helping a bird with a broken wing, and even foraging for wild berries to eat when they believed themselves lost. Verity turned away from the nursery with a smile, to gather her sketch pads and pencils. She went outside toward the eastern end of the property, where a large oak tree had a splendid wooden seat attached as a swing to a sturdy branch. Verity sat on the grass, opened her pad, and started to illustrate the story Ethan told Thomas. She would ask her duke about more of their adventures, or even listen in whenever he regaled the baby with one of his tales, and she would create this memory book for little Thomas. When he was of a reasonable age to understand the stories and knew they were of his father, she would read them to him. He would have them for himself to read over and over, knowing something about the father he lost.

Smiling, she leaned over and began.

~

Artie ambled along the hallway, a proud lift to his steps, a smile on his face, and a kitten curled in his arms. When he saw Ethan, that smile dimmed to be replaced by wariness. Ethan lifted his chin, and the boy hesitated but followed him outside, where they took a stroll along the paved path that led to the lake. Ethan allowed them to walk in silence for several minutes, letting the boy get comfortable with his presence.

"You have been living here for a little over two weeks now, Artie."

He cut him a peculiar glance. "Yes, sir."

"Are you comfortable?"

The boy's eyes widened. "My belly is filled every day, sir. And I ain't cold anymore." Those words hinted that Verity and her sister had faced difficult times financially in the two years he had lived with them. There were days food might have been scarce and the winters cold. His duchess spoke about it briefly, and had mentioned they sold several pieces of their jewelry and practiced strict economies to live as comfortably as possible. It spoke to her character that she had not complained about how exceedingly challenging it must have been for two young ladies, who had grown up in the lap of luxury with an army of servants, to make do in a small cottage with only a cook and day maid to aid them in their daily lives.

Somehow in his grief and responsibility of dealing with inheriting the dukedom, Ethan had not made a link between the 'Catherine' Oscar spoke about and the rare beauty that had been disgraced for having anticipated marriage, and committing the grave sin of loving outside of marriage. That ugly, dark feeling dug into his chest and clawed at him. He pushed it aside until it died away. The chains of guilt were damned burdensome, and he wished he could be callous enough to cut them away with ease, as he had seen others do. The logical part of him knew they would likely one day ease, and he reflected that since his marriage, the burden had been lifting daily.

'I want you to know that wherever Verity and I are, your home is also there. You are now a part of our family."

The boy stopped and gripped the lapels of his jacket in a tight hold. "My father was the local butcher. My mama died birthing me."

Ethan stared at him and waited for Artie to gather his thoughts.

'I ran away from home because of his beatings," he said in a rush. "And I stole food to live, sir."

"You did what you had to do to survive," Ethan said. "There is no shame in it. You were a lad of eight years."

The boy still looked dubious. He gave Ethan a quick sideways look, as if he were trying to understand the man before him.

"Do you wish to return to your father or let him know of your whereabouts?"

"No." A cloud passed over the boy's face. "But...I don't belong here. I feel it in my bones."

"Do you wish to belong?"

A flash of hunger passed over his face. "Yes."

"Do you wish to be educated and prepared for a life where you might make a living, marry well, and have a family of your own?"

The boy nodded.

"Then avail yourself of my resources," Ethan said with a smile. "You do not need to walk around with that worry that you will ever be asked to leave. You are Verity's family—hence, you are also mine. I know Verity has been teaching you your letters and how to read. More must be done. We will start with hiring tutors for reading, geography, arithmetic, fencing, and riding lessons."

The boy's mouth curved into his crooked smile, and the tension about his shoulders eased. He hugged the kitten to his chest in a tender clasp as they strolled and chatted for several minutes about their mutual interests in kite-flying and fishing. When Artie departed, that air of anxiety no longer lingered about him, and he had a confident bounce in his stride.

Ethan walked toward the eastern side of the estate. He had seen Verity run there, as he stood by the windows, telling Thomas about his father. Ethan should be meeting with his estate's steward, but he wanted to see her. He chuckled ruefully, still amazed at the constant feeling of want that pulled him to her presence. Several minutes later, his steps faltered as he spied her sitting on the swing he had loved as a child. She rocked gently in the swing, staring at the sketch pad on the grass.

Today she wore a yellow day dress which clung alluringly to her figure. Wisps of hair escaped her topknot and framed her lovely features, and with a smile, he noted her feet were bare, even of stockings. Glancing around, he saw the discarded boots and white stockings resting by the trunk of the tree.

She looked girlish. Innocent. Sweet. Just lovely. So very opposite to the wanton who had sunk her cunny onto his cock last night and slowly ridden him until he had fisted the sheets and almost begged for mercy. A hot bolt of sensation shot straight to his cock, and he almost cursed to feel himself stirring. Almost every night, he loved his wife most thoroughly, sometimes slow and gentle, other times deep, fast, and hard, as he used her warmth and sweetness to chase away the shadows that clung to him. His wife never seemed to mind when he tupped her hard, and her release at those times was powerful and shattering.

Verity pushed the swing again, and as she lifted her chin, he spied the remnants of tears. Something violent and dark moved through him, and he wanted to slay whoever placed it there. He moved toward her, and her head snapped up. A smile lit up her entire face, striking his heart with her prettiness. Something fierce clutched at his chest, and he released a slow breath. He wanted her to smile at him like that always, to feel the brightness and beauty of it.

Without speaking, Ethan went behind her and pushed her swing so that she soared higher and higher still. She laughed, the sound loud and sparkling. He pushed her for several minutes, letting her soar and feel the wind on her face. Then he slowed his motions, stopping the swing and went and sat beside her.

"You were crying," he said gruffly.

Her breath hitched, and she sat silent for long moments. Ethan did not rush her, trusting that if she wished to reveal her thoughts, she would. If not, he would respect her space and silence.

"I was creating a storybook for Thomas," she said

huskily, lifting her chin to the drawing on the grass. "From the stories you told him. I wanted him to have it, to always remember his father. Then I wondered what story I would tell him of Catherine. Do I tell him she had fallen into a deep melancholy, and that the scandal and pain haunted her so much she abandoned him for a future that did not include him? What do I tell him of his mother, Ethan?"

He closed his eyes against the pain in her tone, regret sitting on his shoulder like a boulder. His duchess rested her head on his shoulders, and they rocked.

"Tell him about the sister you grew up with," he said gruffly. "The one you loved so much you would leave everything behind to be with her in her moment of uncertainty. Tell him about the adventures you had as children. Show him why you loved her."

His wife sighed, and then she smiled. "You are right, my darling."

That endearment jolted him, and then a rush of pleasure filled him.

"Do you want me to find her?"

With a gasp, she sat up and stared at him with widened eyes. "Do you believe you can?"

"I am the Duke of Bainbridge," Ethan said. Then he smiled. "I will try."

"In her letter to me, Catherine said she was going to Paris. That is it, Ethan. That she had met someone, I cannot imagine who, and—"

Verity slapped a hand over her mouth. "There was a scholar who passed through the town. He was from France and was the cousin of the local squire. He was one of the only people pleasant to us, and I saw him once in deep conversation with Catherine. Could it be he that she exchanged letters with? But of course," Verity said excitedly, "Who else could it be?"

He took her hand between his. "Then we will start there. I will hire a team of investigators, the very best, and I will find her for you."

A dark feeling passed through his heart, and he acknowledged that once Catherine knew of Verity's new status, she might very well reveal why she had unceremoniously left the baby on his doorstep. Clearly the lady knew of his part in the affair between her and Oscar; otherwise, how could she have known where to leave her son. He glanced at Verity, and the way she smiled at him then, her eyes sparkling with hope and tender emotions, stopped the words that hovered on his tongue.

Fucking hell.

"What is it," she whispered, touching his jaw. "You look so...savage. What are you thinking, Ethan?"

He hauled her into his arms and took her mouth in a kiss of violent tenderness. She gasped and melted against him. The raw feelings bubbling inside immediately soothed as he accepted her submission to their passion, her trust, and the love he could see in her eyes.

Fourteen

"OH, ETHAN, LOOK," Verity cried, sitting up on the blanket and clapping. "Thomas is walking without falling over or having to hold on."

Sweet relief filled her. She had been worried that Thomas was not yet walking, considering he was already thirteen months old. The family physician the duke had brought to check Thomas over had said the baby was quite fine and developing well, and to simply give him more room to move about, without hovering.

Little Thomas chortled and ran about the lawns as if he had just discovered freedom and had no intention of stopping soon. His nursemaid watched him, even hurrying to gather him up when he took a tumble. He wriggled, and she set him back down with a laugh, and he was off again. Only a few days ago, he had called Verity *mama*, to her shocked delight. Verity had appalled herself by bursting into tears, and Ethan had laughed and hugged her to him.

"He is getting so big," she whispered.

"He is," Ethan said drolly. "Soon he will be wenching and cavorting around town."

With a gasp, she tossed a piece of apple at him, and he laughed, wrapping his arm around her waist and tugging her to him. She landed on his chest with a soft cry.

"No sons of ours will be wenching and cavorting. They will be perfect gentlemen," she said pertly, wrapping her arms around his nape.

Ethan kissed her tenderly. Her heart squeezed. Though her duke was so attentive, and even stared at her with hunger and longing, he had never expressed romantic words. Verity kept reminding herself that he was a practical man and might never give her any such sentiments. Still, she found that she longed to hear the words from him, and be reassured that he might hold some affection for her beyond his dutiful responsibilities to her. Especially when she was already so desperately in love with the man.

"Whatever my duchess says, I will ensure it is done." He reposed on the mountains of cushions, scandalously curving her into the crook of his arms. "Shall we return to reading while Thomas discovers the beauty of his little legs?"

"Yes," she said with a light laugh. Today, the weather was glorious, and they had picnicked on the lawns, taking turns reading *The Orphan of the Rhine* by Elizabeth Sleath. Ethan's voice was perfect for reading, and she found herself enraptured and on edge as she listened to the gothic tale unfold.

~

As she prepared for their evening dinner, Verity debated which of her new gowns to wear. The door to her chamber opened, and Matilda entered. She helped Verity dress in her stays, chemisette, and a lovely rose-colored gown with a charming decolletage. As Matilda styled her hair, Verity noted she appeared anxious.

'Is all well, Matilda?"

She hesitated. 'It is just that, Your Grace, the duke has received a woman caller, and she is scandalously sobbing on him and crying that she cannot believe he is married."

The breath stilled inside Verity's chest. 'I beg your pardon?"

Matilda hurriedly bobbed in an apologetic curtsy. 'I wasn't sure if I was supposed to say anything," she rushed to say, putting in the finishing touches on Verity's chignon.

'I..." Verity took a deep breath. 'It is fine, Matilda. Where is the duke seeing this...lady?"

'In the drawing room, your ladyship."

Verity strolled down the winding staircase and made her way to the drawing room, aware of feeling apprehensive. Ethan had left the door ajar, and some of the tightness eased that she hadn't realized sat on her chest. She stood framed in the doorway, staring at the ravishing red-haired beauty who cried piteously as she stared at the duke, who returned her regard with chilling insouciance.

'You are being cruel, Ethan, darling," she said. 'I traveled from Bath as soon as I heard the news. I did not return to town to receive your missive, ending our liaison. Surely you can forgive me for traveling down without notice, and put me up for the night."

Good heavens. It was his former mistress, and given the lateness of the hour, she expected to sleep under their roof for the night. Though Verity's belly knotted, it would surely be uncharitable to turn the woman away. It was already close to six in the evening, and the sky had taken on an overcast view.

588

"There is an inn not too far from here," he said, "I am certain there will be rooms."

As she was about to announce her presence, the lady said, "Is it that you are afraid for me to meet your wife?"

Ethan arched a brow. "You truly give yourself too much importance."

"I still cannot believe you married her sister," the lady hissed.

"It is no business of yours," he said coolly.

"What if your wife really returns with her pistol," the lady demanded scathingly. "Will you allow her to shoot me?"

"If it is her prerogative," he said casually. "You did attempt to kiss me despite being assured that I am blissfully wedded."

Verity almost choked. He had told the lady she might shoot her. Verity almost laughed, recalling her promise to duel anyone who offended their vows; however, there was a fearful feeling upon her heart. Did this lady know Catherine?

"Ethan," Verity said, hating that her voice trembled.

His back stiffened, and he turned to her. He stared, his brilliant eyes growing distant by the second. The sudden tension in him was palpable.

"Does this lady know my sister?"

The lady in question turned around, her bright brown eyes raking over Verity. She spied jealousy and embarrassment in her gaze and sigh.

"Yes, I know of her, but I have never met her," she said a bit spitefully. "It was the duke who convinced Lord Preston against marrying her. The argument was rather...persuasive, and that is how I knew of it."

"You have overstayed your welcome, Sarah," he said icily. "Get out, or I will have you tossed out."

The lady paled, and her hand fluttered to her throat,

sudden regret lining her face. "Ethan, I am sorry, I do not—"

"Out!"

She jolted, and with a muffled cry, rushed from the room. Verity walked further into the room so the lady might pass her, but she never removed her gaze from Ethan's sudden indecipherable expression. At that moment, he reminded her of the cold, aloof duke she had met the first time she entered this home.

"Is it true?" she whispered, recalling Catherine's tears and questions as to why the earl had not offered for her after their night of impetuous passion.

A slight tremor went through his tautened frame. "Does it matter?"

His answer had a terrible, hollow ache rising in her chest. He should deny this, she thought dazedly. Verity stared at him, a painful sensation gripping her chest. "The reason Lord Preston did not offer for Catherine after...after he had taken her to his bed was that you convinced him otherwise?"

"Yes."

She flinched, the wound in her heart flaying open. "You were the source of my sister's greatest unhappiness."

"Yes," he said with brutal honesty.

She could barely see him through a film of tears. "Why?" she rasped. "Why would you act so callously toward her? What exactly did you do, Ethan?"

His eyes burned through her. "I never met this Catherine that Oscar often spoke of, nor did he ever reveal her full name, I suspect to spare her reputation. We were both six-and-twenty, rakes shy of walking into the traps of marriage-minded mothers and their daughters, determined to remain bachelors until duty required us to marry," he said flatly. "He told me of a girl who came into his room at a house party and confessed her love for him, and how he fell under her charms and could not help himself. When he came to me, babbling about compromising a lady but was uncertain if he was ready for marriage, I told him not to be a fool. It took two to climb into a bed, and she clearly wanted to trap him for marriage. A thing we were not yet ready for."

Verity recoiled. "Catherine had no such notions! They met and danced at several balls and engaged in discourse before...before..."

"He was not publicly courting any lady I know of," he said . His jaw was tight, clenched, as were his hands by his sides. "I did not believe her genuine in whatever feelings she claimed to own for him, the ones he seemed both uncertain and excited about. It was I who convinced him to delay his offer of marriage and follow me to a house that boasted the loveliest courtesans. We drank and indulged in all manner of debauchery, and when we stumbled from that house, Oscar thought it a lark to order the coachman away, and climbed atop the driver's box."

Verity stepped away from him, her heart beating so fast she felt pain. The memory of Catherine's screams and her fainting away at the news of the earl's death almost cleaved Verity into two. "I do not wish to hear anymore," she whispered, or she might scream and rush forward to slap his face.

They stared at each other for painful minutes.

"We raced through the streets of London like two drunken fools," he hissed, his expression a grimace of pained torment. "I did nothing to temper the speed at which Oscar urged his horses, but sat there like an indulgent fool, sipping from a whisky flask. I am still uncertain to this day what the horses hit. But Oscar lost control, the carriage careened, and everything after became bloodied."

Tears slipped down her face, and she wiped them away. "I understand it now," she murmured. "The ease at which you took in Thomas and the ease at which you married *me*. You felt as if you owed Lord Preston...and that you owed Catherine. Tell me, Your Grace, is guilt the only thing holding our marriage together?"

He took a step toward her. "I also feel such regret, Verity. It is not only guilt and grief that haunts me."

Verity's heart shattered, and she gripped the edges of her gown, turned, and ran from him.

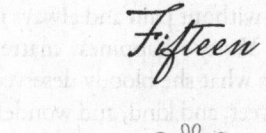

ETHAN NEVER IMAGINED his chest would have been cleaved open with pain at seeing such raw agony in his wife's eyes. That soft whimper of pain and denial would be etched upon his heart forever, reminding him to always take her care into his being.

That he had hurt her...

Sweet mercy. He slapped a hand against his chest and rubbed. That he had hurt her brought him sorrow and a desperate feeling inside to fix everything at once. She mattered more than he had ever admitted to himself, and Ethan felt like a fool at this moment. Verity was... God, she had become so damn important to him.

Fix the past, fix what was happening now...just fix it all, but how could he do that. What was done was done. His actions could not be taken back.

Fix it all.

Those words knocked inside him like an insistent roar, and he took a step after her only to falter, his chest lifting on a harsh breath. She might never want to see him again, kiss him or even welcome him into her bed and heart after today, because he could not fucking undo the past. Ethan shook his head because even if she

593

did not want to speak to him again, that did not matter, as long as she existed without pain and always felt happy with her lot in life. Verity's happiness mattered more than anything. It was what she bloody deserved because she was damn well sweet, and kind, and wonderful.

Good things should happen to incredible people.

Ethan wanted to smash his fist into the wall. This was not something he could ever fix and that means there was no damn reason to chase her.

Wrong.

He could not bear for her to live through her pain and tears without understanding how damned sorry he was. For so much, but most importantly for bringing hurt to her. He couldn't imagine her forgiving him, but he had to tell her that at least. A night should not be allowed to pass without him conveying his feelings to her. She needed to understand that if he could go back and change what he had done that he would do anything he could to prevent her being so hurt by his actions. To prevent the pain it caused her sister and family.

Though marrying Verity had been for mostly the sake of Thomas, their marriage had become so much more than pain, and regret, and atonement.

I am a damn fool.

Without wasting another moment, Ethan chased after his wife.

Verity did not stop until she reached the small grotto, a far distance away from the main house. There she sat on the large stone boulder, rested her forehead on her knees, and took a shuddering breath. The sound of a branch breaking echoed in the silence, but she did not turn around.

"Artie, please, I would like to be alone."

No answer came, but she heard more footsteps. When it faded away, and silence lingered once more, she hugged her knees even tighter and closed her eyes. Tears leaked from beneath her closed lashes, and with a hitch, Verity wept. The sounds were soon raw and harsh. The man she had fallen in love with had been the orchestrator of her family's greatest pain. If not for his interference, Catherine and Oscar might be happily married at this moment. There would have been no scandal, or disgrace...or perhaps death.

She flinched, suddenly understanding the dark guilt attached to his grief. He thought the same.

Oh God.

The only reason he had married her was to atone, and it was for that reason she might never look in his eyes and see more than shadows. She would never see love. Verity felt silly because he had never promised it, but she cried until there were no more tears left in her heart, until she felt dried out and emptied. Thunder rumbled overhead, and she did not move. Rain fell in a light drizzle, and despite the chill, she did not move. She breathed raggedly, her shoulders trembling as the rain slowly soaked her hair and her clothes.

Verity did not believe she would ever move again. A whisper of sound came from behind her, and she twisted around and almost fainted. Ethan sat on the boulder beside her, a mere breath away, and she had not realized.

Awareness rushed through her. The sounds earlier were because he had followed her. And he had sat there while she cried.

"I am sorry, Verity. I am so damn sorry. Please...I..."

He stopped as if he did not know what to say.

"I swear to you I will find Catherine. I will not stop until I do. I will...I will find a way to fix everything."

Peering into his eyes, she saw the deepest pain and regret and fear. Her eyes were too achy to shed more tears, but she wailed at the torment he must feel inside.

There is forgiveness in love.

"You made a mistake, Ethan," she said, "You could never have anticipated the events that happened after. How could anyone have known such consequences would come after? You did not act in malice. Please forgive yourself."

He flinched and closed his eyes, a spasm of anguish cutting deep into his skin. Ethan stood and looked away from her. Wanting him thoroughly focused on her, Verity went to him, placed her hands around his shoulders, and hauled herself up, wrapping her legs around his hips. His eyes snapped open, and she gently touched the corner of his mouth.

"I know what is causing you pain, Ethan. One moment in time, and you lost a person you loved. A dear friend. A friend who had many who loved him, and they also suffered and grieved. You feel guilty at your part in it, and you feel keen regret. I also want you to understand that Oscar could have chosen to ignore your advice and chase after Catherine. It did take two to climb into that bed, and he should have done the honorable thing as a gentleman and made an offer. A man in love would not stay away, and perhaps he would have eventually come around."

His fingers caught a lock of her wet hair. "That chance to return to her was taken from him because..." Ethan's throat worked on a harsh swallow.

"I know," she said softly. "Mistakes are made every day, and regret can live in our hearts for a long time. I cannot know the burden you carry, but if you allow me,

I would share it, and help you carry the weight until it is no longer burdensome."

He stared at her as if she were a rare creature. "You make no sense," her duke rasped.

"I understand my heart, and you will know it in full eventually. Now tell me, this fear I see, what is it for?"

He held her gaze for a long moment. "Losing you. I am fucking petrified of losing you."

The crack in her heart widened. "You cannot lose me," she whispered. "Our marriage is until death parts us."

His hands tightened on her hips and across her back as if he would never allow her to jump from him. "I am afraid to lose your light," he said gruffly. "Your smile, the sweet way you look at me as if you cannot believe I am yours. Because you see, every day, I am shocked that you are mine and so damn grateful for it. I sleep in your arms, and there are no nightmares, only dreams of what our future might hold. I kiss you, and your taste destroys everything horrible that came before it. I...you make me *feel* in ways I cannot understand, Verity. But by God, I know it to be a love that will never dim, but only grows. I want to amuse you, spoil you, protect and cherish you every day that we are together. I love you."

She pressed her forehead to his, startled to feel tears on her face. "I love you, Ethan."

He hugged her to him and buried his face in her neck.

"Love me. Verity," he said into the curve of her throat.

"I do," she gasped. "I do. I love you!"

An almost unbearable ache twisted through her soul as a harsh breath of relief issued from him. They stood like that, uncaring that the rain fell in greater earnest. She leaned back so she could lift his face to hers, and kissed his mouth, tasting him and the chill of the rain. 'No more regrets, Ethan. We will step forward together and give Thomas a wonderful life. We will introduce him to Lord Preston's parents and, if they are interested, allow them to be a part of his life. We will surround him with love and acceptance, and we will tell him of his mother and father. We won't look back on the mistakes but on the loving memories."

'I love you," he said, taking her mouth into a long and deep kiss that lasted for a very long time.

Two years later

Verity smiled as she watched Catherine stroll about the lawns with little Thomas and a small baby girl in a perambulator. It had taken some time, but Ethan's team of investigators had found her living in a small village in Grenoble. Catherine had been married and heavy with child, so she and Verity had exchanged letters for several months, until she paid them a visit only a week ago.

Ethan came up behind her and slipped his hand around her waist, gently resting his hand over Verity's softly rounded belly. She was six months pregnant with their first child, and everyone greatly anticipated the birth of an heir. Despite this, she knew Ethan would be just as happy if they had a daughter.

'She is different," Verity whispered. 'Catherine is happy. I have never thought I would ever see such light-ness in her."

'Her husband is a good man," Ethan said gruffly. 'We went fishing this morning, and it was rather pleasant."

She leaned her head back against him. 'We spoke at length this morning. Catherine…does not wish to take

Thomas with her back to France. She was rather horrified at the notion, promising that was never her intention, nor will it ever be."

A shudder went through Ethan, and she felt the relief in him. Though he had grown to love Thomas as his own son, and had adopted him, he had braced himself to hand him over to his mother, should she prove that she was responsible enough to lovingly take care of her son. When he had just told Verity, she had cried, desperately afraid of losing Thomas , but had accepted that reuniting son and mother might be a possibility.

Though Catherine clearly loved Thomas, she truly felt the best life for him was in England with Verity and Ethan.

"I am selfish because I am so happy to not lose him," she whispered.

"You love him," he said gruffly. "As do I. Catherine was generous enough to forgive my hand in Oscar not offering for her."

"She believes Mr. Langdon is her perfect match and seeing them together, I cannot help but believe it myself."

They stood there, clasped in each other's embrace, watching their family playing on the lawns in the distance. Artie and Thomas chased the cats, and Catherine's husband joined her and their baby daughter on the blankets to watch the spectacle. Verity turned in the cage of his arms, slipped her hand around his neck, and kissed her duke.

The End

More by Stacy

OTHER BOOKS BY STACY

A Rogue in the Making

My One and Only Earl

The Kincaids

Taming Elijah

Tempting Bethany

Lawless: Noah Kincaid

Moonlight Magic: Jenny Kincaid

Rebellious Desires series

Duchess by Day, Mistress by Night

The Earl in my Bed

Wedded by Scandal Series

Accidentally Compromising the Duke

Wicked in His Arms

How to Marry a Marquess

When the Earl Met His Match

Scandalous House of Calydon Series

The Duke's Shotgun Wedding

The Irresistible Miss Peppiwell

Sins of a Duke

The Royal Conquest

Single Titles

Letters to Emily

Wicked Deeds on a Winter Night

The Scandalous Diary of Lily Layton

About the Author

USA Today Bestselling author Stacy Reid writes sensual Historical and Paranormal Romances and is the published author of over twenty books. Her debut novella The Duke's Shotgun Wedding was a 2015 HOLT Award of Merit recipient in the Romance Novella category, and her bestselling Wedded by Scandal series is recommended as Top picks at Night Owl Reviews, Fresh Fiction Reviews, and The Romance Reviews.

Stacy has a warrior way "Never give up on dreams!" When she's not writing, Stacy spends a copious amount of time binge-watching series like The Walking Dead, Altered Carbon, Rise of the Phoenixes, Ten Miles of Peach Blossom, and playing video games with her love. She also has a weakness for ice cream and will have it as her main course.

She is always happy to hear from readers and would love to connect with you via my Website.

To be the first to hear about her new releases, get

cover reveals, and excerpts you won't find anywhere else, sign up for her <u>newsletter</u>, or join her over at <u>Historical Hellions,</u> her fan group!

Thank you...

THANK YOU FROM THE BOTTOM OF
OUR HEARTS FOR READING OUR BOOKS.

Thank
YOU